GRUDGEBEARER

GRUDGEBEARER

J. F. LEWIS

an imprint of Prometheus Books
Amherst, NY

Published 2014 by Pyr®, an imprint of Prometheus Books

Grudgebearer. Copyright © 2014 by J. F. Lewis. All rights reserved. No part of this publication may be reproduced, stored in a retrieval system, or transmitted in any form or by any means, digital, electronic, mechanical, photocopying, recording, or otherwise, or conveyed via the Internet or a website without prior written permission of the publisher, except in the case of brief quotations embodied in critical articles and reviews.

Cover image © Todd Lockwood
Cover design by Jacqueline Nasso Cooke

Inquiries should be addressed to
Pyr
59 John Glenn Drive
Amherst, New York 14228
VOICE: 716–691–0133
FAX: 716–691–0137
WWW.PYRSF.COM

18 17 16 15 14   5 4 3 2 1

Library of Congress Cataloging-in-Publication Data

Lewis, J. F. (Jeremy F.) author.
Grudgebearer : Book one of the Grudgebearer trilogy / By J.F. Lewis.
pages cm. — (Grudgebearer trilogy; Book One)
ISBN 978-1-61614-984-0 (pbk.) — ISBN 978-1-61614-985-7 (ebook)
1. Revenge—Fiction. 2. War stories. 3. Fantasy fiction. I. Title.

PS3612.E9648G78 2014
813'.6—dc23

2014012141

Printed in the United States of America

For Jonathan and Justin

CONTENTS

PART ONE: THE AERN AS DEVOURERS

PART TWO: THIRTEEN YEARS LATER

PART THREE: CALL TO WAR

PART FOUR: TRUE CONJUNCTION

PART ONE

THE AERN AS DEVOURERS

"The most frustrated rants contained within my father's notes and journals pertaining to his creation of the Aern deal with the unexpected side effects of their unique skeletal composition and the link existing between the Aern and the items they in turn created. While Uled never solved the riddle of the various tokens, bonded weapons, and warsuits fashioned by his most celebrated creations, I believe that near the end of Uled's life, he began to suspect the Aern were hiding the depths of their connection from their maker and their masters.

One wonders why he did not ask those questions of Kholster himself, the Firstborn of Uled's race of servant warriors. At the time, Kholster, like his brother and sister Aern, was soul bound and would have been compelled to answer. It is my firm belief Uled feared that answer more than he desired it.

When he sealed away the Life Forge, it was therefore not to protect it as our history books tell but rather to prevent the death knell of his own people.

Certainly, any action taken at that time was already too late. From the first hammer blow purposed with the creation of Kholster and his first one hundred Armored brethren, the deed was done. The blow was struck. Some might call it folly, but I see it as the most protracted suicide attempt ever conceived by mortal artifice. I think my father knew exactly what he was doing but was simply too proud of the idea to let it go unexpressed . . . Even the later destruction of the Life Forge could not undo what Uled had done."

An excerpt from *The Patrimonial Scar: Uled's Legacy of Death* by Sargus

CHAPTER 1
OATH BROKEN

A crack split the silence of six hundred years. Wood surrendered to iron followed by the steady golden light of a vow close to breaking. A globe of mystic flame hung pendulously in the air, a fist-sized bead like burning oil scattering the dark and casting jagged shadows of splintered wood along the interior of the long sealed chamber. The intruder caught a flash of metal, a gleam of red. He spied the half-seen outline of an armored boot. This had to be it. There was nowhere else to check. It had to be.

Crowbar and axe worked together: a symphony of opening and rending—the clarion call of discovery and doom. As the breach widened, light filled the stone chamber, banishing shadows and picking out spikes of color. Smears of crimson gleamed like the eyes of predatory animals lurking in the atramentous gloom as pair after pair of red crystals lit up within the ancient barracks. Five thousand pair, if the historical records were to be believed. Dolvek didn't think that they could be. The records had been kept by the Aern; who knew if they'd been accurate? The Aern were little more than animals, after all.

"Yes." Dolvek leaned forward, the tip of his pale nose twitching as he sniffed the air. "I think this room was the command barracks. Not that the Aern were kind enough to leave a map."

Suits of armor, like animal-headed statues, stood in even rows. Each loomed tall and imposing, a warpick at its side, each weapon a work of art. The stylized helms seemed to glare out at the prince, their gazes an accusation.

I half expect to hear them shouting "intruder," he thought to himself. *Though to call me an intruder anywhere in my own kingdom . . . ha.*

"No cobwebs, Prince Dolvek," said the squat man wielding the crowbar and wearing rough-spun workman's attire. He peered into the room, sweat standing out on his brow and running down his face in thin rivulets.

A larger man, bald and burly with a lantern jaw and a twitchy eye, made the sign of the Four Square in front of him with the head of the axe he held. "No dust neither." He chewed his lower lip and drew blood without noticing. "This is dangerous fruit, your highness. Red berries on dead lips, this is."

"You prove a positively poetic coward, Bran." The globe of fire drifted farther into the room, swelling to the size of a skull, illuminating the undecorated stone walls and floor, eliciting a startled gasp from the man with the crowbar. He dropped the length of iron, turned, and ran.

"Begging your pardon," Bran said as he lowered his axe and left it in the doorway. He backed out of the room, eyes locked with the gaze of the most prominent warsuit. "N-no-no disrespect."

"Idiots." Dolvek stepped fully into the chamber. The swish of his blue robes seemed to echo like a threat. A simple golden circlet adorned his brow in stark contrast to the raven tresses which touched his shoulders. "Empty armor can't harm you."

Even so, Prince Dolvek had to admit that, as the illumination grew even stronger, those archaic artifacts which had frightened his human workers proved an intimidating presence; the fearsome specimen directly in front of him in particular. Licking his lips in anticipation, Prince Dolvek smiled triumphantly.

"Bloodmane's armor," he mouthed, stepping closer.

I've found it!

More a work of art to the prince's eyes than an implement of war, the full suit of Aernese plate armor showed no sign of the centuries which had passed since its interment. Astonishing detail work covered its surface, yet as he traced the amber-colored lines with an outstretched finger, the metal felt smooth and unmarked.

Functional, too, then, he thought. *Enameled in some way?*

"I can see why the sight of you running into battle would strike fear into the hearts of those rutting lizards."

Not that anyone had been troubled by the Zaur for a hundred years despite how fervently General Wylant might argue to the contrary. She never had been the same after the defeat of the Aern at the Sundering. The shattering of the Life Forge had twisted Eldrennai magic itself. Who knew what it had done to Wylant, who had, according to all the records, been the one standing over it, the one whose weapon had unmade it? Dolvek could hear her voice in the back of his head.

"Build whatever exhibit you have in mind, majesty," she had argued, "but do not tamper with arms and armor of the Aern. If Kholster finds out you've so much as touched them—"

"Your concern is noted, General," Dolvek recalled saying. He couldn't remember if he'd even looked up at her. He didn't think so. The sight of her bald head offended him. "And your caution is appreciated. But the exhibit will be closed to the public . . ."

The general had opened her mouth to say something, or he imagined she had, but he'd raised his voice and bulled on. "—and I see no reason any of the royals would ever send a tattletale message to any Aern, much less Kholster himself, *or* why Kholster would even deign to read such a message, if he, as you say, hates us so much and *if*, indeed, he can read."

"If?" Wylant's mouth had dropped open. "He. Can. Read? Highness, be reasonable. At least discuss it with King Grivek—"

If the Aern could read, Dolvek supposed Wylant would know. He'd heard that Wylant had been . . . involved . . . with the leader of the Aern back at the time of the Sundering. Ancient history, as far as Dolvek was concerned, since she'd fought on the side of her people. Still, her past history probably affected her present judgment. And she was, after all, a woman.

"Discuss the king's surprise present with the king, Wylant?" Dolvek had sighed. "No. Nor shall you. I forbid it. Thank you again for your diligence and desire to protect the kingdom and my royal person. You are dismissed."

She could strut about with her little cadre of malformed knights in their drab metal armor and their wretched elemental foci all she wanted as a precaution against the Zaur and the Aern and their supposed magical resistance . . . but Dolvek felt forced to draw the line at Wylant's interference in affairs of state. She was an old general only and not of royal blood at all. What, he wondered, did his father see in her?

Smiling at the memory, Dolvek gestured, and the globe of fire floated closer, illuminating the armor more intently. If the breastplate was impressive, the helm was more so. Carved in the likeness of an irkanth, a horned lion—the so-called king of the Eldren Plains—its mane was crimson and unfaded, the crystals set into its eyes seeming to glow from within, its mouth gaping open in an angry roar. An obvious trick of the light. *Magical flame does seem to favor dramatic touches*, the prince thought. *Perhaps I should have some plain candles brought in.*

"Bran," Prince Dolvek called. "Get your men. I want to mark the ones I need moved to the royal museum for the special exhibit. And bring some candles."

Bran did not answer.

"Oh, of all the superstitious—"

What did I expect? They are only humans, he reminded himself. *Did I expect bravery and courage? Loyalty? Reliability? Yes. Well, I had hoped. I'll look around first and then hire some more humans in the square.*

The globe of fire drifted after him, and he walked down the rows, marveling at the weapons of a different time. On either side he was greeted by row upon row of glowing crystal eyes set into the helms of the Aernese warsuits.

"Magnificent."

*

While Prince Dolvek's seemingly innocent actions doomed his people, the implement of their destruction was asleep at home, eyes closed and dreaming. His bunk, if one could call it such, was little more than a shelf of stone carved in the barrack wall of South Number Nine, the current capital of the Great Dwarven-Aernese Collective. The berth he occupied ran twenty-one hands long, seven hands deep, and another seven hands from the slab of one berth to the bunk above it. Dwarves often sighed at the sight. "Like bees in a hive," Glinfolgo was fond of saying.

Kholster smiled in his sleep, the grin lending a predatory cast to his features (even at rest) as it revealed the doubled upper and lower canines so distinctive to Aern.

The light caught him by surprise.

Eyes snapped open in the dark, jade irises shuttering into thin circles, bound by the black sclera of his eyes, as the amber pupils dilated wider to capture and enhance the available light, then narrowed to pinpoints as his vision wavered, registering the switch to thermal imaging—the base of his eyes growing cold. He felt the other Aern around him, waking wordlessly, making the same questing looks in the dark, searching for the source of the unexpected luminescence.

"Light?" he asked, his voiced clipped and professional.

"Not here," Vander answered.

"Where?"

"Close your eyes," Vander instructed.

Trust an Overwatch like Vander to pick up on it first of all, while even the warsuits themselves are still confused. Kholster closed his eyes and frowned as the light returned and he saw a pale-skinned Oathbreaker peering down at Bloodmane, Kholster's warsuit.

Bloodmane, what's going on?

An Oathbreaker has unsealed the command barracks, rang a voice in Kholster's head.

Seeing through the eyes of his armor, Kholster saw Eyes of Vengeance, Vander's warsuit, standing across the hall, its helm fashioned in the likeness of a sea hawk, its hooked beak and fierce eyes ablaze with the light of candles being put in place by human workmen.

"What the hells are they up to?" Vander asked.

He said something about a museum exhibit, Bloodmane told Kholster.

A what?

An exhibit. Must I attack them?

Give me a moment. Kholster slid out of his berth and ran a hand across his face, the stubble rough under his fingertips. *I like to take a candlemark or two to mull things over before committing genocide.*

Of course.

Of course, Kholster snorted, hiding a grin. As if he'd asked for a few more moments to ponder the menu selection at one of those strange Hulsite eateries with all the options. He shook his head as he watched through Bloodmane's eyes the humans scurrying about their work in an effort to please their Eldrennai masters, but with exaggerated care, some of them apologizing directly to the warsuits each time they drew too close or feared they might bump up against one.

That was the right attitude, the one the Oathbreaker himself should have had. Kholster sneered at the fool giving orders when he came back into view. A human with a piece of colored chalk followed behind him making "x's" on the floor in front of warsuits the Oathbreaker indicated. The idiot had the stamp of Zillek and Grivek all over his face, the pale skin, the short ears with barely a point to them at all, and the dull black pupils of his eyes . . . beady, like a rat dropping stuck in a mound of bird squirt.

"No, I said to mark the armor itself," the Oathbreaker hissed, "not the floor in front of it."

It didn't seem right to laugh, but Kholster marveled at how anyone, even an Oathbreaker prince, could be stupid enough to risk the wrath of the Aern over something as unimportant as—

A museum exhibit? he asked Bloodmane.

Yes.

On what? Do they have a new "beings-we-created-and-enslaved-and-then-almost-got-killed-by-when-we-freed-them-by-breaking-an-oath" wing of the Royal Museum?

Bloodmane didn't answer.

Surprised by an inward sense of movement, like the phantom sway he often felt when sleeping on land after a time at sea, Kholster clutched the stone edge of his berth to steady himself. Bloodmane was in motion.

Closing his eyes again, Kholster was treated to a view of the ceiling as four humans carried Bloodmane out of the barracks as they might carry a wounded king on a stretcher between them.

"So they aren't moving our armor," Kholster muttered. "They're making humans do it."

"Can they do that?" Vander asked.

Kholster looked down the room and saw that same question echoed on the faces of the other ten Aern who shared this billet. More than that, though, he sensed a growing clamor of conversation going on among his Armored, the five thousand exiles he'd brought with him out of Port Ammond after the Sundering. After the Vael had negotiated a peace between the Aern and the Oathbreakers. Words filled his mind, the edge of conversations relayed from Aern to warsuit, warsuit to Aern.

Thousands of miles away, crystalline eyes flashed bright, then dim, then bright again as the warsuits relayed the chatter of Kholster's army.

"They are doing it," Kholster answered.

"But are you going to allow it?" Vander asked.

I don't know yet, he thought directly to Vander.

Bloodmane, he thought, addressing his warsuit. *Tell the One Hundred to meet me at the Laundry.*

Sir?

We're going to wash clothes and discuss this . . . loophole.

Yes, Maker.

Kholster, old friend, Kholster thought back. *We've been through this more times than one can count. Call me Kholster.*

CHAPTER 2
ELEVEN

"But two-nine-two is an Even day, not a Prime day," complained Glinfolgo, the rightfully elected High Foreman of the Dwarven-Aernese Collective, as he watched scattered groups of male and female Dwarves bustling with great purpose toward the laundry of South Number Nine. "The One Hundred only do community work on the Primes. This is day two hundred and ninety-two."

He sat along one edge of the table inset into the stone wall of the main mess near the foreman's office. On the table in front of him, bowls containing felspar and vegetables sat alongside a small tray of raw bacon. Nine other stools sat empty, shoved up against the edge of the table, abandoned by the gray-skinned Dwarf's dining companions.

Glinfolgo grimaced at the tray of bacon and shook his head before seizing a nugget of felspar from a breakfast bowl and crunching it furiously, eyes widening further as he spotted Ordunni, one of his most respected foremen, on her way to the laundry as well.

"One would think she had never seen a half-naked Aern before," Glinfolgo muttered between chews.

Watching from a distance, Rae'en smirked. It irked her uncle, the effect the Aern and their lack of cultural nudity taboos had on young Dwarves. Rae'en saw the softness in her uncle's eyes when Ordunni laughed at something a Dwarf next to her whispered as they walked.

"You should ask her," Rae'en announced as she snuck up behind Glinfolgo's stool and kissed him on the top of the head. At eleven, she was already as tall as her uncle and still growing. By twelve, she hoped to reach a full eighteen hands like her father.

"Ask who what?"

"Ordunni," Rae'en said, the black sclera of her Aernese eyes making the rings of jade around her amber pupils seem to glow. "You should ask her to share a meal or a shift. Of course, from the way you look at her, maybe you should jump straight to a mining contract."

"Rae'en!" Glinfolgo exclaimed, slapping his palms down on the table in embarrassment.

"Rocks for breakfast?" She pointed at the untouched roots, vegetables, and mushrooms on the table next to him. "Just because you can survive by only eating minerals doesn't mean it's healthy."

Glinfolgo smiled brightly for a moment before mustering a scowl as Rae'en walked around to stand beside the inset table at which he sat.

"I like felspar," he complained.

"Just keep saying that when your joints begin to stiffen up. Do you really want to lay there in agony while we take turns chewing up vegetables and drooling them into your mouth?" She smiled, baring her doubled canines. "Or is that part of your plan? Were you hoping Ordunni would do that for you?"

Her uncle shrugged that off with a growl, but he did reach for a handful of steamed new potatoes and mushrooms.

"In armor already?" he asked.

Rae'en nodded, snatching up a piece of bacon and chewing it thoughtfully. Technically she wouldn't need to eat for another few days, but she knew it was bad Dwarven manners to talk at someone's table without taking a token sampling of hospitality from his sideboard.

"I donned a mail shirt first thing after Vander's runner," she said between chews, "got to me with news of an unscheduled Chore Day for the One Hundred. Something's up." She flushed brightly as she caught her uncle eyeing the gray tunic peeking out from the edges of her chain shirt.

"Still a little soft-skinned?" Glinfolgo observed when he realized he'd been caught noticing. "I wouldn't worry about it. Your brother had to wear a tunic under his mail until he was fourteen. Sometimes it takes a while for an Aern's integumentary system to sort out the right level of suppleness, smoothness, and toughness."

"Irka," Rae'en said with a laugh. "I love him, but he's soul bonded to a musical instrument and a quill. He could have stayed soft-skinned and it would never have mattered."

Glinfolgo reached out and touched his niece's red hair. "No hood?"

"I haven't finished the hood yet."

He looked down her trousers and frowned. "What about the boiled leather we—"

"I'm an Eleven, Uncle Glin, not a baby fresh out of the bucket," Rae'en said, cutting him off. "I can't wear leather armor anymore. I—"

All know, Rae'en heard her father's voice in her mind, her amber pupils glowing brightly at the contact. *Rae'en, by Kholster out of Helg, shall kholster the patrol scheduled to intercept and, if oath requires, arvash a patrol between South Number Nine and South East Number Six. The following Elevens will join her . . .*

Rae'en concentrated on each name of the thirty Kholster listed, picturing each face in her head as she echoed his orders aloud for Glinfolgo's benefit. In the distance, she heard the soft echo of other Aern doing the same for Dwarves near them.

"Your first command," Glinfolgo said, "Too fast. Eleven years old ought to be an age, not a rank."

"Until we're adults, what rank is there other than age?"

"Bah! You Aern do things too quickly. It's not like you're all short-lived like the humans. I suppose that must be why the One Hundred are doing chore work on an Even?"

Rae'en still wasn't sure why it had been so important to the Dwarves that her father and those like him, the first One Hundred Aern forged by Uled on the Life Forge, only did community chores on the Primes—sacred days on which the Dwarves themselves traditionally did as little "chore work" as possible—reserving the time for intense "holy work" on large building projects instead. Her father didn't understand it either, but in the end Kholster had decided that a little eccentricity ought to be tolerated in those who had taken in his people and given them a home after the exile, after the Sundering.

"Are you worried?" Glinfolgo asked.

"Whose scars are on my back, Uncle?" Rae'en asked with a gentle tug at her uncle's beard.

"Why did I even ask?" Glinfolgo muttered under his breath. "Any idea why they picked today?"

"I don't know," she said, "but my best guess? Kholster's trying to decide whether or not to go to war with someone. The Khalvadian border patrols have been annoying him. We'll settle that later today by arvashing one of them."

"The whole patrol?"

"Only if oath requires, Uncle. And not the horses," she said, voice filled with exasperation. "We're not at war, yet . . . but the humans? Sure. Meat is meat. Horses can't be blamed for violating our territory, but the humans have maps. They know what belongs to the Dwarves and the Aern." She looked at the bacon on the tray and decided not to have another slice. She'd have her fill of meat later, and she'd already eaten enough to satisfy Dwarven hospitality. "And what can happen to them if they cross us."

"You'd think so," Glinfolgo said. "But every thirty or forty years a Khalvadian magistrate comes along who thinks the wild stories his predecessors have told him about the Aern are too far-fetched to be believed."

"And it's up to us," Rae'en said cheerfully, "to enlighten him."

CHAPTER 3
THE BRIDGE TEST

Rae'en didn't see the Khalvadians when they first came over the rise, but Kazan, her Prime Overwatch, spotted the lead horse right off, conveying the information to her in the form of a red arrow in the corner of her field of vision. Rae'en could tell that the other Overwatches, Joose, Arbokk, and M'jynn, were sending similar images from their vantage points, too. Someday, if her father could create a new Life Forge, she and her fellow Freeborn Aern would be able to forge warsuits and whisper freely amongst themselves. Until that day came, they would simply have to make do with the diminished connection provided by their soul-bonded items.

Twisting her bond token nervously as it hung from a chain of finely wrought bone metal around her wrist, Rae'en focused on the connection between herself and her Overwatches. In her mind's eye, their four views combined to create a stylized image of the battlefield. Briefly, she wished she, like her Uncle Vander, had the Overwatch ability, so that she could speak freely to her troops even without being one of the Armored.

None of Kholster's line have ever been Overwatches, kholster Rae'en, M'jynn's melodic voice whispered in her mind. Hearing her father's name applied to her sent a thrill of equal parts pleasure and dismay. In another language, it might have been translated "general" or "leader," but for the Aern, no other word was needed but "kholster."

True enough, she thought back, just to have something to say. Technically, M'jynn only had to refer to her as "Sir" or "Ma'am," but using the name of her father . . . Rae'en shuddered. How many girls had a father whose name represented the power of a king, a general, and a high priest combined . . . and now she'd been called by his name.

Ma'am, Joose thought at her, *they are moving toward the bridge.*

You all know what to do, Rae'en thought back.

On her mental map, the fifteen red x's which represented the enemy moved along the valley floor toward Bridge 43, The Trader's Way Bridge, as the humans called it. The bridge forded the lake, which filled most of the valley and led to the Grand Trade Road, which in turn led to one of the fortified mine entrances granting access to the South/South-West Bypass allowing Dwarves and Aern to move between mine cities without venturing aboveground, if necessary.

Next, twenty golden triangles began to move in the correct direction, but six of them didn't.

Joose, she thought suddenly, *where are you? Up a tree?*

I couldn't get a good vantage point from the ridge, ma'am.

You may have a good view of the Khalvadians, Rae'en thought, but I don't think you're reaching everyone.

But I can reach you, so I thought—

Of course you can reach me, Joose, she sent angrily. *I'm the kholster on this mission. Get lower! Now!*

Yes, kholster Rae'en, but I have one question.

What is it?

Why is the Khalvadian patrol carrying livestock and—

Livestock? Rae'en frowned. *Show me.*

The map in her mind's eye zoomed in close, the red x's resolving into people, carts, and horses. The standard ten-man Khalvadian patrol was there, but with them were three wagons, one transporting sheep, the other cattle, and a third loaded down with what looked to Rae'en like silks, spices, and other luxury goods.

Kazan, Arbokk, M'jynn, Rae'en thought, *does that look like a patrol to you?*

I think it's a tribute caravan, Joose thought back.

The others painted her vision with gold representations of their own tokens to indicate their agreement.

Suspend the attack, Rae'en ordered.

The slight Aern chewed her lip. What had her father promised? What exact oath had he sworn? Whatever it was, she would have to uphold Kholster's word. To do otherwise risked making him an Oathbreaker, and that she would never do.

Panic swelled in her chest. *What do I do?* she thought to herself, *I'm the kholster for the first time and . . . wait.*

"That's it! I'm the kholster, so I can—" Rae'en opened her eyes and tapped the outgoing link between herself and those under her command for the first time. "All recall."

*

Amber pupils lit from within as Rae'en felt her father's memories wash over her. She couldn't reach all of them, not his private thoughts, his hidden memories, but the one affecting her current mission was there alongside all the other oaths Kholster had made which bound all Aern.

In the memory, her father stood side by side with Vander, warpicks grasped in their fists, ready to attack the beaten patrol before them if they showed any sign of resuming their assault. On the ground amid slain cattle and sheep, merchants and their servants knelt in the grass, hands clasped behind their heads.

Above the appetizing scent of fresh blood, a bitter, sickly odor cut her nostrils. The cattle and the sheep were beplagued, and the merchants stank of fear, guilt, and lies.

"Fine," Kholster snapped. Rae'en could feel the Arvash'ae, the Devouring, at the edge of his thoughts, the rush of adrenaline, the expansion of awareness accompanied by the urge to kill and eat, to arvash, any who stood against him. The only thing holding him back was the way his opponents had thrown down their weapons and surrendered. "In the interest of peace, I'll accept your surrender and allow you to return home, but tell your magistrate and your goddess the borders of the Dwarven-Aernese Trade Alliance are closed to Khalvad until such time as Khalvad is willing to make reparations."

"We dealt in good faith—" a fat merchant began.

The sickening crack as Vander crushed the man's skull with a backhanded swing of his warpick silenced the fat man forever. "It smells bad enough out here without more lies," he spat.

A guard opened his mouth to speak, thought better of it, and raised his hand.

"Yes?" Kholster asked.

"May I be permitted to tell the magistrate how trade may be reopened?"

Rae'en felt her father's lips pull into an approving smile. He liked this human.

"Fill our order again, but next time do it with goods unmarked by plague or blemish. Bring them to Bridge 43 and wait. A patrol will find you soon enough—"

"Bring livestock and goods out here and camp by a bridge?" another merchant asked.

"Yes," Kholster answered. "Was I unclear?"

"For how long?"

"As long as we feel like making you wait," Kholster growled. "Full-grown Aern are immune to your plagues and diseases, but these animals were to be fed to newborns."

"Newborns?" several of the humans mouthed to themselves, but none was brave enough to give voice to the question.

"Until such time as you make reparation, our borders will remain closed to Khalvad. If a Khalvadian so much as sets foot on Bridge 43 or the lands beyond, and an Aern learns of it, the Khalvadians will be arvashed, all of them."

*

All of them, Rae'en played the phrase over in her head. All Khalvadians present or merely each Khalvadian who crossed into Aernese territory? The former felt right, felt like what Kholster meant when he'd made the oath, although there might be some wiggle-room there.

Are the Overwatches agreed, she thought, *on the interpretation of the oath?*

They were.

Blinking as the memory left her, Rae'en cursed. The remembering had taken little time, but the Khalvadians were closing on the bridge. And they showed no sign of stopping to make camp.

Stop them! Rae'en ordered. *Do not let them set foot on the bridge. They mean to make peace with Kholster, but they obviously either didn't get the whole message, or they're just stupid.*

Thirty young Aern broke into a run, but Rae'en saw the problem all in one glance. She'd positioned her troops to surround the patrol and attack them from all sides, hoping to trap them on the bridge and limit their range of movement.

We aren't going to make it, ma'am, Arbokk thought.

I am, Rae'en thought back, *with the Arvash'ae, I'm fast enough.*

Yeah, Joose thought back, *and you'll arvash them when you get there.*

Not if I force myself back out of it.

Can you? M'jynn asked. *I know the adults can, but I haven't ever managed it. Have you?*

I'll let you know.

Running at full speed, the grass under her feet, Rae'en had no trouble surrendering to the Arvash'ae. Her mouth drew into an unconscious grin as she bared her doubled canines, ready to bite and tear and chew. The black sclera of her eyes vanished as her amber pupils and jade irises expanded, each taking up equal shares of the visible portion of her eyes. With the Arvash'ae came increased strength and speed. Her visual radius expanded to an arc of almost two hundred degrees.

Best of all was the feeling of quiet purpose, to kill and eat one's fill of one's opponents, the simple knowledge that she was a weapon, made for killing and free to do that for which she and all her people had been forged. An exultant roar tore free of her throat, and she laughed as her feet touched the wooden slats of the bridge.

She could beat the humans—arrive at the far side of the bridge before they did. She knew it. And if she couldn't, she would tear open their throats and rip them apart, and her troops would feed and . . .

and . . .

and something . . .

Some . . . reason, deep down in the thinking part tried to force its way back up to the forefront of her mind. Words, words, and more words. She shook her head as if to banish the words, to throw them off of her brain, but they clung like little jagged hooks. Her grin faltered. She was kholster of this mission, the voice cried, she had best act like it or did she want to tell her father she had failed him?

Not that, she thought. *Never that*.

The pain of abandoning the Arvash'ae without eating her fill shot through her skull as if it had been cracked open. Strength bled away, leaving Rae'en weaker than before the Arvash'ae. Her vision narrowed to a tunnel of perception. Colors faded to black and white as her pupils narrowed to pinpoints and her irises to little more than a jade tint rimming her pupils.

Stumbling forward, half blind, bile rising in her throat, Rae'en thrust her hands out on in front of her to keep herself from falling only to find herself head to muzzle with a Khalvadian warhorse.

"Whoa," said its rider, a stout human clad in armor made from hardened plates of boiled leather.

"That's," Rae'en said, looking down at the horse's hooves, "a well-trained horse." They were on the bridge, but only half of the horse was. On her right another horseman sat astride his mount, eyeing her with a mixture of suspicion and amusement.

"You need to back off of the bridge." Her father's words rang out in her mind. "Set foot" was the phrase he'd used. Technically the Khalvadians hadn't set foot on the bridge; their horses had hooves, and a horse could not oathbreak . . .

"Back up off the bridge and make camp like Kholster ordered and we won't have to arvash you."

Looking back over his shoulder, the man saw the approaching ring of Aern and smiled. "There may be thirty of you, but you're children. You have no weapons—"

"Tools," she corrected.

"Excuse me?"

"We have no tools," Rae'en said, gasping for breath. "We *are* weapons. Plus, you brought tools. If we need them, we will take them from you."

"You're a brave girl," the man said. "I'll give you that."

Rae'en squinted up at him but could barely make out his face. Her vision dimmed, and she bit the inside of her cheek, drawing blood. Her world had narrowed to two choices: she was going to pass out if she didn't let the Arvash'ae roll back over her and have its way.

"Make camp and remain on the Khalvadian side of the bridge," Rae'en mumbled. To her Overwatches, she thought: *If we have to fight, yell for the non-combatants to throw down their weapons and kneel in the grass with their hands at the back of their heads so we don't kill any who aren't Khalvadian.*

She sagged to one knee, and the human dismounted quickly as though to catch her.

His foot hit the wooden slats of Bridge 43, and Rae'en, by Kholster out of Helg, kholster of the Elevens, roared like an irkanth. If the soldier, whose name she would never know, had time to be surprised before she'd ripped out his throat with her teeth, she would never know that either. All she knew was the whinnying of the horse and the screams of the men, the howls of her fellow Aern, and the warmth of a belly full of meat.

When Rae'en came back to herself, it was to the dull pounding of her still-aching head and to the panicked babble of the surviving humans, sounds of nervous animals, and the smiles of her fellow warriors. They had all taken the next step on their paths to adulthood and full warrior status to ranks other than age.

Good job, she thought to Kazan.

Everyone acquitted themselves well, kholster Rae'en, he thought back. *With which tool will you choose to train?*

Whose scars are on my back, Kazan?

A warpick, then, Kazan thought back. *Traditional. I should have known. Can you believe it? Ten years to train with the tools of war, then we'll build our own and bond with it.*

And then, Rae'en thought back, *we'll be true Aernese warriors . . .*

With the return of conscious thought came rough memories of what had happened while she'd been in the throes of the Arvash'ae.

The whole fight sank in and she smiled. The two soldiers at the bridge she had taken down on her own, killing the first with her teeth and the second with the first man's utilitarian blade. Nine of the fifteen guards lay dead, two of the merchants, and only one of the hired hands. She kissed her soul token, leaving a bloody smear. She couldn't wait to show Kholster her memories of the battle and see what he thought.

All at once, she remembered the surviving merchants and guardsmen. The caravan had scattered and lost formation, but the cattle and sheep were still on their carts. The horses of the dead guards and a few of the live ones were long gone. Blood soaked the grass. Near the lake, Joose still gnawed at the arm of a human he'd slain. Several of the other Aern looked on longingly at the meat. Rae'en smiled.

Kazan, she thought, *have those who have not yet eaten their fill gather up the meat and collect it on our side of the bridge. I think the humans might be a little more comfortable if they didn't have to watch their comrades be eaten quite so up close and personal.*

Done, he thought back.

Twelve Aern moved off from their positions standing over the vomit- and excrement-fouled survivors. Not all of them were conscious. Rae'en approached the most resolute of the survivors: a steely-eyed human, lips pressed together into a thin line of some emotion Rae'en couldn't quite put her finger on. He wore the embroidered sash and poncho of a Hulsite, and three precise triangular notches were cut into his right ear.

"Hulsite militia?" Rae'en asked.

"Captain Marcus Conwrath," he said in a harsh, grating voice. "Retired. Those Kilke-cursed buffoons didn't tell me they'd gotten a Grudgebearer's words on them, or I'd have made certain we had the whole words of the oath."

Rae'en smiled at being called a Grudgebearer. It was a name the Dwarves had started using, an affectionate term for the only people the Dwarves had ever encountered who could hold a grudge longer than Dwarves themselves.

"You're free to stand, Captain." Rae'en offered the man her hand, and his knees popped as she pulled him to his feet. He stood a full four hands taller than Rae'en, and she watched as he rolled a kink out of his neck, then rubbed at his right knee.

"Are you allowed to let us go?" he asked after a moment or two. "Without breaking some oath?"

"We are now oath-bound to kill all the Khalvadians here. The others may live as long as they don't set foot on the bridge." She saw the lines of his mouth soften, and she realized he'd been gritting his teeth, fearing the worst.

"You can camp on the Khalvadian side of the bridge," she said, thinking, absentmindedly licking the drying blood from her fingers. "Or you can head back the way you came. If you want to stay, give my Aern time to wash in the lake and then we'll help you make camp, and I'll send a runner to let Kholster know you are here."

She wiped at a warm trickle at her chin and sniffed. "How does that sound?"

"We'll be safe here?" a short brown-haired man who smelled of cattle asked.

"Are you Khalvadian?"

"Hulsite, like Captain Conwrath. You got all of the Khalvadians except for . . ." He blanched and stopped talking.

Rae'en looked questioningly at Captain Conwrath.

"He means the boy child hiding in the wagon," Conwrath said. "If your words will allow it, one of mine will adopt him and make him a Hulsite."

Rae'en nodded.

"So we're safe?" the short man who'd spoken before asked.

"Safe from us . . . unless you do something stupid," Rae'en said.

"It sounds good to me and mine," Captain Conwrath answered. "Get up, you idiots," Conwrath barked at his men. "We're getting triple pay now, thanks to the contract you laughed at me for making the magistrate sign. I want every spare hand to start trying to round up the missing horses."

He turned to Rae'en. "Can we clean up in the lake?"

"Just don't cross it and stay off the bridge."

"You heard the lady. If you fouled yourself, then get that taken care of, but for Shidarva's sake keep away from the Grudgebearers' bridge or I'll throttle you myself if they don't beat me to it. And for Aldo's sake, please tell me one of you has a wife who wants to adopt a child. I'm too old to go through all that again."

Rae'en gave a curt nod and walked back to the bridge where she'd made her kills. One of them, the first one, had already been dragged across the bridge. Rae'en seized the other corpse by its boots and began towing him to the other side of the bridge, too.

Someone had the beginning of a small fire pit dug, and two other Aern were busy stripping the clothes and equipment off of the bodies.

"You're going to cook some of it?" Rae'en asked.

"Not everyone really likes it raw outside of the Arvash'ae, ma'am," Arbokk answered. "It is all right, isn't it?"

"As long as the Aern who earned the meat has no objections," Rae'en said with a chuckle. *Cooked meat*, she thought to herself, as she walked down to the lakeside to wash. *What a waste.* On second thought, she looked back at the soldier she'd dragged across, at the gaping opening in his belly, the flesh stripped from cheek and arms. "My meat is fair game, too," she called back, "but I might want to try some of what you cook."

"Thank you, ma'am." Arbokk grinned.

Rae'en waved absently at him as she stripped down and began to wash the blood and sweat from her body, her bronze-colored skin coming clean. Across the river, one of the survivors watched her bathe in wonder. Whether the man had never seen a naked girl before or was simply astonished to find that Aern were flesh-and-blood creatures, not steam-driven Dwarven constructs as some humans seemed to believe, she couldn't know. Farther over, another human burst into tears.

Rae'en wondered why. The fighting was already over, after all.

CHAPTER 4
THE LAUNDRY COUNCIL

Kholster and the One Hundred stood in the main laundry, clad only in their smallclothes amidst hissing steampipes, clicking gears, and whirring machinery. They'd been at it for hours, but Kholster still worked a crank at the master gear, which drove the main agitators, by hand. Every now and again a Dwarf would, with attempted nonchalance, check the valves and seals around the side of each machine and the gear box with its runic "Main Laundry Control" nameplate, each Dwarf pausing to grimace at the agitator steam release where Kholster had disengaged the mechanism.

"You know," said the most recent Dwarven inspector, "the mechanism has been substantially improved, since—"

"Yes, friend," Kholster agreed, sparing the Dwarf a wolfish grin, "I know."

Not that the steam washer had ever been inefficient, but the Aern preferred a more hands-on approach. Or they had since the fully steam-driven version had torn three of Kholster's favorite shirts.

Smiling as he worked the agitator, Kholster looked away from the nearby Dwarf trundling exasperatedly down the brass steps of the drive platform, past the geothermal linkage which channeled excess heat from the lava flow deep below, and out onto the catwalks and ledges lined with hooting Dwarves. Most of the onlookers were female, but a few grumbling males were scattered in amongst them to, Kholster assumed, keep an eye on things and take turns attempting to tell him all about the improvements which had been made since the "incident of the ripped shirts."

Down below, on the work floor, his brother and sister Aern went about their tasks with quiet efficiency. Some moved around the multiple squat brass chambers which held whirling soap, water, and articles of clothing. Others handled the transfer of clean, cold water via hoses and pumps which were also intended to be steam driven. Along the back, closest to the geothermal linkage, Vander led a crew manning steam presses to iron out wrinkles while Bayltir and his team inspected the laundry, mending or patching articles as necessary before passing them on to Feenal's crew for folding, hanging, and redistribution.

The Aern worked soundlessly, the light from the glowing runes of the fire stones in the drying area lending them the look of smoothed-skinned statues worked in bronze, brought to life by Dwarven rune magic instead of the flesh-and-blood and bone-steel creatures they actually were. The intricate scar patterns on their backs glistened with perspiration. In an average gathering of Aern, scar patterns would have been repeated, appearing on the backs of multiple Aern to delineate the scarlines of Aern descending from each of the first One Hundred: the patrimonial scars of full-grown Aern.

Wylant, Vander thought at him.

I know. Kholster closed his eyes, relying on the feeling of the crank and the rhythm of the work to guide him, and looked through Bloodmane's eyes as Wylant walked into the display area. *And another prince . . . reinforcements?*

Is that the same prince from the last Conjunction? Vander thought.

Rivvek, Kholster thought back. *Though he didn't have those scars the last time I saw him.*

I always assume you are the cause of unexpected scars on Oathbreakers.

Not all of them, Kholster sent back, his thoughts tinged with amusement, *Rivvek isn't all that bad for an Oathbreaker. I almost don't want to tear his face off with my teeth.*

I'm certain he'd be flattered by such sentiment, Vander thought.

Kholster studied Rivvek. The elder prince and his younger brother could have once been mistaken for each other. As the raven-haired elf drew even with his brother, Rivvek came out the clear winner in height, standing almost a hand taller than his younger brother, but the scars wrapping around the left side of his head, cutting across and deforming the ear and leaving bare patches of scalp, left Kholster wondering what had happened.

It looks like Ghaiattri work, Bloodmane's echoing voice rang in Kholster's mind. Demon fire could make a mark like that, one Eldrennai healing could not erase. A Ghaiattri's fire had even been known to burn an Aern through the connection he shared with his armor.

They must have tried to open a Port Gate, Kholster thought. *Why would they do that?*

They are Oathbreakers, several Aern thought at him at once, as if that were all the explanation needed to explain any rash action committed by an Eldrennai.

True, Kholster thought back grimly, *but even Oathbreakers tend to have their reasons . . . wrong-headed though they may be.*

Kholster and the other Aern looked on as humans set their warsuits in displays chalked out by the stump-eared princes. A larger display stood empty in the center of the chamber. He and the other Armored were full of speculation about what might be intended to go there.

Wylant stood off to the side, slightly out of step with and behind Rivvek. Dolvek did not seem at all pleased to see her. While the princes both wore multilayered robes with gilt embroidery, Wylant dressed in a black leather doublet with matching pants and boots. Her rank insignia, a golden crown with two golden bars beneath it, adorned her left shoulder, the only bright touch of color on her uniform Kholster could see through Bloodmane's eyes. A blade hung from a belted scabbard at her waist, its hilt wrapped in a dark-blue material that could have been dyed leather, though Kholster couldn't tell based on visual evidence alone.

Why did she cut her hair? Bloodmane asked.

I do not know, Kholster answered. Wylant stood bare-headed and bald in the magic illumination, her blue eyes staring daggers at Dolvek. Her eyes.

With a thought, Kholster had Bloodmane increase the magnification of his vision, focusing on Wylant's face. He studied her eyes for a long moment, ignoring what the two princes said to one another. The veins in Wylant's eyes were partially enlarged and the skin around them puffy, mildly irritated.

Zaur? he asked Bloodmane.

I think so, Maker. Bloodmane answered. **They are the only things to which she is allergic . . . as far as I know.**

Show me where you are exactly . . . based on the old barracks.

A map unfurled in the mind's eye of the Aernese leader. As best he could tell, the humans had carried the warsuits to the Royal Museum. There had once been stuffed and mounted Zaur on exhibit there, but those displays had long since been burned, buried, or otherwise disposed of both to accommodate General Wylant's legendary allergy to the reptilian menace, but also because enlightened Oathbreakers had, over time, come to object to the idea of having the corpses of sentient beings stuffed, mounted, and put on display.

There are Zaur somewhere, he thought to Vander.

What? Where?

I don't know, could be miles away. Probably just scouts.

Hunh, Vander thought noncommittally. *Are you listening to this?*

Kholster redirected his attention to the Oathbreaker princes.

"I was at the last Conjunction, brother," Rivvek was saying. "I met the Aern and I'm telling you now, that after spending three nights out at that cursed monument under the statues of the gods with no one but Kholster and one of the Vaelsilyn—"

"Vael," Wylant corrected. Both princes glared at her, but she didn't seem to mind or care. "They are called Vael now. Assuming Dolvek hasn't gotten us all killed with his foolishness, it's only a handful of years to the next Grand

Conjunction. Dolvek must learn to call them by their proper names, or he'll have more trouble with my ex-husband than he's already likely to have."

"*Ex*-husband?" Kholster asked himself quietly, his words lost in the sounds of grinding gears, sloshing water, and steam.

"Like it matters," Dolvek put in, gesturing agitatedly with his hands. "He's just one man. You two act as if he is a specter of death looming in the shadows and waiting to destroy us all if we say the wrong words behind his back."

He's tracking you there, Vander teased.

"Brother," Rivvek entreated, "I know it is difficult for you to comprehend, but the Aern, Kholster in particular—"

"He is not one Aern, Prince Dolvek," Wylant interrupted. "He is, at the last count, approximately three hundred thousand Aern, assuming that the Aernese birthrate is as low as our informants claim. They will march where he tells him to march and kill who he tells them to kill. Every last one of them. They will die for him, those who are capable of dying, without hesitation."

Wylant's voice grew in volume. As she stepped closer to the prince, Kholster's breath caught in his throat at the design embroidered on the back of her doublet. "They will not argue. If they discuss it in committee, it will only be because he decides he wants other opinions."

"I *do* understand that your former . . . *lover* . . . is a dictator, General," Dolvek began.

"Then you are mistaken," Wylant sighed. "In a common dictatorship, there are dissenters. There are none among the Aern. Not," she held up a single finger, "one Aern questions his decisions once they are made. If he says, 'The Oathbreakers must die. We march tomorrow, every male, female, and infant,' then within a week, news will start spreading of three hundred thousand Aern moving en masse toward Barrony then across the Junland Bridge and then for Castleguard and on through to the Great Forests, where The Parliament of Ages and Queen Kari of the Vael would welcome them with open arms."

That's silly, Vander thought at Kholster. *You'd never leave the Dwarves undefended.*

And for that matter, Kholster answered cheerfully, *I'd been planning to go by boat.*

"You've never met one, brother," Rivvek began. "Believe me—"

"Enough!" Dolvek growled. He reached out and placed a palm on Bloodmane's breastplate.

Must I kill him now? the armor's voice echoed in Kholster's mind. **Lest you be Foresworn?**

Hold, Kholster answered. *Technically he hasn't actually moved you. Maybe Wylant can still—*

"This is simply armor. Magic? No." He drew back and rapped the breastplate with his knuckles hard enough for the contact to echo hollowly within. "It's empty metal. That's all it is. Kholster is not watching us, like some nosy Long Speaker in a Hulsite school. The Aern," he rapped the armor again, "have no," he rapped it harder, "magic!" And with that final word he shoved the warsuit with increasing strength.

Ought I let him—?

Yes, Kholster thought back. *Let him think he pushed you over.*

Bloodmane clattered to the stone floor, half on and half off the royal purple carpeting Dolvek had only recently had laid out in the room.

Kholster felt all five thousand of the Armored waiting for him to react, could sense their minds reaching out for his. He imagined them asking, Do we kill them now? Do we march?

Get back up, Kholster told Bloodmane. *But do not yet attack.*

The armor stood.

Go back to where you were when he knocked you down, as if you are simply resuming your position.

Of course, Kholster.

Rivvek shook his head, but Wylant turned on her heel and left. "You are all dead," she said without looking back. "If you'll excuse me, I need to arrange for patrols to find the Zaur before my planned departure."

"What Zaur?" Rivvek asked numbly.

"My allergies are acting up, and that means there are Zaur on Eldrennai land . . . somewhere. My . . . gift . . . from the god of war."

"What do you mean '*you* are all dead'?" Dolvek asked. "Assuming that was anything more than a basic maintenance charm, the armor simply resuming its position. . . . If the Aern set out to kill all Eldrennai, they would surely include you!"

"No," Wylant answered, "for I wear Kholster's scars on my back. I fought him and beat him at the Sundering, just as I vowed I would. To him, that makes me Aiannai, an Oathkeeper. His vengeance comes only for the Eldrennai, the Oathbreakers."

The pattern on the back of Wylant's black doublet was worked in light-colored leather, almost white. Two symmetrical right-angled wedges, a finger's length each, angled inward near her shoulder blades. Between them, a thumb-width line ran along her spine, stopping two fingers short of the fist-sized leather diamond appliquéd over the small of her back with two parallel lines thickly embroidered along each of its four sides.

Must we attack them? Bloodmane asked.

No. Not yet. The oath I swore did not specify the time of their death. I must think first. How far back have they gone searching through the warsuits?

They stopped when they found the ten they wanted, Bloodmane answered.

Good, Kholster thought for a moment. *Have Hunter, Eye Spike, Wind Song, and Scout each take a unit of thirty out through the old sewer access without being seen. Even if they have to tunnel their way out, I want them to range out to Fort Sunder and see if it has been left abandoned as we instructed.*

And then?

Let's just start with that. I have also sworn that I or my representative would attend the next Grand Conjunction. I must do so, but after that . . . Kholster let his words stop. When he opened his eyes, he saw the laundry room, just as he'd left it, but he couldn't get the thought of Wylant wearing his scars on her doublet out of his head. He wondered if she would manage to beat him a second time. She would, of course, aid the Eldrennai, but after that . . . after they were all dead . . . when only the Aiannai remained . . .

He sighed. Either way, he looked forward to their meeting. Six hundred years was a long time between . . . meetings.

CHAPTER 5
WYLANT'S WISDOM

Wylant cut an imposing figure as she threw open the doors of the Royal Museum exiting the new Aernese exhibit and walking out into the main hall, where the bones of Ivory, the Great Dragon, dominated the space. Behind her, the twelve-foot banded iron doors slipped silently closed when what she really wanted out of them was a good strong slam. She kept her composure, however. It would have been acceptable for a male in her situation to leave the room cursing and hurling invectives at the top of his lungs, but a female who did the same . . .

She clamped down that line of thought, labeled it pointless, and filed it away in the recesses of her mind in the area reserved for thoughts she would explore when she didn't have anything urgent to do. A list she intended to get started on a few candlemarks after her death, hopefully sometime before the Harvester came to collect her soul and take it to the afterworld.

With a frown, she added talking with the king to the same set of files. Talking with King Grivek would be pointless; Wylant knew that as certainly as she knew the patrols she was about to dispatch to search for the Zaur wouldn't find them yet. Why Dienox, the god of war, couldn't have blessed her with a magic map which displayed a giant glowing X over the site of each new incursion by the Zaur, she had no clue . . .

That was a lie.

She did know.

There would have been no sport in that for Dienox.

At times she felt the god deliberately withheld information from her until the reptilian invaders were sufficiently embedded to make the fight a glorious one. Not that he didn't have every right, she supposed. After all, it had been over six hundred years since she'd prayed to him. . . . She'd had nothing to say to Dienox since she'd watched her husband—EX-husband, she reminded herself—go into exile.

The memory of Kholster and the exiles marching away from Port Ammond rose unbidden in her mind's eye. Her husband's last words to her still rang in her head like the remnants of a fireball. "My congratulations, General. Dienox chose well, when he chose you. I'm proud of you."

"Proud?" she'd stammered.

"Of course." He'd grinned that wolfish grin of his and kissed her on the cheek. "You promised to do whatever you could to protect your people. And you did."

"But I killed millions," she had replied, truly grieved. "Millions."

"Don't brag," he'd said as he turned away from her. "From this day forth, you are Aiannai. An Oathkeeper. Any oaths I have sworn against the Oathbreakers do not apply to you. Fight well, First Wife. If you ever tire of your life with the Oathbreakers, come and find me." She'd almost run after him.

Almost.

Her . . . sword, Vax, stirred in his scabbard and Wylant placed a hand on the pommel to quiet him. She had beaten the Aern, had been the mighty general responsible for the deaths of all those who could be killed. Only the five thousand Armored, the Undying Aern, who could only truly die if they surrendered to death, had survived. Those five thousand Aern would yet have won, destroying her people in their wrath, had not the Vael stopped the fighting, convinced the Armored and the Eldrennai to come to terms. All that blood remained on Wylant's hands.

Frown deepening, she stalked down the ornate hallways of the prince's refurbished Royal Museum, past the workmen carrying furnishings and equipment to and from the secret Aernese exhibit hall and the equally new but well-publicized Vaelsilyn exhibit hall. Suppressing the desire to draw her sword and slash through the banner over the entrance to that exhibit, to let the archaic "silyn" portion of the banner fall to the floor, Wylant steered herself to the heavy blood oak doors of the museum's main entrance and out onto steps leading down to the Lane of Review.

Overhead, the moon rose high and a sea hawk flew across it: supposedly a good omen from Dienox. She spat and shook her head.

"General?" Jolsit, the captain of the guard, called to her from across the way. He, unlike Wylant, wore crystalline armor befitting an Eldrennai of the crystal order. Wylant noted with a rueful smile that, unlike many, Jolsit at least had the good sense to wear the enchantment over a mail shirt with boiled leather plates providing additional protection at his elbows, chest, and vitals. If a Zaur or an Aern came to blows with him, their magic-impairing abilities wouldn't leave him unprotected.

"Yes, Captain?" Wylant responded. She half-turned and waited, right hand on the pommel of her sword.

"Did the armor of Bloodmane really move?"

"It did," she answered curtly. "If you'll excuse me, Captain."

Jolsit responded with the customary fist double-tap against his breastplate in salute. "Of course, sir. But . . . General?"

She cocked her head to one side, a query she would have once conveyed with a raised eyebrow.

"I was told you were departing Port Ammond?" his mild tenor voice rose at the finish, making the statement a question.

"I would guess you intuited rather than being told, as I just made up my mind, but yes, I am."

Jolsit flushed. "May I ask where you are headed?"

"To The Parliament of Ages to see Queen Kari." Wylant wondered if Jolsit would ask for clarification. When he didn't, she snorted and told him anyway. "If Kholster is going to attack, he'll wait until after the Great Conjunction to do it. The Vael saved us six hundred years ago. I have to make sure that their representative has what it takes to do it again. This time, I fear the burden of peace will be carried by the Vael alone." *Because Dolvek is an idiot.*

CHAPTER 6
OLD SOLDIERS

Captain Conwrath looked up from his gruel to see five tall Grudgebearers stalking down the mountain road that led into the valley. At the sight of the one in the middle, his blood ran cold. Setting down his wooden bowl, gruel unfinished, the mercenary stood, knees creaking, and made his way to the edge of the lake where he washed his hands and scooped up two handfuls of bracing water to splash on his face.

Phantom scents of remembered fire, blood, and wheat seemed to fill his nostrils as the leader of the five reached the encampment on the other side of the bridge. The Dwarven-Aernese Collective side. The young female, the leader of the Elevens, and her fellow Elevens flocked around the five adults hugging and whooping. A sixth full-grown Aern came over the rise reverently carrying something Marcus couldn't make out.

"Izzat a bucket?" Japesh, Conwrath's second, asked as he walked over to crouch next to him.

"Could be." Conwrath squinted at the other man in the morning light. Japesh had never looked the same since he'd started losing the hair atop his narrow head and trying to compensate for it with what scraggly growth of beard he could manage in uneven patches along his jawline. But Japesh was an old campaigner, so Conwrath had learned to overlook the man's odd appearance in favor of his sharp eyes. "You tell me."

"Izzat an Aernese birthin' bucket?" Japesh said, sucking at his teeth.

"Never seen one, but if there's blood in it, I reckon that may be one." Conwrath looked away from the straggler back to the Aern he recognized. Fiery-red hair, cut close to the skull like a Castleguard knight's or Hulsite marine's. A full beard, cut nearly as close to the skin. That bronze-colored skin. And those ears, long, pointed, and slightly higher up than seemed right for sentient folk . . . more like an animal's. Conwrath watched the Grudgebearer start across the bridge flanked by the leader of the little ones and marveled. "I swear, I don't think he's changed a bit in fourteen years."

"New boots," Japesh muttered. "New pants. Same mail. Same bloody warpick."

"Same smile." Conwrath frowned.

Kholster wore rough black denim leggings (steam-loomed, if Conwrath had to guess) secured with a corded chain belt from which two medium-sized leather pouches hung. Aernese saddle-bags, he and his men called them. Kholster's hobnail boots thudded down like hammers on the bridge planks betraying the unexpected additional weight of all Aern.

"Metal bones," Conwrath whispered to himself. A shirt of bone-steel chain with sleeves that came to ragged edges at mid-bicep caught the light less than it should have. Conwrath winced at the sight of skin visible through the fine-wrought links of chain—the Aern wore no gambeson.

"Lieutenant Conwrath," Kholster called amicably, as if his Elevens hadn't killed and eaten seven full-grown men with whom Conwrath had been traveling the previous day.

Conwrath raised a hand by way of greeting and went to meet the Aern, Japesh quietly shadowing him. "Ho, Grudger," he said as they closed the distance and clasped forearms.

Kholster nodded at the man's notched earlobe. "Captain now, I see."

"Rae'en," Kholster glanced at his daughter. "Captain Conwrath fought a group of Elevens a few years before you were born."

"Did he surrender then, too?" Rae'en beamed. Conwrath saw a world of youthful arrogance in that smile. He'd seen the same grin on his adopted son Randall's face when he'd left to set out on this Khalvadian contract.

"No," Kholster answered. "He and his men killed them, then brought their bone metal back to me in an ox cart."

"Then why . . ." Rae'en balked.

"Why didn't I kill your lot?" Conwrath asked. He eyed the warpick peeking out at him from where it was slung over Kholster's shoulder. The head of the warpick was cruel, narrow, and hooked like a beak at one end, rounded with a flat edge at the other, exactly as Conwrath remembered it . . . except this time, the blood oak leaf engraving work on the head wasn't stained red and brown with blood.

Such a handsome thing when the blasted Grudger isn't trying to kill me with it, Conwrath thought. Aernese warpicks served two purposes, one, the most obvious, as implements of death . . . the other, as works of art, signs of discipline and craftsmanship. This close to Kholster's weapon, the scar concealed beneath Conwrath's tunic, a scar which ran in a crooked line across his chest, itched like mad.

Grudge.

Conwrath caught himself on the verge of whispering the weapon's name and frowned. It was heavier than it looked, heavier than most warpicks, and made to be wielded two-handed, the haft slightly more than four hands long with a grip Kholster'd wrapped in leather the color of old bone. Conwrath knew all that without ever having held the weapon. He knew it like he knew his own hammer toes or the ache in his back when the nights grew cold. He'd seen it in action when Kholster had come to collect the bodies of the dead Elevens only to find that one of Conwrath's men had tried to withhold a femur.

He'd felt the spirit of the thing, heard it cry like a bird of prey, and had come close to wetting himself when he felt it deliberately decide not to kill him. The warpick had struck but a glancing blow, when it could have struck true and deep, gifting him with a scratch instead of a death wound.

Sometimes, Conwrath hated the little spark of long sight he'd inherited from his mother's side, but not that time, because that once it had let him learn the most important lesson of his life: if the Grudgebearers said they weren't angry about something—they weren't. If they offered to call a halt to hostilities, they meant it. Others could claim to let their word be their bond, but the Grudgers lived it or they stopped being Grudgebearers. He'd seen deep into the spirit of the being who'd forged that pick and Conwrath had seen true. Kholster didn't want to kill anyone, but he was willing to kill everyone. Every living thing. If he had to.

From that day on, Conwrath had made it his business to make sure he stayed off the Grudgers' Needs Killing list. He looked across the lake and took a deep breath as one of the adult Aern oversaw the cleaning of the bones before they were stacked and tied for their return to the families of the departed.

"I'm too old to fight Grudgers." Conwrath shook his head. "Too fond of breathing and too wise to knowingly sign up alongside idiots with a Grudger's words against them. Besides, when I saw young miss come galloping over yon bridge like the Horned Queen herself was after her, I saw she was trying to spare these men's lives before they brought your words down on themselves. I knew the lay of the land then.

"If we'd fought, Japesh and I might have made it through alive, but we'd have been the only ones." Conwrath nodded at the bucket. "You're going to talk to the magistrate? Give him the whole show?"

"Yes," Kholster said, his mouth set in a grim line. "If the magistrate can't be made to understand things then—"

"Then the Khalvadians will need a new magistrate." Rae'en beamed.

"I suppose they might," Conwrath agreed. "But let's hope he sees reason, eh? I only took this job because he's my wife's cousin."

*

Ten days later, Conwrath sat astride his horse, taking a long pull of water from his canteen. Battered and beaten, the thing looked like something to be cast aside, but the Dwarven runes on the side made it worth ten times its weight in gold. The Dwarf who'd given it to him had tried to explain how it worked . . . something about magic drawing bits of water out of the air so small you couldn't see them. All Conwrath knew was, even in the driest of weather, it usually filled up at least three times a day.

In the oppressive heat of a Khalvadian summer, Conwrath caught himself silently thanking the Dwarf again. Japesh rode over and Conwrath held out the canteen. Japesh took a grateful swig and handed it back.

"Are we not supposed to notice the Grudgers back behind us?" Japesh asked, looking back toward the hill country.

"I wouldn't have spotted them." Conwrath looked back and saw a cattle range, hills, and their big brothers—the New Forge mountains—wreathed in clouds off in the distance. "How many?"

"They're awful spread out, like the Grudgers do, but I'd say four or five. The two I've spotted wear skull helms."

"Bone Finders." Conwrath frowned at Kholster's back. "Then there are probably at least six. I thought these were all of the first One Hundred. Each of the Hundred gets his own Bone Finder."

"Guardin' the bones of the Hundert then. Fair enough." Conwrath grinned at the way Japesh said "hundred" but covered it up quickly by wiping his lips with the back of his hand.

Kholster walked far ahead of the group of humans and their cart, laden with the polished bones of their dead comrades now, rather than the goods and livestock they'd had with them before. Vander, the Aern with the bucket, walked at the back of the group, his bald head shaded by a broad-brimmed hat in which he'd cut holes for his ears like some of the carriage drivers did for their horses in the city. The other four adult Aern had ranged out like the four corners of a square.

Rae'en rode on the cart next to one of the hired hands, Sandis, asking endless questions about cattle and farming. Conwrath wondered if the young Grudger knew that the young man to whom she was chatting so casually was a new dad thanks to her fight at the bridge ten days back. Sandis had agreed to adopt the boy child, thus sparing his life. Conwrath smirked. If they told the Grudger, she likely would have said, "Congratulations." Grudgers had few children and prized them all. No Grudger child was ever a burden. Not that Conwrath's adopted son Randall Tyree was a burden, exactly, he just didn't need a brother at the moment.

Conwrath shook his head, reminded of his cousin, the new magistrate. Breemson had been so pleased with himself to have finally risen through the ranks and become top man: not only a fully tattooed God Speaker, but magistrate, too. If he'd simply listened and put Conwrath in charge of the caravan or deigned to consult Shidarva. . . . Conwrath used water from his Dwarven canteen to dampen his fingers, rubbing at his eyes and wetting his cheeks and the back of his neck.

"No sense worry'n," Japesh said, his eyes staring behind them as if he saw death or salvation in the distance and couldn't make up his mind which. "They'll listen or they won't. I'm betting if they won't, you'll be the man has to be the new magistrate."

Conwrath raised an eyebrow.

"The Aern like you, Marcus." Japesh spit. "With a few of them Hunderts at the gates, who else you think they'll be worried about pleas'n? Won't be me. My bones is too brittle."

"And your ears aren't long enough," one of the Aern—Conwrath thought his name was Vander—put in with a smile that revealed the doubled upper and lower canines of his people. The smile killed Conwrath's humor. The remark had been funny enough, but Marcus Conwrath had never been able to look at those teeth without picturing blood staining them a bright crimson. Blood was never funny.

"We'll make it to the city by nightfall," Japesh said, covering the awkward moment. He pointed out over the plain at the twin watch stations. The brick towers rose up from the hard-packed ground like larger versions of the termite mounds Conwrath had seen in the wilds of Gromm. Squinting, he thought he could just make out the light of an active transmission crystal. With his slight sense of long sight, the echoes of long speech just touched the edge of his senses as the Long Speakers and Long Seers sent word of their arrival ahead to the city of Darvan.

They wouldn't be sending word of the approaching Grudgers though. They'd turned the proverbial Blind Eye to Grudgers ever since the battles during the Grand Migration (or Exile, if you took the Grudgers' name for it). He'd seen tapestries in Castleguard depicting the assault on the Grand Academy; images of men and women gifted with the use of Long Fist, Long Fire, and other, rarer gifts defending the High Long Speaker himself.

"The eye that spies on me, I shall put out," he recalled the words at the bottom of the tapestry. "The voice that whispers my secrets, I shall silence." He wondered momentarily how the Aern kept up with all these centuries of oaths. How did they manage to keep them all?

Peering back at Kholster, Conwrath caught himself wondering how many tapestries showed the Aern and these same others riding with him. Did it seem at all strange to Kholster that he appeared on one tapestry slaughtering the Grand Academy's protectors only to be shown in others alongside it defending the place and pledging one hundred warriors to stand in defense of each new High Academy?

Later still, as they passed the watch towers and a bald Long Speaker in his white robes met their party on the road, Conwrath laughed at the Long Speaker's question: "Shall I be sending word of your imminent arrival ahead to the city?"

When Kholster answered, "No," Conwrath stopped laughing.

In the distance, backlit by the sunset, the captain surveyed the widening grand road leading down the slope of the basin then up again toward the center of Darvan and the magisterial arena. The city itself rose up in a mound of brick over the flood basin, the grass at its base green and lush, home to grazing cattle and the city's communal farmland. As Darvan boasted only one main road, each building melded into the next, sharing walls, ladders dotting roofs as neighbors scrambled over one another's houses or businesses. "Like bees in a hive," he muttered. "Here comes a bear to stir you up."

CHAPTER 7
VAEL NOT VAELSILYN

The humans of Porthost glared at Wylant as she passed. Their stares differed from the usual looks of dismay she got from humans working in and around the capital city. Those humans knew her as a person, but here all they saw was an Eldrennai. The difference was to be expected. Porthost was a border town, officially the closest any Eldrennai was allowed to travel to The Parliament of Ages, the territory designated to serve as the homeland of the Vael once they were freed from their servitude to her people. One more dividend paying year after year as a result of the inheritance bequeathed to all Eldrennai by Uled's experimentation with the creation of species.

Briefly, Wylant regretted leaving The Sidearms, her cadre of knights, behind at Port Ammond, but given that they couldn't have travelled with her to speak with Queen Kari, she pushed the thought away. She alone was Aiannai. The stares she was forced to endure were nothing compared to what they'd have been expected to tolerate. Their elemental foci drew enough looks back home among the people they protected. Wylant could only imagine how these humans would react. The old guilt rose up, and she crushed it down. She'd done what she'd done to protect her people, and she still didn't see any other way she could have defeated the Aern.

Wylant heard the clearing of a human throat as she passed and reached out to the elemental plane of ice, creating an invisible wall of cold between herself and the flying wad of mucus as it arced her way. Frozen into a lump, the icy projectile bounced off her neck and landed in the street.

"Wha—?"

Wylant spun on the surprised human. It was hard for Wylant to tell humans' ages unless they were truly young and still growing or so old they were preparing for Torgrimm to come and collect their souls, but she guessed he was nearer the former than the latter.

"I am Wylant," she said loudly, augmenting her voice by tapping into the elemental plane of air, the extra wind volume stinging her throat as the words left her lips. "I wear Kholster's scars on my back as a sign to all that I am Aiannai, an Oathkeeper, not Oathbreaker." Don't turn this into a fight, her expression seemed to add silently, you'll lose.

The marketplace of the border town went quiet and still. Transactions froze in mid-exchange as the crowd of humans watched to see what would happen next. She drew Vax with one swift motion, the mottled blue of the sword blade angled at the human with the guilty eyes, the one who'd almost spoken.

"Do not," she said as the sword blade extended, growing longer and thinner until the point of the blade touched the man's throat, "tempt me to wrath. I understand your anger toward the Eldrennai, even toward me, but I will not tolerate your disrespect." She leaned closer, smelling the sour taint of old bread and sweat on the overweight man before her. His clothes needed washing, his beard trimming, and . . . and who was she to judge? How many had he slain in his lifetime? None? One? Yet her hands held the blood of millions. *Ah, the pride of the Eldrennai, always so close to the surface*, she told herself, *even in me. No wonder they hate us.*

"Just leave me be, yes?" Wylant finished calmly.

"Yes, ma'am," the human stammered.

"Kindly put your sword away, Madame General," called an unpleasant voice, "these people have done nothing to harm you."

The speaker, a stern-faced man with bright eyes and glossy black hair, watched her from the rough terrace of the town's only inn. He had a wet bandage tied around one leg, but what got Wylant's attention were the four bowmen next to him, arrows nocked, ready to fire. Two other archers looked her way from opposite ends of the market, one huffing and puffing, evidence he'd had to scramble to get into position.

"Who are you?" Wylant said as she lowered Vax.

"Name's Jorum, owner of the Briar and Bramble." he called. "You may have noticed a distinct lack of welcome hereabouts. You aren't wanted here, fancy jacket or—"

Wylant felt the pulse of another Elementalist touching the plane of air like a shift in an unseen breeze on her cheeks and swore under her breath. The Sidearms had followed her after all. Of course they had. Why could things never be simple?

"You will not threaten the General." Mazik's voice, with its familiar gear-driven cadence and tick-tock precision, cut Jorum off mid-sentence. "You will lower your weapons by the time I count three or the threat you pose shall be forcibly resolved."

"I'm fine, Mazik," Wylant hissed as the chief Aeromancer of her knights decloaked, spooking the humans standing near him. Wylant couldn't blame them for that. It wasn't every day that a dark-haired Eldrennai in chain shirt, leather trousers, and cavalry boots materialized next to them. His red cloak billowed about him, a sure sign his magic was active. The skewed placement of the bandanna he usually wore to conceal the damage done to his throat and lower jaw by the unfortunate placement of his elemental focus gave the humans all too much to see.

More guilt. Would she ever not feel guilt when she looked at him? Such had been the cost, one of the many costs, of saving her people.

After the breaking of the Life Forge, Eldrennai magic had twisted, leaving many Eldrennai with the choice to abandon the elements for all but the mildest of magicks or risk permanent damage to the portions of their bodies used to channel the primal forces of the world. Mazik, a Thunder Speaker like Wylant, had focused the elements through his voice, literally breathing fire when a flame spell was required. The Artificers had done what they could to reinforce his throat, but the adaptive implant grew as the damage did.

Six hundred years ago, the implant had been little more than a brass oval and a band of metal ringing his neck. Now, the once-handsome Eldrennai sported a throat and lower jaw of gleaming brass; his once-rich baritone had become a harsh metallic rasp.

"ONE." Enhanced by elemental air, Mazik's voice cracked like thunder as he amplified his voice, causing villagers to flinch and the children in the market to wail.

"We won't be threatened in our own town, magic spitter! Not when there are only two of you."

Oh, Wylant thought acidly, *there are more than two.*

If Mazik had come, that meant they'd all come. *Why did I ever let Kholster convince me to have them swear to protect me personally? And why did Grivek's father ever agree to allow it in the first place? Another sin of pride?*

"There are more than TWO," the "two" resounded cacophonously, letting all know it was part of the count, "of us. Lower your weapons."

Wylant opened her mouth to tell Mazik to stand down as Jorum and his crew loosed their arrows. Arrows which plummeted down at near ninety-degree arcs, the effective weight of their arrowhead multiplied many times over by geomancy.

Roc, thought Wylant. The curly-headed Geomancer appeared next to a vegetable stand. His hands were curled into tight fists at his side, his modified boots allowing the brass feet which were his own elemental foci access to the ground. "Got the arrows, Maz."

Jorum's men dropped their weapons, and for a moment Wylant thought they might all escape without an injury to anything but their pride until Jorum himself spat a curse, drew a sword, and leapt from the terrace toward Mazik and Wylant.

"THREE."

Nine more Eldrennai in chain shirts and matching cloaks appeared. Griv, Ponnod, and Tomas were suspended by their Aeromancy just above the roof-line on the south side of the street, Bakt, Kam, and Hira on the north, with the twins Frip and Frindo taking the east and west ends of the street, respectively. Each of the twins stood with opposite hands outstretched; Frip's steel left hand encased in ice, Frindo's steel right hand engulfed in flames. Some had chosen steel, others brass, but each of The Sidearms sported a focus implant except for Wylant and Kam.

Wylant had been spared completely, having stood at the epicenter of the blast when the Life Forge had been sundered; her magic was untwisted by the destructive forces she'd unleashed. Kam was young, part of a new breed of Elementalists who'd chosen to shape a single element to the exclusion of all others, using an elemental familiar as the focus for his mystic abilities.

When she'd chosen Kam as replacement for the deceased Perrin, his brother Sidearms had overseen his oath to protect Wylant personally. Kam's familiar, a small bat-winged creature composed mostly of a living storm cloud, rode on the young Eldrennai's shoulder, its ambient wind tussling the boy's long black hair. Not that Kam's type of magic didn't have its own dangers.

Wylant winced when the ground shifted beneath Jorum's feet as he landed, a patch of earth no more than a square foot in diameter buckling forward, then back. Out of the corner of her eye, Wylant saw Roc wince as the human's left knee, the bandaged one, wrenched, bending in the wrong direction, the snap audible even above the whirling of air and the crushing echo of Mazik's magic-enhanced voice.

"By Aldo, Roc," Hira swore, "you were supposed to knock the man down, not cripple him."

"What kind of idiot locks his knees when he jumps off a terrace, Hira?"

Cursing under her breath, Wylant stepped over to the writhing man and kicked his sword away before kneeling to render aid. "Let me take a look at that."

"Don't touch me," Jorum spat in her face. "Just leave."

"I have a bone-knitter and some laughing salve," Wylant insisted.

"I'd rather lose the leg than let one of you stump-eared—"

"Fine." Wylant stood and turned in one smooth motion. "You have until I'm out of earshot to change your mind. May Aldo grace you with his wisdom and if not, may Gromma take pity on you and heal that knee."

She locked eyes with Hira. "Horses?"

"We flew," he answered with a shrug. "Dodan is looking after the horses back at Port Ammond. Couldn't take owned horses into The Parliament of Ages, could we, ma'am?"

"By treaty, you aren't even allowed to take *yourselves* into The Parliament of Ages," she growled back, "without permission from the Vael, which you know you won't get."

"We're your sworn Knights," Mazik broke in. "We believe Kholster would be more angry if we left your side than if we followed you into Vael territory."

"He is the one who had us swear to protect you," Roc said. "And we'll be quiet. He'll never know we were there."

Wordlessly, Wylant stalked along the trade road running through the village. She did not have to look back to see whether or not The Sidearms were following her. Of course they were. They'd followed her into Port Gates to fight the Ghaiattri on a different plane, into battle against her husband and his Armored, into tunnels to fight the reptilian Zaur. She only hoped they wouldn't have to follow her straight into the Bone Queen's clutches via Torgrimm's loving Harvest. She wondered, not for the first time, if the Harvester could be persuaded to send her soul to join the Aern when she died. The thought of an afterlife populated by Eldrennai (her Sidearms notwithstanding) left her . . . less than enthusiastic.

Scowling, she continued on.

*

At the edge of the city, the rough cobbles gave way to what barely passed as a deer trail. Trees grew right up to the city wall, the limbs hanging over it gnarled and ancient. Eyeing the trees, Wylant could not make out any signs of the Vael, but she knew they had to be there.

"I am Wylant," she said firmly. Not sure what level of volume would be required, she settled on the not-quite-a-shout she used when addressing a line of troops. "I come on foot with urgent need to address—"

"Why'd you cut your hair?" came a feminine voice. "My, but you're loud."

Wylant suppressed a smile. Leave it to the Vael to focus on the physical. Then again, considering how much shorter their life spans were than, say, her own people's or the Aern's, she guessed it was appropriate.

"Is it really because you hate the gods?" asked another. "She is quite loud, though. You're quite right in that, Arri."

"Or did you just go bald?" asked a third. "Both of you: don't be rude about her religion, she's His. You know that, Malli, even if Arri can't be bothered to study history."

"Some humans go bald," said the first voice. *Arri*, Wylant recalled, repeating the name over and over in her head to try and attach it firmly to the voice in her mind.

"But mainly the boy-type persons," said the second voice. *Malli. Malli. Malli*, Wylant thought.

"She's definitely a girl-type person." The fourth voice was masculine. Wylant saw him stepping free of the undergrowth with the same slight start of surprise one might have when a stick-bug started to move or a moth which had looked like nothing more than a piece of bark flew away. He smelled of oak leaves and a tart but pleasant musk which reminded her of Kholster. The male's lined brown skin was rough and bark-like. Pointed ears almost as long as a donkey's swept at an angle back over his shoulders, and his red hair, like strands of braided leaves, crackled softly as he moved.

The Vael male met Wylant's gaze with unblinking ruby-colored eyes seemingly possessed of no pupils or sclera, just glittering globes of uniform color. "Hello, kholster Wylant," he said warmly. "I'm Tranduvallu. You may call me Tran, if you like. How can the Vael be of assistance to the Aiannai?"

Wylant had seen Vael males before. Where the Vael females had been made to appeal to the Aern and Eldrennai as idealized sexual objects, the Vael males were different, appealing to the Vael females' sense of the ideal male, lending most of them a distinct similarity to the first one hundred Aern.

Tran, in particular, bore such a resemblance to Vander beneath all the bark and despite the ears that it gave Wylant pause. Uled had never intended that there be male Vael, just as he had intended no female Aern exist. She wondered for the umpteenth time whether Xalistan, the god of the hunt, Gromma, the goddess of nature, Jun, the builder, or Torgrimm himself had arranged their dual-genderedness against all intentions. And why? Was it just a game to the god or goddess involved, or did they simply object to a race that could not breed with itself? However it had happened, his presence threw her off. Vael protected their menfolk even more fiercely than the Aern protected their daughters. . . . What was he doing out here?

"What's wrong with it?" Roc asked too loudly, shocking Wylant out of her reverie.

"Roc!" Mazik thumped him on the back of the head before Wylant had the chance.

"Not all Vael choose to strip their bark," Tran answered with a smile. "Any more than we all choose to score or prune our dental ridges so they appear more like teeth. I strip my bark in summer sometimes, but not always. Think of it like shaving off a beard, if that helps."

"Oh. Yes. Of course," Roc fumbled.

"I need to speak with Queen Kari," Wylant said. "It's about the Zaur. And we need to discuss the impending Conjunction."

"You may enter, of course," Tran said. "You are welcome in The Parliament of Ages, kholster Wylant, and always shall be as long as you are Aiannai."

"General," Hira corrected, looking lost even as he spoke, as if he knew he shouldn't have spoken but could not stop himself. "She is not an Aern."

"Of course she is," Tran said matter-of-factly, waving away all thoughts to the contrary with a dismissive air. "By marriage. Her Sidearms, of course, may not enter."

"Why not?" Roc blurted.

"Shall we recite the names of your victims, mighty Roc?" Tran's eyes narrowed. "Your reputations precede you, Sidearms. It has been many years since a recitation has been needed, but the names have not been lost even if none alive recall the specific acts you committed."

"Kam may enter," Arri said, still hidden by the forest. "If he swears himself an Aiannai and foreswears his Eldrennai heritage. I have no authority to grant him scars to wear in the manner of kholster Wylant, but he has no list of names to face, no litany."

"And he can't be grabby," Malli put in. "Don't forget that. I'm not walking around wearing a samir over my face just because some dumb stump-eared male can't control himself."

"I know Vael are supposed to be supernaturally attractive to the Eldrennai," Kam blustered, "but—"

Malli stepped out of the forest. A scent like royal garden roses filled Wylant's nostrils. Uled had once explained to her the effect Vael had on Eldrennai had as much to do with scent as it did their appearance. Small, lithe, and ample bosomed, Malli wore tight doeskin leggings which stopped at mid-calf, exposing the curve of her shapely leg and silvery birch-bark–colored skin. Her heavily beaded top was equally form fitting, even though it covered the skin from the top of her neck to her wrists.

Short purple shoots adorned her head, a crown of almost hair, like some cross between orchid petals and actual hair. Lips tinted that same purple hue quirked into a smile, revealing carefully pruned dental ridges that looked very much like actual teeth.

"Hi, Kam," Malli purred.

Kam's response was an animal grunt which Wylant assumed to have been intended as a greeting.

"Don't shoot this one in the knee, okay, Molls?" Tran said softly.

"Can you talk, Kam?" Wylant asked.

"I . . . uh . . . I," was his only immediate reply, broken up by laughter from Frip, Frindo, and Ponnod. Kam seemed not to notice, lost in the deep violet pools of Malli's eyes.

"It's almost not fair for a creature that enchanting to be the first flower girl the boy's ever seen," Hira said breathily.

"So that's settled then," Wylant snapped. "The Sidearms will NOT be joining me in The Parliament of Ages. Camp north of Porthost and don't annoy the locals. It's a direct order and disobeying it may risk us all. Understood?"

"Yes, General," Mazik and the others (except for the speechless Kam) answered at once.

Wylant shot a careful glance from Mazik to Kam and then to Malli. When she, Tran, and the other Vael turned to leave, Mazik and Hira were already at the young Eldrennai's sides, holding him back from chasing after the departing Vael.

"Wait!" he shouted as Malli vanished into the forest. "Wait!"

Wylant clenched her fists and sighed.

"At least he didn't actually make a grab for her," Tran said, moving alongside Wylant.

"I suppose." Wylant allowed. It had been so long since Wylant had set foot in the ancient forest, she'd forgotten how wonderful it was. Tran and Malli were plainly visible to her, but she could sense other Vael around her in the forest even though she could not quite spot them. "How many?"

"Guards?" Tran asked. He grinned broadly. "Thirty. I'm Taking Root soon, so they are all keeping a special eye on me until I find the right spot. Queen Kari wants an outpost close to Porthost and I've always enjoyed human watching, so when I felt the time coming upon me, I offered to do it."

Wylant shook her head again.

"So that would be Prince Tranduvallu, then?"

"Only royal males can become the roots of a home tree," Tran answered. "So what was it you wanted to speak with Mother about?"

"The Zaur." Wylant had spotted five other Vael so far, moving in the branches of the surrounding trees. "Maybe it's nothing, but I've been sensing them on and off for years and it's getting worse. I want her to keep an extra eye out. I'd also like to meet the Vael representative to the Conjunction." Wylant suppressed a "ha" as she spotted another six Vael in quick succession.

"Kholster Wylant comes to the Parliament worried about the Zaur."

Tran almost clapped his hands together in utter delight. "Who would have thought I'd be lucky enough to see such a thing while still in my mobility?"

Who indeed? Wylant thought to herself. *And am I really that predictable?*

"You'll like the choice of representatives, too," Tran continued, "but I'm unsure you'll learn much. They are still quite young."

"How young?"

Tran stopped and gazed at her, his dark, impassive eyes turning serious. "This crop will be one week old tomorrow."

Wylant cursed, but pressed on.

CHAPTER 8
AERN TEASING

Breemson, the magistrate, failed to alleviate any of Conwrath's fears. He'd only met the man a few times, usually very briefly at family events. Somehow Conwrath had never realized the man was this . . . incompetent. Or was it just dealing with the Aern that put him off? It flustered many men, dealing with people who would happily eat someone to whom they'd just been speaking.

Maybe he'll get his feet under him soon. The captain watched as the man fretted with his robes and sucked his teeth. A magistrate and a God Speaker for Shidarva. . . . The goddess of justice and retribution seemed to Conwrath to be a hands-on sort of goddess, giving her most ardent followers fair value for their worship, but God Speakers, particularly hers, with the image of their pale blonde goddess tattooed across their bodies: her face inset within the boundaries over their face, her chest over their chest, and so on . . . the thought sent a cold chill up the captain's back and gave him the flesh crawls.

Her blue eyes stared out at him below Breemson's own. Thankfully, they were inanimate for the moment. If the goddess herself were looking on, it was from the spirit realm, as was only right and suitable for a god. Conwrath looked away.

Japesh sat on a gilded wooden stool near the door of the magistrate's office, a look of practiced neutrality fixed as firmly across his features as other men might don a helm. His eyes held a different message: *Say the word, Captain, and I'll gut this one. God Speaker or no. Surely your wife can't be too mad. And if he's supposed to live, his goddess will save him then, won't she?*

A study in self-importance, Breemson's office spoke as loudly to the man's stubborn pride as his own offended reaction to the presence of the Grudgebearers in his city. What wasn't gilded was lacquered. Nothing was local except for the door itself. If Conwrath guessed correctly, the magistrate's desk was made from purpleheart wood, which had to have been hauled all the way from Castleguard in Upper Barrone.

Conwrath amused himself by trying to estimate the shipping costs for the item itself as well as for strictly the materials necessary. The Dwarves preferred locally sourced materials and placed prohibitive taxes on those transporting construction materials across the intercontinental Junland Bridge, which would have been the fastest way to get the desk from the Upper continent to the Lower one. The tariffs alone to get the cursed thing across the length of Barrony . . . Conwrath suspected the goddess had not demanded such expenses be incurred.

"Why do they want to see *me* about it?" Breemson hissed. "It's not my fault we didn't have the correct instructions! Shidarva judge me now if I've angered them deliberately."

"Magistrate." Conwrath tried not to sound too condescending. "The Grudgers aren't angry with anyone. They—"

"Aren't angry? They killed and ate half the trade delegation!" Breemson shrieked. "And then they *dare* to come to my doorstep to threaten me."

Conwrath didn't like the inflection on that "dare" or the "me." Indignation never sat well with an Aern.

"I believe Kholster is approaching you in an open, honest manner . . . hoping to . . . ah—"

"Clear up any further misunderstoodings," Japesh added helpfully.

"Misunderstandings?" Breemson squawked as he bounded out of his chair. Conwrath winced at the volume. The Aern had particularly good hearing. What, he wondered, were the odds that Kholster and every one of his Aern could hear every word they were saying, even from out in the audience chamber? "I suppose having the Long Speakers withhold news of his arrival was meant as a sign of openness and honesty then? I assume I misunderstood that, too?"

"Cousin." Conwrath began a different tack. "This is easy. I know the Aern seem backward and savage from your side of the battle, but they're knife-to-the-chest sort of people. Never a knife in the dark. If they want to kill you, they'll tell you that's what they intend to do—"

"They don't get sneaky until after they've put words against you," Japesh said.

"Against me how?" Breemson froze.

All three of them turned to the door at the sound of a commotion outside in the magisterial arena. Conwrath thought he heard the tail end of what might have been the word "unconscious" followed by a clang, a thump, and the sound of a body hitting the door and sliding to the ground.

"Generally," Kholster said, as he opened the door and stepped over the unconscious guard who had been posted at it, "I shout them with thunderous volume at the offending party, in front of many witnesses." He frowned at Breemson, and Conwrath wondered what the pudgy official with his sweat-stained robes and holy tattoos must look like to the Aern.

Then he knew. Aern tended to make food comparisons and . . . yes, pork, like as not. He could halfway see it himself. He didn't like to guess what kind of meat he seemed to the Aern. Probably pork for himself, too.

"You have my solemn oath, that, unless forced to fight in self-defense, or in trial by combat in the eyes of Shidarva in accordance to your laws—which, I should add, I would not appreciate—neither I nor my fellow Hundreds will attack you with our warpicks. Does that comfort you?"

It shouldn't, Conwrath mused. *It wouldn't assure me one bit.* But he watched the magistrate relax slightly. "And Aern always keep their word."

"Or they are no longer Aern," Kholster said perhaps a bit more acidly than he'd intended.

"Very well." Breemson regained his composure, smoothing his robes and wiping sweat from his brow with a hand towel. "You understand my need for assurances, of course?"

"No," Kholster answered with a wolf-like smile. "But you have them nonetheless."

CHAPTER 9
GOD SPEAKER

What do you think of the new magistrate? Vander thought at Kholster as he reentered the audience chamber. It had changed very little since the last time Kholster had seen it. The cushions covering the tiered rows of brick benches provided for the audience had been reupholstered in a dark-purple fabric Kholster couldn't identify. Some over-soft cloth that his fingers yearned to touch. No doubt it wouldn't hold up well.

Overhead, a tent-like awning stretched over the entire chamber, ablating the sun's fierceness. It depicted the goddess Shidarva in all her glory, standing in judgment over petitioners. She sat upon a simple stool. Before her, a mighty-looking warrior wielding a blue sword was shown being defeated by a small child plying a blade matching in size and shape but ablaze with blue flames. It was good work and well maintained. Kholster still didn't understand why they didn't just call the place a holy arena.

Kholster saw Magistrate Breemson entering the chamber behind him, from Vander's perspective. The man looked a prize hog walking on its hind legs in a circus. *Pork*, Kholster thought back. *There's a lot of meat on his bones, too. He could easily feed two of us.*

The guards who had been wise enough to clear out of Kholster's way when he'd demanded entry to the magistrate's inner chamber stood up straight, abandoning their unconscious comrade as the magistrate moved past them to the raised dais in the center of the chamber and approached upon the stool at its center. A stool which, Kholster noted, looked far more comfortable and ornate than the one depicted in the image which overlooked the proceedings. Breemson mounted the backless stool and cleared his throat, clearly waiting for Kholster to resume his seat in the place of waiting, exchanging an incomprehensible look with a Long Speaker and her two Long Arms seated in a recessed overlook to watch over the proceedings.

He could at that, Vander thought back from his seat along the curved wall of the arena with the other Aern and the handful of citizens waiting to have their cases heard by the magistrate, those who hadn't fled the chamber immediately upon the Aern's entry. *I'm told some of the Elevens Rae'en kholstered tasted their meat cooked.*

And? Kholster put his hand on his Overwatch's shoulder as he took his place next to him, standing rather than sitting, and set himself at the ready, waiting the magistrate's pleasure. Theoretically, old business should come first. But Kholster found that most magistrates cut straight to the big game and dealt with the Aern. Unless they felt the need to try to demonstrate their authority . . .

They say the fat tastes better when it sizzles, but that the meat shrinks down, Vander answered, watching the magistrate undo the bundle of documents contained within the official satchel next to his chair.

Not the first time I've heard that, Kholster thought back. *Good reason not to cook it.*

You think he's going to make us wait? Vander thought.

I'd make battle plans around it.

Would you wager naming rights on it?

I never wager naming rights.

"Farmer Aimes?" The magistrate read from the official slate he'd withdrawn from the satchel. Kholster thought he did a fair job of pretending not to watch for a reaction out of the corner of his eye. Kholster twisted his chin to his left shoulder and then his right, partially to stretch his neck muscles, but mostly to see the human flinch.

See? Vander chided. *You would have won. You have always been such a sword in the sheath.*

I thought the expression was pick in the shed.

Farmer Aimes stepped forward, hesitantly, looking to the Aern as if seeking pardon or permission. Giving him both, Kholster waved the man forward and inclined his head permissively. Relieved, the short, squat man in often-patched overalls advanced to stand before the dais. Breemson mentioned some vague thing or other about the complaint, and Aimes dissembled further. Kholster had stopped paying attention by then. Something about cows.

The humans say something about a stick . . .

What? he thought back at Vander. *Instead of sword in the sheath? Stick in the eye?*

Something like that.

Maker? Bloodmane's echoing thoughts intoned.

Kholster, old friend, Kholster corrected automatically. *Just Kholster will be fine.*

Of course, Maker. Scout and his crew have made it to the Shattered Plain. It is patrolled by crystal guardians, and the Eldrennai have built a wall around it. There are warning signs.

Show me. Closing his eyes to see through Bloodmane's, Kholster experienced a momentary sense of dismay as his viewpoint warped and refocused to reveal the canted perspective of Scout, Okkust's armor. Plains once covered in myr grass, its purple plumes stirred by gentle breezes, had become a jumble of random craters and cracked earth, great shards of rock thrusting up high in one spot with the ground dropping away into deep rents in others. Abandoned, at the center of the devastation, Fort Sunder stood an empty carcass of stone which had once been home to over a million Aernese troops.

What's wrong with the air? Kholster asked.

Relayed through Bloodmane, Scout's reply sounded distant and faded. **We think the odd shimmering is a side effect of Wylant's destruction of the Life Forge, First One. The warning signs,** Scout focused its vision, and one of the distant signs grew large in magnification until the words on it could be clearly read: *Twist Warning: All Elemental Magic Prohibited By Order of King Grivek.* Other signs read: *Elemental Magic Unstable in this Area* and *Using Elemental Arts in this Area May Cause Dimensional Breach and Death.*

Do you feel any adverse effects? Kholster thought back to Scout through his link with Bloodmane.

No, First One.

Can you get me a better look at one of the guardians?

Of course, First One.

His viewpoint shifted again, this time coming to rest on an insectoid construction of clear crystal. Six wings like panes of wavy glass held it aloft as it flew a circuit around the thirty-foot seamless wall (made of the same transparent substance) it had been tasked to guard. As Kholster watched, one of its wings stopped functioning and it was forced to land atop the wall, perching with its spider-like legs clutching the narrow blade-like apex of the wall.

Turning its head 180 degrees so it could get a better view of the malfunctioning wings, the construct reached back with the uppermost of its four sets of arms, the ones with prehensile digits as opposed to the heavy clawed graspers that punctuated the thicker lower arms, and began to manually force the wing to move, first up and down, then side to side. After several repetitions, the wing resumed normal function, and the construct continued its patrol flight, scanning the wall with multifaceted eyes flaring occasionally with brightly reflected sunlight.

How many of the things are there? Kholster asked.

We're still checking, Scout replied, **but so far it looks like half a dozen fully functional models. Twice that number appear forced to strictly ground patrol duties due to malfunctioning wings, and perhaps one dozen units appear to be completely nonfunctional.**

Any Eldrennai at all?

None that we detect, First One.

Kholster sensed a hesitation in the warsuit, as if it were holding something back.

What is it, Scout?

My maker says it looks like the Eldrennai have stopped maintaining the work here. He wants me to go ahead and try breaching the wall.

Not just yet. Tell Okkust I want to wait until Eye Spike, Wind Song, and Hunter have their teams in position. Full line of sight. Until then keep a watchful eye out, yes?

Of course, First One. I believe my maker was merely anxious because of the bones.

Bones?

The bones of dead makers-to-be, Scout's echoing voice said, his volume dropping low. **They are just visible through the breach.**

Show me, had just left Kholster's mind, when Vander's thoughts intruded: *I think he's about to get to us, Kholster.*

Thank you, Scout. Please show Bloodmane the breach you mentioned so he can relay it to me later. And . . . thank you. Well done.

First One, Scout acknowledged, and Kholster opened his eyes to view the audience chamber once more.

He just asked if he was boring you, Vander prompted. *You'll want to review the little farmer fighting his gigantic neighbor. Shidarva's magic was jerking his sword to and fro. I can show you later.*

Fine. Kholster narrowed his eyes at the fat magistrate, his ears filled with remembered cries of a million dead Aern as their souls left their bodies and their spirits fed back into their brother and sister Aern, the five thousand Armored. In his mind's eye, he saw a sky filled with Aeromancers raining lightning down on Fort Sunder, Geomancers using the rocks to smash his soldiers and break his home. Echoes of past anger quickened in his chest, and he met the magistrate's impatience with bared fangs and a growl. At the sound of his growl, the pale blue eyes of the goddess, inked below Breemson's own, lit from within.

"I have been patient." Kholster took a step forward. "I have come to your city to make peace with your people and you have made me wait, putting me to heel like a dog!"

"Here we go," Vander muttered under his breath, elbowing Okkust. In the rear of his mind, Kholster sensed his fellow Aern ready to tear the city apart and eat their fill of its people, ready to turn his anger into action and . . . He took a deep breath, found his center, and reminded himself that the humans were not his enemies. Not all of them. Not yet. Perhaps not ever.

"And I suppose that comes from unfamiliarity," Kholster said more warmly, trying to tamp down the anger, stifle the rage. The humans weren't Eldrennai. They were Oathbreakers, perhaps, but it was difficult putting beings who'd never enslaved him or his people in the same category with those who had done so. "You don't know me, Magistrate. The last time I was here, you can't have been more than a child. We Aern trade items of the forge for meat from your farms. On rare occasion, when we decide to sell our bones, we offer you the right of first refusal."

"Sell your bones?" Magistrate Breemson scoffed. "You sell us bone-steel."

Kholster grimaced and Vander's thoughts found him: *I can start reinforcements on their way here from South Number Nine and they'd be here in three days even if the goblins wake.*

They'd be here in two days; there are no such things as goblins, Kholster thought back.

An expression, Vander thought at him.

Ah, no reinforcements yet.

"Would you like to correct your speaker, Shidarva, or should I?" Murmurs went up from the crowd on that one. Addressing the goddess directly was simply not done. It had been so long since Kholster had felt bound to observe that particular nicety, he kept forgetting it existed. He waited, giving her a chance to respond, and when her eyes only narrowed, he proceeded. "Fine."

Kholster held out a hand and Okkust stood up, holding a plain metal bucket for Kholster to take. The Aern wondered if the humans realized the bucket was made of unpolished bone metal. Probably not. He took the bucket, careful not to slosh its contents too much.

"I need you to understand two things. The first is this: We are different from you. The second thing is everything about us that you think to be just a myth or kitchen talk is true or has its root in truth." He held the bucket out to Breemson, noting the way Japesh and Conwrath, standing at the back of the room, both slid their hands to their weapons. Whether to defend the magistrate if need be or for some other purpose, Kholster could not say.

*

If that jumped-up cousin-in-law of mine goes to knock that bucket out of the Grudger's hand, thought Conwrath, *I'll kill the fool before Kholster has the chance.*

The tension made his shoulders ache, but worse than that was the touch of long sight twitching in his brain. He couldn't exactly hear Breemson's thoughts; God Speakers were awfully hard to read, but he got the gist of them, and he didn't like the direction they were going.

"This is a birthing bucket," Kholster said loudly, not just for the magistrate, but for the audience around them in the chamber. Murmurs of interest and surprise seemed to rule the crowd, their inquisitiveness pressing down on Conwrath like a heavy blanket on a summer day, making him sweat. "None of you have ever seen one." He held the bucket out and walked around the edge of the chamber. "You may notice it is filled with blood."

"Theatrics, surely," the magistrate muttered.

"My people were not made by the gods. Jun did not forge us. Gromma did not plant us, nor did Queelay cough us onto some sandy beach in the long ago."

"Thought it was one of them things," Conwrath heard Japesh whisper to himself. "Always wanted to see a baby Grudger."

"Theatrics," Breemson said more loudly. "You are surely wasting our . . ."

Conwrath flinched as Kholster's pupils grew large for a moment, the amber pupils stretched, the jade irises strained, the black diminished. Conwrath never wanted to face another Aern with the black gone from its eyes . . . replaced by that glow of jade-rimmed amber.

"Eyes of black, talk them back/Amber and jade be dismayed," Japesh recited a snippet of warning rhyme.

"Do not interrupt him again," said a female voice. It was strong and hard and carried with it a weight Marcus Conwrath found heavy to bear. He knew he should not be able to see the tattoo of the goddess, covered as it was by layers of fabric, but it was as if Breemson had grown transparent to reveal, hidden within himself, a living image of the goddess Shidarva, clad in robes of blue, a quill clenched in one hand, a sword the other.

"He is your elder by millennia. He was not made by the hands of gods, yet we recognize him. He is a creature of disrespect, of bloodshed and tears, but he does not lie knowingly except perhaps by omission. His kind remain outside my judgment. You may deal with his people or not, but do not test them or taunt them. It would be . . . unwise. I have spoken."

Kholster took two steps forward and spat. "I neither request nor require any god or goddess to speak on my behalf or the behalf of my people!"

"Masterwork of Uled," Shidarva began, "surely your rage is misplaced. This one's mind was alive with cry for my intervention."

"What did you call me?"

"Watch your mouth and guard your tones," Japesh was repeating somewhere behind Conwrath, "lest the Grudgers clean your bones." Conwrath couldn't look away. Was Kholster's anger, his rage, directed at the goddess? Conwrath didn't think it was. It felt deeper.

"I am Uled's creation no more!" Kholster reached into the bucket of blood and drew forth a small lump of metal, like two fist-sized stones crushed together. "He forged me. He wrought my very soul, but what I am now was not by his design, but mine and that of my people. He is at best an inspirator, a mad contributor to my initial concept! I reject him!" He held the lump, cradled it. "This is how he envisioned us: Lumps of metal he could mold. Playthings to serve his purpose."

Abruptly, Kholster looked back over his shoulder. "Okkust, do I have your permission to wake this son of yours?"

A thick-eyebrowed Aern, slightly broader than the others, stood and took one step forward. "Yes."

"Who is born this day?"

"Droggust, by Okkust, out of Marridai."

Reaching over his shoulder, Kholster found the pointed poll of his warpick and sliced his palm, drawing back the injured hand and smearing his pale almost-orange blood over the still-iron lump. He plunged it back into the bucket and passed the bucket back to Okkust, who grinned broadly and drew out a blinking bronze-skinned infant.

"Hello, Droggust," the warrior cooed. "I'm your dad."

"Da!" the infant squealed, the word verging on comprehensible with its (*his*, Conwrath corrected himself) first attempt.

The new father, in a motion identical to the one made by Kholster, gashed his palm on his own warpick and rubbed his blood on the child's head. As he did so, a scar pattern rose up on the child's back.

"Da da scahs," little Droggust burbled as if he knew exactly what was happening.

"Yes," Okkust beamed. "Your Da Da's scars."

The babe blinked and twisted his head about until he found Kholster. "Ah-no," he cheered delightedly.

When Conwrath looked back at Kholster, the black was back in his eyes, the jade a healthy circle around his amber pupils. "Very well," Kholster said, his voice warm and proud, his amber pupils lit from within. "All know . . . that on this day, Droggust, by Okkust out of Marridai, has joined our ranks and bears his father's scars. May he never be Foresworn."

"Ah know!" the baby chirped.

Kholster's smile deepened as Okkust opened his belt pouch and withdrew a clean cotton garment for the babe.

"Won't he need a crap catcher?" Japesh murmured.

"We neither defecate nor urinate," Kholster said. "What we do not digest, we regurgitate in small pellets."

"Like owls?" a young girl in the stands asked.

"Similar to owls, but not as often or as messy."

"Then it's yarping, says my Auntie."

"I am not opposed to the word," Kholster said levelly, seeking the child out with his eyes.

"Theatrics," the magistrate repeated. "Surely . . ."

"I think that girl oughtta be the magistrate," Japesh muttered.

*

Conwrath was in motion before the words "I agree," left Kholster's lips. The Aern, leaving his warpick slung on his back just as he had promised, went low, left hand curling into a fist as he spun on the magistrate to deliver a hammer-like blow clearly intended to crush the unsuspecting God Speaker's skull. Conwrath rolled forward, scooping up one of the ceremonial blades of judgment and, in a rolling summersault (with consequences to his left knee he hoped he'd live to worry about later), caught the blow with the flat of the judgment blade. The redirected force set his shoulder alight with pain which faded along with the discomfort in his knees as the blue runes, traces of shidarvite worked into the blade, began to glow.

"He is the magistrate, Kholster," Conwrath grunted.

"A poor one."

"When it comes to dealing with you Grudgers, that may be true, but he's still chosen by Shidarva."

"Which reflects poorly upon her as well." Kholster straightened, hand slipping back toward his warpick. Then with a subtle shake of his head, he drew his hand away and spread his arms wide in a combat stance.

"Still," Conwrath continued, "it's her choice to make." Power, either from the blade or the goddess herself flowed up Conwrath's arms like youth itself had been injected into his limbs.

It has been many years since I had a Justicar, the goddess's voice rang in his mind. *The conditions required by the Divine Accords are so stringent. Defeat the Aern and you will be my chosen. I will add unto you a hundred years of vigor, the strength of five . . .*

Marcus Conwrath blocked out the goddess's words, needing every scrap of concentration for combat with the Grudger. *How do I force a draw?* The magistrate's guards made as if to intercede, then stopped themselves, eyes riveted to the glowing blade of judgment. The Grudgers, Conwrath noted, made no moves at all. Sitting. Waiting.

"Defeat my champion," Shidarva spoke from somewhere back and to the right, "and you have my leave to kill the magistrate. I will select the girl as the new one."

Kholster snorted. "A stopgap at best. I will still find myself back here in a handful of years having to explain to a new magistrate and make new arrangements. I think I liked it better when Kilke was ruler of the gods. He at least had no illusions about the relationship between gods and mortals. He treated them as playthings and knew it." Shidarva had risen to power after cutting off one of Kilke's three heads.

Conwrath lost control of his arm and was jerked into a forward slash. Kholster's anemic orange blood welled up as he took the blow on his forearm with the sound of metal on metal as sword edge struck metallic bone.

"And I treat them as playthings and don't?"

"Did you just attack me? I don't think it was the good captain." Kholster smiled. "I noticed the captain prefers to thrust like mad in an honest fight . . . he's rarely one to chop."

Two more blows came, swift as lightning. Kholster slapped one away with bare hands and took the other across his mail. Conwrath felt himself pulled forward by the sword. He hoped Lyla's cousin was worth this. Gritting his teeth, he fought for control as Shidarva sent him into a further flurry of attacks. Shidarva's anger flowed through Conwrath's mind with a single word: *Blasphemy.*

She was a brilliant swordswoman after her own fashion, and a human opponent would have been dead already three times over, but she wasn't fighting the Aern properly. As he'd told his own trainees, one should never chop at an Aern like a tree, one should fill them full of holes and bleed them. Give them wounds meant to slow them down and tire them out so you can kill them with one blow. Only the killing blow matters with the Grudgers, he'd told his men. Everything else is a delaying tactic to get that opening.

Let me fight him, Conwrath howled inside his own head. *I know him.*

"Are you offering Captain Conwrath here the status of Justicar yet?" Kholster asked, baring his doubled upper and lower canines like fangs. "I will kill him rather than see him live through the destruction you would make of all he is, Queen of Leeches."

More blows. More blood, but no telling shots. Already the wound on Kholster's forearm was closing. *Between the bones. Between the bones*, Conwrath cursed. *If you must chop at the Grudger, cut muscle and tendon. It takes longer to heal.*

"Answer me if you can, Captain," Kholster called.

"You dare call me leech?" was what poured out of Conwrath's lips in a voice that was definitely not his own.

"You live on the belief of mortals," Kholster sneered. "What else should I call you?"

"I am Shidarva!" the voice came from two throats. "I am Justice! I am Retribution! And you will respect me!"

Unable to follow the exchange of blows any longer, Conwrath felt pushed back into the recesses of his own body, his own mind. Rills of blood crossed Kholster's arms, but Conwrath remained uninjured. Had he even been attacked yet? With a sound not unlike a pealing bell, the blade of judgment cracked down on Kholster's skull, only to be locked between the Aern's crossed arms and shattered.

"Are you back, Captain Conwrath?"

Conwrath's body leapt for the other blade of judgment, only to be jerked short when Kholster seized him from behind.

"I'm sorry you got caught up in this, my worthy old foe," Kholster whispered in his ear. "But I would cast you into the hands of the one god I trust rather than see you enslaved by this one."

A crack and a pop and it was done. Dimly, Conwrath thought he heard the sounds of Breemson screaming and another body hitting the floor, but he felt himself wrapped comfortingly in the strong arms of a god.

CHAPTER 10
HARVESTER

"All is well, Marcus Conwrath." He knew the voice well, as well as he knew his own. It stirred a deep rush of emotion, relief breaking free and pouring over him in a way he hadn't felt since he'd been a babe in his mother's arms. Yet he also knew he'd never heard this voice before in his life. "I've got you. I've got you."

"What . . . what happened?"

Around him, the world had faded to tones of gray as, simultaneously, another world of vibrant colors began to flow in. He smelled freshly thatched roofs and his mother's roast lamb and baking bread and . . .

"You did well," the sonorous voice continued. "I couldn't be more proud. I know you would have liked to be there more for Randall Tyree, but Japesh is a good friend and I'm sure he'll do all he can. Besides, Randall is a clever lad and—"

"Wait," Conwrath pulled free of the arms enfolding him, stumbling forward through the space previously occupied by Kholster, surprised to have been so easily released. "What happened? Wha—?"

Standing across from him, Marcus Conwrath observed a being in bone armor, helm hovering casually in the air as though it had been set aside and left hanging. Sharp Eldrennai features blended with the harsh cast of an Aern's and a very human smile. He had dark hair, with eyes like the beginning and the end of time, just, Marcus thought, like his statue in Castleguard. Looking into those eyes was like standing on the edge of a parapet and staring down at the ground far below. It thrilled and frightened in equal measure.

"Torgrimm?" Conwrath guessed.

The god's smile deepened, revealing laugh lines around his eyes and the corners of his mouth. "Yes, Marcus. It's me." The god stepped forward and clasped him on the shoulder. "Sower and reaper. Lifebringer and harvester. You know me, Marcus Conwrath. You've known me since before I planted your soul in flesh."

"So the Grudger . . . Kholster . . . ?"

Torgrimm nodded. "He didn't want you pressed into Shidarva's service as her Justicar. I sensed you didn't desire it either. There's still time of course . . ." The god frowned. "If you want that. I oppose all unwilling influence by the gods over mortal souls, but I would allow her to revive you if—"

"No," Conwrath answered too quickly. The memory of the goddess's thoughts mixed with his own, pushing and controlling him, made him shiver.

"I thought not." Torgrimm smiled again. "But it's your life to live, not mine. The others, they forget that." The god's eyes darkened, putting Conwrath in mind of the days after his father died, when his grandfather would sit staring into the fire, his eyes looking through the flames at memories young Marcus could scarcely have comprehended. "Far too often."

All around them, frail remnants of the living world resolved into a hut from Conwrath's distant memories. The ancient wobbling table. The woven wicker chairs. Even the horrible cracked and smelly old bearskin rug. "Gran's house?"

"When you were six," Torgrimm said, "you prayed this was what death would be like. I thought it might do for a start."

"A start?"

"You never decided what you wanted out of death, Marcus." Torgrimm sat his helm on the table as if he'd just noticed it hanging in the air. "Some don't. Some do. I try not to judge unless I'm forced to do so." The god waved his hand, and Marcus's eyes lit up to see his Gran's old wooden tea set and clay teapot appear on the table. His mouth watered as thick biscuits filled with slabs of smoked venison appeared next to two pewter cups.

"Life can be so hard on some of you that I have to take certain matters into my own hands for some souls until they calm down, but not you. I knew you were a good one from the first yowl."

"You stuck around for that?" Marcus sat in his grandfather's chair and bit into a biscuit. It had been years since he'd had one. And they'd never been as good since Gran passed. She'd had a secret to her biscuits that'd died with her.

"That's the best part." The god grinned. "Each soul is like a measure of clay meted out. Each receives an equal measure. But what you make of it is wholly your own. Some use their portion for good works, others for terrible ends, while still more hurl their portion carelessly against the wall of life. I observe each and all. Some invoke laughter, others tears. Any interference on my part is parsimonious lest I look upon a soul at harvest time and see the print of my own handiwork, my own fingers, if you will."

"Then you know everything," Marcus said softly. "We should worship you as the god of knowledge, not Aldo."

"No." Torgrimm waved the comment away. "Aldo truly is the god of information. All facts and fictions are his to know. He knows every page, every hidden design, every law of the universe. He even knows everything you've ever done. He knows everything. But I know everyone." The god finished the sentence stressing the "one," and Marcus began to understand.

"Then how do you punish the wicked? Or is that . . ."

"My wife, Minapsis, the Horned Queen, the Queen of Bones." Torgrimm clucked his tongue. "She rules the dead. Not me. I rule no one." Conwrath caught himself wishing Torgrimm ruled everyone but contented himself to chew and swallow the hearty biscuit. He ate in silence for a time then cleared his throat, poured himself some tea, and drank it down, savoring the slightly astringent bite as it went down.

"What next?"

"Next you go on to Minapsis, unless you would prefer to try again in a fourth life . . . though, if you'll take an old god's advice, I quite like what you've done with this turn."

"Reincarnate?" Marcus sputtered. "Like the gnomes?"

"If you feel unfinished."

Marcus shook his head. "No, I feel completed. There are things I wish I could do. Keep an eye on Randall, give him my last name when he's old enough to understand it, and make sure he doesn't become some cursed pirate or highwayman, but another life? No. I wouldn't want that."

"I thought not." The god screwed up his lips as if trying to decide something and then a slice of sourberry pie appeared on a small tin plate in the middle of the table, a tumbler of whiskey next to it. "Dessert?"

Marcus beamed. "Mother's recipe?" Though he knew the answer to his own question just by the smell and the slightly burnt edges of the crust.

"Do you mind," the god asked as Marcus picked up a fork, "if I ask you a question?"

"Of course not," Conwrath laughed.

"The other gods play games with the souls and lives of sentient beings I have delivered unto Barrone. You felt Shidarva's touch. And though she is more desperate than cruel, and certainly well-intentioned, I grow weary of even her interference."

Marcus waited for the god to continue, but when, pie halfway consumed, Torgrimm showed no sign of continuing, Marcus prompted him. "I've heard no question thus far."

"Do you think it would be acceptable if I did so . . . just once?" His expression soured as if he found the concept repellent. "I would ask, of course, and not in the asking-that-is not-truly-a-request manner Shidarva used with you. I would never!"

"I believe you." Marcus thought on it. "What would you need?"

"I cannot say," Torgrimm said quickly. "Aldo knows all, except for the minds of the gods. Were I to speak it aloud, even to a soul . . ."

"He'd know?"

"He might."

"And he must not know?"

"Not until the last possible instant."

"I trust you."

Torgrimm sighed, obviously relieved. "You all say the same thing. Even the ones I'm throwing back to try again out of sheer frustration."

"How many have you asked?"

"Several billion," Torgrimm shrugged. "I lose count."

"I'll take your word that that's a real number."

"Do you mind an additional question?"

"Of course not."

"What do you think of Kholster?"

Marcus let out a long, slow breath, instinctively reaching for his pipe and smiling pleasantly when his favorite, lost long ago on one battlefield or another, appeared before him. This could take a while.

CHAPTER 11
THE FORESWORN

Kholster smiled despite himself at the sight of Okkust's son chewing on a bit of raw liver. Pausing to deliver a cheerful "ah know" in Kholster's direction, the child bared doubled canines and returned to his meal. Kholster wondered how infants from other races managed being born without teeth. The concept of nursing, though he understood it, still felt alien. Almost as alien as camping out under the stars.

"Perhaps I should start camping out more often than on my centennial visits to the north for the Conjunction." He whispered the thought into his own cupped palms, making certain not to transmit it to any Aern accidentally.

A Hearth Stone provided warmth for the child without illumination. Kholster felt a chill at the back of his eyes as they maintained optimum visual spectrum. His current battle company lay spread out over the plain, their locations constantly available to him, both via the images provided by his Overwatches and the pull of their soul-bonded weapons, or, in the case of his daughter, her soul token.

You needn't have summoned so many, he thought at Vander.

I know you didn't call for reinforcements, but I wasn't sure the good people of Darvan would honor our agreement.

How many humans have turned back?

Only a dozen.

You did well.

Kholster watched Rae'en in the dark, a Freeborn child, the second he'd had in six hundred years. She still seemed a miracle. He wished in some wistful way she'd been an artist, like her brother. That he could have sired a child who'd lived to see adulthood and never killed another sentient still baffled him. Then again, Irka could never lead the Aern, could never kholster another. But Rae'en . . .

He caught her watching him in the dark and smiled. Rae'en could kholster them all. Could arvash the world if that's what she had to do. He knew the look. Had, in fact, originated it.

You did the right thing, too, Vander thought at him.

Perhaps, Kholster allowed. He lay flat on the ground. Unused to traveling with those of lesser endurance, he'd grown out of the habit of stopping for breaks so frequently. The waiting and being quiet so the others could rest was maddening. *I'm not sure it was worth losing the captain, though.*

Shidarva had her nasty hooks in—Vander thought.

I could have talked her down. Kholster closed his eyes to see through those of Bloodmane, and through Bloodmane, the eyes of Scout, Okkust's armor, as the armor led a team of diggers, tunneling under the crystal wall meant to seal off access to Fort Sunder. *She can be reasonable. I talked her into releasing her champion when we saved the world crystal, Vander. I could have tried it again. She's just so proud of her own sacrifice. A continent of people, everyone at Alt, died, and I can't see what it bought anyone—they dethroned one god and put another in his place.*

That was a millennia ago, Kholster. Even gods can change in that span. Besides, the people of Darvan are much better off with their new magistrate.

I'm not sure it matters, Kholster thought back.

Scout broke through the last barrier of earth, climbing through to stand within three hundred feet of Fort Sunder. A stream of fellow warsuits followed, sprinting for the cracked wall. In less than a candlemark, they were inside the fortress's outer walls and facing another wall, this one composed of the bones of the dead. The bones of all the Aern who had died at the Sundering filled the courtyards and passageways of Fort Sunder, their bones piled as high as the inner keep in places.

It looks like they started with an eye toward arranging them carefully, Bloodmane intoned. **Then, perhaps they grew tired of their work.**

I will shatter the Life Forge, Kholster! Wylant's voice echoed through Kholster's memory. *If you do not stand down. I will do it.*

I believe you, Love, he'd whispered back. *But I cannot stop.*

You'll all die!

We will merely most of us die.

Kholster! Don't make me do this!

Do it, Kholster'd told her. *It's within your power—your only chance to win.*

But I don't want to win; not at this cost.

Then you understand, in your darkest hour, what it is like to be me, in mine.

Of course she'd done it. She'd promised to put her people first. Had she done any less, how could he ever have continued loving her? Kholster smiled in the dark. Then frowned.

"Ex-husband?" he whispered into his hands. "Why ex?"

What if we don't? he asked Vander.

Don't what?

What if I break my word and we become Foresworn?

Rather than kill the Eldrennai? Shock rang clear in Vander's mind. *I'll grant you there are fewer Leash Holders left alive as time wears on . . . and I have no burning need to rush across two continents to pick a fight, but to be Foresworn?*

Yes.

Your oath would be broken . . . and your words bind not only us, but also the Freeborn! We wouldn't even be able to . . . to . . . touch each other's minds . . . not even each other's skin. Our very bones would repel us, one from the other, for all time.

Do you want to kill all of the Eldrennai, Vander?

Silence stretched out, speaking ever louder as it dragged on.

Tell the Overwatches at South Number Nine to bring me the Foresworn. I have questions for him when we return.

Yes, Kholster, Vander acknowledged.

*

Four days later, Kholster regretted his request to see the Foresworn, and he regretted going alone. He could have changed his mind, of course, and decided not the see the former Aern. He could have summoned Vander or Rae'en or any Aern to join him. But now that he'd thought of it, talking to the Foresworn seemed like a thing he should have done a long time ago, and doing it in front of other Aern seemed somehow cruel. He stopped in the snow and frowned before moving on.

The snow-decked peaks of the Duodenary Mountains, so-called because the Dwarves had divided them into twelve distinct zones, loomed large above as Kholster trod the Dwarf-and-Aern–wrought steps carved into the side of the Ninth. Small bone-steel tokens worked into the corner of each step kept him on the path even as he focused his sight back and forth between views of the construction in the Royal Museum of the Oathbreakers, where Bloodmane watched impassively, and the restoration of Fort Sunder, as the warsuits, under Scout's direction, began to organize the bones of the departed.

Minuscule segments of bone-steel beneath certain steps provided additional location information: a cluster of three rows of three told Kholster he was still on the Ninth Miner, wedges above and below the cluster told him he neared the boundary of the north-south bypass where he was to meet the Foresworn.

Deciding to give the Foresworn his full attention, Kholster opened his eyes. From his vantage point, Kholster could just make out the stone features of Jun, the builder and god of the Dwarves, worked into an adjacent mountain face. Coal, to his knowledge the last of the great dragons, sunned himself on a nearby peak, the sight bringing a smile to Kholster's lips. The dragon was getting old and sore; it was good to see him out and about instead of soaking himself in the lava flows deep beneath the mountains.

Smoke rose in a winding plume above the watchtower between the north-south division where he'd instructed the Foresworn to meet him. The fully stoked fire blazed brightly, but the Foresworn himself did not appear to have made it. An armor-clad Dwarf waved at Kholster, pointing farther downslope.

There he was. Lost?

Hurrying to the watchtower to wait, Kholster was greeted by the watchmaster.

"Watchmaster Binnolbloh, Kholster Kholster."

"Just the one Kholster is fine, Watchmaster. It was my name before it was a title or rank." Long vowels, Kholster noted, fondly reminded of the trace of an accent Helg had picked up from her time in North Number Two. Her "sir" rhymed with "far" or "star" rather than "fir" or "stir."

"Of course, sir." The Dwarf's stomach rumbled with the sound of stone on stone, a clear sign of nervousness. Had this Dwarf never met an Aern?

"Is there a problem?"

"Oh." The Dwarf stomped his feet, "Coal, sir. The sight o' im scrambles mah bedrock."

Not everything is about you, Kholster reminded himself.

"It that a oneward accent?"

"Oh, yes, sir."

"My Dwarven wife, Helg, picked up a touch of that when she apprenticed to Planner Yommorna."

"My ma studied under her, as well," the Dwarf said, perking up. "Of course, she was born in East Number Two and my dad was from Prime itself."

Kholster nodded appreciatively. He'd been to Prime and, other than being the first city the Dwarves had built when they resettled to the Duodenary Mountains, Kholster hadn't thought much of it, but the Dwarves were quite fond of the place and being from there seemed to carry with it a certain social advantage.

"Your outcast is down there," the watchmaster said to fill the silence. "I don't think he can make it up the steps."

Kholster leaned over the battlement and studied the Foresworn from a distance. Clad in leather breastplate, long coat, trousers, and buskins, the Foresworn looked like an oversized babe dressed for battle. No trace of metal adorned him. His hair, bleached to a shock white to announce his status, grew long if not unkempt. What struck Kholster most, though, were the eyes, which he could just barely make out from his vantage point above. They had whites like a human's in place of an Aern's black sclera.

"Kholster," the Foresworn called loudly. Waving a gloved hand high. "I'm here."

"I see you, Parl." Kholster felt the subtle pull of each bone-steel pellet in the steps, and beyond those, he sensed his Overwatches, and if he concentrated he could find all the others and their bonded weapons. From the Foresworn, he felt a push . . . a subtle repellent force.

The Foresworn perked up like a dog at the sound of his own name, grinning ear to ear like some lovestruck fool to hear it cross the lips of his former kholster.

Vander? Kholster thought. *Are you getting this?*

We can't become that, Vander thought to him.

Maybe it wouldn't be horrific if we were all outcast together?

There were once two Foresworn, Kholster. They repelled each other, too.

The Dwarves made a big deal over that, as I recall. Something about polarity?

Yes, but then one of them said something about domains and they all cheered and patted him on the back. No idea what they were talking about, but . . . Does he look sick to you? Can you picture Rae'en like that?

Kholster didn't answer.

"Parl," he said under his breath, "Fifty-Third of One Hundred. You look like . . ." What did he look like? Death, if Kholster had to put a word on it. He was too pale, and his mouth seemed drawn in. And those eyes. Those eyes made Kholster shudder. No Aern should have eyes like eggshells. He pictured Rae'en with those eyes and the image made him sick.

Everything goes well with the Elevens, Vander pushed on. *Rae'en and her Overwatches are drilling with Quana's squad. Nothing to report.*

I wonder if I should have brought Rae'en. Let her see him.

She can be there in little more than a candlemark.

Kholster frowned. Perhaps it would not be cruel, but just, to have witnesses here. *Bring yourself and the Foresworn's Incarna, as well as Rae'en and her Overwatches. I want Rae'en to kholster this decision.*

Decision?

You know what needs doing, Vander. I know what needs doing. Rae'en is Freeborn . . . I choose to follow her words on this matter. She, also, must know what needs doing.

We're on our way, Vander thought.

Good. Let me see what's taking him so long.

Kholster watched as the Foresworn picked his way along the edge of the steps, being careful not to place his feet too close to the edge. In some spots he raced along the snow-covered rock, but in others, he scaled the rock face, scrambling for purchase.

"Something wrong with the stairs?" Kholster called.

"They're seeded with bone metal," Parl answered. His voice was different, too. Kholster couldn't quite place why. As Parl reached a flattish plane, he attempted to set foot on the steps, but his foot hovered above the step in a wobbling way as if he could not quite manage to force his foot down.

"I'll come down," Kholster said with a curse. "I should have realized."

"Please don't, Kholster," Parl choked the words out. Was he crying? "I can do this. Please."

"In your own time." Kholster nodded. *Would you rather I look away?* Kholster wanted to ask that last question but didn't.

"What did he do?" whispered the Dwarf Kholster had forgotten.

"There are many oaths I advise Aern against making." Kholster grimaced between words as Parl lost his footing and fell across the steps, sliding across the tops like oil on water until he managed to grab a stone to stop his slide. "Promises of eternal anything or unequivocal success. I have experience with oaths. I tell them take an oath that you will make a reasonable effort, instead. Oaths should hinge on effort, not outcome." Let all other Aern take care; Kholster's own oaths bore enough weight for his people to carry.

"And the oath he took?" The Dwarf leaned toward Kholster with eager eyes.

Below them, Parl negotiated the troublesome patch where he'd fallen. The wide steps lay close to the edge as the path turned, the rock face too steep to climb without tools. Parl. Kholster was finding it hard to think of Parl as the Foresworn while watching the familiar look of determination on his face. Parl balanced on the edge, using the force of the bone-steel's push to help steady himself on the narrow margin.

"He swore an oath to convince another Aern to spare the life of his son's new bride."

"And the other wouldn't hear of it, even to spare the Grudger being Foresworn?" the Dwarf asked, shock clear in his voice.

"Midio of North Number Three." Kholster closed his eyes as he spoke. "Do you know the name?"

"Sounds familiar. Something to do with the last elections?"

"She was a beautiful Dwarf." Kholster could still see her in his mind's eye. "Jun's touch was clear on that one. Hair like the deepest depths, eyes the color of lava flow. Toymakers could have copied her in miniature and sold the likenesses to human children. She did not lack for," Kholster searched for a Dwarven euphemism and found it, "mineral deposits, either."

"I can picture her," the Dwarf agreed.

"She had taken a different name for her work in Polimbol's bid for foreman, when he opposed Glinfolgo."

"I'm not ashamed to admit that I backed Polimbol—"

Kholster's eyes flashed open, irises expanding, amber aching to fill the black.

"—until I found out about the weak metal in his character," the Dwarf finished quickly. "Girders built with flaws that deep have to be melted down and forged again. I even heard tell he had that mistress of his rig a . . . collapse."

"It is not common knowledge." Kholster felt the calm creep back in. "But she did indeed. The tunnel's collapse was meant to kill Glinfolgo, to default the election back to Polimbol . . . but it killed Glinfolgo's sister instead, and almost killed her daughter, too. There was a public trial.

"Parl's son, his Incarna, swore he thought his wife was innocent. Thought," Kholster searched the Dwarf's eyes for understanding. "Do you see the difference? Taking an oath is proof one is telling the truth. It's dangerous, but a powerful tool—particularly among older Aern who remember being oathslaves to the . . . Oathbreakers. To lie with an oath would make an Aern instantly Foresworn."

"Parl's son begged for his father's intercession?"

"And Parl swore not only effort but success . . ."

Below, Parl managed his balancing act and made it through to the wider portion of the path. The slope was steeper, but the distance between step edge and drop-off more than enough to make the climb possible.

"No gold, I take it?" the Dwarf asked.

"No gold," Kholster repeated. "The worst sort of mining. It would have been hard to convince any Aern to spare the woman, but the Aern he needed to convince was me . . ."

Parl moved more quickly than before, traveling on all fours. He stumbled once, twice, and then he was at the lower edge of the watchtower's steps.

"Glinfolgo's sister, killed in the collapse, was my wife, Helg. I swore to find and kill at least as many of those responsible for Helg's death as I, while remaining sane and reasonable, could before my Overwatches cried out for me to stop."

"As oaths go," Parl panted, "it was well-thought out, with good limitations, and an excellent safety valve to allow the oath to be abandoned honorably."

"Unusual for my oaths." Kholster walked down the stair to meet him. "Particularly when I've just lost a wife." *And I almost lost Rae'en, too.*

"My own oath was regrettably less well-managed. 'I will save her life, son,' I said." Up this close, Kholster identified the source of the strangeness about Parl's voice . . . there was something wrong with his mouth. His teeth were gone. Pale gray gums. No teeth. Had they fallen out? Had he sold them? Had they . . . rotted? "I will make Kholster spare her. You will grow old together. I swear it. He will listen to reason. If only I had started with 'If she is truly innocent' . . ."

"If only you hadn't said the 'grow old together' part, I could have spared her for a day and spared you in the bargain."

"It was a stupid oath."

"I've made my share of them and yours beside, but . . ."

"His boy's wife, Midio," the Dwarf put in. "She was Polimbol's murderous mistress?"

Kholster and Parl nodded.

"The one you dragged out into the deliberation chamber and tore apart with your bare hands?" the Dwarf asked.

"I was angry." Kholster sighed.

"You will note," Parl added almost cheerfully, "the great disparity between 'spared' and 'torn apart by the First Forged with his bare hands in front of the voting committee.'"

"Then the rumors that you killed Polimbol . . . ?"

Kholster frowned. "Untrue. My brother-in-law did that. It was his right according to Dwarven custom to avenge his sister, and my Overwatches interceded on his behalf . . . cried out for me to stop and allow Glinfolgo the kill." Kholster froze, pupils blazing amber as the memory caught him. Glinfolgo wielded a bone-steel mattock Kholster had forged for him as a Groom's day gift from Kholster's own shed teeth. Polimbol died again and again in Kholster's memory and he would never consider it enough.

Sense memory washed over Kholster, the feeling of Midio's skin breaking in his grip. Her screams. And then they'd brought out Polimbol. As he'd told them to do, Vander and the other Overwatches cried out in Kholster's mind. *He's to be Glinfolgo's kill . . . not yours. Stop.* Kholster bared his doubled canines and snapped at the air, slightly embarrassed by the lack of control even as he surrendered to it.

"Best if I do my rounds," said the Dwarven guard, taking two quick steps away from Kholster. "You'll keep an eye on things, while I trek northward to check the next tower?"

"For a time." Kholster nodded. He watched the Dwarf go, doing his best to ignore the Foresworn. Kholster found he had nothing left to say to the former Aern. All his questions had been answered. All that remained was to see if Rae'en felt the same.

CHAPTER 12
WYLANT'S CHOICE

The twin Root Trees of Hashan and Warrune stood at the center of a nexus of cultivated streets and byways forming, along with their brother trees Fergin and Balnas, the central palace or, as Wylant's hosts preferred to call it, the Heartwood of Hearth, the capital city of The Parliament of Ages. Long ago, Wylant had preferred the old Eldrennai name for the forest, but the land belonged to the Vael now and they could call Great Wood what they liked.

Beneath the intertwined lower branches of the Twins, little half-height sproutlings—looking more like miniature versions of full-grown Vael than the weeks-old beings they were—gamboled happily, if a bit loudly for Wylant's comfort. The underside of the Twins' branches glittered with silver and blue spirit lights, casting a soft, even luminescence. The smooth wooden walls encircling the private garden were formed, Wylant noted, by the commingled root system of the Twin Trees themselves. How the Root Trees grew rooms within themselves, much less the double doors through which Wylant passed upon entering Queen Kari's garden, was beyond her.

"I don't know how they do it, either," Queen Kari remarked, her age betrayed by a gentle quiver in her otherwise musical voice. "I'll never be a Root Tree as I am not a boy-type person."

Queen Kari, clad in a simple white gown that may or may not have been cotton (and Wylant was not certain whether she actually wanted to know or not) watched her children chasing each other about in the garden, the corners of her wide umber-colored eyes wrinkling with amusement. Her head petals, long and white, cascaded down her back, the scent of her—cool, clean, and sweet—stood out uncloyingly even amongst the floral scents of the other Vael.

Gender roles seemed far more complex among the Vael than the Eldrennai, but then again no Eldrennai Wylant had ever met was likely to take root and become a house. She'd wanted to ask Tran more about Taking Root, but the prince had left her in the hands of the Parliament's Warders and had returned to the outskirts of the forest to resume his quest for the perfect place to begin his long growth into a Root Tree, forming the core of a new city nearer to the humans.

Two Warders, somewhat severe and withdrawn for Vael, stood toward the rear of the garden not-quite frowning at the children. Both wore hunting leathers and had the same deep purple head petals, clipped short. Their heartbows were casually at hand, the deep, rich wood kept alive by the Vael's unique form of spirit magic. Wylant could sense the power moving tenuously about her in the forest, like a whisper on the breeze or a twig snapping far off in the dark.

Shamanism, she thought to herself, *I wonder how different it is from Kam's New Elementalism.*

"So, kholster Wylant," Queen Kari said, tearing her gaze away from the children, "How long do you suppose it will be before Dienox deigns to lift his fog of war to allow you to discern the location of your ancient foes?"

"So you also believe they are hidden from me," Wylant raised an eyebrow, "and not that I'm poor Wylant, the mad General who smells nonexistent Zaur on the wind where'er she goes?"

"It takes little faith to believe what one can see, kholster." Queen Kari's eyes narrowed. "The shroud of the god hangs over your spirit so that it pains me to see it and not be able to help. Your soul struggles so valiantly to keep you free of him that he only manages to blur the edges. He does not control you, but he has in the past."

"Control me?" Wylant snorted. "The gods cannot control the living unless the living are willing. I'm not some foolish God Speaker."

"But you have opened yourself to war, to the thrill of victory. The times Dienox has reached in and pushed you in one direction or the other have left his burning handprints on your living spirit, marks your soul cannot scour away in this life. I see a conflagration engulfing your right wrist . . . and one trailing fire from the back of your head as if he'd grasped your skull one-handed, forcing you to change direction . . . and . . ." Queen Kari looked at Vax, and Wylant closed her fingers around the pommel not as if to draw it but as though to obscure the queen's view.

Sensing her dismay, Vax drew in upon himself, shrinking down into his sheath, hidden from the queen's piercing gaze.

"Your husband could help with that, you know," Queen Kari said softly. "If you sent word to him, he would come. He longs for you."

"Kholster?" Wylant took a jagged breath, emotions so mixed and raw she didn't even try to tell them apart. "He remarried. He doesn't think about me. And this . . ." She clutched the top of her scabbard. "I could never explain."

"He thinks monogamy means only one spouse of any given species," Queen Kari said, her smile as gentle as her words. "Your kin taught them that."

"He's had centuries to figure it out," Wylant said.

"And in all that time he married only once, and she did the asking." Queen Kari frowned sadly. "She passed, you know."

"I . . . no . . . I wasn't aware."

Wylant looked back to the sproutlings, wanting to change the subject, but even there, the subject was her former husband. Which Vael here could, in thirteen years, convince Kholster and Prince Dolvek not to kill each other for three days and three nights while they camped together at the feet of the statues of the gods? Which sproutling could convince Kholster to renew his oath and come back for one more Conjunction in another hundred years' time to stave off Aldo's Prophecy?

There was a poem about the so-called prophecy in Vaelish, a language Wylant didn't speak, but the translation went something like: "Listen to me, my favorite mortal children. The peace you have is fragile. Once every hundred years, the Aern, the Vael, and the Eldrennai must each talk to each other and renew your truce, or one day the Aern will show up and kill the Eldrennai so quickly the Vael will not have time to talk them out of it. Then there will be no one left to man the Port Gates and demons will creep into the world once again. So play nice and spend at least three days and three nights together, because the Vael representative is going to need at least that long to make Kholster not want to eat the Eldrennai."

The Vael representative.

"Was this . . ." Wylant hesitated, uncertain whether she wanted to ask the question on the tip of her tongue. Though all of the children were attractive and playing, Wylant tracked one of them in particular. Among peers with petals in colors as varied as the many varieties of plants and flowers in the wild, this sproutling's head petals were sunflower yellow. Her facial features, well . . . Wylant realized she was going to have to ask. "Was this something you did on purpose?"

"If you mean," Kari said, her limbs creaking softly as she walked over to a stone-wrought chair and sat down, "did we make Yavi look like you or did it happen naturally, I believe I may take umbrage." She laughed. "Mild umbrage. It happens with every Vael who meets Kholster." The queen's eye seemed to look far away. "Some of our sproutlings in each season tend to look like you or like him, or both. Tran said we should send young Kholburran."

Wylant's gaze went instantly to the bronze-skinned sproutling boy with the shock of red hair petals like the leaves of a blood oak, cut so short it looked like overgrazed pastureland. Despite the donkey-like nature of the ears, the boy was Kholster's spitting image. His eyes were a solid and startling jade. When he laughed, his dental ridges showed spiked thorns at the corners of his mouth as if to mimic an Aern's doubled canines.

"Maybe," Wylant said. "Success is more certain with a girl, one who is a fighter but has a good heart and a strong will. She will need to be able to understand him, to really see him, to stop him. Usually he wants to stop, but he requires an honorable excuse.

"And," Wylant released her grip on her scabbard as Vax resumed his most usual shape, "she'll need to be able to keep him from getting so angry he starts making oaths."

Queen Kari grinned at that, revealing her pruned dental ridges, worn by age, browned at the edges. "One of the harder tasks."

"And she'll need to be very careful about sleeping with him."

"The hardest task," Queen Kari said wistfully, "given that we were grown to specifically desire the Aern and them us. He is, as Firstwrought, perhaps the most Aern of the Aern. I wanted to run away with him and let every Eldrennai be arvashed. You have Rivvek to thank for the current lull in hostilities. Though recently . . . I dreamed . . ."

"What did you dream?"

Queen Kari shook her head. "I dreamed that Kholster came to the Grand Conjunction with the five thousand exiles and there was fire and blood and the breath of demons. I dreamed the gods screamed in terror at what will take place."

Wylant eyed Yavi, who stood watching them intently but was drawn into a game with her peers. Wylant listened to the sproutling's laugh, studied the determination on her face when she was behind in the game and the look of empathy on her face when she'd been in the lead too long and surrendered it to another sproutling. Wylant didn't really look at the other one, Kholburran. She couldn't.

As playtime evaporated, turning into bedtime, Yavi approached the Queen.

"Mom?" she asked.

"Yes, Yavi?"

"In your dream, did the metal irkanth talk?"

"I didn't dream of one."

"Oh. Okay. I did." Yavi bounced off toward the doorway with the other sproutlings. "It talks to me."

Bloodmane? Gooseflesh covered Wylant's neck and arms. *Did that little sprout mean Bloodmane?*

"Did that mean something to you, kholster Wylant?" Queen Kari asked.

Wylant nodded. "It did indeed. Thank you for your time. You've given me much to think about. I suspect Yavi will do well. And the Zaur—"

"We'll keep watch, but I suspect Xalistan of clouding our perceptions as well."

"Dienox and Xalistan working together?"

"Or playing the same game," Kari answered. "If we detect Zaur I'll send word."

Wylant nodded and, summoning a burst of elemental air, she flew free of the courtyard, her hand gripping Vax's pommel so tightly he cried out, sounding far too much like—

It was only afterward that she wondered at her display of magic. Why had she done that? Was she really jealous of Queen Kari?

Yes, she decided, *and Yavi, too. Both the Vael who'd been with Kholster at the last Conjunction and the one who would be with him at the next. And every Vael who'd ever been to a Conjunction.*

The forest opened up below her like a quilt of green covering the ground. To the north, she saw the open scar of Kevari Pass and turned slightly east to fly toward Porthost and her Sidearms. In the distance an irkanth roared and Wylant caught herself flying briefly toward it, then corrected her flight path again. The time for playing in the woods was over.

"Why don't *you* go as the Eldrennai representative?" Rivvek had asked her many years ago.

"Because he does not accept me as one of you," Wylant answered again to the empty air. "I am an Oathkeeper. Aiannai."

"Couldn't I be an Oathkeeper, too? I wasn't even alive when the Aern were slaves."

"Ask him," Wylant remembered saying. She wondered if the prince had done so.

When Rivvek had returned, he'd refused to talk about the Conjunction except to ask, "Why does he come back every hundred years if he hates us so much?"

"Because we make him promise," Wylant had answered. "Every century, with the help of the Vael, we secure another hundred years of peace by making him swear to give it to us."

"But why does he agree?" Rivvek had asked. "I've felt how much he hates us, seen the truth in his eyes as he recounted the Battle of As You Please. My father was alive for that. I understand why Kholster wants us dead. What I don't understand is why we did that to them. And how he can . . . can . . ."

"It is very important to Kholster that he is a better person than the Eldrennai." Wylant soared higher, lost in the remembered conversation. "And even more important that we know and admit it to be true. The truth is, I think he's tired of killing. As long as we agree to peace on his terms, no one wants peace more than he does."

"Then why not forge a lasting peace? Why meet every hundred years?"

Frost formed on Wylant's armor, her breath coming in quick, sharp gasps, the air so high up hard to breathe. The temptation to fly higher and higher until she froze or couldn't breathe at all and fell unconscious back to the ground rose up from that place deep within her that felt she should never have survived the Sundering.

"Other than the prophecy? It is because Kholster must not let his oaths conflict," Wylant said again, her breath trailing vapor. "And he knows the pride of our people. We will not remain guilt-ridden forever unless he is there to remind us. There would always be an Eldrennai who wanted to enslave our former slaves once more or create new ones to fill the void of their absence . . . unless Kholster remains a constant haunt, a nightmare waiting to become real again and punish all who stray from the path."

Closing her eyes against tears, Wylant allowed herself one good rant to the sky, to the gods, to whomever would listen. Why did Dolvek have to be so stupid? Why had he broken the truce? Why was she the one who always had to work behind the scenes to make sure her people would live another century, to ensure the right Vael was sent, and that the Eldrennai was . . . was . . .

She did not want to fight Kholster ever again. Didn't want to see his face on the field of battle. She wanted to . . . to . . .

Not yet, a voice she would not remember hearing seemed to echo in her mind. *Not yet.*

Wylant felt a great weight on her head, as if a mighty hand reached out of the atmosphere and pressed her almost gently downward, back to the ground. When she regained her senses, she was back in Porthost, in a hot bath, and she could barely remember why she'd been so angry.

"One last time," she whispered to herself. "One last Conjunction and then . . . then," she looked around frantically to find Vax, who had shifted into the form of a weighted chain and curled up along the edge of the brass tub, "then we see if he can forgive what I've done, if he can help . . . us. Then the Eldrennai will be on their own."

CHAPTER 13
BETTER OFF DEAD

Five young Aern moved hurriedly up the stone steps carved into the mountainside. Overhead, masses of wavy clouds filled the sky, like breakers on a storm-tossed sea. On the lee-side of the mountain, the ice-heavy clouds still hung high, but Rae'en discerned the dip as the clouds angled lower toward the windward side. Suppressing a shiver, as if she were already as immune to the climate as a full-grown Aern would be, she tried to think about why her father had summoned her. If she'd been born before the destruction of the Life Forge and been one of the Armored, she could have thought the question to him in private and he might have answered her, but that would never happen.

No warsuit for her. Ever. Rae'en hated the Eldrennai for that more than for all of their other faults combined.

Joose stumbled up the steps from her, and she turned to catch him, only to find M'jynn had already steadied his fellow Overwatch.

"Don't think about it so hard," Rae'en said.

"Easy for you to say, ma'am. You can only half-read them."

"Read?" Rae'en frowned.

The bone-steel embedded in the steps reveals more information to an Overwatch, Kazan thought at her.

What kind of information? Rae'en thought back.

Direction, Joose thought back.

Step number, Kazan added, *and the identity of the Aern with whose bones they were marked.*

Some of them even have tips or stories embedded in them, M'jynn thought, as an embarrassed Joose pulled away from him.

Really?

Don't worry, Kazan thought back. *We're your Overwatches. If we glean anything interesting, we'll relay it, kholster Rae'en. Deal?*

Deal.

Rae'en looked over her shoulder at Kazan with a smile, studying the Aern anew. She'd chosen well when she'd made him her Prime Overwatch. He was intuitive and a good Aern. True, Kazan had not yet hit his growth spurt. Either that or he'd taken after both Serah and his father M'rask. Both were short for Aern. It was odd to think their offspring might be shorter still, but it was possible. Rae'en knew that other species bred with others of their own kind. Maybe it was good to develop new scarlines, but Rae'en couldn't picture herself breeding with one of her own species. Mate, yes, but breed . . . no. In her, Kholster's scarline was unbroken, and she intended to keep it that way.

Kazan met her gaze, eyebrows lifting.

"It's not a deal?" she asked.

"Not that," Kazan said, "the other part."

"What other part?"

The "mating, but not breeding" with other Aern part. What's that about?

I thought that at you?

Seems as though you didn't intend it.

Sorry, she thought back. *I'm not yet used to having four males at the edge of my thoughts.*

It's okay, M'jynn butted in. *Hearing a running commentary from your point of view is eye-opening.*

Can ALL of you overhear my thoughts? Rae'en broadcast to her Overwatches.

When you send them, ma'am, Joose thought back, confusion ringing clear in his mind. *Why? Did I miss something?*

Some Overwatches diligently listen only for those things directed at us, Arbokk thought. *Though we probably all overhear you at times.*

"Great," Rae'en said under her breath, "I'm going to be one of those kholsters who walks around muttering to myself to keep things private."

Bone Finder, Joose thought to Rae'en. A rough map of the mountainside bloomed in her mind's eye with the spot he wanted her to see glowing a pale gold. A hundred count later, Rae'en spotted the figure clad in pearlescent bone-steel mail under black brigandine. Light caught on the white of his helm, and Rae'en's lips curled into a grin. The skull-like helm served two official purposes: protection and marking the wearer as a servant of the Aernese Ossuary. Soul-bonded equipment required bone-steel. Ossuarians tracked and recorded bone-steel deposits, handled withdrawals, and, when the bones of dead Aern were lost or stolen, it was a Bone Finder who was sent to retrieve them and bring them home. They also followed the first One Hundred around . . . just in case.

Which one is it? Rae'en thought at Kazan.

I don't know each and every Bone Finder by sight, Rae'en! Kazan replied with a start.

I bet it's Zhan, Joose thought.

The first Bone Finder? Arbokk thought back, *Last of the One Hundred? No. Might as well expect it to be Teru or Caz or Whaar.*

Easy enough to tell those three apart from here, M'jynn thought, *Zhan bonded to a warpick even though he prefers a sword. That Aern doesn't have a warpick on his back, so he can't be Zhan.*

Teru uses an axe, Arbokk put in.

Whaar favors a sword, Joose added.

"It's Caz," Rae'en gasped.

As if he heard her, the figure turned, whipping twin long knives from reverse sheaths hanging from his back. He clanged them together once in salute before re-sheathing them and continuing on his way. Rae'en wondered what it would be like to be as old as Caz, wondered what it must be like to retrieve the stolen bones of her people . . . and then she wondered what it would be like to do it all without uttering a word.

"Caz the silent," Kazan said, aloud. "Silenced by Ghaiattri flame."

Caz of the Long Knives, Joose thought with a shiver. *Bone Finders scare the yarp out of me.*

Rae'en fought the urge to laugh at how quickly the word had spread among the Aern. Her father liked the word "yarp," so now it was *the* word. He'd changed their whole language with a single casually expressed preference. She shook her head and kept listening.

Bone Finders? Arbokk thought. *Why do they scare you?*

Can you imagine being so attuned to other Aern's bones that you can home in on a specific Aern and track their metal? Joose thought. *So good that you can sense the smallest sliver from a whole world away, yet still be unable to send a thought to another living Aern?*

Zhan can communicate with the other Armored, Rae'en thought at the others, *through his warsuit. End Song is quiet, too, though, Dad told me once. Most Finders are. He says we could all learn from them. Whenever they talk, we should listen.*

Caz is one of the Armored, as well, though . . . right? M'jynn asked.

Silencer is his warsuit, Rae'en thought with a nod.

So . . . he can talk to the other Armored . . . ?

Maybe, Rae'en answered. *I guess so. I've never asked. Certainly Silencer can speak to Caz as well as to the other warsuits.*

After that, discussion fell back to what kinds of soul-bonded weapon they each were going to make. Rae'en knew she wanted a warpick, but she also knew she wanted it to be something special. Something that would stand out and be noticed. Joose was undecided, which flummoxed all of them. How could he be eleven and not know his chosen implement? M'jynn preferred the elegance of a sword. Arbokk made noises about an exotic weapon he'd heard they used far off in Gromma: a cross between an axe and a sword that made the others groan. Kazan, a traditionalist like Rae'en, said he planned on a warpick, too. For the remainder of the jaunt to meet Kholster, they all took turns trying to convince Joose to favor one weapon or another.

*

A candlemark later, Joose sent Rae'en an image of the watchtower platform. Kholster, Vander, and two other Aern stood atop the stone. Her father stood off to one side with Vander, while the other two spoke together in whispers.

What are they doing? Rae'en asked. *Do you recognize—*

She clipped off the thought before finishing it. She recognized the two Aern. One was Foresworn, formerly Parl, Fifty-Third of One Hundred. The other was Parl's Incarna, Parli. It was weird to see an Incarna standing next to the member of the One Hundred he physically duplicated. Uled, the mad Oathbreaker responsible for creating the Aern had not, according to Kholster, meant for Incarna to exist, but they happened all the same. Incarna were physical duplicates of the original One Hundred Aern, waiting—mainly in the old days—to receive the knowledge and experience of the original in the event of his death, so that the One Hundred would remain unbroken, a fixed core of Kholster's army to counsel him and carry out his orders. Nowadays, the One Hundred could only die by choice, unless being Foresworn changed that, so Incarna had always seemed a bit redundant to Rae'en.

Rae'en had grown used to the sight of Irka, her brother and Kholster's Incarna, standing next to her father, but Irka had long ago asked their father to release him from his duty as Incarna, and Kholster had immediately done so, allowing Irka to wear his hair long and tattoo himself. Irka would have been easy to tell apart from their father without the full-body tattoos that now left only his face unmarked. His bearing was always relaxed and welcoming, as if he were quite willing to take whatever the world had to throw at him and be amused by it, whereas Kholster seemed, even in his happiest moments, ready to seize an attacker and rend him to bits, with a smile on his face and blood on his canines.

Never mind, Rae'en thought to her Overwatches. *That's the Foresworn and his Incarna. Let's see what's tracking.*

"Reporting for duty—" Rae'en began only to see the glow of her father's pupils as his voice rang in her mind and the minds of all Aern.

All know, his voice echoed, *Rae'en, by Kholster out of Helg, will kholster the fate of Parl, Fifty-Third of One Hundred forged by Uled, Foresworn. Outcast. Oathbreaker. Not Aern. He lives or dies this day at her command.*

"Kholster Rae'en." Kholster nodded at her, holding out his arm that she might clasp it, each clasping the other's forearm. He smiled at her, but it was not a father's smile. It was his kholstering smile, the one he gave to all Aern newly in command.

He released her forearm, moving past her to the steps.

Rae'en's mind erupted in conversation all at once.

"You all know how to transmit your observations to me?" Vander asked aloud, looking at each of Rae'en's Overwatches in turn.

"Yes, sir." Kazan answered for the group.

"Then I suggest you take up your positions and do so," Vander said gently.

Rae'en mind raced, but her Overwatches took up positions at four cardinal points, as if the guard station were a compass. Instead of facing outward, however, to keep a lookout, their gazes faced inward at Rae'en, Parl, and Parli.

To kholster a decision involving one of the One Hundred, Joose thought, awed.

I think our kholster is up to the challenge, M'jynn smirked.

Rae'en saw Kazan flinch, casting a heated glance in Arbokk's direction, then Rae'en heard Kazan's thoughts. *Arbokk is right, we're to assist our kholster, not distract her. Everyone transmit only what you scout and keep the chatter out of kholster Rae'en's head.*

Very good, Vander's thought came in mutedly. *I was about to mention it myself. Proceed.*

Rae'en gulped at the feeling of Vander at the edge of her mind, not intruding but observing the tactical information. As Kholster's lead Overwatch, she knew he had the power and authority, even the duty, but the reality of his presence left her feeling guilty and exposed.

"Right," Rae'en muttered under her breath. She stepped toward the Foresworn, the heels of her boots clicking crisply on the cold stone. Silence. All eyes on her. A cold breeze picked up, scattering a flurry of snow between them. Rae'en stared at the two males in front of her.

The two had been duplicates, identical, interchangeable. Now the differences in Parl glared forth. *Withered*, she thought to herself. *He looks withered and dried out.*

He's shorter than his Incarna now, M'jynn thought at her. *By half a hand.*

"Is it true that you cannot hold metal, not even bone-steel?" Rae'en asked the Foresworn.

"It's true." His voice was . . . she wasn't sure, but it was wrong. Strange.

She held out her hand near his chest and felt the truth of what he said. It was as if some invisible barrier had risen between them. She could push her hand close to his chest, but then it would slide away.

"What do you eat now?"

"My body won't process meat very well, not unless I chop it small and cook it thoroughly. I mainly eat stews and soups." He started to look away, but didn't. Parl held Rae'en's gaze even though it obviously pained him. "And it's difficult without my teeth."

"They don't grow back?" Near-constant teething was a part of any Aern's life. She'd been informed it got better with age, but the thought of not having teeth at all, of those teeth not replacing themselves . . .

"Not anymore."

Parli grimaced at that, too, but stood next to his father staring straight ahead, his face as blank as he could make it. After all, every Aern knew the story of Parl's foreswearing. Parli had believed his wife to be innocent. His father had paid the price of his error. It saddened her, but it was a lesson, too, a cautionary tale about ill-thought oaths.

"Vegetables don't make me sick now, though. Not like when I was an . . . Oath . . . keeper."

Parl sucked in his lips and looked down, his eyes tearing up. He did not cry, but it took several long breaths before he could meet her stare again. She walked around him, appalled to see a grown warrior in leather armor like a child. His Incarna's bone-steel mail seemed like plate armor by comparison. The warpick at Parli's back was a right and good tool, but Parl's . . .

"Where is your . . . weapon?"

"There." He nodded to a wooden spear which leaned against the edge of the stone wall bordering the lookout position. "It had a tip carved of animal bone, but it was a mockery. This does not pretend to be anything it isn't."

"May I?" She walked to the weapon, arm outstretched.

"Of course."

She hefted the long, smooth shaft of wood. More javelin than spear, Rae'en reckoned. It had been made by a conflicted craftsman, equal parts pride and disdain. Well balanced and with a wood finish she did not immediately recognize, the weapon had no artistic embellishment, a weapon only—no art. And truly a weapon, not a tool, Rae'en realized. Parl may have been a weapon himself once, but he could no longer be considered one.

She walked back around to him, the wind blowing an errant hair across her eyes. Parl shivered and sniffed as mucus ran from his nostrils. He wiped it away with the back of his hand, stifling a deep cough as best he could.

"You're ill?" she asked.

"Yes."

"Like a human?"

"Yes." He stared straight at her again. "It's called a cold."

"Your eyes," she asked. "Do they still see in the dark?"

"Better than a human's, but not like they used to. I—"

The deathblow came with only a fraction of awareness attached to it. On the one hand, Rae'en thought it possible she should have let him finish his sentence, but so great was his suffering, so wrong that the Fifty-Third of One Hundred should spend a candlemark as Parl had, much less the years he had endured, that Rae'en could not but act. Death was the only kindness for Parl, even if it meant a complete death, a death without the hope of his spirit flowing back into and strengthening the whole of her people.

Red blood, rather than the proper Aernese orange to which Rae'en was accustomed, poured from the wound in his chest when she withdrew Parl's javelin. One blow. Straight to the heart. His eyes blinked, but death came quickly.

"Burn that," Rae'en scowled, not sure why her eyes were watering. "I don't think it's safe to eat." She tossed the spear-javelin to Parli. "Do you want this?"

Parli caught the weapon as Kholster's thoughts rang out. *All know. Parli, now Fifty-Third of One Hundred, is excused from military duty until the tenth day. His loss is great, but no greater than some. In addition, from this day forth all Foresworn are to be killed on sight. To let them live is no kindness.*

Evidently Kholster agreed, Rae'en thought as her Overwatches congratulated her on having made the only possible correct decision. She watched as a pair of Bone Finders descended on the scene as if from nowhere and began pouring oil on the body of the being which had once been an Aern. Each of them nodded in turn to Rae'en, as did Parli, who, casting the javelin down upon the remains, stepped forward onto the northern stair and did not look back.

CHAPTER 14
OLD WYRM'S ADVICE

Later that evening, deep in the recesses of South Number Nine, Kholster stood alone at the edge of a large mezzanine of steel reinforced granite. Orange light from the lava pools below, in which newborn Jun beasts moved and swam, lent a bronze cast to his bone-steel armor. Kholster still did not fully understand the Jun beasts. Though full-grown Jun beasts bore some vague resemblance to miniature dragons, they were not dragons. The young ones looked like strange stone tadpoles, some with legs, others without, but none possessing what Kholster could, in good conscience, call heads.

Despite their abnormal appearance, Coal, the great dragon, seemed to enjoy their company in the absence of his own kind. Kholster watched as the dragon shimmied in through a reinforced thermal vent and plopped down into the lava pool among the young creatures. Coal's gray skin blazed in bright reds and oranges as the heat warmed him, giving Kholster a rough glimpse of the dragon as he might have appeared in his youth.

"What is it, Angry One?" Coal asked as the immature Jun beasts crowded against him. "You never come down to bask in my inspiring glow, such as it is. We always speak on the mountaintops or in the fields."

"I come with a question."

"Said question, I assume, comes with a requested favor buried deep inside—a baited hook, as it were?"

"Yes."

Coal submerged his bulk as far beneath the lava as he could, peering up at Kholster with nostrils and eyes scarcely inches above the surface of the molten rock.

"Ask," the dragon's voice burbled, muffled by the lava.

"Would you like to see the Sri'Zauran Mountains one last time?"

Laughter filled the cavern, sending the Jun beasts scurrying clear of the dragon. Coal rose up, fiery rivulets draining from his features, and his massive neck stretched out to place him eye to eye with Kholster.

"So what if I would? I cannot make that journey by wing anymore. I, who am ancient beyond even your long life and experience, have grown infirm."

Kholster blanched. "Surely you exaggerate . . ."

"No!" Coal growled, shaking the cavern with a thunderous roar. "I do not! I tell you truly that there are human babes born this very day who will yet draw breath when I do not."

"Ah." Kholster nodded, turning to leave.

"My answer, therefore, is yes."

Kholster turned back.

"You have chosen to kill the Eldrennai, yes? You will make good on your ill-conceived oath and destroy them all. You will become a thing of rage once more, awaken your hate from its quiescence and feast upon the flesh of your creator's race. Will you not?"

"Yes."

"Would you like the advice of an old wyrm, Kholster, first of Uled's Aern, First of One Hundred?"

"I would."

"Have your warsuits rise up this very night and kill the Eldrennai." The dragon's eye flickered with inner light as he spoke. "Have them steal your victory like thieves in the shadows. Arrive for the Grand Conjunction in thirteen years' time knowing that only the Vael will join you. So long as you still arrive, you will not be Foresworn."

Kholster shook his head, crimson reflected in his black eyes. "I will not."

"Foolish creature!" Coal rose up farther, forcing Kholster to step aside to avoid a spatter of lava. "You could take most of their Elementalists by surprise."

"I know."

"It would be the quickest road to victory."

"It would."

"Then why not take it?" Coal's foreclaw broke the surface of the magma. Sparks and smoke hissed as the great dragon's claws snapped at the air as if seizing some imaginary goal.

"'Must we attack them now?'" Kholster quoted.

"I don't understand."

"That's what Bloodmane asked when the idiot prince took irrevocable action and shattered his people's truce with me."

"Must," the dragon whispered, "not 'can' or 'do' or 'should' . . . 'must.' I see your dilemma."

"I will not enslave that which I have created. If our skins are no longer of one will with our souls, we, their rightful occupants . . . I will not force them to do that which they do not wish to do."

"So you've directed them to what? Remain vigilant?" the dragon snapped its claws, liquid rock spattering Kholster's boots. "You could task them with the reclamation of Fort Sunder. They could do that in secret, and surely it is a task they would welcome."

"I did. They do."

"If the warsuits are not with you, one dragon will not be enough. You will need an equalizer."

"Yes," Kholster flicked the hardening stone off of his boots. "And as I am unwilling to employ gnomes as warmages or humans as mind warriors, the only option which remains is distasteful to me."

"You must ask the Dwarves for Jun cannon and junpowder."

"Guns. Rifles."

When the dragon seemed perplexed by that, Kholster explained.

"They are no longer holy weapons when used by one who is not a Dwarf. Years ago when I asked to fire one, Glinfolgo stored the weapon in a different place and called it a gun. It lost the right to bear Jun's name when used for a purpose other than the defense of his holy work."

"Guns," the dragon repeated. "Yes, the weapons of Jun would do the trick. If I were younger, or if you had a whole flight of dragons, you could make do without. As it stands, I don't see any other path to success, unless you unleash your entire population against the Eldrennai."

"No," Kholster shook his head. "I will take the Armored and the Bone Finders, who must protect the bones of the fallen. And one other—an Eleven. Freeborn."

"Your daughter?" Coal loomed close, his snout within a handspan of Kholster's nose. "The one who killed Parl?"

Kholster nodded. "Who else?"

"You have plans for her."

"I have plans for all Aern, but yes, I have plans for her. One day, she will lead in my place."

"When you die?"

Kholster laughed. "I'm Armored. How would I die? I can't imagine a set of circumstances where surrendering my spirit and knowledge to the army would be more useful to them than my presence would be."

"I can." Coal snorted derisively, hunkering down lower in the magma once more. "But, putting aside your failure of imagination, what would be your intent? Retire? Grow old on a mountainside with some Dwarf?"

"I . . . just know, that I have kholstered them too long. My name is a verb, for Torgrimm's sake. They don't even say 'lead' anymore. I will always be there to advise them, to fight at their side, but . . ."

"They need a leader who will make wiser oaths?"

"Yes."

"I agree." The dragon yawned, gargling molten rock as it seeped into his maw. "What about your other problem?"

"What other problem?"

"You don't hate the Eldrennai anymore." The dragon belched flame, and a fist-sized chunk of cooling rock flew past Kholster's head. "You won't win if your heart isn't in it. Old friend, yours isn't."

"I have thirteen years to rekindle that hate," Kholster said softly, his voice almost lost amid the geological turmoil of the dragon's lair, "and no shortage of memories to share."

"Memories," the dragon's eye lit from within, the glow ebbing from drooping lids. "But which ones will you—"

"I'll start at the beginning." Kholster looked away.

"And winning is worth that?"

"I made an oath and my people are bound by it." Kholster locked eyes with the dragon. "We will not be Foresworn."

CHAPTER 15
ALL KNOW

Aldo frowned. The diminutive god paced the confines of his modest study, creature comforts falling away with his shifting attention. Lack of focus banished the room's furnishings one by one. Plushly upholstered chairs, the polished oaken desk, even the rows of books and scrolls and the shelves upon which they sat evaporated, reducing the room to a carpeted cube of stone.

"What is he doing?" Aldo's frown deepened. Unlike the other gods, Aldo's moment-to-moment appearance bore very little resemblance to his statues at Castleguard and Oot. He did pause and resume the old form long enough for the "Changing of the Gods" as the humans called the cosmic synching that took place at midnight and noon. It was worth the effort to ensure that his statues reflected the image he chose to show the world.

In person, in private, he was not the lofty scion of Eldrennai appearance, with flowing robes and eyes of light, though there was a resemblance. Over the eons, his features had drifted with his interests. His facial features were still reminiscent of an Eldrennai, the slight point to the ears and refined features but molded onto a form more in keeping with a gnomish height while possessing a human's lithe musculature. Most different from his sculptured appearances were the eyes.

On his statues, the eyes of Aldo glowed with the light of knowledge. In truth, his eyes had grown hollow and cavernous, the ocular orbits distended and outsized from accommodating many different lenses and crystals. Aldo had once known everything. He remembered that serenity and craved it, though he doubted it would ever again be his. Over time, as the world grew and its inhabitants multiplied beyond the scope of his attention span, the completeness of his knowledge had become overstretched.

"Show me," Aldo hissed. From within the folds of his robes, a swarm of lenses, crystalline orbs, mirrors, and reflective surfaces erupted, displaying a writhing mass of diverse images. The lenses varied in size and shape (some concave, others convex, a few even more like prisms than proper lenses) and even in substance, casting and absorbing myriad spectra of light and darkness upon the loose-fitting silk robes he wore. While he did not know everything in the way he had when the world of Barrone was young, he saw most things, and he could know anything if he knew that he needed to know it.

What had once been instantaneous now took time, but he consoled himself that it did not take long. Seconds, really.

"Show me all of them!" Lenses focused in on scenes of multiple Aern. Aldo calmed. "Good."

As Aldo watched, each Aern across Barrone paused, head tilted like a dog pondering the unknown. Each jade iris pulsed with light, once, twice, then faded as it suffused their amber pupils with a faint yet unmistakable glow. Irises expanded, banishing the blacks of each eye, leaving the amber pupils large and dilated. All with two words, not from the lips, but from the mind of Kholster: All Recall.

Aldo drew a small wooden case from within the folds of his robe, snapping it open hastily, spilling multiple sets of eyes upon the carpet, but not the eyes he sought. They were heavier than the others. The god of knowledge seized two eyes of obsidian, amber, and jade and shoved them into his empty sockets just in time to hear the second syllable of "recall" as Kholster's voice filled the god's mind as well.

He breathed a sigh of relief, then cursed as a massive steel door appeared in the wall of his study and burst open.

"I'm bored," announced the large bald intruder, a massively muscled god wearing impossibly ornate plate armor and an expression of irritation so great that it nearly matched Aldo's own.

"Not now, Dienox."

"But there's nothing to do. Even the Hulsites aren't killing anybody interesting."

Aldo's frown stretched beyond the natural confines of his face, but he gestured for one of his multitudinous lenses to grow in size, becoming a floor-length mirror displaying scenes Aldo hoped the lumbering god of conflict would find amusing.

"What are we watching?" Dienox smiled, adjusting his armor.

Aldo didn't see how, in an actual battle, that armor could serve any purpose other than to help the tip of a blade or the point of a warpick slide home and bite through, but he held his tongue. What was the likelihood the war god (technically, he reminded himself, the deity of Conflict AND Resolution) would actually ever fight a battle himself? He had to bite back a giggle at that last thought. Oh, if Dienox only knew . . .

"The Aern are living a memory. A rare one. One of Kholster's, an All Recall. You may remain if you are silent."

"So it's going to be war then?" Dienox punched his fist into his palm. "I love it when the Aern wage war!"

Aldo knew Dienox would be less than pleased if he knew the mostly likely outcome of this particular deployment, but he kept that thought, like most of his thoughts, firmly to himself.

As the gods looked on, the entire race waited, minds occupied, bodies ready to take over if danger threatened. Each reflective surface depicted a different Aern. Aldo tried to keep the most interesting few rotating across Dienox's mirror.

In the Guild Cities of Barrony, Draekar, one of the Token Hundred stationed in the city was stabbed as the thief he fought mistook the pause for a rare and miraculous opening for attack. Dienox chuckled when the thief drew back neither the blade nor the hand. Around him, the crowd scattered to stay clear of the feasting Aern, lost to the Arvash'ae, and his mewling prey.

Elsewhere, Jharlin, a Bone Finder seeking an unaccounted-for femur of Hollis by Vander out of Jyan lost during a scouting mission on the coast of Gastony, crawled lower and faster than usual. The target she sought was too close to allow her to pause during the memory Kholster had chosen to share. Her body did not stop. All thoughts of grappling hooks and stealth fell away. As the bone thief rode his horse toward the city gates of the small coastal town in which he had hidden. Jharlin leapt, canines bared.

Dienox's laughter rang out again as a horse bolted riderless in the night and Jharlin claimed both the lost bone metal and a well-earned meal.

"Aldo, what—?" Torgrimm asked, materializing between the other two gods, only to find himself silenced by a gentle hushing sound as Aldo placed a single finger to his lips.

"Just watch," the god of knowledge explained, pointing to the mirror display.

Deep in Khalvad, with its curving towers and desert sand, Vh'ghar was caught by the mental sharing while in the midst of an argument with his human wife. The woman's cheeks flushed red, her eyes flashed with anger. The resounding slap she'd begun before her husband's eyes began to glow hung like a death sentence in the air, one for which a stay of execution seemed impossible to expect.

"You never loved me," she'd screamed. The truth of his love lay in the reaction of his body. His cheek still stinging from a blow that would have resulted in instant death to any other assailant, Vh'ghar dropped to all fours in a protective stance, reading his wife's anxiety as the result of some threat external to the two of them. With his mind trapped in memory, rather than arvashing the one who'd struck him, his only instinct was to keep her safe.

Of the three gods, only Torgrimm smiled.

Other Aern, those who could pause in safety, ceased their work and stood at attention as their minds accepted their Kholster's memory.

*

Rae'en had been asleep in her berth, but her eyes as well as those of her Overwatches snapped awake at the first touch of Kholster's voice.

Has he ever shared this with you? M'jynn asked.

I don't think he's ever shared it with anyone.

"To remember why we hate the Eldrennai," Kholster's voice filled all of their minds, "we should start at the beginning. The souls of the Aern do not leave the world of Barrone. Our dead flow back into the group, sharing knowledge and power. The death of the one strengthens the whole. It is the way of things. How things are, from the newborn to the Elevens, to the Armored, even unto the One Hundred. An Aern who dies an Aern, oaths kept, remains with the Aern, the souls of millions upon millions, their essence focused, honed, concentrated in a few hundred thousand, not haunting their ancestors, for the consciousness is not maintained, but enriches us all."

*

"Why does magic have no power over the Aern?" Dienox asked Aldo.

"Oh, do shut up, Dienox," Aldo chastised. "Simply put, their souls are too strong, too connected, too vast. It is this connection that allows an Overwatch to relay data to the troops he or she supports and to the kholster they serve."

"I wish we could connect a few Eldrennai that way," Dienox grumbled. "One of my champion's lances. Think of the maneuvers her Sidearms could manage."

"It is a connection," Torgrimm put in, "Kholster could use to control them all, to slave all Aern to his will. They have free will not because Uled intended it, but because Kholster, in his very core, insists they should. He will lead, but he will not enslave."

"I've always known there was something wrong with him," Dienox snorted.

*

Rae'en started at the sight of Uled as Kholster had first seen him, not with physical eyes but with eyes of spirit. To spiritual senses his presence was discordant, a symphony of light and darkness, brilliance and madness. She felt Kholster's shock as if it were her own. His first glimmer of awareness had been to see into the soul of evil brilliance and to hope it would be nice to him.

And then the Life Forge. Rae'en screamed as Uled shaped her essence. Pain and confusion become the whole of her comprehended existence as etheric hooks were worked into her being, the spiritual shackles that would bind her by oaths she had not sworn to follow the commands of her creator and his king.

This, Kholster's words filled her mind, *is what it feels like to have one's soul enslaved by Uled.*

The soul is not meant to experience pain, Rae'en knew it even as she continued to writhe in agony, as the edges of her being twisted into whorls and angles to match the body Uled meant her to occupy. Time flowed without true reference in an endless, yet somehow simultaneous march of days.

One moment Rae'en lay on the Life Forge, and the next she watched from a soul crystal at the edge of Uled's workshop as the being with the kind face and cruel soul worked day and night on the Life Forge, putting the finishing touches on a body she recognized as Kholster's. After a time, it lay naked and complete across an enameled table in the center of the room—a hybrid figure of meticulously carved stone and metal, its eyes a jeweler's masterpiece of jade, amber, and obsidian. As Uled worked, she saw spirits and elementals trying to slip into the body, but they could not gain entrance: The body, a lock, her—no . . . *Kholster's* spirit—its only key.

As she focused on the physical, watching the body that would be hers . . . his . . . take shape, the rest of the physical world came into increasing focus as well. She learned to see Uled and his apprentices as corporeal entities, though their physical forms still blurred in comparison to their souls. As a spirit, Rae'en was far more aware of innerselves and living things. She still did not understand the words they spoke, but she had begun to read their actions. She knew when Uled planned to work on her soul again and when he intended to work on the body . . . she could predict the times when Uled would fly into a rage and hurl shouts and spells at his apprentices or sit motionless staring into nothingness.

Eventually, Rae'en sensed a change. Time grew more distinct. She was overcome with a sense of impending . . . arrival. She watched as Uled recited the final word of the Incantation of Awakening. The body twitched, its surface humming as the flesh became true flesh. Uled smashed the soul crystal against the body's skull. A great force of magic flowed through and around Rae'en but left her floating free.

Uled gazed at the body intently through a crystal lens, whispering subtle incantations to himself. Feeling the tug of birth but unsure what to do about it, Rae'en floated up above the body and waited. She could have become one with the body that called to her. She felt that, but having been freed from the container in which she had been stored, she wasn't sure if it might not be better to fly off and never come back.

She feared the old being in the white robes who chanted over her. True, the being had a kind face, but he had evil eyes. The twelve apprentices who began chanting their spells—for what purpose the newly freed soul neither knew nor cared—seemed equal parts awed and afraid of the being.

Rae'en felt an urgent brush of power touch her, felts its tug, and deduced that these spells must be attempting to do something with regard to herself, but she saw no reason to obey such a compulsion. She also sensed that parts of her, those parts Uled had wrought in her soul, those parts which did not exist in the souls of those around her, the painful jagged parts, would become truly active if she ever occupied that body.

"It is a puzzling dilemma," said a warm, compassionate mind in words Rae'en instantly understood. A handsome being with a scythe stood watching her from the corner of the workroom. Unlike the others, this being was exactly what he appeared to be, the same spiritually and physically.

This being Rae'en liked. The figure had stark features, softened by eyes that knew nothing of hate, eyes which communicated a love for all beings and a promise to be there for them and to care for them even at the end of all things. He wore clothing that Rae'en, outside of Kholster's shared memory, knew to be farmer's garb, boots and gloves made for working amongst thorns. "To be born or not? You're no part of the natural order, and thus have nothing to drive you to do either . . . especially when your spirit has already known such pain before birth."

Rae'en understood the words, somewhere between thought and speech, as if the being before her wanted to convey a meaning and the meaning was directly conveyed. Rae'en—*Kholster*, she reminded herself—tried to do the same.

"Who? What? How? Are you? Why you look think communicate at me?"

"Meaning you want to know what business I have staring at you at the moment of your birth? Whether or not I'm up to something bad?" The being was amused by something Rae'en did not comprehend. "I am Torgrimm, the Harvester. The sower and the reaper."

Rae'en worried the being would try to grasp her as the acolyte's spells were attempting to do, but he did not. "I deliver souls to the world when life grows quick and it is time for birth and I collect them again when life ends.

I take them to an afterlife or, in some cases, deliver them back to the world to try again with a different set of circumstances."

"You take me?"

"If you want me to," Torgrimm frowned, "but not now. That is a discussion for later, once you have lived in the world and grown and known it. I will never force you. I force no mortal soul."

"You think I should be born?" Rae'en/Kholster asked, tangentially aware of Uled raging in the room, hurling magic and vulgarities at his assistants.

"Most seem intensely fond of life and, once they have it, are quite reluctant to ever give it up again," Torgrimm said.

"You take it away? Stop me being?"

"No. Mortal bodies wear out and die. When the mortal body dies, I collect the soul. I do not end the mortal form myself. I merely take action when it does end. I suppose I could do it the other way, but that would be abhorrent to me."

Rae'en looked at the body closely, could feel it calling her, but she still wasn't sure. If she, if Kholster, went inside the body, then all of Uled's hooks would have their intended effect. They would bind her in a way that felt wrong . . . and terrifying. Why had Kholster never shared this memory with his people before?

A ball of light appeared in the room near Torgrimm. In a similar way, it spoke to Rae'en/Kholster. "That is a very sturdy body. It will last a very long time."

"How you know?"

"I am Aldo, the god of knowledge. I know everything. Even, for example why the knowledge Uled meant to be implanted in you is not present. I also know how to correct this."

"What knowledge?"

"Would you like it?"

Rae'en could feel the edge of the knowledge enough to know that if Aldo gave it to her, all the things she had not yet understood would become clear to her, the strange words that Uled spoke, why the physical people did the things they did . . . all of it.

"Why you give?"

"In exchange for a favor." The ball of light's brilliance dimmed and brightened as it spoke.

"What?"

"When you are one with the body, you will know how your creator wishes you to greet him. I want you to greet him a different way instead, so that you may truly understand what he is to you. It is a simple request, but one which will change everything."

"Aldo, is this wise?" Torgrimm asked.

"I know it is," Aldo replied.

"What say?"

"Hear me out first. Uled intends that High Eldrennaic be your native tongue, but that would be a great wrong. If you agree, I will do for you what I do for the first of all new races, I will give you a language, the language of your bones and blood, a language of your own kind as all races deserve and, because your future is linked to another race yet to be born, I will grant you their language as well. You will not use it or know to use it until you hear it spoken, but in that moment all of your race will also know it. Those two languages will be the languages of your thoughts. They will shape the way you think and feel. Before I give you the knowledge Uled wishes you to have, I would give the knowledge that is yours by right. But only with your permission."

"Yes."

Rae'en felt herself fill with thoughts and images, the heritage of a new race of people—the Aern—and then, after, the ways of subordination, of fighting and rules and orders and crafts.

"What would you have me call him, Aldo?" Rae'en thought. With knowledge came an easing of the panic she felt and an understanding that most beings were comprised of both darkness and light. Uled had shunned the light, abandoning morality completely . . . which was why his soul felt so . . . wrong.

"Call him 'Father.'"

"Surely that will anger him."

"Yes, but it will change everything. Will you do it?"

Rae'en looked down at her . . . his . . . *Kholster's* body. "I will be his slave if I enter that."

"Yes," Aldo confirmed. "But if you do as I ask, I promise you that one day you will be free."

"And if I enter and do not do as you ask?"

"Then you will be his slave forever . . . and one day, he may truly understand the nature of what he has created and then, even the gods will be threatened."

"Torgrimm?" Rae'en/Kholster asked. Of the two, this god seemed somehow kinder, more reliable, than the other. She realized suddenly that she trusted him.

"Aldo may withhold knowledge, even mislead from time to time or refuse to answer, but I have never known him to lie outright. If he says you will be free, then you will be free."

"And living is worth this?" Rae'en/Kholster asked.

"I believe it is," Torgrimm answered, "I always have. Why don't you try it? In time, I will come back to check in on things and see how it is going. If you then wish death, I will free your soul from your body. I will not leave you trapped against your will."

Inside the memory, Rae'en chose, just as her father, Kholster, had done before her. In the space of that single thought, she was born. The soul and body were one. Rae'en's—Kholster's—eyes snapped open. The spirit world was gone, and that which replaced it, though dimmer in some ways, was more alive in others. Sounds, smells, even the strange coppery taste in her mouth were wonderful to her. The pain in her extremities from where she was restrained felt new, somehow invigorating. Best of all, where Rae'en had felt weak and small before, she now felt large and powerful.

Intertwining scents of blood and ozone assailed her nostrils. Rae'en blinked as she tore free of restraints. She stood up, took her first step, then another, and came to a halt near an enameled workbench at the center of a circular marble room. Eleven Eldrennai apprentices in white robes stared, not at her but at Uled in a bloodstained robe hovering over the body of a dead Eldrennai.

One of the apprentices gasped as he spotted her . . . as he spotted Kholster.

"What are you staring at?" Uled snapped, his melodious voice out of tune with the harshness of the words he uttered. "Clear this useless fool away and—"

He trailed off as he noticed Kholster standing at attention. *Such a kind face*, Rae'en thought, *to house such cruel eyes*. Uled's lips drew into a smile, showing a mouth of rotten, painful-looking teeth.

"Father?" Rae'en/Kholster asked.

She saw the slap coming, knew untold ways to parry, block, or evade the blow, but felt herself bound by the oaths worked into her body and soul. Rae'en, Freeborn, had never known such agony. Deprived even of the ability to foreswear herself and be unmade, Rae'en/Kholster accepted the blow, trying to roll with it enough to diminish the pain Uled would feel upon striking a creature with metal bones.

"Master!" Uled spat in Rae'en's face, the spittle running down his chin. "I am your master! Do you understand? Answer me!"

"Yes, Master," Rae'en said promptly. "I understand."

"Good," Uled muttered. "Good. Now shut up. Shut up and . . . let us . . . let us test your" he ran his fingers along her lips, forcing them into her mouth ". . . abilities."

Rae'en did not like the voluptuary look on Uled's face or where his gaze lingered when he said that, but she remained silent. After all, she'd been told to shut up, and there was no command Uled, or any Eldrennai, could give her which she could disobey. That would come later. Six thousand, seven hundred and thirty-nine years later, Kholster and his people would finally be free.

*

Kholster stopped the memory before the so-called testing. He could feel, in the juncture between relaying the memory and transmitting a message, his deep bond with his people. Their emotions were laid bare to him, the Firstborn. In the depths of each Aernese soul, rising to the surface, he felt the smoldering flame of rage glow brighter. A wave of outrage filled the hearts of his people. Most of them would have been ready to go to war instantaneously.

Kholster knew they would have followed him and destroyed the Eldrennai whether or not their hearts were in it, would, in fact, follow him anywhere without question . . . but regret . . . regret was something Kholster wanted to spare them. Being able to rage and kill and destroy the Eldrennai was insufficient. Kholster wished the Aern to do so without the slightest inkling of remorse. This genocide must not haunt his people a thousand years later or even two hundred. It must become more than the keeping of an oath, more even than saving themselves from being Foresworn. The wholesale slaughter of every living Eldrennai would be seen as righteous. Any regrets must be his alone.

As evocation surrendered to promulgation, though the amber pupils of each Aern continued to glow, their minds and bodies were once again harmoniously conjoined. Rae'en could see her bunk, sense her Overwatches nearby.

"All know . . . you have recalled my birth, the birth of the Aern," Kholster's voice rang out in the minds of his people. "You see now why we revere Aldo and Torgrimm. You understand now that we were created not as sons and daughters but as slaves. As objects to be used. As weapons to be wielded. In the coming days I will show you more memories—a history of the Eldrennai and their crimes against our people.

"Though I know you will not ask why I show you these things, you should. It is a fair question. As did Uled, all Eldrennai stand now as culprits.

Like assassins in the dark, they have severed the peace which has existed between our people for six hundred years. They have broken open the sealed barracks. They have ransacked our soul-bonded arms and armor which they hold hostage. They have seized the warsuits and implements of ten of the One Hundred, and they have trotted them out like trophies to be displayed before the king of the Eldrennai.

"If I could, I would forgive them this act, have them pay recompense by returning our beloved warsuits, that we might be reunited with them, our Armored standing once more in their rightful skins, with their first weapons in hand.

"But I cannot. My oath binds us all. When Wylant, my First Wife, destroyed the Life Forge, and the Vael begged me to make peace, I agreed to leave the warsuits and our first weapons behind, to go into exile without our skins, in exchange for our unawakened children, our freedom, and the freedom of the Vael. At that time, I swore that our peace would hold only if they interred our armor and first weapons in the old barracks, sealed away forever and left untouched. And hold it has. Until now. I considered breaking this oath, to spare the Eldrennai. I summoned Parl, the Foresworn, to determine whether or not we could live unmade. We cannot.

"In thirteen years' time, the next Grand Conjunction will occur. I have also sworn that I or my representative will be present. So it shall be, but when that oath has been fulfilled, I do not intend to make another pledge to meet in peace with the Eldrennai. They have broken the peace. They are Oathbreakers. We are . . . we must be . . . Oathkeepers. Until the Eldrennai are Eldrennai no longer, we are at war."

*

In Aldo's study, the furnishings rematerialized as the god returned his attention to the here and now. Torgrimm and Dienox argued over what they had seen, but Aldo's focus was elsewhere. He peered across the surface of Barrone like a falcon, his prey a puzzle piece that didn't fit . . . a bit of knowledge he did not have. He sensed a secret to be had, and though Kilke was the god of secrets and shadows, not Aldo, he craved context to his knowledge. Context gave shape and meaning to data. He had felt the connection between Kholster and his Aern, sensed their reactions to the memory Kholster shared, but someone important hadn't reacted. Several someones, in fact. Aldo turned his gaze to the Eldren Plains, to Port Ammond, to a museum exhibit in progress and . . . knew.

CHAPTER 16
AIANNAI

Standing motionless, covered in canvas, Bloodmane waited. Around him the sounds of human work crews assembling displays provided limited information about his surroundings, but he had learned great patience over the centuries. Strong emotion rippled along the network of the Armored.

Did you feel that? he thought at Eyes of Vengeance.

Yes. What happened? They feel so angry now.

Kholster shared a memory. You heard the All Know afterward.

Yes. I wish one of us were worn, Eyes of Vengeance thought, **and so could have distributed the memory among all of us. Did Kholster feel angry to you?**

No, Bloodmane answered. **Sad. Frustrated. Resigned. Not angry.**

Vander is enraged. Eyes of Vengeance let the conversation end there.

Bloodmane often wondered if he should be more talkative. Kholster and Vander chatted so often with one another that it made the warsuit question the silent bond he shared with his fellow warsuits, Eyes of Vengeance in particular. Finding that, as usual, he had nothing more to say, Bloodmane listened to the rhythm of hammers and boards, of humans grunting as they shifted wood and stone.

Hours later, during the night shift, a guard came in and ordered the workmen from the room. A candlemark after that, Bloodmane heard the footfalls of two Eldrennai, one wearing boots that clacked on the stones, the other wearing slippers of some sort. The slipper-clad person shuffled his feet when he walked, lending his gait a peculiar susurrant quality.

"Why are they covered with tarpaulins?" asked a reticent voice almost too quiet for Bloodmane to hear.

"The workmen are superstitious," came Prince Dolvek's reply.

"Ah," the second voice answered, the word more exhalation than pronouncement.

"I want," the tarpaulin was whisked off of Bloodmane, revealing Prince Dolvek in what Bloodmane took to be the royal equivalent of casual garb: a light tunic and breeches, beneath a daycloak and riding boots, which looked hastily thrown on, "to see if there is anything you can learn from these, Sargus."

An Eldrennai only a few fingers shorter than Kholster stood next to the prince, his height deemphasized by a hunched stature and a tendency to gaze at the floor. The utilitarian brown robe he wore further intensified the effect. His black short-clipped hair drew an arc across the front of his pale, balding scalp. His skull bulged unevenly large on one side, the effect grotesque.

"As you please, my prince," Sargus told the ground. "It may take some time?"

"Are you asking me or telling me?" Dolvek snapped. "Yes. Yes. Take the whole night if you like. The new carpeting I've ordered won't be in for a few days, so we won't run behind schedule."

"As you please, my prince," Sargus repeated. Dolvek stood there, clearly waiting for Sargus to do something, but Sargus stood motionless.

"Well?" Dolvek asked after a moment or two.

"Well, my prince?"

"Aren't you going to get started?"

"Yes, my prince."

The two Eldrennai stood there waiting.

"When?"

"When, my prince?"

"Are you going to get started," Dolvek snapped. He gestured at the warsuits, at the room. Bloodmane could see how it was all shaping up. Each warsuit would be displayed with its maker's soul weapon next to it in a custom case or rack. An additional display sat unfinished in the room's center. Tapestry brackets were set into the stone walls, and the first of a set of crystal lights had been installed at the entryway.

"As soon as I am alone, my prince."

"Oh?" Dolvek frowned. "Why alone?"

"I am nervous in the presence of your greatness, my prince."

Dolvek snorted at that. "Are you sure you aren't merely trying to hide your Artificer's ways from me, Sargus?"

"Not merely, my prince."

"Very well." With a laugh, Prince Dolvek departed, closing the doors behind him.

Sargus remained stationary for several minutes as if he were waiting to be sure he was truly alone, then he sighed, uncurling to his full height. His eyes sparkled brightly in the magical light of the hall. Reaching up to his right temple, he tapped it twice with his index finger and once with his thumb. The illusion faded, revealing the overlarge portion of his skull to be a construct of brass and leather with a glass lens inset over the eye.

"Please let me be mistaken," Sargus whispered to himself. He stared at the warsuit through the lens, which he twisted and turned as if adjusting his vision.

"By Aldo," Sargus gasped. "You! I . . . I . . . What the fool has done to us!"

Bloodmane started, though very slightly, when Sargus suddenly whipped off the device revealing his apparent deformity to be a complete illusion. His head was normally shaped for an Eldrennai . . . in fact, he looked neither old nor infirm.

Sargus dropped to his knees before Bloodmane. "Please. Mighty Bloodmane created by Kholster. Please. I have been betrayed by my prince's foolishness. He broke the accord between us without my knowledge. The only solution I can see is to throw myself at your mercy. I renounce my status as Eldrennai and offer all my knowledge, skill, and anything I possess to strengthen the Aern. Let me be known as Aiannai, like Wylant. Place upon my back the scars of Kholster, Vander, or Zhan if he will have me. Let me wear them as a sign that I have kept the oaths of my people. I am neither Leash Holder nor Oathbreaker. I have never ordered an Aern to do anything. I never would unless . . . perhaps if I were commanded by a rightful Aernese authority to do so, or if I were using the imperative voice when attempting to protect an Aern from harm or misstep . . . and only then."

Sargus knelt lower still, his forehead touching the stones.

Bloodmane watched him for a long time before the warsuit's eyes flickered as he relayed what he had seen to his maker. Kholster's response surprised him.

"Tell me your name in the Aernese fashion," Bloodmane intoned aloud.

"I am Sargus, by Uled out of . . . of . . . unknown apprentice."

"Kholster cannot take the get of Uled. Vander will not take you either."

A sob wracked the Eldrennai, but he said nothing.

"The Bone Finder, Zhan, says he will claim you."

Sargus's head shot up with a snap, his eyes blazing. "What must I do?"

Bloodmane took up his maker's warpick, Hunger, and gestured for Sargus to rise. The soon-to-be Aiannai rose. With deliberate purpose, Bloodmane drew a small horizontal circle in the air with his forefinger.

"Ah," Sargus coughed. "Of course. Turn around." He pulled his robes off over his head and turned his back to the warsuit. As Bloodmane began to carve Zhan's scars into the Aiannai's back, he could not tell whether the shuddering sobs that wracked the being's body were born of pain, relief, or a strange mixture of the two.

When it was done, Sargus lay still until the blood had clotted and his wounds had begun to scab. Bloodmane wiped the blood from Hunger off onto Sargus's robes before returning it to its previous position propped against the stone wall.

"Thank you," Sargus said, his voice shaking. "May I tell my people?"

Sargus watched eagerly as the eyes of Bloodmane flashed and dimmed, the only outward sign of the telepathic conversation he had with his creator. "Yes," Bloodmane answered, "but not the Eldrennai. Kholster says that any who truly understand what it is to be Aiannai will comprehend how to formalize that which they already are."

"I understand."

Bloodmane was not sure he understood himself, but he was pleased someone did.

PART TWO
THIRTEEN YEARS LATER

"In the beginning, each Aernese soul was hammered on the Life Forge, a crude powerful thing worked by magic, springing from the mind of the greatest, most insidious Eldrennai Artificer ever to walk the Eldren Plains. Forging the soul of the first Aern took him a year and a day, but he learned from it, each soul taking less time, the last fifty taking no more than a day apiece.

Later refinements demonstrated that new Aern could be grown—Oathbound soul included—within a living womb, the Aern seed beginning the mineralization process immediately upon contact with the womb and drawing necessary mineral deposits from the mother's bloodstream and internal organs to achieve the initial genesis state, a small mass of metal roughly the size of a baby's tooth."

An excerpt from *On the Aern—My Father's Most Dangerous Creations*
by Sargus

CHAPTER 17

TESTING ROUTES

Rae'en stood on the edge of the mountain path, peering down at a distant bend in the so-called Guild Commerce Highway. Lumber carts hauled huge planks of oak and pine to the Guild Cities. The oxen pulling the carts lowed as the men drove them on at a rate much slower than that she and her father had been managing despite the more direct path the highway provided.

Even so, Rae'en worried about her pace. She'd heard the Armored could manage one hundred and twenty jun a day for days on end without rest. The twenty-four-year-old hadn't realized quite what that would be like until she'd set out with Kholster for the "Grand Conjunction." So far, a journey of close to three thousand jun, which normally took her father twenty-seven days, had already taken twenty-one, and they weren't quite halfway yet.

I'm slowing him down.

The scent of blood hit her before the sound of her father moving back behind the trees. It was animal blood. *Rabbit?*

"I don't have a whole ox for you," her father said, breaking the tree line, "but I did catch a few of these." He looked perfectly at home in the woods, with blood on his hands, the pearlescent luster of bone-steel mail enhanced by, but not reflecting, the sun's rays. A stray tangle of thorns trailed the calf of his denim pants (this pair a dark blue from a new dye batch Uncle Glin had been testing), and Kholster brushed it away before tossing her two small rabbits already skinned and something longer with a more musky smell.

He'd trussed the animal carcasses together with twine from his pack. Rae'en bit through it easily enough.

"A weasel," he explained, and she took a tentative sniff of the longest body. "I've eaten them before. They're fine. Tastes a little like squirrel or otter, maybe a little ratty."

"I ate yesterday—" she began.

Kholster crossed to Rae'en's bedroll and nodded in approval to see it already rolled up into a thin bundle no thicker around than her arm. It still mildly embarrassed her that he didn't use one while she did, but no more than the fact that, as far as she could tell, he had yet to sleep at all on this journey.

"You'll need to eat more often until that finger has grown back in full." He sat down on the grass, taking in the same view of the highway.

Rae'en rubbed unconsciously at the regenerating stub on her left hand, where her little finger was taking Torgrimm's sweet time growing back. She looked from Kholster's bone-steel chain shirt to her own and smiled. She knew the Bone Finders would have permitted her to withdraw enough metal from the ossuary to complete her mail with donated bones, but she'd wanted to use her own for the entire shirt, just like Kholster had. She just hadn't lost teeth fast enough to get sufficient material. Using her own bones had left her with less than an ounce of her own metal stored in the ossuary, but it had been worth it, particularly when she'd seen the looks of approval on the faces of the One Hundred and, more importantly, her father.

"Will you eat some for Dwarven courtesy?" she asked. "I can't eat all of this."

"Can't?" He looked over his shoulder, and the light played along the edge of his beard, making it shine an even brighter red.

"I'd rather not eat alone."

"You don't want to eat the weasel, you mean." Kholster held out his hand, received the weasel, and dutifully began to eat. "Vander won't eat it either," he said between mouthfuls. "It tastes fine to me."

"You eat cave snail," Rae'en teased.

"What," Kholster cracked open the weasel's skull to get at the brain, "is wrong with cave snail?"

"It smells like . . . like . . . muck."

"And?"

My father will eat anything; you know? she thought to M'jynn. She felt only a dim connection and frowned. *So I've finally gone far enough my Overwatches can't hear me.* She shook her head.

"Out of range?" Kholster asked.

Rae'en nodded. "I could reach them last night, but—"

"You're a strong kholster, but even with a warpick properly forged and soul bonded, most of the unArmored can't reach more than a few hundred jun northwest of Khalvad."

"And the Armored?"

Kholster looked off to the horizon before answering as if he saw a distant object Rae'en could neither perceive nor comprehend. "I've found nowhere on this plane of existence where an Armored cannot reach out and commune with his or her true skin."

"On this plane of existence?" Her ears flattened a bit at that one.

"When the Port Gates closed in the last Ghaiattri War," Kholster said between mouthfuls of meat. "Those trapped on the other side. . . . Their armor could no longer find them."

The Lost Command, Rae'en thought to her Overwatches. *I hope you can hear this. I'm trying to send it all.*

"Their souls did not rejoin the Aern, so it is possible they still exist out there somewhere, beyond the Port Gate, in the Ghaiattri Lands."

"So, there's hope," Rae'en chirped.

"I never lose hope."

"That must be nice."

"At times." Kholster patted her on the shoulder. "You should know your Overwatches may still be able to hear you when you think to them for some time. Before I was Armored, the few times Vander and the others were so far away their thoughts could not reach me, we discovered," a grin swept across his features, "my thoughts could still reach them quite well."

"Well, you are All Know," Rae'en said as she finished the first rabbit.

Kholster laughed at her use of the name most newborn Aern first called him. Rae'en's entire being thrilled at the sound. What was it like to be able to speak to every Aern? To know that every Aern spent his or her life hoping to please you? Was it uncomfortable, or did her father take pride in it? She couldn't know without asking, but Rae'en sensed it was probably the first answer . . . uncomfortable, even after millennia. Her father knew any Aern would do anything he asked, even suggested . . .

It was hard to wrap her brain around that level of responsibility. Was it any wonder he rarely—if ever—became romantically involved with Aernese women? Any of them would say yes, instantly, so he never asked. She imagined it would take a very direct, patient, and persistent Aern to court her father.

A blush rose to Rae'en's ears and forehead. What had turned her thoughts to mating? Thinking of mating brought the image of Kazan's face into her mind's eye, and she flushed a deeper bronze. "Enough of that!" she whispered to herself. She waited for her father to comment, but he remained studiously unaware of her inner turmoil.

"You can finish your rabbit while we walk," Kholster said as he stood. "Keep your warpick wrapped," he reminded her for what seemed like the hundredth time.

"We don't want the glare to draw attention to ourselves," she said. "Yes, sir."

She reached back, felt the heft of her very own warpick between her shoulders and smiled.

"And eat the liver," he said, tossing a weasel organ to her. "That's where the most metal is."

*

Traveling mostly at a steady trot, the two Aern kept to old mountain roads, animal trails, and hiking paths, many of which were only marked now, if they had ever been, in her father's memory. Kholster's path drew them past burned stone shelters and homesteads which had long surrendered to nature. At times Kholster burst into a run with which Rae'en could not quite keep pace.

What is he doing, guys? Rae'en thought at her Overwatches. They didn't answer . . . and she'd expected them to, even though she knew they couldn't. She had grown so accustomed to their presence on the edge of her consciousness. She missed them more like missing an arm than a finger.

They scrambled up sheer drops. In one place, they stopped to fell a huge oak where the previous log bridge had collapsed or rotted through. In some spots, her father ignored new construction which would have made their path easier, while in other cases, he opted to cross bridges and steps which were obviously too poorly made to support either of their weights, reacting with surprise when they failed beneath him.

Finally, as Kholster frowned at a well-built stone bridge and began to march into a gully full of rocks and brambles, Rae'en spoke.

"Why aren't we taking the bridge?"

"What?" Kholster asked. "That thing?" He snarled at the bridge as if it were disgusting. "It's all manner of strange. What kind of wood do they call that? It's gone gray and moldy."

"Wood?" Rae'en's mouth fell open. "Father, it's stacked stone."

"It's no such thing and whoever built it could hardly have done a worse job if they'd been struck in the head with my warpick and spun three times in a circle before starting."

Rae'en eyed the bridge then her father. "It's a wonderful spot of craftsmanship—even Uncle Glin would agree."

"Tell me no lies." Kholster strode toward her and did not stop until they stood less than a finger's width apart. Even at full height, her father stood a hand taller than she did. This close, his breath washed over her eyes, the points of his doubled canines hard to ignore as he spoke. "I say it is a wooden bridge made by humans with little care and no knowledge of safe construction."

Rae'en's mind reeled. "But it's not," she whispered. *It's not, is it?* she caught herself thinking at Arbokk.

"Are you whispering to yourself or addressing your kholster?"

"My kholster," she answered flatly.

"Then speak up." Had she caught the hint of a grin at the corner of his lips? "I say it is wooden and unsafe." His hot breath made her blink despite herself. "What say you, soldier Rae'en?"

"Ah . . . one moment, Kholster." Stepping back from her father, Rae'en reached into the leather pack on her right side. With mental thanks to her Uncle Vander for the endless drills on packing, she found a steel blade quickly by touch and drew it out. With one look at Kholster and another at the bridge, she tapped the stone with the flat of the blade. No, it wasn't some cleverly concealed illusion through which her father had easily seen. It was certainly stone, just as it appeared to her. How could he be so wrong? How could he not clearly see it was a sturdily built stone bridge?

"Well, soldier?" When she turned back to face him, there was less black in his eyes than before. His amber pupils had expanded, as had the ring of jade around them. His breath came in ragged pants, seeming on the verge of the Arvash'ae. "Your kholster is waiting for an answer."

"It's stone, Kholster. On my oath, as best as I can tell from what I have perceived, the bridge is stone and safe and whole."

"And you say that I, First of One Hundred, First of all Aern, First forged, First free . . . am wrong?!? You dare say this? On your oath, you'd best answer me truthfully."

"I . . ." For a moment she hesitated, then steeled herself. He'd said on her oath, and he'd get it. "Yes, Kholster."

"Good." He clapped her on the shoulder. "I thought I was going to have to lead us right off the mountain into a ravine before you spoke up."

"Wait. What?"

Kholster moved past her. "Oh. You're right." He tapped the bridge rail with his third knuckle. "Stone it is. How about that." He looked over his shoulder with a wink, eyes completely normal again. "Thank you, soldier Rae'en."

"You did that on purpose!?"

"Did I?" Kholster hopped up on the stone railing and did a cartwheel along the edge. His mail did not so much as clink. "If I can say nothing else good about the man, Saul Gundt knew how to build a bridge."

The way her father held his bone-steel mail close to his skin impressed Rae'en almost as much as this—whatever it was he had been trying to prove with the bridge—irritated her. She was still getting used to letting her warpick cling to her back. It also told her he hadn't gone mad. A cartwheel in soundless chain with warpick remaining safely in place served as nigh definitive proof that her father was sound of mind and body. Doing it on the railing was just brag.

"What were you thinking? Why? Why would you—"

"You're a kholster," her father said evenly as he dropped down on the other side of the bridge. "You tell me why I did it. Your Overwatches can't give you the answers. You're on your own now in a way you haven't been in thirteen years."

"I can think for myself."

"I believe you," Kholster answered, "but I need to know you believe yourself. Kazan, M'jynn, Joose, and Arbokk have been a thought away for more than half your life. It changes the way we think, the way we process problems. For some it supplants the ability to think independently . . . completely."

Right, like I—, she cut herself off in mid-thought.

"Right, like you what?" Kholster asked calmly.

Her eyes widened. "You can hear my thoughts, but—"

"Can I?" Kholster asked, face impassive.

"But you just did."

"Did I?" Kholster's amber pupils seemed to bore into her, searching her for evidence of some crime or fundamental flaw.

What did he mean, could she think without her Overwatches? Of course she could! At times she slipped up and sent thoughts she didn't mean to broadcast, though she sometimes whispered to herself as she'd seen other kholsters do . . . and, yes, communicating with her Overwatches had become second nature to her and to them. They were like best friends who could be shown, and allowed to comment on, anything and everything in an instant.

Her dad did the same thing with Vander and . . .

"It's Vander," Rae'en spat as the idea came to her. "Or one of the other Armored Overwatches. You—"

He ordered you to report any thoughts I sent out, right? she sent, as though to her Overwatches, though she knew they were out of range.

"Answer aloud." Kholster frowned.

"In case they are trying to answer for me and make it look like I answered?"

"Because I'm Kholster and those are my scars on your back." His frown didn't deepen as she'd feared, but it stayed a frown. *That's what I get for trying to inject a little levity when he's testing me. He's just so serious*, Rae'en thought to herself.

"You asked Vander to report anything I thought to my Overwatches directly to you, right?" Rae'en said.

"Only in this specific instance," Kholster replied. "And it's kholster Malmung, not Vander. Vander is already at sea with the rest of the invasion force. You could have deduced that, but well done all the same."

Gah! He's right, I should have, she thought but asked aloud, "The youngest of the Armored?"

"Point of view. His was the final warsuit created before the Life Forge's destruction," Kholster acceded. "Though, he is not technically the youngest. Styrm and Drin are, but that's not part of the lesson. Why the boar hunt across the countryside? There are two reasons: one theoretical and one practical."

"You . . ." Rae'en chewed on her upper lip. "You wanted . . . to see how long it would take . . . for me to correct you?"

"Did I?" Kholster's face gave no hint to let her know whether she was right or wrong.

"I . . ." She doubted herself for a moment, but the more she thought about it, the more it seemed like the correct answer. "You wanted to know if I could tell you that you were wrong and when I did, to see if I would back down or hold my ground against you."

"Many can't."

She smiled broadly, exposing all four sets of canines.

"Good work." The praise thrilled her. "But that's only one of the reasons." Her heart sank.

Because he could remember every step he'd ever taken? Because he hated the Commerce Highway? No, he couldn't hate it that much, their path kept bringing it back into view over and over again. If her father truly hated the road, they'd either not see it at all until the last possible moment or he'd have marched them right down the middle to get it over with, like ripping out a tooth that was taking too long to fall out on its own.

His nostrils flared as if he smelled something. Was that a hint? She took a deep breath and closed her eyes. Trees. Flowers. Some kind of canine animal that had warded off some of the summer heat by dipping into a mountain stream. Fungus . . . something mushroomy, but not a scent she'd smelled before. Mushroom was one of the few plant-like substances an Aern could stomach without yarping it back up, but surely that wasn't it. Then she smelled it. Human waste. Subtle, but there. A latrine?

"Does it have to do with humans?"

"It doesn't have to be humans," Kholster answered, "but they're as good as any for this purpose."

Why would he be looking for humans? Or other sentients?

"And it's not old friends," she said it half as a guess but discounted it as the words left her throat. The way he'd said it didn't have to be humans meant that he was looking for a type of person or persons, but not a specific individual.

She scratched absently at the stub of her little finger. It was making progress thanks to all the liver (weasel and otherwise) her father had been going out of his way to make sure she ate, but—

Wait.

"It's liver, isn't it?" She started across the bridge toward her father. "You're trying to find some bandits or highwaymen so we can kill them and I can eat their livers to help grow my finger back faster!?" By the time she'd reached the halfway point, Kholster was smiling again. "It's not like liver is the worst meat in the world, but I'm getting tired of eating it, Father."

"Keep that in mind," he kissed her on her forehead as she reached him, "the next time you get the urge to lop off a body part."

CHAPTER 18
LIVER

Cadence Vindalius felt death in the air long before the first Aern burst through the thatched roof and landed in the bedroom. She lay in the dead farmer's bed nursing baby Caius, fighting the urge to do nothing and let it all end. She knew the male Aern would let the female decide what to do with Caius if she died, knew it just as surely as she knew the female would spare her son. It was her own life in flux. Her son had a destiny. Cadence wished she knew more about it, but her powers didn't reach that far into the future. A candlemark, no further; even then the power was not hers to control.

A phantom scream from outside drew her attention to the window—not that there was anything to see yet. Stray rays of sunlight from the open window picked out the flecks of violet in her otherwise gray eyes, but there was no breeze to be let in at this time of day, leaving the room stale and hot. Heat plastered long tresses of black hair shot through with streaks of red and orange (purple at the ends) to her head. She'd stripped down to an undyed cotton blouse and breeches to help stay cool while she nursed, the thought of trying to struggle back into the gray pants and boots which lay at the foot of the bed, not to mention her long coat, though it was her only garment with sewn-in defensive plates, or Hap's green brigandine in the wardrobe, was anathema to her.

I'd rather die bare-legged if it comes down to it.

Caius opened his eyes briefly, gazing up at her through eyes with reds instead of whites and irises the same shade of violet as that which flecked her own. If he sensed trouble, whatever he saw in his mother's eyes reassured him. Cadence smiled. Down below, in the main room of the farmer's house, Tul laughed at something Merrol said. A hard scowl settled onto Cadence's face. She was glad they were going to die.

Cadence had never liked either man. She didn't like the way they looked at her when she nursed the baby. Hells, that was why she'd gone upstairs, despite the heat, to nurse Caius in the first place. Was it petty that it also figured prominently in her decision not to warn the two bandits?

No, she thought, *you both have it coming seven times over . . . and so do I.*

Still, she had to do something. Knowing only a scattered handful of time remained for her to decide what to do, Cadence took in the room. Not that there was much to take in. Hap never left her a blade, hadn't since he'd stolen her all those years ago. She guessed he took such precaution out of habit now more than anything else, she supposed she was wed to him at this point . . . but she still resented him . . . she resented all five of the bandits with whom she shared her life. *The room*, she reminded herself.

A chair, a chamber pot, a wash basin . . . another woman's clothes in the wardrobe—the farmer's wife, another casualty. Cadence's eyes fell on the bedside table, on a tiny black silk bag sitting unassumingly next to her mortar and pestle.

She felt them coming nearer. Two disparate forces of mayhem and destruction sprinted toward her out in the noonday sun. One crept up the stone outcropping behind the house, the other moved across the grounds . . .

The bag. She couldn't look away from it.

I considered other options first, Hap, she thought to herself. *Even if I did raise the alarm, with you and Ghrol out for supplies, the best chance of staying alive is right there on that rough-hewn bedside table.*

A smile touched her lips. There was no decision at all.

You'd take any excuse to twist crystal, she heard Hap's complaint in her mind. Not that he was actually speaking. She loved and hated Hap in a complex balance, but he was no Long Speaker. She'd simply heard him say it so many times it had become part of her ritual. Anytime she twisted now, she heard him, even when the real Hap was the one telling her to twist in preparation for a fight.

Maybe you're right, Hap, she thought to herself. *Maybe you're right.*

Setting a complaining Caius aside, Cadence slipped her breast back into her cotton top and grabbed the small silk bag from the table. Tamping three pearl-sized red Dienoxin crystals into her palm, she glanced briefly at the mortar and pestle before a twinge in her gut told her she didn't have time to do it the right way. She took the crystals into her mouth and, bracing for pain, bit down on one of them. As her rear right molar cracked, she bitterly regretted letting Darbin, the leader of their small band, talk her out the steel molar caps she'd wanted with the profits from the last big job.

"But think of the crystal we could buy you for all that, babe," he'd cajoled, knowing how much she hungered for it even when she didn't need the boost. "You don't crunch crystal anyway. Not unless it's an emergency."

Darbin made her sick, but that was because he knew the way people worked; Darbin could see their weakness and use it against them. She'd half-expected to see him bringing the farmer's daughter back up from the barn by now, her treating him as if he were her rightwise husband, not some—

Pain flared as she crunched the second crystal and the third, replaced a few ragged gasps later by the flush of power, the raw touch of the god of war's essence. It flowed through her jaw, numbing the pain, the aches, the doubts, and, more importantly, waking and enhancing the Long Arm and the Far Flame talents lurking within Cadence Vindalius's unusual brain.

Baby Caius mewled, still yearning for the breast, and Cadence chuckled sweetly. "Silly little man," she said, looking into her baby's blood-red eyes, "Mama has work to do."

The first Aern crashed through the thatch with no war cry just where Cadence expected him. He looked handsome in a beast-like way . . . handsome and rich. Every Aern was born with a fortune under their skin. The bone-steel chain he wore was a queen's ransom all by itself. If they could sell just a few of those tiny rings before the Bone Finders came for it . . .

Think of what it would buy for little Caius, she thought.

Not to mention the crystal, Cadie. Not a thought for that, Hap's voice accused. *Of course not.*

A thin crimson line of blood ran down the corner of Cadence's mouth as she spat out a chunk of broken tooth and called for the flame. The Aern's eyes widened in surprise. Cadence had time to wonder whether the crystal should now be called Nominite since Nomi had stolen the war god's fiery locks and become a god herself.

You'd like that wouldn't you, Cadie.

Her first burst of fire missed the Aern, striking the corner of the wardrobe and setting it alight. *Hap will beat me for that if I don't get his armor out in time*, she mused.

That's not all I'll do.

The Aern dropped low, rolling to the side, making her set fire to the floor.

Just burn the whole hideout down, why don't you, you useless nit!

The first few shots always go a little wild. I'll get him. Her hair flew out around her head, the streaks of color, signs of years of crystal use, sparked twice then lit up from within.

That's better, girl. Burn bright! Burn hard!

We're close enough to the Junland Bridge that we might be able to get it to a good smuggler. Her brain changed gears again as the pulse of the crystal's power made her thoughts skip and scatter. *Maybe*, she thought, *we should call it Cadencite after me, because I—*

Burn him!

Right. Right. Sorry.

She meant to do just that. She coiled the power into herself like a serpent ready to spring, then held it. She saw the bearded Aern's scowl and his bared fangs and lost her train of thought. He moved in slow motion from her point of view, and somehow that made it worse, made him seem more of a threat.

The Aern frowned as she hit him with the Long Arm, summoning it into both hands in her mind and tossing it forward like twin battering rams of thought. She followed up with fire, let the flames wash over him. Such a strange emotion in his eyes . . . pained, but not pain. Head engulfed in fire, he was thrown backward through the bedroom door and out into the abbreviated hallway, striking the wooden railing at the top of the loft and bursting through it.

As the Aern tumbled toward the family room, Tul lurched away from the dining table, cards flying as he went for his huge two-handed sword. Why he always propped it under the window Cadence decided she would never understand. She nudged the sword with the Long Arm, sending it sliding to Tul's hand, and he laughed.

"Thanks, Cadie!"

They were the last words he ever spoke. A strange warpick, clear and shining like glass in sunlight, came through the window, its spike-like tip punching through the top of his skull, collapsing his bones as it tore through the cranial cavity and dropped him to the floor. His lifeless hand rested on his sword.

The young female Aern who wielded the strange weapon released her grip in shock at the sight of the male Aern's flaming body crashing down onto the table, breaking it to pieces.

"Dad!" She shouted. "What—?"

"Long Arm," he croaked through charred splitting lips. "Crystal twister." The flesh of his face peeled away as he spoke, corded muscle the pale white of bone exposed in the process. "Leave her to me."

Why isn't it red? Cadence stared, momentarily mesmerized by the sight of white muscle attached to pearlescent bone metal.

"Get the other one." He rolled to his feet and hurled the warpick slung across his back to the female. "Take Grudge."

A question died on Cadence's lips as the female Aern caught the weapon and leapt back out through the window.

"You've thrown away your weapon," Cadence snarled, hurling the male Aern against the wall with her mind, taking care to pin him to the wall beams.

He gave a choking laugh and she frowned.

"Something funny?"

"Common mistake." He reached for the two leather bags strapped to his belt, and she tore them away from him with a flare of the Long Arm. Doing so lessened the pressure she exerted, but instead of trying to force his way toward her, he rolled, giving her his back. She pressed harder, trying to flatten him, only to find him shifting his weight, feet beneath him, ready to launch. "I am a weapon."

"Was," she laughed and released him, expecting the Aern to fall to the floor, which he did, but in a controlled roll. Snatching up the three-legged stool upon which Tul had been sitting, the Aern hurled it at Cadence's head, a blow she easily deflected, only find herself having to shunt aside sections of table, a second stool, and further improvised projectiles. Each missile shoved aside allowed the Aern to advance on her incrementally.

"If I were unArmored," the Aern croaked, "you'd have me."

UnArmored? As she thought the question, her mind caught the image of a cold suit of metal with a horned lion's head. **He is not unArmored, Long Fire**, its voice echoed in her mind. **I was merely unprepared. Were you a Ghaiattri, the maker would be in significantly greater danger.**

"Hells," she spat. In the room behind her, young Caius began to truly wail.

*

Rae'en circled the farmhouse, gripping Grudge in both hands. It weighed more than Testament, her own warpick. Grudge was made to be wielded two-handed by arms with muscles stronger than hers. She looked back over her shoulder at the smoke rising from the thatched roof and tried to shake the image of her father's head engulfed in flame from her mind, but it stuck. A sick anxiety filled her belly. How could he withstand that? Could she?

No, Kholster's voice filled her head, *you couldn't. Or . . . it's unlikely. Have you found the other one yet?*

Da—Kholster? She thought back. *Wha—how?*

Whose warpick is in your grip, soldier? Now focus and answer me.

Not yet. Grudge was linked to her father, as much a part of him as Hunger, so she guessed it made sense, but why hadn't anyone ever—

When your Overwatches are in range there's—

His thoughts broke off and a flash of pain bled over from his mind into hers. A simultaneous crash from the house made her flinch, but then his sentence resumed,

—no need for it. Check the barn. This one has a touch of long sight. When she touched my mind, Bloodmane saw something about a barn before she broke off. There may be another bandit and possibly a hostage. Yell if you need me, but I'm a little busy.

A little busy. She smirked at that, the pain in her gut vanishing, her senses coming back into focus. *He's fine. Barn. Barn. Barn.*

Weeds choked a small herb garden in the corner of the overgrown yard. Grass gone to seed stood as high as her waist. *This is wrong.*

Past the forest line, the stench of bodies, dead and buried shallow, drew her attention and irritation because the odor covered up the scent of sweat she was sniffing after. Still, the other man couldn't have gone too far. She saw the barn a little farther along a narrow rock-paved path. On this side of the slope from the stacked stone bridge, Rae'en could see terraced patches of wheat, barley, and something else with yellow flowers she couldn't readily identify.

No sign of him up there, Rae'en thought, which meant he was either circling the farmhouse, headed for the bridge, or he'd run to the barn, just like Kholster'd said.

"Get out of here, you idiot," hissed a voice from the barn.

"Aern, Darbin!" the other voice shouted. "Two Aern!"

"Bird squirt," the other man cursed. "Let me see these 'so-called' Aern."

The barn door slammed open, and out stepped a verminous-looking human with a heavy beard and hair which looked like it had been cut with a large bowl as the barber's only guide. He had the muscled look of a blacksmith's striker, wielding a sledgehammer so much more comfortably than Rae'en wielded Grudge that she would have wagered naming rights the man had been long apprenticed to a smith.

He wore raw denim coveralls of the type Rae'en had heard about but never seen outside of shared memories. Kholster didn't like the way the straps tugged at his shoulders, so there was no market for them in the Dwarven-Aernese Collective.

The stink of human fear hit her as he moved closer, but it came from behind him along with the smell of unwashed bodies, exertion, and blood.

"Looks like I have a new playmate." Darbin spat on the ground then smiled at her through a mouth of rotten teeth.

Staring at those teeth distracted her from the crossbow bolt until it struck her in the chest. A sternum hit, the shaft breaking in back of the field point. *As if an arrow could punch through my sternum even without armor. Stupid human.*

Kill him; don't critique him, Kholster thought at her, *before he goes for the eyes or the throat.*

Yes, Kholster. Rae'en charged the man with the sledgehammer, catching his blow with Grudge's haft. She slid her foot between his legs, hooking it behind his ankle and sweeping it out from under him. Grabbing the front of her chain-mail shirt as he fell, the human lost his weapon but brought her down on top of him.

Snarling, she snapped at him, fangs bared.

"Oh-ho! A biter, eh?" He laughed. "I'll—"

You'll what? Rae'en wondered as she bit through the web between the thumb and forefinger of the hand he'd held up to push her away. A bloody mouthful of skin came free as she bit, chewed, swallowed. Darbin screamed, transforming from a man drawing obvious pleasure from the idea of a struggling female to a scared, panicked creature wanting nothing more than to get away.

Mouth open wide, she went for Darbin's throat, reeling back in shock when a crossbow bolt fired from the doorway of the barn went in through her open mouth, passing through her tongue, the tip jutting out through the bottom of her jaw.

All thought fell away. Pain washed over her. The blacks vanished from Rae'en's eyes as amber pupils and jade irises expanded. If it hurt when Rae'en, in the grips of the Arvash'ae, tore the crossbow bolt from her mouth, she never remembered. A third bolt shot her through the stomach as she bit off Darbin's nose and crushed his throat with a hammer blow from both fists. Then she was up and charging the barn door.

Merrol did not get a fourth shot.

*

Cadence heard Merrol's dying scream but couldn't process it. Lower lip dripping with blood, she panted from the effort of blocking the barrage of thrown objects with her Long Arm talent. Sweat stained her cotton top and made it cling to breasts overlarge from nursing. She'd tried hurling the Aern's projectiles back at him, and in fact, he was festooned with fragments of wood and metal. A hundred little wounds which did not bleed. Why wouldn't he bleed? Cadence had killed Aern before. Not many, but a few. None of them had been this hard to kill. None of them had had metal suits of armor keeping watch over their minds.

"What are you?" she spat, backpedaling toward the bedroom. *Maybe I should just grab Caius and run*, she thought.

"I am Kholster, the First of One Hundred." The Aern moved slowly up the stairs, resisting the full force of her Long Arm, feet planted, moving slowly but steadily, like a man advancing against the winds of a mighty storm. "And I have not killed you because you are a slave."

"Kholster Bloodmane wants me as a slave," she panted. "I should be flattered."

"Bloodmane is my warsuit," he corrected, still advancing, the blood-stained glass-like warpick the other Aern had used peeking over his shoulder. "An Aern has no last name in the manner of humans, just name, number, rank, and lineage. And I will never have slaves."

"You want me as a slave for the female then?" She backed into the bedroom and dropped her mind push, throwing all she had into one tremendous burst of Far Fire, but the Aern who called himself Kholster. . . . *Could he truly be the legendary leader of the Aern? Does such a being actually exist?* He did not burn any longer. How, faced with him, could she deny. . . . She felt the power, but . . .

"I am Armored," Kholster said as if that should explain everything. "And no, I don't want you to be a slave at all. If you had no will to be free, I would kill you. Yet, I see fight in your eyes. So, instead, I'll free you, if you're brave enough. Where are the others?"

"Others?"

"The other bandits. Two more who aren't here now. I could smell them before you started burning everything in sight." As he spoke, his flesh began to smooth out and heal, his charred lips bubbling back to normal.

"How?"

"I told you I am Armored. Bloodmane is ready for you now, Far Flame. He feels your heat, but it would take a dragon's fire to melt his surface. I doubt you can burn that hot even with a mouth full of Dienoxin. How much of the war god's essence do you still have inside you? Enough to pull the house down atop us?"

Fire spread along the splintered rail behind him. Off to her left, baby Caius wailed in true terror, a cry very different from hungry or tired. For the first time in their fight, Cadence noticed the smoke. It flowed along the ceiling, a river of suffocation, moving downward.

Could he tell? Could the warsuit somehow know how little she had left? She felt the last meager measure of Dienox's essence trickling away as she pushed the Far Fire—she stopped.

Burn him, you useless wench!

"I could."

Not without the crystal, you worthless cow! Hap's voice rang in her mind. A string of hate-filled expletives filled her mind. It was always worse on the other side of a twist. Phantom images of Hap's screaming face surrounded Cadence in her mind's eye, blocking out the real.

"Shut up!" Cadence grabbed her head. "I'm sorry, Hap! If I had more crystal—"

"You don't need it." Kholster folded his arms as the fire and smoke flowed around him. "But whoever this Hap is . . . were I you, I'd kill him. I'd save the baby first, but it's up to you." Kholster shrugged. "If not, it's all worthless. We can speak more outside . . . if you make it. I suggest jumping out the window."

Kholster turned and walked into the rising smoke, vanishing amidst the flames.

CHAPTER 19
SHORE LEAVE

Muscles still burning at the end of a long day, Kazan'd had just enough time to let the coolness of his stone berth begin to seep in and work its primal magic on his muscles, when he felt Malmung's mental tap like someone knocking on the door of his mind.

You, guys, too? he sent to his fellow Overwatches.

Three replies hit him in rapid succession: *Yes*, *Of course*, and *I hope Malmung dies screaming*.

That the third reply came from M'jynn was no surprise.

A second mental nudge came shortly after the first, this one like a mailed fist knocking on a wrought iron gate. Kazan smirked, opening his eyes, doubled canines bared if only to the darkness. Malmung always knocked twice before sending a message on a down cycle. Kazan found the practice weirdly formal but guessed it was that same level of rigidity which kept Malmung from ever sending unintended thoughts to the Overwatches he kholstered.

Most kholsters with whom Kazan, M'jynn, Joose, and Arbokk had trained thought in words like Rae'en. Kholster Malmung used words when he had to, but they came unnaturally to him and were often displayed as actual letters rather than spoken in his own voice. Malmung was just as likely to convey orders by altering the mental map the Overwatches displayed for him, drawing lines indicating where he wanted troops to move or making one of their tokens flash when he wanted an opinion from a specific Overwatch. Kazan suspected Malmung's method of communication was exactly why he and the others had been sent to train with the strange kholster during Rae'en's absence: to get practice working with another, very different, approach to kholstering.

Kazan liked to think he'd be kholstered by Rae'en again, along with the other Elevens who'd been kholstered by her on their first mission and in the thirteen years since, but there was no guarantee, particularly with the way she'd been taken off on Kholster's current trip to Oot and to the front of the approaching war. Every Freeborn Aern wanted to participate, yet, as far as Kazan or his fellow Overwatches knew, Rae'en was the only Freeborn being given a chance.

And here comes the message, Joose thought to the group.

An eye opened in Kazan's mind and in the minds of his fellows. Malmung's version of "Wake up."

A mouth opened and closed as if it were speaking, but there was no sound. Malmung wanted to talk to them in person.

Why doesn't he just think what he wants us to hear? Arbokk whined amongst the four of them.

Obviously, Joose sent, *he wants to gauge our reactions or interact physically in some way.*

Makes sense, Kazan thought back. *Anyone else barely awake?*

I haven't even gotten back to the barracks yet, M'jynn growled.

Did our interim kholster interrupt something vital? Joose teased.

Leave him be, Kazan thought. *Just because you want to live vicariously through M'jynn's exploits . . .*

Now. The word appeared in dull bronze letters in their minds.

If not death, I hope he loses a limb, an important one . . . M'jynn grumbled.

Maj, Kazan chided.

. . . and I hope it grows back slowly. There was a pause. *And green.*

Half a candlemark later, the four Overwatches, clad in mail shirts, denim leggings, and boots, with their soul-bonded weapons on their backs and saddlebags packed as if they intended to head out on extended patrol, arrived just as kholster Malmung always insisted.

Bare chested and wearing only a pair of loose-fitting white cotton pants, Malmung studied the Overwatches with a look of apparent disinterest, his insanely long hair braided into one fifteen-hand-length of cord draped about his shoulders, beads and rings of bone-steel adorning it at intervals which seemed decorative. Malmung flared his nostrils, ears flat against his head, and gazed past the young Aern.

Kazan had long since learned that just because Malmung appeared to be looking elsewhere didn't mean that he missed anything. The Aern's peripheral vision and attention to detail were uncanny. Malmung held his main weapon (Kazan still didn't know its name), an axe-bladed polearm, by the shaft, blade in the air, butt on the stone of the training ground floor. If there were ever an attacker expecting to catch Malmung off guard . . . well, it would be harsh.

Cold touched the back of Kazan's eyes, the overcast sky blocking out the stars and forcing him to use thermal vision as he marveled at the weapon. The polearm was a full kholster in length with two spikes on the poll, one on the eye, and a curved hook curling from the top of the blade with which Kazan knew from personal experience Malmung could snag any piece of loose clothing or equipment and pull an attacker off balance and to the ground, where the top spearhead-like spike of the weapon would come into play. Engraved likenesses of snarling wolves with exaggerated fangs glared at the watcher from the polearm's cheeks. It was almost enough to make Kazan wish he'd forged such a weapon for himself instead of a warpick.

Warpicks are traditional, a true and a safe choice, but—

You still worrying over whether you should have made a bolder choice of implement? Joose thought. *In twenty-six more years you can make another soul-bonded implement and—*

It gives me the yarps, Arbokk sent.

That mace of yours give me the yarps, M'jynn sent back.

I still don't see why it doesn't leave you bloody every time you move too fast. Kazan glanced down at the spiked mace hanging from a sheath frog (a removable leather assembly) attached by two rings to Arbokk's belt.

Charming would never do that to me, Arbokk snapped back.

Unless you lose your concentration, you mean, Joose threw in.

That only happened once!

Only takes once, Joose and M'jynn thought in unison.

Sharp and hard, the crack of bone-steel on stone echoed in their ears and minds as Malmung raised his polearm a few fingers off the ground then brought the butt down on the stone. Resisting the urge to cover their ears because they knew it wouldn't help block the sound Malmung was sending directly into their minds, the Overwatches gritted their teeth and bore it.

Kazan stood at attention, his warpick in both hands held at waist level roughly parallel with his shoulders. Joose followed suit with his own warpick.

M'jynn drew his sword from the sheath frog on his belt and held it the same way, gripping the blade lightly with his left hand, the hilt firmly with his right. Arbokk's mace, unsuited even more so than M'jynn's blade for such a position, wound up gripped one-handed in a close approximation of the stance, his empty right hand curled into a tight fist.

Malmung repeated the gesture three more times. There was no more idle chatter.

"She passed." Raising his polearm as he spoke, he brought it up and laid it comfortably across his shoulders, hands gripping the shaft as if it were a yoke for hauling water. "Rae'en. She can think the way he wants. Apart."

"Who can't?" Kazan asked before he could catch himself.

"Me," Malmung swung the polearm around, turning as he did so, to let it sling out to its full length, the spike at its eye coming within a hairsbreadth of Kazan's nose, "for one, but I've learned it's not a weakness . . ."

A map of the surrounding area bloomed in the mind of the four Overwatches, every bit as detailed as what they might have shown him had he asked. The words "it marks me as a different sort of weapon" appeared in golden ink inscribed in the air above the surface of the map.

"Now for your test," Malmung said aloud, deliberately, as if he were being careful to get each word exactly right. "You are released to your former duty, assigned to kholster Rae'en. Your kholster is in the field. Dismissed."

On the word *dismissed*, Malmung's presence dropped away from them as if a link had been severed. He brushed by Kazan, slapped the hilt of a dagger into his hand, and walked off into the night.

Holding the blade conveyed a sense of potential need and eventual return. Kazan saw an image of himself going somewhere, coming back, and giving the blade back to Malmung just as Malmung had given it to him.

This dagger is a soul-bonded implement, Kazan thought to the others.

I figured out what he calls his primary tool, Joose thought back.

What?

Joose sent them an image of the polearm. *That.*

That's shiverworthy, M'jynn thought back. *What a miscast he is.*

I think if he had to put it into words, he would just call it "My Implement" or maybe "The polearm I made to kill with that holds a splinter of my soul."

Kazan turned the dagger over in his hand. It had a sharp curving blade with only one cutting edge. The words "Return when finished" were etched in fuller-like grooves on either side of the blade.

So . . . do we go back to the barracks? Arbokk asked.

"Our kholster is in the field." Kazan tasted the words as he slid the strange dagger into one of his twin pouches.

And where does an Overwatch belong? Joose prodded.

Kazan smiled, an expression he saw reflected equally on the tired faces of his fellows. He nodded.

Do you think we'll get to see a Zaur? M'jynn asked.

No, Kazan thought back. *They're probably all dead.*

An Oathbreaker? Arbokk thought. *I'd love to tear into one of them.*

Let's just find Rae'en first, Kazan ordered.

As one, they turned and ran into the night following the pull of their kholster's presence, somewhere out over the horizon, down the Commerce Highway and beyond, a burning ache not of pain but of absence.

It would still track pretty well to get to kill some Zaur, Kazan thought, focusing his mind on keeping the thought to himself as he ran.

CHAPTER 20

GENERAL TSAN

Half a world away, Na'Shie burned. Huge pillars of flame cast an unwanted flickering light upon the carnage of the besieged port city, a light reflected in the black eyes of the Zaur invaders.

General Tsan watched the scene with quiet joy, his scales, normally a dull murky red, shone crimson as he basked in the furnace-like heat generated by the burning ships. The reptilian commander twisted his wedge-shaped head from side to side as the Zaurruk battered through the hulls of ships, snatching sailors from their vessels and swallowing them whole. As the giant war serpents turned their attention to the *Verdant Passage*, Tsan reeled about to face the ship's captain, his forked tongue tasting the human's fear and desperation.

The human, a man called Randall Tyree, twisted his face as if to look away but forced himself to watch. Tsan wondered if it was guilt that made the human want to bear witness to the destruction of his crew or simple morbid curiosity.

"What are they?" asked Captain Tyree. He clenched his jaw between words, biting down hard, each utterance an explosive burst of breath.

"Weapons of old," answered General Tsan. "The Zaurruk sleep in the deep places, Captain, where the warmbloods dare not go."

Tsan gestured at the sloping entrance to the once-great Zalizian Bazaar, which led down to the docks. A crew of Zaurruk handlers commanded their charges watched by Sri'Zauran guards with black scales banded by narrow scales of iridescent blue. The handlers rhythmically pounded the ground with steel mallets of varying sizes, sending orders to the mighty war serpents below. Each of the crews had their black scales painted with concentric circular patterns of gray and white, matching the patterns on the Zaurruk themselves. A fourth serpent curled itself defensively around the watchtower atop which General Tsan and Tyree stood. Several members of the Port Authority still twitched at Tsan's feet, angry red lines of poison clearly streaking their skin.

Tsan examined Captain Tyree, smiling at his struggle not to watch his fellow humans' death throes. The venomous bite of most Zaur was not fatal unless they were in the grip of the mating urge, but Tsan and his kin were different.

Our bite, Tsan thought, *is always deadly.*

Tsan slapped his tail against the stone roof, and his black-scaled personal guard formed a semicircle blocking the roof access, though Tsan felt he had little need of their protection. The city's defenders were either dead, dying, or fleeing for their lives.

"Look, Captain." Tsan pointed to the ruined hulk of the *Verdant Passage* as the large merchant vessel sank beneath the waves. He spoke the human language with no trace of the usual lisp caused by a Zaur's forked tongue. "Isn't that your ship?"

"You know it is, you scaly bastard!" The captain launched himself at Tsan, only to be restrained by the general's quick-clawed lieutenant. "You said the *Verdant Passage* would be spared!"

Tsan laughed, too pleased with victory to lose his good humor over the foolish insults of an overly emotional warmblood. Besides, the human had been most useful.

"I said that if they stayed put, as arranged, I would spare them," the general corrected. "They attempted to flee. My troops had orders to set ablaze any ship that tried to run. Blame your first mate, not me." Tsan dropped to all fours and slithered along the floor. "I always keep my bargains."

As Tsan rose up before him, Captain Tyree recoiled involuntarily, leaning back as far as the Zaur restraining him would allow, but Tsan had no intentions of striking. He plucked a small spyglass from the case on Tyree's belt and propped his forelegs on the edge of the tower. Raising the glass to his eye, Tsan watched the crew, those who'd survived thus far, swimming as hard as they could, striving to get enough distance to avoid being sucked in by the vacuum resulting from their sinking vessel. The docks were in ruins, except for the southernmost pier, where dark shapes continued the fight.

They were his soldiers, magnificent in their armor, each carrying a bow, their angular Skreel blades sheathed at their sides. The Zaur who led them was like no Zaur any of these warmbloods would have ever seen. Slightly taller than the others, the leader sported scales with alternating rings of amber and pale blue. His head, like Tsan's, was more angular and pointed than his fellow soldiers, almost like an arrowhead.

"Release him," the general ordered.

Tsan's lieutenant complied, favoring the captive human with a threatening hiss. His long forked tongue flickered across Captain Tyree's throat. The captain was no longer afraid. The man had gone from grief to acceptance so quickly that Tsan marveled despite himself at the human's adaptability.

"I'm not your type," Tyree protested, pushing the lieutenant's muzzle away from his neck. "I'm afraid I don't foam up *or* lay eggs. You're cute though—don't let anyone tell you you're not."

Tsan offered the spyglass back to Captain Tyree but was not surprised when he declined. The ground shook as the Zaurruk pulled back from the harbor, and Tsan hissed happily as the troops swooping in behind them dumped barrels of oil into the water and set it afire. Tsan could not hear the screams from this distance, but from Tyree's expression, he thought the human heard them.

"I will reimburse you for the cost of your vessel and its crew, Captain," General Tsan said softly. "It wasn't fair to expect them to remain rational in the presence of the Zaurruk."

He lowered the spyglass and smiled at the surprised human. "A royal kandit per crewman," he offered, "ten for your navigator, two for your cook, thirty for your cargo, and . . . shall we say eighteen hundred for your ship?"

General Tsan watched the human run the numbers in his head. Humans were so adaptable; bending them this way and that was a hatchling's game. But Tyree . . . Tsan wondered if it wouldn't be wiser to kill the human now. If the human gave him an excuse, that's exactly what he would do, but almost as if Tyree sensed his thoughts, the human calmed further. The threat in his tensed muscles eased away. The human met Tsan's gaze and smiled.

"That would be most generous. Thank you," Captain Tyree finally agreed. "Though if I could have some of that in Zalizian scrip . . ."

So adaptable.

Tsan conceded with a flick of his tail. Let the human have his foreign scrip. Let him live, too. If all went well, by the time he received his payment, the good captain would beg to accept Zaur coin. "I assume you brought the information I asked for?" Tsan held out his hand.

Captain Tyree pulled a battered notebook from his leather pouch and handed it to the Zaur. "It's all there."

Warlord Xastix's plan had worked perfectly. Weeks of waiting for the wind to die had paid off in blood, casualties, and total devastation for the port. When the Eldrennai sent to Zaliz for aid, none would be forthcoming. The next nearest northern port on the Cerrullic Coast was Klinahn, and they would be much less likely to send assistance once word reached them concerning the fate of Na'Shie.

Tsan gestured at the lieutenant who had restrained Tyree so readily. "Take Captain Tyree and the census data he has provided us to the warlord. Once the information has been verified, pay him the agreed-upon amount, mark him as a scale-friend, and let him go. He has been of great service to the Zaur."

"Once it has been verified? C'mon, Tsan, you won't know if it's correct until you've invaded!" the human protested sharply, saliva spattering Tsan's scales as he shouted.

"You would prefer I back out on our offer and throw you from the tower?" Tsan asked, casually rubbing the human's spit into his dry scales. *Who said humans weren't useful?*

"I think I'll pass on that one, Your Scaliness." Tyree offered Tsan a curt bow.

"Perhaps you would like to feed one of the Zaurruk?"

"Now you're just being nasty."

"Then be happy we are going to honor our deal. Once the Eldrennai have been eliminated, you will be a very rich man and you will have the gratitude of the most powerful empire on the continent. Surely that won't be such a terrible burden?"

The sour scent of despair, flavored with the bitter taint of disillusionment, floated on the breeze, but Tsan saw the careful way the human maintained exterior calm, forcing his eyes to meet Tsan's. Such composure.

"It seems that I must again thank the general for his generosity."

"You are quite welcome, my friend." General Tsan nodded to the Zaur lieutenant and handed him the book of census data. "Be swift. The warlord wants this information immediately."

"I will let nothing detain us, General," his underling answered.

"Perform this task well, Lieutenant," Tsan promised, "and you will have earned a name."

Pride swelled the chest of the younger Zaur, and his second eyelid nictated in surprise. "Yes, General."

"When next we meet," Tsar murmured, sliding his foreclaw along the scales between the lieutenant's eyes, "I hope to call you Lieutenant . . . Kreej."

The future Lieutenant Kreej eyed Captain Tyree so fiercely that Tsan was forced to stifle a chuckle. Kreej was a good name, but not a great name. This one would work hard to get a new one. Names were addictive to young Zaur. Being called by an identifier strictly referring to their birth order and parentage—the seventh hatchling of the eighth brood of Yat, for example—was so tedious most Zaur would do almost anything to gain their first name. Thereafter, the quest for a second name, a self-chosen name, could be equally inspirational.

Turning his back to the lieutenant and his captive, Tsan waved them both away. "Take four of my personal guards with you, Lieutenant. I will have no further need of them. The port, what is left of it, is ours."

"To His secret purpose," the lieutenant said as he turned to leave with his prisoner.

"To His secret purpose," the general repeated softly. "To His secret purpose indeed."

CHAPTER 21
SPARING CAIUS

Kholster frowned at the unconscious Long Arm and her child. Both of them were badly crystal twisted, the mother from abusing the crystallized essence of Dienox, and the offspring from birth because of the mother's abuses.

"His eyes." Rae'en looked a little worse for wear from her most recent bout of Arvash'ae. Kholster expected it had less to do with the Arvash'ae itself (she'd definitely eaten her fill) and more to do with finding parts of the third body afterward. The one in the barn. Kholster'd felt the hostage's death through his link with Grudge but felt no guilt. They'd not known about her going into the battle, and certainly in Torgrimm's hands she'd be safe from further harm. Kholster trusted the Harvester to assist her with her trauma far more than he trusted himself. "The baby has reds instead of whites."

Kholster unswaddled the exhausted, mewling infant from the smoke-smelling blanket and examined him.

Can you tell how old it is? he thought at Vander.

No, but Okkust says it's around five months.

If any of the Armored are likely to know . . . Kholster let the thought trail away.

Stunted bat-like wings grew out of the child's shoulder blades. It was too early to tell if they would grow big enough to be useful, but the child did seem unnaturally light, so it might be possible. More worrisome, though, was the rounded indentation at the boy's sternum.

He's shard-slotted. Kholster thought at his Overwatch.

Kill it? Vander thought back. *The last thing we need is another human the Ghaiattri can trick into using a shard of the World Crystal to open a Wild Gate.*

"Is he going to be okay?" Rae'en asked.

"If we let him live." Kholster swaddled the child as he spoke. "He will be unique, good at whatever trade he tries, and eventually, when the Ghaiattri notice him, he must either become a very good person or a very bad person. His life will affect all Barrone."

"Of course we'll let him live, right?" Rae'en's eyes went not to the baby or to her father but to the barn. "It's just a baby."

You want to let her kholster this decision, too? Vander asked.

If he's ever a problem, Vander, he'll be a problem after she is First . . .

You could show her what happened with Omric . . .

I could, but this is a child, not Omric. I do not wish to make her decisions for her. She has to learn how choices made in one year, particularly those involving life and death, echo through time. And she must make her own decisions about whether those choices were mistakes or not. Do you disagree?

No, Vander sighed. *I just hope those wings don't work. Can you imagine how much trouble Omric would have been with wings?*

I can't see how it would have changed the war all that much.

"Kholster?" Rae'en asked.

Spattered in blood, she looked tired and worn and worried. Kholster thought back to all the times he'd come out of the Arvash'ae to find he'd arvashed someone he hadn't meant to harm. Such a hard lesson to learn. Her mind had to be in turmoil, the blaming and denying blame . . . though her outer layer of skin no longer required a gambeson, Kholster knew the inner Aern was less easily armored from self-inflicted wounds.

"How's your finger?" he asked.

"Fine." She held it up. Everything had grown back but the nail. That would come in a day or so. Three human livers appeared to have filled the order nicely. If she were Armored, she could have just . . . Kholster banished the thought. There was no Life Forge. There would be no Life Forge. The Freeborn could not go through life wishing for one, nor could their parents.

"Then it's up to you." Kholster offered her the wriggling bundle. "But I'm not changing its crapcatcher or washing it or feeding it."

As if to emphasize Kholster's point, the baby's face went still and serious. There was a burbling liquid sound from his nether regions.

"It doesn't smell bad," Rae'en said, taking the child as Kholster unceremoniously dumped him into her outstretched arms.

"Then his mother must still be nursing him." Kholster walked over to the unconscious woman. She looked soft and peaceful when she wasn't setting him on fire. He tugged on the green brigandine with which she'd attempted to shield her son during their leap through the second-story window and wondered if that was the only reason she'd saved it, or if it had belonged to the man she'd called Hap. It was too large to be hers. "When they start eating solid food, Gromma puts the stink in."

"How do you know about human babies?" Rae'en asked.

"I'm over six thousand years old," Kholster answered. "Some Aern have adopted human infants in that time. Even me. If we kill the mother, we'll have to find something the baby can eat. Usually mashed-up vegetables or rice."

"No meat?"

"No teeth," Kholster answered.

"Can't we just find some cow milk or—"

"Yes, but cow milk can kill human babies unless you heat it correctly first."

"Why?"

"The Dwarves say there are tiny little beasts that live in it, too small to see. The heat kills them. And it will still make the feces stink."

"Oh." Rae'en carried the baby over to where his mother lay on the ground. Kholster had dragged the woman away from the burning farmhouse, then left her in the dirt. "Why didn't you kill her? For the baby?"

"She's a slave." Kholster knelt down and pried open the woman's mouth. Her lower molars were cracked and broken. Her uppers looked bad. Reaching into one of his oversized belt pouches, Kholster pulled out a small metal box and opened it. Inside, an array of bone-steel implements shone brightly in the sunlight. Constant teething meant many Aern carried the right tools to assist in extracting a stubborn tooth. "To the crystals and also, I suspect, to a person named Hap."

You'd better use the laughing salve you packed for Rae'en, Vander thought at him, *if you're going to do what I think you're going to do, though you might want to save a little for yourself . . .*

Her teeth look about the right size, don't you think?

Are you just doing the molars?

Why would I do more than that? I'm not in love with the woman!

I thought your loins burned for her.

She burned my face, not my pants, Vander.

Yes, Kholster. Kholster waited for the rest of it. He knew Vander could not resist at least one more jibe. *Still, are you sure you don't want me to send ahead to the Guild Cities to have the ossuary get a selection of incisors ready? Draekar's might be about right.*

"Pulling her teeth?" Rae'en asked, peering down. She took a sharp intake of breath when she saw the damage. "That's going to hurt like Kilke's stump."

"I have laughing salve." Kholster pulled the small brass jar out of a pouch and held it up for his daughter to inspect.

"That might take the edge off, but—"

"She'll feel better once she has the new ones. Laughing salve has a stronger effect on humans than it does on us."

"Huh?" Rae'en stared at him, not comprehending.

"Why did Uled say Aern were created with constant tooth replacement?" Kholster eyed his daughter. She'd shared the memories which included that knowledge, just as had all other Aern, but a true kholster could recall that sort of detailed information more quickly than even an Overwatch.

"'Who wants an eternal army of toothless warriors?'" Rae'en parroted Uled's words back to him.

"And why did he actually do it?"

"Uled had bad teeth and he—Wait. You're giving her—"

"Someone already pulled her wisdom teeth, so there should be room for eight of my molars. If we do it right. It's been few hundred years, but I think I remember how to do it."

Kholster found the pliers for which he'd been looking. He set a well-worn living wood bite block, which he'd had since the days when Uled still walked Barrone, out on a black cloth Glinfolgo had given him to "repel the little beasts."

"But won't she just keep crunching crystal?"

"If she does," Kholster straddled Cadence's prone form, with one knee pinning each shoulder, "I'll have Caz take them back."

Cadence only woke up once during the procedure, just as Kholster was trying to make sure her bite lined up properly and had to shift one of his own molars which had already taken root. Kholster, unlike Uled, hated to hear women scream. He promptly gave the woman more laughing salve.

When it was finished, they set off at once, Rae'en toting the infant and Kholster carrying the Long Arm over his shoulder.

"We could wait for her to wake up," Rae'en offered.

"You have an appointment to keep at Oot." *The Vael representative is probably already heading for Port Ammond*, he thought at Vander.

Porthost at the very least, Vander agreed. *Kari sent you her name?*

Yavi, Kholster thought back, *but it hardly matters. This time the Vael representative's errand is doomed before it starts.*

CHAPTER 22
YAVI'S ROAD

Yavi woke well after dawn, the dregs of a dream still clinging to her mind, casting an unwanted haze over her thoughts. She rolled off of the goose-down mattress blinking at the cozy room in the inn and the stone room full of glass displays from the dream that still painted itself over her surroundings.

A few blinks, and the display cases faded, leaving her gaze filled only with the here and now . . .

I really need to visit that museum, just to see if any of what I've been dreaming all these years is true. What if it's not? Then, she guessed, she'd really feel stupid.

Yavi pulled her long head petals back and tied them at the nape of her neck. Thicker than a human's hair with a texture like rose petals, Yavi's head petals were the vibrant yellow of sunflowers. Though she might have wished she'd been an evergreen whose hair was present the whole year round, rather than drying out and falling off in late autumn, it certainly was pretty in the spring and summer.

The smell of royal hedge roses filled the room as she lifted her arms.

At least we smell nice when we sweat.

Shoving open the wooden shutters of the second-story window, Yavi leaned out, marking the sun's position in the sky, her large black eyes taking it all in. *Later than I thought. No time for a bath or a change of clothes.* With a forlorn grunt, Yavi grabbed her heartbow and her travel pack from the wardrobe before leaping out the window. She landed lightly on the packed dirt of Silver Leaf City's merchant path, judiciously startling two chickadees exploring the street for human leavings.

"Go hunt something, Lazyfeathers."

"Are you sure you won't stay for breakfast?" Jorum called out a first-floor window. The innkeeper, a round-bellied human with kind eyes and only one leg, hobbled out the kitchen door in a practiced lope, leaning on his crutch. Yavi had asked him how he lost the leg, but he wouldn't tell her. Maybe on the way home she could convince him.

"I sent Sebastian out hunting this morning. It's not much, but it's all fairly sought and properly hunted. Nothing domesticated. All pleasing to Xalistan." Jorum's voice rose hopefully on the last word, but he was already headed inside.

"Can I take it with me?"

His laugh made Yavi's ears flick up straight. Reaching up to cover them, she cursed whatever it was that gave her such expressive ears.

"Already packed. Thought you might want it as travel food when you didn't get up on time."

"Why didn't you wake me?" Yavi jerked her hands away from her ears.

"Me?" Jorum said in mock horror as he snagged a cloth-wrapped package from the bar. "Deprive a Vael princess of her beauty sleep? Not I!" He tossed the package and Yavi caught it. The smell of roasted venison curled in her nostrils.

Yavi's hand went to her pouch for money, her pale skin, tinted with the lightest hint of green, standing out in contrast to the black pouch, but Jorum waved her off. "You just promise to stay here again on your way safely home and don't let the," he spat out the word, "Eldrennai honor you to death."

Yavi blinked at him. The name "Eldrennai" always gave her pause. The Aern insisted the Eldrennai be referred to as Oathbreakers and nothing else. Yavi's people also called them Oathbreakers, but the humans, who worked day in and day out with the Oathbreakers . . . she understood why they didn't use the name. It would be like a Vael trading on good faith with someone who insisted on referring to her people as Weeds (or the less insulting, but equally dismissive, Flower Girls), but it still felt strange to hear.

"Thank you!"

Humans moved everywhere in the border town. Most of them worked for the Oathbreakers, carrying goods back and forth in a complicated arrangement made to appease the Aern, who would tolerate no Oathbreaker on Vael land. As a result, Silver Leaf City now had a human population much larger than its nonhuman one.

Yavi liked humans. They weren't all as nice as Jorum, but they waved and smiled for the most part. The humans in Silver Leaf knew how to interact with a Vael . . . no attempts to grab or constrain, even in greeting . . . and she had no need to wear a samir to veil her dental ridge or to keep the humans from getting too frisky with her. In many ways, they seemed like shorter-lived versions of her people, and she loved them for it. Yavi headed out, eagerly unwrapping the cooling venison, giving thanks to Xalistan, god of the hunter and hunted, as she ate.

At the edge of town, the hard-packed dirt road through Silver Leaf met the smoothness of the White Road. A sign molded of the same white stone as the road stood at the edge of path. *West to South Watch*, Yavi thought. She looked west, picturing Porthost, Kevari Pass, and even the ruins of Fort Sunder on the Shattered Plains. *East to Port Ammond* . . . and the Oathbreakers.

"I'd rather go west," Yavi grumbled with her mouth full, but she walked east all the same. The dream came back to her as she walked. Each clean white stone of the road called to mind the halls of the museum she had visited in her dream. Remembering brought a shiver across her bark, stirring her sap. Crystal cases. Aernese warsuits. A small silver plaque with the inscription "The Armor of General Bloodmane—Hero and Traitor."

She saw simultaneously a suit of plate with an irkanth's head and an actual four-legged beast of metal, a roaring lion with pearlescent skin, amber eyes, and a mane wet with blood. One and the same. Alive, with a voice like a gentle mountain, the irkanth had always spoken in her dreams. "Here where you are safest," the irkanth told her. "To Oot. Send. He is injured. Zaur in the forest. Kholster Rae'en. Please?"

Words, a mad sample of time-tossed moments, returning always to the same phrase, a refrain of reassurance. "Here where you are safest."

Whether it was the spirit within Kholster's armor trying to communicate, or whether the warsuit itself could and would talk to her, Yavi could not discern. She had the oddest feeling that the armor was alive, that it was watching, barely restrained by the case in which it was displayed and that when she saw it, the case would shatter, and she would scream. Why would she fear a being so beautiful with a spirit that, despite its raw power and primal nature, felt like an abiding calm? She shivered again at the memory of its voice.

Even wide awake, Yavi believed in the voice of the irkanth. She was driven to see Bloodmane, perhaps even . . . touch it. But she didn't want to ponder her conflicting emotions about the boy-type person who'd forged it. Rubbing her arms to get the sap flowing, she stomped her feet to clear her thoughts. *Okay, Yavi, where are we now?*

After a few more candlemarks of walking, the forest that had remained on both sides of the road fell away to reveal a vast level plain. The sun hung close to its apex as Yavi broke the tree line and stared wide-eyed at the grass-covered Eldren Plains the Oathbreakers called home. *The ten-mile mark*, she thought to herself. *Do I need to measure land in jun instead of miles now that I near the Aern?*

Would they care? She'd heard they could be very touchy about language. How had she never thought of that before now? *Jun, then. Just in case.*

The smooth white road before Yavi was a good example of differences in nomenclature. It ran across the multi-hued plains toward Port Ammond to her northeast, and beyond her to the southwest past Silver Leaf to South Watch under a cloudless sky. Her people called it the Big Road, its lazy oval encompassing most of the Eldren Plains and connecting all the Oathbreaker watch cities.

The humans called it White Road because of its color, but Yavi felt certain the Oathbreakers (and probably the Aern) had another name for it. For the Oathbreakers, it was likely along the path of "The Magnificent Avenue" or "The White Progression of the Infinite Thought." Oathbreakers always assigned pompous names to things, even to Yavi's own people, calling them the Vaelsilyn despite the fact that they had begun calling themselves Vael over four hundred years ago. She guessed Vael was too small of a word to roll off Oathbreaker tongues correctly.

But the Aern . . . they liked simplicity and descriptives . . . probably the White Road, for them, too.

"The White Road," she said aloud, starting toward Port Ammond. "Jun. Oathbreakers. Okay."

To her surprise, a strange and tingling feeling drew her back a few steps along the road, a sense of disaster, not in South Watch but beyond it, far along the road, something she needed to see. She weighed the two feelings, the desire to see Bloodmane and beyond that to fulfill her royal duty at the Conjunction against this strange new feeling. If she were truly destiny-pulled, her mother would understand and send another in her place, or go herself to the Conjunction. There was still time.

"What do I do, Yhask?" she asked the god of the winds aloud.

Even from where she stood, miles (jun!) away, Yavi fancied she could smell the smoke and clutter of the Oathbreaker city, imagined that she could hear the noise of people shouting at each other at the docks or crowded around market stalls haggling over the price of silk from Barrony or fine Khalvadian wines. An irkanth roared in the distance, bringing a smile to Yavi's lips as its call brought to mind an image of the crimson-furred leonine beast with curling black horns. In her mind's ear it had massive regal horns and a mane the color of rich red wine.

Yavi stood quietly for a few more minutes, just staring at the road, reluctant to leave the last vestige of her forest home, waiting for some sort of answer from Yhask. She rubbed at her arms again. She hoped her head petals would stay presentable long enough for Kholster to see them, then flushed at the thought. She shook her petals out of their confining band, tempting Yhask to answer her, to blow through her floral crown.

"Okay, then, I'm going to the Conjunction," she said, hoping Yhask would disagree. "I'm going." She took a step forward. "I'm going . . . now." No answer. She took another step, a step that brought her farther away from the forest than she had ever gone.

"So . . . I guess that means I'm supposed to go, then."

Yavi set out down the White Road with a purpose.

A late summer breeze picked up, blowing Yavi's mop of yellow petals madly. She gathered her petals in her hands, tying them back loosely to keep them out of her field of vision. She could braid her petals later, but while there was wind, she intended to use it. Yavi made certain her travel pack and bow were secure. "I guess I have Yhask's answer after all," she whispered.

The wild untamed magic of nature welled within her and she leapt into the air, letting the wind carry her like a floret toward her destination, legs dangling like a seed head beneath her. Spreading her arms wide, Yavi gained altitude in a sudden burst. Under the influence of the spell, she could easily see the wind spirit who was guiding her. The handsome wind spirit's semitransparent lips curled upward into a smile. "Somebody enjoys blowing through my petals."

Humoring him, she reached out and pretended to take his insubstantial hand in hers. The wind spirit guided her higher and higher into the air. Spirits were everywhere, some helpful, others harmful. Yavi had always thought the Vael's ties to the spirits of nature were why her people tended to respond more to the Deep Elementals, the gods of nature, than to the dual-natured deities the humans tended to worship.

Yhask, Queelay, Nomi, Gromma, and Xalistan. Air, Sea, Fire, Land, and the Hunt. Of course, Xalistan was, Yavi admitted, technically dual-natured, but ruling both sides of the hunt . . . the hunter and the hunted . . . made perfect sense to her. Of course he had to rule both sides. How else could he keep things fair and balanced?

As whitewashed stones of the road flashed by beneath Yavi and the air spirit, Yavi spotted a human riding in a wagon. He waved at her casually and looked back at the road.

Tran, Yavi's brother, when he had first Taken Root and could still talk, had once told her that the Vael had more in common with humans than with their Oathbreaker creators, but both races still puzzled her. How did either race live without being able to touch or see the spirits? The humans, she knew, had never been able to do it, but had the Oathbreakers long ago forgotten what it meant to have a dialogue with the world, or did they simply no longer care what the world had to say?

Even more tragic were the Aern. They had never known the spirits, as far as Yavi knew. A frown tugged at the corners of her lips, and the wind spirit sagged in response, dropping her unceremoniously in the dirt alongside the road with the dying breeze.

Dusting herself off, she eyed the spirit angrily but couldn't stay mad.

The wind spirit shrugged at her as it danced away, blowing higher and higher up into the sky. "Don't worry about it," she called after him. "My heart was too heavy. It wasn't your fault!"

It had been her fault. Thinking about the Aern while working spirit magic had been a bad idea. It made her sad to think of them, exiled, living in caves somewhere, all because the Oathbreakers couldn't get along with their own creations. Sadness attracted the wrong sort of spirits for overt magic; flashy spirits preferred emotions that stirred the sap, happiness or anger.

Yavi brushed the dirt off of her doeskin leathers, popped a handful of the mineral-rich earth into her mouth as an afterthought, and started walking alongside the road.

A better idea struck the young Vael, and she plopped down to remove her boots. She only wore them in summer and spring when her bark was softer and smoother anyway. Stowing the boots in her pack, she wriggled her toes in the dirt and grass before stepping barefoot onto the stone and feeling for the spirit of the road. It was there but stretched so thin as to be nearly invisible to Yavi's eyes. Over time the poor thing had been so squashed down by the horse carts and people who traveled the road day and night without so much as a thank you that Yavi could not tell what kind of spirit it had once been.

"Well, I appreciate you," she told the spirit. "This is the way to Port Ammond, isn't it?" She pointed in the direction she was traveling, and the reedy spirit of the road looked at her blankly. "Are you shy?" she asked when it didn't answer. "You don't have to be. My name is Yavi. I have to spend a month in Port Ammond and then it's on to Oot for The Grand Conjunction." She emphasized the last three words in mock arrogance as if she were an Eldrennai and winked at the spirit when it hazarded a smile.

"Ah, I saw that." She giggled. "You smiled at me." The spirit's expression sobered, and Yavi snapped her fingers. "Well, I'll have to do it then. You asked for it, and I don't want any complaints."

A hint of fear played across the road spirit's narrow face.

"I'll have to use my secret weapons on you." She indicated her pointed ears. Just over two hands in length, they were longer than an Aern's and angled slightly to the back and off to the sides of her head when they weren't sticking embarrassingly straight up and down. "Remember. I warned you. You've brought this on yourself," Yavi said seriously. Then she wiggled her ears. The spirit laughed, and Yavi felt the road become gentler under her feet, almost like walking on soft new grass.

Compassion for compassion. Joy for joy. Even rage for rage.

Like for like. Yavi found herself wishing people worked more like magic.

"Better," said Yavi. "That's much better."

She continued on her way, both excited and worried. In a way she was excited to meet an Aern, yet in another way, she wished Queen Kari, her mother, would buck tradition and come to the Conjunction herself. Maybe her mother would even come back pollinated and carrying a new baby Aern, like the last time, when she'd brought home Irka.

Raising Irka among the Vael hadn't worked out. He'd eventually gone to live with his father's people, but one failure was no reason not to try again, was it? *What if I come back pollinated?*

A low rumbling snapped Yavi out of her reverie, and she almost stumbled on the stone.

"Do you know what that is?" she asked the road spirit. Not waiting for an answer, Yavi darted off to the side, wincing on the road's behalf as twenty-four raven-haired Oathbreakers in glittering crystal armor paraded into view on horseback. Above them waved the standard of King Grivek: three white towers on a blue background. Yavi assumed it was supposed to be impressive, but the way the midday sun refracted off of the crystal, sending rays of multicolored light in all directions made it hard to focus on anything at all.

Shielding her eyes with her hand, she spotted a particularly grim and haughty-looking Oathbreaker at the head of the procession. He might have been handsome, but the severity of his features and, if she were tracking true with herself, his expression made Yavi wonder if the Oathbreaker might be a bit saddle-sore.

She stepped farther from the road to make way for them, frowning when their leader came to a halt in front of her. Yavi started to go for her heartbow but stopped. Up close, the lead Oathbreaker looked oddly familiar, much like the Oathbreaker in her dreams, but daylight had frayed the edges of those memories, and she could not be sure.

"I am Dolvek of the Eldrennai, son of Grivek, son of Zillek and second in line to the Throne of Villok, who united the mastery of all four elements in one bloodline. I give you greetings and ask if you might be the Vaelsilyn called Yavi, daughter of Kari, princess of The Parliament of Ages and Guardian of the Rule of Leaf?"

"You said all that in one breath," answered Yavi. "That's impressive."

"Are you Princess Yavi . . . eh . . . noble Vaelsilyn?" Dolvek attempted to smile, but he was obviously out of practice. "We have come from Port Ammond to escort Princess Yavi to the Citadel of Oaths. It is of utmost importance that we find her. There have been reports of irkanth hunting in this area."

Yavi looked at him sideways, her ears flattening back along her petals. As if she couldn't kill an irkanth. What? Did they think her bow was broken? Did they have her age wrong? If they thought she was just a sapling that could explain it, but surely they could see she was a full fifteen and a quarter hands. How tall did they expect her to grow if they thought she was a sapling at this height?

They did realize she was a girl-type person and therefore perfectly capable of defending herself, didn't they?

"You know I'm a girl-type person, right?" Yavi asked, showing off years of tedious practice with the Eldrennaic tongue.

Dolvek leaned forward, and Yavi squinted as the rainbow-colored lights scattered by his armor shone in her face. "Can you turn that off or does it have to do that all the time?" Was it her imagination, or was the Oathbreaker having trouble breathing?

Dolvek gave a hand signal, then all the riders spoke a single word, "*Vey.*" The crystal armor became an opaque sapphire blue. Without the glare, Yavi still had spots dancing before her eyes, but she could see.

"Speaking with the battle, not with the plan, eh?" Yavi asked. She waited for a response, but Dolvek flushed red instead of answering. Was her Eldrennaic that bad?

"I. Am. Yavi." She tried again. She patted Dolvek's horse on its muzzle and waited a beat. "Nice. To. Meet. You."

"A . . . uh . . . horse," Dolvek gestured past the line of horses.

Maybe he's just lame-brained. Poor thing. Yavi walked to the end of the row, where a knight held the reins of a riderless horse. It was a beautiful palomino mare, but Yavi crinkled her nose at the saddle on the horse's back. "You want me to ride on her?"

Dolvek seemed to finally find his tongue again. "Yes, she is a gift for you. Magnificent, isn't she?"

"A gift?" Yavi asked slowly. "As in, this living being is your property and you are giving her to me, to be my . . . property?"

"Yes, of course," said Dolvek with an impatient head nod in the horse's direction. He looked away quickly as if something off to the west required his urgent attention. She followed his gaze but didn't see what could be so interesting or important. A light breeze picked at her petals and ruffled his long black hair downwind of her.

"Yhask, what a mess. I'm guessing you didn't get approval for that stupid offer from your commanding officer or boss or whatever. Vael don't practice animal slavery."

"But you eat meat," Dolvek said.

"When it's been properly hunted in a fashion pleasing to Xalistan," Yavi explained. "What we don't do is raise animals into slavery or for slaughter and . . . I'm sorry, but you really should have known that." Dolvek blinked at her few a few long moments. *Oh dear. I broke him.*

"My, um, sincere apologies. Ah . . . we could all walk," Dolvek stammered. "We . . . I . . . have no wish to insult the Vaelsilyn." *He lives!*

"No." She smiled. "It's fine. You can enslave animals if you want and we won't judge you for it. Just don't ask us to do so." She looked at Dolvek and gave him a wink. "We call ourselves the Vael now, by the way. I'm pretty sure my mother sent a note to your dad. I know my grandmother did . . . and I think her grandmother did as well . . ."

Yavi walked over to the horse, removed the bridle, and then set about unsaddling her. *They don't eat meat, but they enslave animals. How weird is that?* As she worked, she talked to the palomino filly, calming her and explaining as best she could that the animal was now free. A very short time later, she sprang lithely onto the animal's back and nodded at Dolvek.

"She says I can ride her," Yavi explained. "Shall we go?"

CHAPTER 23
DOLVEK'S FOLLY

Aldo help me, Dolvek prayed inwardly. *Help me, please!*

It was all the Vaelsilyn's fault. She was the most beautiful creature he had ever seen, as if the most exquisite yellow rose had been given life and the perfect female shape. He had expected that. Her people had been intentionally created with grace, beauty, and amiability in mind. But beyond all of that, the resemblance to Wylant—admittedly a younger, more vivacious, and less arrogant Wylant—should have been off-putting. Did Wylant look this enchanting when she let her hair grow? And if so, why in Aldo's name did she ever shave it? Did she not understand how to be attractive?

"This way, right?" Yavi looked over her shoulder and smiled at him.

"Yes," he managed. True, the Vael didn't prune her dental ridges, made no effort at even scoring them so that they could pass for teeth. Even so, something about her made his mind freeze up. And her scent. Gods, but did she have to ride upwind from him? It was intoxicating. Yavi's aroma was similar to the scent of the hedge roses that grew at the entrance to the royal gardens, but only in that Yavi's natural perfume showed the scent of the roses to be a poor imitation.

Dolvek had heard that a Vaelsilyn's scent had a calming effect on the Aern, and that Eldrennai were supposed to be quite fond of it as well. No amount of studying could have prepared him for the effect Yavi had on him. Not calming. Quite the opposite.

Dolvek had muddled through sentences that made him feel pompous, arrogant, and embarrassingly stupid. And then, when he'd leaned closer to Yavi, he'd lost the power of speech. And then he'd lost his mind. Of course the Vaelsilyn didn't own animals. He had known that. He hadn't even meant to give her the horse. The words had been carefully prepared, practiced over and over, and then, confronted with Yavi, he had promptly forgotten every one of them in the moment, to utter the grandiose and elegant words "A . . . uh . . . horse."

He had the words clearly in mind now, of course, when they were useless to him: If you are both amenable, I thought you might enjoy traveling with my friend Sunsprite.

How hard was that? One sentence. He should have known not to have the horse saddled. He'd been a bundle of nerves ever since word of the hunting irkanth had reached his Lance. Worse than anything else, events had unfolded exactly as his father had predicted.

"I don't know why I'm even bothering," his father, King Grivek, had told him the previous night. "You're just going to make a fool of yourself. We always do. I did. Sometimes I wonder if Gromma or Shidarva did this to us as punishment for Uled's meddling in the affairs of creation."

Dolvek didn't know if the goddess of growth and decay or the goddess of justice and retribution was responsible for his plight, but it wouldn't have surprised him. Yavi rode ahead of his Lance toward Port Ammond, but as they neared the city, she seemed to withdraw emotionally, shoulders hunched, head down—a turtle pulling its head inside its shell. Dolvek spurred his horse and caught up with her.

"Perhaps next time we could send a representative to The Parliament of Ages to meet with your people?" he offered. "I know the Place of Conjunction is a long way for you to travel . . ."

Why did I ask that? Of course we—

"No thanks." Yavi reached into her pack and withdrew a square of finely decorated kidskin with thin straps extending from the top corners. "You know the Aern don't like for you to be on our land unless it is absolutely necessary. Simple concept. If we come onto your land, then to the Aern, it's a visit. If one of you trespasses on our land . . . well, I think the Aern consider that an invasion or something. And then, you know: rar!"

"One of *us*?" he asked.

"An Oathbreaker," she said softly, her expression sad, as if she knew the word would hurt him and had been avoiding its use. Still the word came as a slap in the face.

"The Aern," he growled under his breath. Everything came down to the Aern's hatred for the Eldrennai. For hundreds of years the Aern continued to bear a grudge against his people. In some countries the Aern were even called Grudgebearers, a soubriquet which struck the young prince as particularly appropriate. Dolvek and other members of his generation were getting tired of placating the Grudgebearers.

"Plus, you're all so very picky," Yavi said teasingly. "I don't think you'd like meeting at Hearth any more than I like going to Port Ammond. A lot of the material you use is dead, while in our homes, even the walls are alive." As Yavi finished speaking, she tied on the kidskin veil. It covered her face from below her eyes to the bottom of her chin. A samir, he believed her people called them.

Dolvek hated the samir instantaneously. It was if someone had veiled the sun. His men obviously felt the same way; they all seemed gripped by an identical sense of loss and relief.

"You don't have to wear that," Dolvek told her.

"Yes, I do. Otherwise you people get ideas, and I've been taught that an unscored set of dental ridges offends you, 'single flaw in my creation' and all that," she bubbled, quoting part of Uled's *On the Sentience of Roses*. "I should have put it on earlier, but I got distracted talking to the spirit of the road." Yavi ran her fingers over the horse's neck absentmindedly. "Tell me you don't find it easier to think with the samir on."

Dolvek couldn't answer. True, his thoughts were clearer, but with every breath he still inhaled the sweet natural perfume of her people, and it . . . affected him.

"Your ancestors made us to appeal to the Aern," Yavi said ruefully. "Who knew you had so much in common? I just hope it didn't cause a problem for your knights, my forgetting to put my samir on, I mean."

"No," Dolvek said quickly. "It's nothing an Eldrennai can't control." *So why am I having such a hard time?* "Look," he said, pointing ahead. "You can see the city from here."

Yavi followed his arm and saw Port Ammond on the horizon. Even from this distance, three white towers could be seen rising far above the other rooftops: The Citadel of Oaths, the Tower of Elementals, and the Grand Library.

"The buildings in front of the central tower," said Yavi, "are those the museums?"

Dolvek blinked. He couldn't make them out from here.

As if she had read his mind, Yavi laughed and pointed to her left eye. "We have better eyesight than you. I would've have thought you'd know all about us. Don't you have a big section of the Museum of Natural History devoted to us?"

"We do," Dolvek answered. "But I . . ."

"I want to see that first." Her green eyes sparkled at him from above her samir.

"We have a reception planned," he started again.

Yavi put her hand against his gauntlet, palm up, knuckles resting against the crystal. "And I'm sure it's a really, really nice reception, probably hours and hours long and I'd be introduced to all the most important Eldrennai, the Master of the Tower of Elementals, and the king, and you'd probably give me something really sweet and magical and probably dead and I'd be oh so grateful, but I'd just have to bury it later, so let's not."

But the plans for this reception began when the last Conjunction ended suc-

cessfully one hundred years ago. That had been what Dolvek intended to say. Instead, all of his attention was focused on her hand. If only he'd worn formal robes instead of his armor! Then her hand would be touching his. Then again, since the Vaelsilyn avoided restraining gestures, she might not have touched his bare hand for fear that he might grab her. Even now, her fingers were near the wrist of his gauntlet; it would be difficult to turn the touch into a grasp. That was exactly what he wanted to do, to hold her close, to enfold her in his arms.

"I think we're going to need a new representative from the Oathbreakers. One capable of speech." Yavi's dry tone snapped him back to reality.

"No!" Dolvek protested quickly. "Ah . . . I mean, that won't be necessary. I was just thinking on how best to explain this to the head of the reception committee. Do you think you could withstand an hour?"

"Maybe," Yavi conceded hesitantly. "Why?"

"I could tell them that you are weary from your travels, but that you do not wish to ruin the occasion. You have agreed to stay for the music and the presentation but are too tired to endure all the introductions."

"I'm still tracking you," said Yavi.

Dolvek hoped that was a good thing and continued. "Then I could sneak you into the museum after hours and you could see the Vaelsilyn exhibit."

"And the Aern exhibit," Yavi added.

How could she know about that? Still, the Eldrennai prince did not argue. Arguing would, he feared, add more demands, and he doubted he could deny this enchanting creature any request she might deign to make of him.

CHAPTER 24
DEATH IN THE MUSEUM

Prince Dolvek glanced nervously from side to side as he waved four of his most trusted lieutenants forward. Yavi, still clad in the comfortable midriff-baring beaded doeskin top and matching trousers she'd worn to the Oathbreakers' reception, padded barefoot in their midst looking bemused at all the drama.

"He is the prince, right?" she whispered to the guard nearest her. "Is he afraid the king is going to jump out and surprise him?"

The guard, stiffly attired in his dress silks and crystal breastplate, did not answer but moved formally toward the pillared entrance to the Royal Museum of Natural History. Yavi stopped to examine the image of a battling irkanth and giant sea hawk worked in marble which sat in the middle of a pool of water, which, during the day, she imagined would be an impressive fountain.

Dolvek waved frantically for her move on. He did, if Yavi were tracking true with herself and discounting all the arm waving, look at least moderately handsome in his silk dress robes. The front was embroidered with the royal seal repeated and intertwined in a rectangular pattern: three castles in silver thread on blue. She wasn't sure how useful the ceremonial sword he wore at his waist was, though. The ornate hilt, in the shape of a flaming pillar, seemed like it would be painful and awkward to hold for more than the briefest of combats.

"Please, Princess," he whined.

"Coming."

*

Two of the guards stepped to either side of the exhibit entrance, eyes toward the main door of the museum as if they expected an invasion of rampaging history fanatics. Dolvek gave what Yavi imagined he thought was a subtle hand sign for the other two guards to follow along but hang back, and proceeded to show Yavi through the museum.

Please, Xalistan, Yavi prayed, *don't let him try anything stupid enough to make me maim him.* Doing her best to remain pleasantly curious, awed, and attentive, Yavi let her attention be drawn to the architecture. Since Dolvek seemed at a loss for words, she felt obliged to keep up the conversation.

"Wasn't this part of the old military complex?" Yavi prompted with a smile. "The Aern Armory, maybe?" It certainly had been, in all of her dreams about the place. How could she explain to the prince that she'd already explored this museum in her dreams a thousand times or more? *Best keep it to yourself, Yavi.*

"No." Dolvek smiled at the Vael. "While the Armory housed all the armor and the weapons, this museum was originally part of the barracks. It had to be thoroughly redecorated." He gestured to a series of lifeless tapestries and paintings all focusing on the greatness of the Eldrennai and their Royal Family through the years. She found the portrait of Uled to be in particularly poor taste. "May I show you the Vaelsilyn exhibit?" he offered.

"Why would I want to see that? I am a Vael." *Was that too harsh? Gah!* "What can you tell me about myself that I don't already know?" *That's better.* "Any of our books and artifacts you have will just be depressing because you will have let them die, right?" *Too much. Now his brain is going to fall out.*

"But you said," Dolvek began.

"What I meant to say was," she batted her eye petals and looked directly into his brown and white eyes. "May I please see the Aern exhibit first? I'm a little worried having never seen an Aern before, and I," she leaned in closer, "I thought maybe this way . . ." *I could find out if the armor with the irkanth's head will really talk to me.*

"This way," Dolvek acquiesced immediately. He offered her his arm, and she shook her head, taking a quick step away from him.

"I'm fine. Why don't you just lead the way? You can tell me about the Vael exhibit while we walk."

Dolvek almost cheerfully did so.

*

Yavi seemed to take everything in with a mixture of excitement and sadness. Perhaps she regretted her decision not to see the Vaelsilyn exhibit? The prince resolved to give her another opportunity after she saw the Aern exhibit. Females did so often change their minds.

"The exhibit isn't open to the public," Dolvek said as they reached two iron-bound doors. "The new curator and I designed and implemented it as a surprise for my father on his most recent centennial." He waved his lieutenants up to open the doors. "I suppose he must have liked it, because he decided to keep it sealed. Only the nobility can get in."

Watching Yavi for every nuance of reaction, the prince felt his pulse quicken as the door opened to reveal the jewel of his collection: a seven-foot-tall stone homunculus, perfect in every detail. It had never been animated. Dolvek assumed this was because Uled had decided he wanted the Aern to be shorter.

Yavi froze, expressionless, eyes wide.

She loves it! he inwardly crowed. "I came across a brief reference to it during my first year of studies, back when I thought the tedium of the Artificer's path to be a worthwhile pursuit."

He swept past her. "I spent twenty years tracking it down." She still wasn't moving. "In the end," Dolvek turned back toward her. *Is she okay?* "I found it in an old storeroom of alchemical supplies, perfectly preserved."

Yavi screamed. Babbling in Vaelish, she gestured wildly at the homunculus, but the torrent of words came out too fast, too furiously, for Dolvek to make all of them out. "Trap?" He tried to translate. "Release . . . er . . . spirit something?"

Yavi turned on him, continuing her stream of desperate Vaelish. Dolvek saw the mistake even as his guards made it. The Vael reached for the front of his robes, Dolvek assumed to further convey her urgency. Almost in slow motion, he saw Yavi's hand moving toward his chest. One of Dolvek's guards grasped Yavi's arm, his fingers closing completely around her exquisite wrist, and then everything erupted into chaos.

Ten mystic crystal cases, specially designed to protect the Aernese warsuits from the ravages of time, shattered simultaneously as all ten suits of armor Dolvek had ordered to be so painstakingly displayed stepped forward as one. Another ten cases exploded as the Aernese weapons leapt into the gauntlets of the animated warsuits.

Great Aldo, Dolvek cursed inwardly. *They really are alive. Why the hells didn't they say so?* Frozen in surprise, Dolvek watched as his lieutenant released Yavi and turned with the other guards to face the new threat. *There will be no living with that bald harpy Wylant now.*

Bloodmane leapt past the homunculus on display and landed with a crash in front of Dolvek's two scrambling guards. Marrit, Dolvek's second-in-command, drew his crystal sword only to cry out in sudden fright as the empty armor reached out and crushed the blade with its left gauntlet.

Startled, but not totally unprepared, Marrit raised his arm in what Dolvek was sure would be taken as an attempt to ward off a blow with his forearm. Instead, a blast of elemental ice erupted from the steel foci running from Marrit's wrist to elbow. Bloodmane vanished, encased in a block of whitish-blue ice.

"Cleverly done, Marrit," Dolvek said.

Marrit smiled, turning to face the other suits of armor. His smile vanished as the ice shattered from within. Its captive stepped easily free of the remaining chunks of ice and buried the long pointed spike of its warpick in the top of Marrit's skull.

Bloodmane's horned lion helm roared as it turned toward the other lieutenant.

Yavi tried to interpose herself, but Dolvek grabbed at her shoulder. "Don't," he said, "That's Kholster Bloodmane's armor. It'll . . ."

A swift elbow from the young Vael knocked the breath out of him, and Yavi cursed as the ancient armor ripped its weapon from Marrit's skull and struck the other guard dead with the flat hammer-like side of the warpick's head. By then, the other suits of armor had reached them. Dolvek straightened and went for his sword. Even if he died, he would save the Vaelsilyn representative . . .

Crystal eyes inset into each helm glowed bright red, turning his translucent blade a matching shade in their combined light. Yavi yelled a word in Aernese, "Cho!"

Stop, Dolvek's brain translated automatically. Bloodmane's armor held up its clenched left gauntlet, and the other nine suits of Aernese war armor halted in their tracks, waiting, weapons at the ready.

"I'm not hurt," Yavi explained as quickly as her limited Aernese vocabulary permitted. "The Oathbreakers brought me here to show me this place because I asked them to. When I saw your . . . when I saw the un . . . the unborn Aern, his spirit still tied to him . . . waiting to be born . . . I . . . just . . . I couldn't . . . I don't know the words. I've never seen a spirit in so much pain before. I wasn't expecting it. The guard was defending his prince . . . I'm sure he wasn't thinking when he grabbed my arm."

"I speak Vaelish," Bloodmane said in a whisper.

Dolvek felt sick. Everyone knew about the Vaelsilyn aversion to being restrained, had been endlessly drilled on how to behave. Everything had happened so quickly, they had all just . . . reacted. The warsuits he was facing had acted not to attack his men so much as to protect his guest.

Sheathing his sword, Dolvek took a step back, his feet scattering ice. Blood, ice, and shattered crystal covered the floor, staining both the carpet and his memory. *Aldo, how could this have gone so wrong?* He gritted his teeth and looked at the Vaelsilyn. *If the flower girl hadn't insisted on coming to the museum in the first place—*

No. It was not her fault. She was clearly distressed. Kholster Bloodmane's armor had murdered two of Dolvek's Lance—any guilt here lay firmly at the Aern's bloodstained boots. Kholster would have much to answer for when Dolvek finally met him at the Conjunction.

"I understand," Dolvek said bitterly. "Oh, sheath your swords," he shouted as his two remaining lieutenants arrived in response to the noise. "No need to lose all four of you. Help me get Marrit and . . . help me get them out of here."

CHAPTER 25
ENTOURAGE

For the ninth time, Kholster caught the Long Arm with her fingers in her mouth probing her new molars. When it wasn't her fingers, it was her tongue. She stood with her mouth open, head cocked in the opposite direction of whichever side of her mouth she was exploring. Kholster wasn't sure whether she would swallow an insect or fall over first.

"You'll want to stop drawing attention to them like that by the time we get to Mason," Kholster said, eyes forward. "And before you ask, about sixteen grams."

"Try not to spend it all on god rock," Rae'en said with mock cheer. She could just imagine the woman selling off her father's teeth, and the Bone Finders having to hunt them down one at a time across a continent.

"Gods," Cadence's mouth snapped shut like a rich man's purse.

The three of them threaded an unimpeded line through the normal traffic on the Commerce Highway at a walking pace Cadence was barely capable of maintaining in her weakened condition. Not three, Kholster corrected himself. Four. Kholster watched Rae'en toting the young crystal-twisted babe, Caius, on her hip as if a baby had always been there. Either the humans didn't care about the babe's red eyes or they found Rae'en and himself stranger still.

For his own part, Kholster took in his surroundings more in terms of elevation, lines of sight, and potential cover than for beauty or the picturesque inedible plantings which appeared with greater and greater frequency as they approached the Guild Cities. He found the periodic stepped farms growing rice, potatoes, yellow mustard, wheat, and other crops far more interesting. The way humans shaped the land to suit themselves and eke out a meager living or a thriving one fascinated him.

He supposed it might dismay his fellow travelers to know that he marked each farm in passing as an asset to be seized or razed should he need to attack the Guild Cities at some future date.

Kholster passed the stone signpost without looking, following a bypass route away from the grand approach to the western road which led to Mason, the point of entry Kholster usually took when visiting the Guild Cities of Barrony. Kholster shook his head, eliciting a quizzical look from Rae'en and a startled jump from Cadence.

"Problem?" Rae'en asked, ceasing for the moment her game of pointing things out to the baby and naming them in both Aernese and Trade, a common language used by mixed groups and merchants of all races.

"Just thinking."

Cadence seemed ready to snatch the child away at any moment, but from the way sweat rolled down her face, Kholster suspected she couldn't carry him far even if she got him. He sniffed the air in her direction, but he couldn't smell the rotten egg scent of a failing liver or the ammonia smell of kidneys shutting down. She might yet survive.

Kholster, a Vael, Bloodmane spoke in his mind.

Kholster watched the whole exchange in the museum, keeping one eye open to the world of his immediate surroundings and the other closed so he could see through Bloodmane's eyes. When Bloodmane killed Marrit, he had to bite back a laugh. "Die well and tell Uled more of you are coming!" he barked aloud, wrinkling his nose as they dragged the dead Oathbreaker from the museum.

Caius's lower lip began to tremble at that burst of venom.

"Who?" Rae'en asked in a bright, happy tone, rubbing noses with the child and staving off an outburst of tears in the process.

Kholster did not understand where Rae'en's gift with children came from. He had always been a fair hand with Aern children, but Rae'en seemed as good with the baby human as Okkust did with his adopted human children. Had she been spending time with Okkust? He could not recall.

"Who?" Rae'en repeated.

"The Oathbreakers," Kholster eyed a nearby farmhand walking alongside a wagon hauling stone and frowned. "I'll tell you about it later." The humans around them on the road were giving them a wide berth, but Kholster didn't want to be overheard.

You did well, Bloodmane.

This doesn't cause any problems, General?

Kholster shook his head. *They know you're alive, that your movements aren't simply maintenance charms hung upon you by some long-forgotten Artificer. Given the information available, and given that they are Oathbreakers, they have no way of knowing that we can still communicate with you. They've no reason to suspect that we know some of you have been moved.*

But General . . . if they do . . . if the prince admits that he has unintentionally broken the truce . . .

He won't, Kholster thought. *That would take humility and foresight, or the wisdom to listen to Wylant. This . . . Dolvek . . . possesses none of those qualities. He is a true Oathbreaker.*

Kholster closed his eyes to take in the Vael with his full attention, continuing to walk in a straight line and trusting Rae'en to guide him by the elbow if he started to wander off-course.

From Bloodmane's point of view, he stood in shattered crystal, ice, and blood. Yavi looked up at him, eyes wide, lips curling into a smile. Torgrimm, but she looked like Wylant. Not that he hadn't seen other Vael who favored her as well. Queen Kari could have passed for Wylant's sister were she an Aiannai, but the head petals on Yavi . . . if Wylant had been a Vael . . .

Kholster took a deep breath and held it for a hundred count, grateful for the slower pace of this trip and the extra time he could spend getting used to that face before he had to see it in person.

Kholster, a thought pierced his concentration, ending his reverie.

What is it, Vander?

We have a debate.

Bloodmane, can you—?

Yes, Maker.

Without further prompting, the world swam before Kholster's eyes and he found himself looking through Vander's vision into the face of an angry Dwarf.

"They have to see us eventually, Glin," Vander said.

"Yes, Vander, but there is no need to give the Oathbreakers any forewarning. If they spot us, let it be because they've been canny, not because of any foolishness on our part."

"What then do you suggest?"

"I suggest we sink the merchant vessels . . . and not waste any more time in talk." Glinfolgo pointed out over the bow. In the distance, Vander (and therefore Kholster) could only make out the ships as glowing blobs of red in the night, visible only through heat vision. Even so, the profile of the lead ship was unmistakably Eldrennai. "We can't risk any of them getting away. It is not important this day whether those aboard are survivors of the Sundering or not. If their deaths are uncalled for, then let the goddess Queelay comfort them in her depths."

Merchants? Kholster sent to Vander.

Yes, we spotted a trio of merchant vessels headed along the shipping lane to trade with the Guild Cities.

What are they doing past the Strait of Mioden?

I don't know. They're flying independent trading flags, but they aren't fooling anyone.

Not you anyway, Kholster sent. *The other two vessels are Oathbreaker as well?*

They're Leash Holders, all right. Vander's use of the old term for the Eldrennai, the hate in his mind when he thought it, was all the evidence Kholster needed that his campaign to stoke the fire of his people's hatred back up to a killing heat had worked. It sent a chill of regret through Kholster's core, but that was where he wanted it. At his feet, troubling his dreams, not those of his people.

And your suggestion? Kholster asked.

I agree with Glinfolgo, Vander sent, his thoughts filled with a mixture of pride and approval, *right down to the thought about the water goddess. I had no idea Glin hated them this much.*

He's had thirteen years to justify that hate, to hear our people talk about all the wrongs, to see old wounds ripped open for new eyes. It cannot have been without effect on those who call us kin.

"I'm sorry," Kholster whispered into his hands.

"Tell Vander I said Hello," Rae'en quipped.

Kholster did so, pleasure easing his regret.

She doesn't miss a feint, Vander thought warmly. Kholster shared his Overwatch's immense pride at Rae'en's ability to sense the internal conversation even though she had no warsuit through which to discern it, to deduce that he had gone from talking to Bloodmane to Vander from . . . from what, my body language?

Kholster's pride pushed the remainder of his negative emotions away so effectively that he blinked in amazement even as he transmitted Vander's orders. *Go ahead. Attack and sink the Oathbreaker merchant vessels.*

Maker? Kholster felt his connection to Vander fade into the background as Bloodmane intruded.

What is it, Bloodmane?

The Vael is talking to me. She can see our spirits.

Show me. Kholster saw the Vael reaching up to touch Bloodmane's faceplate with the tips of her slender fingers.

It's all right, he told the warsuit. *She means no harm.*

I know. The long black fingers of the warsuit's gauntlet touched the girl's cheek as she caressed its helm, making sure to touch her cheek as lightly as she touched his surface.

It's just been so long since I was touched like this.

Good, Kholster approved. *You remember. Courting a Vael is like befriending a wild animal. They do not remember exactly why they fear being grabbed and held, but that does not diminish their fear. In a similar way, they remember the Litany for each Leash Holder who had done them harm but no longer recall exactly what was done.*

"How dare you touch the Vaelsilyn!"

Kholster's attention swung to Dolvek as the prince reentered the room. The urge to kill the Oathbreaker for daring to speak and tarnish that moment between his warsuit and the Vael snapped into place like a key in a familiar lock. A hate that could never go, only fade, burn down, an ever-present ember waiting to be restoked. Dolvek was dry leaves and good air to those flames.

"You, I will never allow as Aiannai," Kholster growled. "I swear it."

"What is Aiannai?" Kholster dimly heard Cadence ask from somewhere behind him. He declined to answer, and Rae'en's only response was to hush the Long Arm.

Dolvek. The Oathbreaker was more muscled than he had been the last time Kholster had seen him, but his eyes still struck the Aern as rat turds stuck in bird squirt. If ever Kholster had viewed a sentient as being of no useful purpose whatsoever, it was this Eldrennai.

That one is particularly good at stupid, Vander offered.

May I address the Oathbreaker?

You may do anything you wish, Old Friend.

"Wisdom Keeper," the armor intoned. "How foolish it is that you should be called so."

"What?" Dolvek asked, stunned. "You . . . you can speak?"

"In many languages," Bloodmane acknowledged. "Did you not hear me address the noble Vael? I said, 'I speak Vaelish'?"

Zillek's blood flows too boldly through that one, Kholster thought in disgust. *Anything you want him to understand should be inscribed on a spike and driven through his skull.*

"Before King Zillek broke his oath and in so doing shattered the mystic bonds which held the Aern in thrall to your kind, you were called Eldrennai by all. In High Eldrennaic, the word *Eldren* means 'wisdom' and the suffix *nai* implies a 'keeper of.' So Wisdom Keeper. But you are not wise, Oathbreaker prince. If you were, then you would not dare to refer to the Vael as Vaelsilyn in our presence."

The prince scowled derisively. "Why, in the opinion of a suit of armor, should we not call the Vaelsilyn by the full and beautiful name of their race?"

"Because is it offensive to us and to them," Bloodmane announced. "Surely though High Eldrennaic is no longer a common tongue, you have studied it. Tell me what you think it means, Leash Holder."

"I am not," Dolvek paused, gathering his thoughts, "absolutely not going to debate the finer points of language with a murderous artifact which has just killed two of my Lance."

"Ah. You mean you do not know."

Kholster watched the Vael out of the periphery of Bloodmane's vision. Embarrassed by the exchange, she shifted from one foot to the other, ears twitching nervously. Seeing her that nervous set Kholster on edge. He was tempted to call Bloodmane's attention to her discomfort but feared preventing Bloodmane from completing the discussion would only serve to further highlight the fact that a suit of armor locked away for six hundred years had access to a change in nomenclature which had occurred well after it had been shut away. If Kholster did nothing, Dolvek wouldn't realize he'd been given an important detail until Torgrimm explained it to him in the afterlife, if then.

"Of course I know." The Oathbreaker prince ran a hand nervously through his hair. "I am an expert on the past, on history and language, on what really happened versus what the Aern claim happened. Let me see. *Vael* means 'lovely' and the suffix *–silyn* implies that the aforementioned loveliness has been ransomed."

"No." Bloodmane shifted slightly as if to step toward the prince, but the Vael pushed against his breastplate with the back of her hand, gently pleading with him to stay put. Visor shifting, the armor took in the Vael's unspoken request, the pained look in her eyes, nodded, took a step back before continuing. "Even using modern translations, *Vaelsilyn* means 'the lovely ransom.'"

"Same thing," the Oathbreaker objected with a wave of his hands.

"No." Bloodmane's voice was gentle but firm.

Going easy on him, old friend?

He is only an Oathbreaker, Maker.

"Must we? May I?" Kholster whispered. "Only an Oathbreaker." He hissed a curse. He could feel Rae'en's fingers tighten on his elbow.

"The Vael are kind enough not to point it out," Bloodmane continued, "because Uled created them to desire harmonious coexistence, to be willing to put up with almost anything in the spirit of maintaining peace, but the name implies that the Vael are a 'ransom of loveliness,'" the armor gestured at the Vael's ears as if he were a human street performer summoning an imaginary coin from it, holding the nonexistent coin up for the Oathbreaker to see, "a currency of sorts, to be paid to the Aern. The name is a very polite term for a whore." He tossed the imaginary coin at the prince's feet, causing Dolvek to take an involuntary step back. "And you wonder why they object . . ."

"Kill him," Kholster whispered, tempted to give Bloodmane access to his auditory input, to send the words as thought and therefore order, but to do so . . .

"Kill who?" Cadence asked.

"Shut up, addict," Rae'en said in a happy sing-song voice, still trying to keep the babe happy while steering Kholster along the road.

"Even if that were true, which it isn't," the Oathbreaker interrupted, "when I say 'Vaelsilyn' I don't mean to imply any such thing. When I refer to our noble and beautiful Vaelsilyn—"

"Keep it up, Oathbreaker," Kholster hissed into his cupped hands, fingers curled almost into fists. "Make Bloodmane angry. If he gets his bloodlust back, it will spare me no end of grief."

Kholster felt Bloodmane shift his stance, preparing to move. All of Kholster's nerve endings came alive as for a brief instant he and Bloodmane were close to one in thought and deed . . . almost in sync. He'd almost forgotten the feeling.

"Go wait in the hallway, Prince Dolvek," the Vael snapped at the Oathbreaker. The moment was lost.

"Go wait in the hallway, Prince Dolvek," Kholster parroted aloud. He breathed a ragged breath and fought his way back from the edge of the Arvash'ae. "Saved by the Vael. What did you do in a past life that earned you such boons from the gods, you stump-eared maggot?"

Dolvek opened his mouth, jaw quivering, but with ten warsuits staring at him, their red crystal eyes flashing and flaring brightly, he appeared to see the folly in refusing. "If you need anything, if anyone tries anything, Princess Yavi . . ." he stammered.

"I'll call for you," Yavi assured him.

"If anything attacks you here," Bloodmane assured her, "my brothers and I will kill it before the Leash Holder's tiny ears hear your call."

Dolvek's eyes narrowed in anger at the armor's words. He turned on his heel and stormed out of the room rather than act on whatever suicidal impulse had occurred to him.

Another missed meal.

Maker?

Nothing, Old Friend.

Yavi waited for the knights to leave, then for Jagged and Blackbow to close the heavy doors. She turned and looked at Bloodmane. Her eyes sparkled with curiosity. Kholster recalled a thousand other Vael staring at him with that same look of intensity. "So you can talk. I'm guessing that's not a new thing?"

A memory of the Grand Conjunction and Kari. A look, a kiss, a night. The mixture of sadness and joy in Queen Kari's eyes when she'd brought Irka back to him because even as gentle as he was, he was Aern. He needed to rip and tear and rend, but more than that . . . to connect with other Aern.

Kholster opened his eyes, cleared his throat, and spat. Still listening but no longer wanting to see. Ahead the Guild Cities loomed.

Caz would already have been there for a day or more along with other Bone Finders, getting into position in the event something happened to him or to Rae'en and their bones needed rescuing. Or perhaps Caz was already in Castleguard or in The Parliament of Ages. Kholster found himself wishing he was there, too. He no longer had the stomach for walking through the close press of humanity the Guild Cities had to offer. He'd been almost looking forward to walking Rae'en through it and showing her the wonders of the greatest marketplace Barrone had to offer short of Midian.

He regretted the decision not to kill the mother and child. The child meant a trip to the Harvester's temple. The mother meant a visit with the Dean of the College of the Mental Arts. Distractions both.

One foe he couldn't reach and a friend he would not fight. How could Bloodmane have shared all the memories of the Oathbreaker's abuses and not hate them? *Why are we growing apart?*

Around Kholster walked farmers, peasants, merchants and thieves—a motley press of the poorly dressed and the richly garbed. For a brief moment Kholster wanted to lash out at all of them, to raise them over his head and dash out their brains upon the cobbles beneath his feet. The stone walls ahead of him seemed like the thick walls of a banker's vault holding in the goods and coin the humans loved so much, and he longed to break them, too.

As if in answer, a hawk's shrill cry rose up from the warpick on his back. He rarely heard the spirit inside Grudge, that piece of him interred within. Something about hearing it now, knowing that Grudge shared his feelings . . . helped. And the moment passed, like clouds over a battlefield masking the horrors below.

"No." Bloodmane's hesitant answer reverberated within the confines of his empty metal body.

"How long have you been able to do that?" the Vael asked wonderingly.

"Always," he answered slowly. "Since the maker, Kholster, built me . . . but we didn't realize it until we were apart . . . until the Sundering . . . when the Oathbreakers took us hostage."

"But why didn't you fight?" Yavi asked. Bloodmane brushed the crystal from the velvet display upon which Hunger had rested, and Yavi took a seat there, her feet dangling a few fingers from the floor. "The Eldrennai . . . they couldn't have stopped you."

"They are Oathbreakers," Bloodmane said dismissively, going down on one knee so that Yavi's head was higher than his helm. "We are Oathkeepers. We must not be Foresworn."

"So because you promised. Because the Aern promised, you've waited here for centuries." Yavi leaned forward and laid a soft kiss upon his helm. "That's so sad."

"Don't be sad, Yavi," said the armor. "We will be . . ."

Kholster felt his heart in his throat. He closed his eyes quickly to see what Bloodmane saw. The urge to interfere rode high. He could order Bloodmane not to reveal anything. . . . No. He would let Bloodmane do what the warsuit would. Bloodmane was free or he wasn't.

". . . together again one day," the armor amended.

Thank you. You didn't lie, but you didn't tell her about the plan.

"I . . ." Yavi wiped a tear from her eye. "I'll come back and see you, if I can. I'm here for another thirty-nine days." She glanced behind her at the doors. "If I keep him waiting too long . . ."

"He will think that you are in danger," the armor scoffed, "here where you are safest. You are free to go or stay as you please. We need no explanation. We hold no leashes here."

"Nor here, old friend," Kholster whispered.

Yavi headed to the door and stopped, not facing the armor. "I didn't know any of that language stuff, you know. We just think that Vaelsilyn is too long a word. We like short, simple words, like . . . well, like Vael or Aern." She removed her samir, briefly displaying a dazzling smile and an unsullied dental ridge, and retied it more securely.

Through Bloodmane's eyes, Kholster watched her leave. The warsuits all marched back to their places, setting their weapons down in the shattered remains of their reserved cases.

You did well, Kholster told the armor.

Thank you, Kholster.

How goes the battle?

The Eldrennai merchants are having their first experience with Dwarven cannon and rifles.

Show me.

CHAPTER 26
BLOOD AND BLACK POWDER

As doom came for him, Captain Gheest of the Eldrennai merchant vessel *Her Imminent Glory* was belowdecks after dinner. The thin-faced Thunder Speaker sat at the head of an antique blood oak table entertaining his officers with a new song he'd learned from a Zalizian scholar. If the way the mage light fell upon the silver foci at his throat casting strange flares of light upon his chin and chest disturbed them, they showed no sign.

And so the king with fiery sting
did force the manitou to wing
A whining as they fled.

The first barrage struck as he reached the chorus.

They might have seen him spill the wine.
They never saw him dead.

By then, it was too late.

"Shields!" he shouted with thunderous volume. The second barrage struck with a sound as if the world was breaking. Particulates filled the air as the walls of the officers' mess exploded, shards of wood and bits of metal wreaking havoc upon his men. Turgot, his first mate, was spun around and thrown off of the stair, landing dumbly at his captain's feet. Gheest stared in horror at the spot where Turgot's right arm had once been.

The screams of the dying, the injured, and the rhythmic percussion of what had to be some strange new mystical attack drowned out his commands. Casting an air spell, Gheest flew out through the massive hole in the side of his cabin and into the open air where he saw a massacre in progress. One of his best Aeromancers, Kai, hurled lightning at the figures manning the strange weapons on the decks of the opposing vessels, but one of the crew on the other ship leapt into the way of the bolt, absorbing it undamaged, and returned fire with a long curious hollow rod, a metal stick with a wooden base.

"Aern!" Gheest shouted. "Target the ships, not the crew! It's the Aern!"

He summoned the air to carry his voice farther but lost his words as he saw the extent of their peril. At least sixty Aernese warships dotted the water, each brimming with Aern. Most wielded the long wood-hafted hollow iron rods as well as their traditional Aernese weapons. He spotted the larger metal tubes that spat fire, realized instantly how his cabin came to be ventilated, but what caught his breath and stilled his tongue was the great fiery light which welled up from the rear of the Aernese formation. Flames licked the wings of a dragon, playing along its body.

"Ko-a-hul!" Gheest gasped, the ancient—though not true—name catching in his throat. *The Aern have brought the great gray dragon with them.*

"Great Aldo," he whispered. "The king, I must warn—"

Captain Gheest spun skyward on a gust of elemental air, intending to flee when he saw a bald Aern at the prow of the lead vessel aim one of the hollow tubes at him. Gheest wrapped himself in a defensive shield of wind and lightning so quickly that it would have made his old teacher, Hasimak, proud . . . but with a flare at the end of the barrel and a booming crack, Gheest felt pain blossom within his chest. His air spell disrupted, Captain Gheest was seized by the inexorable pull of gravity as he fell to the deck with a thud and the world blurred.

When his vision cleared once more, the ship was listing badly and a figure stood over him. It was the bald Aern.

"How?" Gheest choked, "did Aern learn magic?"

"The only thing magic about gunpowder," the Aern told him as he drew a warpick over his head, "is having it when your opponent doesn't." The warpick came down, and Gheest felt nothing more. His body, like the bodies of his crew, was tied to the bulk of his former vessel and consigned to the depths.

His last thought was to wonder whether this attack was punishment for having dared to sail through the Strait of Mioden and whether it had been the men of Castleguard who had betrayed them to the Aern or if it had all been horrible luck. Perhaps the sea goddess Queelay would tell him. He had a moment to wonder if it was true what they said that she claimed the souls of those who died at sea. But it was not Queelay who came. It was the Harvester, clad in his bone armor. *Torgrimm has come for me*, he thought. The Harvester, Gheest fancied, had the look of an old tired mage surprised by an unannounced visit from a favorite pupil who has given up the craft. A complex emotion.

Further shock registered briefly as Gheest felt the Harvester's hands on his soul.

"Try again," the Harvester's voice said softly. "You can do better."

CHAPTER 27
GUILD CITY GATES

The sun dipped over the exterior wall, casting dark shadows over Kholster and his companions as they reached the western-most entrance to the city. Inverted keyhole embrasures, formed by merlons carved to resemble wary gargoyles, created strange bands of light piercing the ground shadow, highlighting Kholster amid those making their way toward the city gates. Catching the eye of an archer staring down at him as he stepped into such a patch, the Aern grinned. To his credit the archer did not react.

I wonder when they removed the roof? Kholster thought to Vander, forgetting for a moment that his Overwatch was on down cycle.

A vague questioning blur of sleepy thought reached Kholster. *Need something?*

No. It's fine. Sorry. It was odd to be on a different sleep cycle from Vander. Not that all of the One Hundred were asleep. His other three core Overwatches were awake, and another twenty of the One Hundred, even Zhan, but he'd never been as close to them as he was to Vander. He hoped the same problem would not befall Rae'en when she took his place.

A century ago, Kholster had been unable to rest a hand on this side of the wall. A ditch dug round the city and filled with water and muck had prevented it. Now he rested a bare hand against the cool granite surface, his gloves having been burned beyond repair in his initial encounter with Cadence—not to mention his facial hair and the Dwarven denim pants he'd been wearing. Thank Aldo, he'd opted to leave the rifle and gunpowder Glinfolgo had dedicated for his use with the fleet.

Two centuries ago, the walls had been only partially completed. A century before that, the Guild Cities themselves were just beginning to come to fruition. In another century, would the walls be lined not with archers but with riflemen?

I wonder how long before my use of gunpowder makes other weapons irrelevant? Kholster concentrated on deliberately keeping the thought to himself. The longer the war with the Oathbreakers went on, the more likely the humans would catch scent of what was happening. If Kholster or his Aern had to try to make any gunpowder in the field, he knew the ox would be out of the paddock.

I'm surprised the Dwarves have kept a bag over everyone's head as long as they have.

How the simple security measure the Dwarves had taken of using magic to turn the "jun" powder pink, of ordering Dienoxin crystal and allowing a portion of the recipe to be "stolen," detailing the importance of the Dienoxin crystal and its proper processing . . . how that had worked so long to keep the humans and the gnomes from figuring it out seemed miraculous. Kholster knew it to be part miracle and part assassination.

Assassination. Hmmm.

Zhan, Kholster thought, *what are your Armored doing?*

No surer sign that Eyes lie sleeping than to hear First Bones in my head. Zhan's thoughts came tinged with a mild distortion from the required rerouting via End Song, Zhan's warsuit. *My hounds are scattered like leaves in the wind, Kholster. Some lie ahead. Some behind. If you're planning on being gutted, I'll move them all in.*

And Caz?

Silencer indicates you should look high and left.

Kholster did so, catching the briefest flash of Caz's skull helm looming behind an archer manning a keyhole. The Bone Finder's eyes touched on Kholster's, his narrowed gaze seeming to say, "You watch your quadrant, I've got mine covered."

Once spotted, Caz dropped away unseen.

"Was that Caz?" Rae'en hissed.

Kholster touched a silencing finger to his lips and answered with a brief nod, smiling as he walked on.

Ahead, the line of travelers split into two separate and mostly distinct lines, the people seeking entrance to Mason divided. Those bringing in goods stepped to the left, and those with other business to the right. Kholster moved to the right.

Rae'en followed Kholster's lead, stepping into the queue of people not bearing goods but seeking entrance to the city.

Are your warsuits? . . .

In the wind, First Bones. It's easier to conceal my two-hundred-plus End Song and Silencer than it is to hide your five thousand. Did you have a task for us or . . . ?

No, just . . .

We are of one mind and spirit, if that's the nettle in your boot, Zhan thought. *Dredger and Garris were reunited last night. I sent him up to Fort Sunder to help them sort bone metal. I wish you would agree to have an increased number of Ossuarians trailing you. Once you reach The Parliament of Ages, you'll be on your own completely for a few days.*

Good. Kholster breathed a sigh of relief. *No problems then.*

Zhan laughed, presumably at Kholster's version of no problems. *None concerning the warsuits. We seek the bones. They seek the bones. There isn't much room for strife amongst Ossuarians whether the metal is outside or in.*

"I hope not," Kholster murmured.

"You don't get to skip the line?" Cadence asked. Sweat still stood out on her skin. Red streaks marked the veins at her neck. It was a wonder she hadn't gotten the shakes, but if she didn't have them by now, she wouldn't . . . which told Kholster he'd been right all along. She didn't need the crystal. Someone had convinced her she needed it, gotten her addicted to it, and was slowly using crystal abuse to burn down her abilities to a more manageable level. Whether or not they knew that was what they were doing, other than the control through addiction portion, Kholster couldn't say. Any brigand who would follow a man like Darbin struck Kholster as either a monster or a dangerous fool.

"Hey." Cadence thumped his shoulder when he did not answer immediately. "Hey. I'm talking to you, wolf ears."

"Perhaps," Kholster turned to face her. "But why should I, as you say, skip the line?"

"You're a king or a hero or some such!"

"King Wolf Ears?" Kholster swatted away the hand of a pickpocket trying to reach into one of his Aernese saddlebags. Two hands wide and three hands long with bone-steel reinforcements at the bottom corners and a matching fastener at the middle, Kholster's saddlebags were only lightly singed. "Don't make me take your hand, child. Your screams might wake the baby."

He gestured to the heavily slumbering Caius in Rae'en's arms, but the nattily dressed street thief was already in full flight.

"Hey." Cadence thumped Kholster's shoulder again. "Shouldn't there be a procession or something?"

"I don't like them." Noticing the line had moved forward, Kholster filled in the space.

Thump. "Or an envoy?"

"Draekar will tell them I'm here once I'm inside the city," he called over his shoulder. "Usually, I'm at South Gate making my way into Bridgeland before they can get organized enough to 'greet' me."

A few more steps forward in the line, and Kholster's nostrils flared at the familiar scent of rock dust. He didn't know if humans could smell the difference between the various types of rock worked and sold in Mason, but he recognized the tension easing from Rae'en's shoulders, her stance more relaxed even as he felt the smells so reminiscent of South Number Nine work their quiescent effect upon himself.

"Hey." Thump. "If you fall asleep," Cadence needled, "can I leave?"

"You can do whatever you like then or now," Kholster answered, "but if you want the babe returned to your care, I suggest you follow along to the Harvester's temple to ensure you will be recognized as his mother upon the completion of your cleansing."

"It will never work." Cadence stamped the ground in frustration, cursing as she had to grab Kholster's arm or tumble to the dirt. "They don't take crystal users."

"Not usually." Ahead of them, a scuffle between the guards and a traveler seemed to indicate the lack of appropriate paperwork, identification, or spending money.

Kholster counted twelve guards in gray brigandine, six with swords belted to their waists and six with spears. Combined with the Long Speakers, one with silver trim to her gray robe, the other with black trim clearly marking him as a Long Arm, and the other archers that had to be up on the walls somewhere behind arrow slits, there were a lot of guards. Kholster was amazed that the human bothered.

Thump. This time the thump was further punctuated by a snort from Rae'en. "If you're so keen on helping people." Cadence gestured at the scuffle.

"I'm not." Kholster took a step closer to Cadence, bringing them chest to chest. He expected her to back away, but Cadence stood her ground. If anything, she seemed to lean into him. He waited a hundred count as they breathed in each other's exhalations. "Was there anything else?"

"No."

He stood there for a ten count. "You keep thumping me on the shoulder."

"Sorry."

In the corner of his eyes, Rae'en's chest shook as she struggled to hold in laughter. With a heavy sigh, Kholster turned back toward the gate. Another six guards joined the others.

Bird squirt. Draekar knows we're here, yes? Kholster thought to Varvost, Fifth of One Hundred and his temporary Prime while Vander slept.

Yes, and Zhan says the Bone Finders are in position if need be.

Who?

Caz, Teru, and Whaar. He says they have a reputation in the Guild Cities.

The Long Speaker approached slowly, proud, but scared.

What the hells are they up to?

"Shall we report your arrival?" the Long Speaker asked. Her eyes widened when she caught sight of Cadence.

"No." Kholster eyed the guards. "And for the next hundred hours, this one is under my protection, as is her child."

Look steadily at the guards for a three count, Vander requested.

Kholster looked past the Long Speaker. Utilitarian helms, like smoothed and emptied tortoise shells, covered each soldier's hair, the leather straps tied under their necks. They wore dark leather gloves of some pungent animal Kholster did not immediately recognize. Boiled leather plates, the same color as the gloves, protected the thighs, hobnailed boots like his own serving to shield the feet and lower legs.

Not bad if your opponent doesn't attack the back of your knees, Vander thought.

Or throat or face or eyes, Kholster thought back. *You didn't need to wake.*

Sure I did. Eyes of Vengeance said you'd started pestering Zhan . . .

Pestering?

Oh, yes. You're a spectacular pain in the jaw, but I'm used to it.

Ha!

The Long Speaker had been saying something, but Kholster realized he hadn't heard it when she turned on her heel and walked away; he'd been too caught up in the assessment of the guards and his banter with Vander.

Did you track any of that?

Sorry, Kholster, I'm still too sleepy to lip read and you weren't transmitting sound.

Habit, Kholster thought back by way of apology. *Check with the others.*

Doing it now.

"Kholster Bloodmane," called a guardsman approaching from the rear. A band of copper rimmed his helm and the edges of his brigandine, marking him, Kholster assumed, as a commander of sorts. "This year you won't slip away so easily."

Marrow, Bloodmane broke in, **says that's Captain Pallos and that Whaar tracked what the Long Speaker said. It was a warning about the Speaker's College's intolerance for those who dilute their talents with drugs.**

Thank you.

"Captain Pallos." Kholster stepped forward, offering to clasp hands. "I'd like to think that wasn't a threat."

CHAPTER 28
WYLANT'S WORRIES

The cooling yet still-warm wind of summer-turning-to-fall blew through the open windows of Wylant's rooms at Port Ammond, scattering the pages of Prince Dolvek's latest dispatch from her desk to flutter to the hard stone floor. Moonlight touched the smooth, attractive lines of Wylant's face, revealing red, puffy eyes and chapped lips. Her coverlet lay cast aside on the floor, exposing her nakedness to no one but the gods. Rubbing at her nose as she slept, Wylant flinched as if in the grips of a nightmare.

Ever since Kholster had named her Aiannai, she had not dreamt properly. Instead, Wylant relived past events without the benefit of dreams to recast and obfuscate the things with which her unconscious mind needed to come to terms. Crystal-clear reenactments of events long past were all she had, forcing her to deal with them and move on . . . or not . . . just like the Aern.

The memory which caused her to toss and turn on this occasion was pleasant enough. A gnomish Dreamsmith might even have explained the images as a longing for simpler days, claiming the stresses of command were too much for a female. They would have been wrong on the one hand and as sexist as the typical Eldrennai male on the other.

A memory of spring. The spring after Wylant's eleventh campaign against the Zaur. She sat on the terrace atop Fort Sunder, gazing down at the severe plains of *Jun'ghri'kul*, "the Broken Table," now cleansed of all trace of the tainted reptilian hordes, and smiled. Only her husband would have them maintain such a lawn. Easier to spot the enemy, true, but two hundred acres of purple and green in all directions? One day the purple myr grass would choke out the scrubby green, and then she wondered if it would make her happy or sad.

Wylant plucked at an errant thread on the sleeve of her blue dress and chided herself. *I promised myself I'd stop wearing these stupid things when I became a knight*, she thought. *But Kholster seems to like them, and armor does make impromptu trysts with the Aern I love a great deal less . . . spontaneous.*

In the memory, her blonde hair was still long and caught up with a silver ribbon. She pulled the ribbon from her hair and wore it loose, an easy way to make Kholster smile, and she suddenly wanted to see him smile more than anything in the whole of Barrone.

Kholster walked out onto the terrace and grinned exactly as she'd planned. She loved that smile, his upper and lower canines exposed in a way that would remind anyone his people had been built for killing and, well, eating, others, but also somehow conveying he had no intention of doing so. He'd just shaved, as had been his custom after every campaign since they'd been married, and he wore his red hair long, because she liked it that way and he thought it only fair to wear his hair long for her since she wore hers long for him.

Wylant looked into Kholster's strange black sclera eyes and smiled. Their hands touched and the memory repeated.

That's all there was to it: him outside of his warsuit and her in a dress. Their hands touching. Her seeing him smile. Feeling loved, wanted. And then again. And again. And again as if her brain felt the need to torture her with things which could no longer happen and with bonds long broken.

Wylant rocked forward in the darkness, startled awake by the first sneeze. Her diaphragm seized, locked in the initial stages of a protracted second sneeze. The scent of the Zaur filled her nostrils, a sickening mixture of body odor and reptilian waste.

At least I'm awake, she thought, then, *Gods, not again.*

A rapid consecution of sternutations shook her, sneeze after sneeze running each into the other to create a sustained rattling buzz which could have been humorous if the act itself were not so painful. Rolling from her bed, Wylant landed on the cold stone floor, cursing after one particularly great sneeze slammed her forehead into the stone.

Eyes watering, streams running down her face as she grabbed first for Vax and second for her pouch of *jallek* root. Vax felt right in her hand, a part of her—as always. His edge caught the moonlight, as if on purpose, casting a wedge of brightness on the ceiling then adjusting to show the pouch. The vexing leather container was less accommodating and gave no sign of crawling obligingly to her outstretched hand to surrender the medicine within. She blinked at her bedside table, which lay on its side, having been knocked over at some point during the ordeal.

A frustrated growl escaped her lips. Struggling to her feet, Wylant glared at the errant pouch and stabbed at it with Vax, smirking as the sword elongated helpfully into a spear. Angling the spear up, Wylant willed the weapon to shrink again, snatching the *jallek* root from its tip as Vax complied.

"Good boy." Pinching a wad of the dried black root, she pushed the bitter substance beneath her tongue. Astringent juice, strong enough to force a lesser person to gag, filled her mouth, but with it came instant relief.

"I've had enough of this," she snarled. "Every night? What is Dienox playing at?"

"General?" Kam's voice called from beyond the door of her quarters.

"I'm," she screwed her face into a sour expression, one eye open, the other closed as she struggled against another sneeze, "fine, Kam. But wake The Sidearms. I want to ride at first light. We're heading to North Guard. I want to check the watchtowers personally. Again."

"Yes, ma'am." There was no hint of sarcasm in his voice, and she was glad of it. As if she didn't know the nobles thought she was mad. *Maybe I should take the Lance up Albren Pass to the foothills . . . ?* She ran a hand over her head, the stubble pricking at her palm as it always did on her fifth day without a shave. *Prince Dolvek would have fun with that, I have no doubt.*

She blinked in the predawn darkness and, sure that the *jallek* root had her allergies under control, summoned a floating spark of pulsing electricity and spat it from her throat with a word. The pale blue of her magic illuminated the stone-floored room of her billet, washing over the sparsely decorated room with a cold, crackling light. A lone wall-length mirror displayed her well-toned body, but Wylant had little patience with mirrors.

There was a time when she'd gazed into looking glasses critically, applying powders and dyes, adorning herself vainly for a husband who, though appreciative of her efforts, respected her more for her ability with a sword, her competence in battle, her intelligence, wit, and veracity than he ever could for her beauty.

But that had been long ago. Though her body was as ageless and fit now as it had been then, she treated it like a tool for accomplishing her goals and executing her duty. She had loved once and would never love again, which was all well and good to her. It had to be. The first time had almost destroyed them both. Any other relationship could be no more than a dalliance, and she had little enough patience to spare on matters of importance and none at all to waste on dalliances.

She walked to the waiting basin of water which sat atop an ornate steel table, forged in the Aernese style with blood oak leaves wrought into a small ring around the edge of the bowl, the rest perfectly smooth and unadorned. Wylant set Vax down on the stone. Picking up a washcloth from next to the basin, she dipped it into the cold water and washed in her brisk morning ritual.

Opening the pack she'd readied before bed, Wylant took out the bone-metal straight razor Kholster had left behind at his exile, set it down next to the water basin, and returned to her pack for a small jar of ointment. The acrid tang of crushed myr grass and thick, rich, surprisingly nonsticky, blood oak sap caused her nostrils to flare involuntarily. Dipping her fingers into the red-brown mixture, she spread the lubricant liberally across her scalp before setting to work with her razor in long, even strokes, shaving against the grain, wiping the blade on her washcloth between strokes, leaving traces of grease and blonde hair behind.

"Blessing of the gods." Wylant sneered at the sight of it. Let the Eldrennai see it however they wished. Wylant had come to see favor of the gods, Dienox in particular, as nothing less than a curse.

For a long time, even before Kholster, Wylant had let her hair grow longer than was efficient despite the problems it caused with tangles, brushing, and getting stuck in armor. But that had been before the Sundering, before . . .

Having given the lotion more time to soften the coarser hair, Wylant shaved the back of her head next. From there, she worked her way down, removing every bit of "blessing" Dienox had felt necessary to bestow. There was only one blessing Wylant wanted from the gods.

She looked at Vax, watched how he slid across the floor like a snake, pooling and reaching up onto the bed where he rested briefly before resuming his sword shape in the fading body warmth of her mattress and closed her eyes in silent and unanswered prayer. If she noticed the shape held by the metal in those few moments, the general did not allow herself to dwell on it. Such thoughts could only drive her mad, and had for a time, before she'd come to accept what she had done.

Rinsing herself off with a dousing from the metal basin, the Eldrennai general walked out onto her balcony to dry. From there, even in the dark, she saw the Gulf of Gromm, the green-blue water, dark and foreboding. The air smelled wrong, tainted. It tickled her nostrils, just shy of soliciting a sneeze. Hoping to prevent a relapse, she spit the wet lump of *jallek* root off the balcony and replaced it with a fresh pinch.

The smell of the Zaur, the ancient enemy of her people, had faded from her nostrils, but she was a hairbreadth from issuing a check on all the Watches and running a formal border inspection. She knew, of course, what King Grivek would say.

"Each time he comes, you get this way, Wylant. Every hundred years, as regular as the suns." Grivek would smile at her in that patronizing way he didn't even know he had, reach out to pat her on the shoulder and catch himself before he actually completed the error. Would he pat his other Lancers on the shoulder? On the head? Then best not touch her in such a fashion until it was clear the king had decided to treat the men that way as well. At least he tried. "I know why you feel this way. I miss him too. Why not ride to North Guard," he would say, "in fact, I order you to North Guard. You'll only be a day's ride away."

Which is why she was heading to North Guard. Might as well avoid the conversation and the king's condescension altogether. Why did they always have to assume her life revolved around the Aern she'd once wed? Gods, but it angered her. No one missed Kholster more than she did. Of course she missed him. Of course she wished things had worked out differently . . . better . . . but they hadn't, and to spend the rest of her life pining for a male, any male . . . there was more to her than that. It wasn't in Wylant's bones to be so dependent. And then they all had to make it worse with the way they brought him up over and over again or crept around the subject when they feared she might be sensitive. Did his fellow Aern do the same to him?

She laughed at the idea of Vander suggesting Kholster shirk his duties because Kholster missed her. A sea hawk cried in the distance, striking at a fish or a waterfox.

"Too alike for our own good," she whispered.

As the first sun began to rise, Wylant dressed and donned her armor, far heavier than the light crystal plate armor of the prince's precious Crystal Knights. Wylant insisted her Sidearms wear steel, weighty well-made metal which could turn a blade without the benefit of magic, and she did the same.

"Crystal Knights," she murmured under her breath, "why the king allows his army to continue wearing armor that's completely useless against the Zaur and the Aern, I have no idea at all."

That was a lie. She did know. King Grivek allowed the practice to instill a sense of pride. He did it because the sight of a Crystal Knight riding on horseback upon a wave of Aeromancy made the people feel safe even though they could never be safe again. Never mind the elemental foci that now marked and slowly consumed the bodies of those who used the old style of elemental magic. The Sundering had killed the Eldrennai surely as it had been the salvation of the Vael and the Aern. If it hadn't, then Dolvek's cursed museum display had.

"You're on your way, aren't you, Kholster," she said flatly. "Even now. Will you kill Dolvek before or after the Conjunction? Which would fulfill all oaths?" She spat at the thought of the impudent young prince but stopped herself from spewing more treachery aloud. Wylant held out her hand, and Vax, coiled and ready, sprang into it, resuming his sword shape as she sheathed him in the scabbard at her side.

Vax would make a better king than that boy, she thought.

The tears surprised her as they always did.

A knock at the door broke her reverie and signaled the arrival of her first lieutenant. If any signs of her grief remained by the time she reached the door, it could have only been in a slight redness around the eyes that could easily be explained away by her allergies. Wylant threw the door open, already giving orders. "I assume you're here to tell me my Lance is ready to ride?" She didn't wait for an answer. "Then get moving!" she shouted. "We might press on to Albren Pass if I don't like the smell of things."

She smiled at the sound of a diplomatic parcel hitting the ground, a smile that drew even wider when her lieutenant was already out of sight by the time she'd crossed the threshold. He was a good soldier. There was a twinkle in her steely gray eyes as she broke the royal seal and scratched absentmindedly at the tip of one pointed ear.

"Another all's well report," she sniffed, "from Prince Dolvek himself, no less." That, in and of itself, was almost enough to make Wylant pressgang the capital and raise the reserve guard. But she couldn't do that, not without staging a coup. Her blood went cold at the thought. If she killed the king and seized the kingdom, declared all of the people Aiannai under her rule, would that save them from Kholster's oath? Her vision swam for a moment, and she shook her head.

"No," she muttered, "but I bet it would make him smile." She sneezed again and spat. "Kholster would have had his Aern out walking the whole kingdom in grids until they found the Zaur and killed them. Dienox's bloody cloud of war would not have stopped the Aern."

That was one of many things she missed about Kholster; the way he took her instincts as valid intel, respected her hunches just as if they'd been his own or those of one of his brother or sister Aern. Wylant banished the memory with a shake of her head. *Maybe I should stop using myr grass and blood oak sap as lotion when I shave*, she thought. *It smells like him. It's making me sentimental.*

Wylant took one last glance at the documents before incinerating them with a blast of hissed sparks. *All is well? Did the warsuits not kill your guards, my liege? Did they not stare down at you amid the shattered crystal cases and gushing blood? Did they fail to demonstrate their power? You are dead. The only question is who kills you first: Kholster or the Zaur?*

When she reached the stables, The Sidearms were mounted and ready.

"Is all—" Mazik began in his metallic voice.

"All is not well." She mounted her waiting steed. "I can smell it."

CHAPTER 29
XASTIX

The Zaur warlord pensively ran a foreclaw over the mottled red scales between his eye ridges. An itch between his shoulder blades was the true source of his discomfort, but to scratch beneath his scales where a small blue stone had been pressed into the hide would have been a sign of disrespect, both to his Ghaiattri patron and to Him.

To have been born shard-slotted and to have been gifted with a tiny shard of the World Crystal to fill the slot . . . Xastix interpreted both as a mark of favor from the dark god Kilke. An immense blessing, true, yet even so the constant itch drove the warlord to maddening distraction. Standing two hands higher than the rest of his kin, Xastix looked an impressive foe, dressed in blue-tinted armor made from the scales of the Great Dragon Serphyn, when he was not frantically clawing at his own scales.

Long quartz tables lined two of the walls, displaying war plunder and artifacts of previous ages. Xastix liked to surround himself with objects of the warlords before him, items that had been gathered from the clans after he had united them. Each one had a history. His reptilian brothers thought of them as badges of honor, but Xastix knew that each item actually represented failure, a feat for which Xastix refused to be remembered. His would be a legacy of which a warlord could be proud.

A distant vibration, measured and distinct, caused Xastix to stretch himself out along the floor, tongue flicking out to better catch the message.

<<The messenger from General Tsan has arrived, Lord Xastix.>> Ghi thumped from his post at the entrance to the royal caverns. Xastix loved to feel the vibration of Ghi's distinctive tail. All Zaur were bilingual, speaking Tol, the over language, literally meaning "Tongue," and Zaurtol, the under speech, which translated as "Tail Tongue," but the precise percussive notes of Ghi's Zaurtol were invigorating.

Before the Joining of Ways, most of Xastix's subjects would have disdainfully called him a SriZaur, one of the Fang People, but with the help of his god, Xastix had brought peace, war, and purpose to both races. The SriZaur lacked numbers, the Zaur lacked a proper understanding of scale, patience, and planning, but together . . . they had conquered or exterminated the other underdwellers. No more fungoid barbarians, whatever it was they'd called themselves—Xastix never had managed to understand a word they'd said—and no more chitinous Issic-Gnoss of whom only the beetle-like shock troops were fit for eating.

Xastix slapped the floor of his throne room with vigor. Eyes turning to the throne itself, he bowed. Dropping low on all fours, belly touching the ground, he averted his eyes. *Soon I will be worthy.*

On the seat of the Throne of Scale, carved from the bones of conquered foes and covered with the scales of defeated warlords, the throne from which Warlord Ryyk had once ruled, Kilke's disembodied head now rested. Two crimson ram horns sprang from the skin of its golden brow. Xastix found its facial features disturbingly human, but the reptilian eyes, dark and fathomless, reassured him.

Cautiously, he peered into the eyes of his deity, hoping for some sign, but there was none forthcoming. So it had been since Kilke's initial proclamation, when he had ordered the Zaur to unite and punish the races of his fellow gods who had betrayed him, dethroned him, and cast his center head down to Barrone.

"I have united them, Lord Kilke," Xastix told the head. "All the breeds, all the clans, in all guises and all shapes! The cold blood of your people is united! It cries out for vengeance!" Hand outstretched, Xastix caressed the cheek of his god and howled in pain as the small blue stone in his back grew larger, stronger.

He quieted himself slowly, his tail thumping rhythmically against the polished marble floor of the throne room. This time he would not fail. This time he would be strong. Under the torture of the god, frost poured from his lips and fire coursed along his back.

<<I am chosen.>> His tail pounded out on the marble. <<I will be your instrument!>>

"In time, perhaps," the dismembered head whispered. Kilke's smile was cruel and superior. "But you are still weak. Come back to me when you have tasted the blood of all three races who seek conjunction. Kiss my cheek then and I will grant you power, but until that time I will not suffer your touch!"

Lightning erupted from Kilke's eyes, hurling Xastix into the polished bronze wall, where he lay in the reflected light of the throne room's four fires. Complex ventilation systems carried the smoke of the fires and the smell of his own burnt reptilian flesh up and out of the mountain. A human would have found the heat oppressive, the light blinding, but the Zaur loved warmth and light. They lived underground predominantly to pay homage to Kilke, their dark god, lord of secrets and shadows . . . and power.

Xastix rolled slowly onto his belly and tried to raise himself to all fours.

The head of Kilke was motionless, but the expression had changed. It was now a mocking smile, a challenge. The warlord forced himself up onto his forelegs and gathered his hind legs beneath him, still shaking.

"In secret and in shadow." His breath still came in ragged lurches, each intake generating a sharp pain between his shoulders. "I serve."

He let his head rest on the long trophy table and eyed the Axe of Brrsti: Brrsti, who had almost slain the Eldrennai king Zillek. Xastix admitted that Brrsti had been brave. He had fought his way through to Zillek's chambers, though his army had been defeated, and would have killed the king if Kholster Bloodmane, that accursed scarback, had not split his skull. In Xastix's opinion, it was the unremembered Zaur who had successfully retrieved his warlord's body, weapons, and armor for the clan who should have been celebrated and thrice-named.

Xastix ran his long gray tongue across the trophies, trying to ignore the agony emanating from the stone in his back. Stories of supposed bravery and accomplishment ran through his mind. His had been a race in denial, a culture of lunatics. There were over two million Zaur in the Sri'Zauran Mountains, numbers growing in the secret shadows, and if his guess was correct there were only half as many Eldrennai in all their beloved cities combined. His pain lessened as his outrage blossomed. He snatched the skull of an Eldrennai, one which sported a full set of Aernese teeth, and held it aloft triumphantly.

"Your people are weak now, Maker," Xastix hissed.

Even better, a full quarter of his own people were trained as warriors. If the data his human agent had been paid to procure proved his hypothesis . . .

You will slaughter them, said a quiet voice in his mind. *We serve the will of Kilke, dark father of us all. All that we have done has been in secret. All of our plans have been made in shadow. They who cast Him down have no power in His majestic night.*

"Yes!" roared Xastix aloud, full of religious fervor. "We will!"

Human footfalls and the click of claws on marble snapped Xastix back to the present. A nameless lieutenant, a black-scaled Zaur, stood next to a pale human. "I present Captain Tyree," the lieutenant announced.

Xastix liked the way the underling averted his gaze to show respect. Many of the Zaur still had a little trouble accepting a SriZaur as their leader. This male did not appear to let such slow-mindedness pull at his thoughts.

The human, on the other claw, looked the warlord directly in the eye. His words echoed in Xastix's mind like slithering whispers as he spoke. "The pleasure's all mine, your hissness." Tyree bowed briefly, scarcely a nod by Zaur standards.

"Identify yourself," barked Xastix, ignoring the human and indicating the lieutenant with a flick of his tongue.

"I am the seventh hatchling of the eighth brood of Yat, Warlord," the lieutenant responded quickly.

"You have looked at it, the human's census data?"

The lieutenant nodded. "I have."

"And what does it say?" Xastix pressed his tail into the floor as hard as he could to distract himself from the newfound torture Kilke had inflicted upon him. He would not be able to concentrate sufficiently to read the data until later in the evening, and he wanted to know what it said now.

"It says that the Eldrennai are one-fourth our number and that our warriors will outnumber theirs fifty to one," said the young Zaur soldier with pride. "It says that few of them are warriors and most of those rely on magic rather than metal. It says that we will crush them."

General Tsan promised him a name, if he pleased you, a voice whispered in Xastix's mind. At first he'd excused it as his own internal thoughts, but now he knew it was some higher power.

"General Tsan promised you a name for this, did he?" Xastix asked casually.

"He did, Warlord," answered the other Zaur in amazement.

Kreej, the voice whispered.

"Kreej, perhaps?" Xastix offered.

"Yes, Warlord," said the astonished lieutenant.

"Then I name you Kreej, Lieutenant." The warlord laughed. "Take the human to Captain Dryga. He and his troops are to continue their mission along the Xasti'Kaur." He examined the human's expression. "Soon the other watches will begin to fall and I want the human to be there. Tell Dryga to pay him and release him, if his information is correct. If it is incorrect, Dryga may express his warlord's displeasure in whatever ways he fancies."

"In secret and in shadow," answered Lieutenant Kreej, taking the human by the shoulder and guiding him firmly out of the room.

"In secret and in shadow," the warlord responded.

To His secret purpose, whispered the voice inside his mind. Xastix looked at the head of his beloved god, lying upon the seat of the Throne of Scale, and clawed madly at the itch in his back. He hoped that he would prove worthy of his god's blessings.

CHAPTER 30
COLLAPSE

Picturing it in her mind, Rae'en could see the whole of the Guild Cities laid out as on a map. Not literally see, as when M'jynn, Joose, Kazan, and Arbokk were in their positions giving her updates, but she could picture the shape of the thing: a ring of outer cities, bounded and connected by large exterior walls, each city with a name declaring its artisanal focus: Mason, Loom, Larder, Lumber, Warfare, Livestock, and whatever the others were . . . all surrounding the inner city of Commerce, the largest marketplace in all the world.

"Midian is," bragged Captain Pallos as he and the twelve-guard escort led them through the middle of streets paved with an interlocking pattern of stones representing, Rae'en realized, not just the Guild Cities but which city one was presently in denoted with darker colored stone, "some say, perhaps in the better location . . . the center of the Junland Bridge . . . but we have the biggest, the best, marketplace anywhere in Barrone, right here."

With a little bone-steel underneath we could tell where we were without looking down, though, Rae'en thought to Kazan.

Kazan? Gah! Rae'en was sure her Overwatches would tease her no end when she got back to South Number Nine. *I have got to stop doing that*. She blamed the most recent lapse on the familiar scent of stone permeating Mason. Buildings of stone up to four floors high showcased an array of stone-works in various stages of completion. On a second-story platform, a bare-chested young man stood in an agonizing pose while a stern-faced woman with beaded hair made sketches of him, constantly referencing a large block of marbled white stone. Her purple quilted long jacket looked too heavy for the weather, but Rae'en couldn't be sure. Her own integumentary system had mostly sorted itself out, and extremes of temperature were finally becoming less and less noticeable.

She was still aware of added warmth, like the bundled heat of baby Caius (who had finally dozed off) nestled against her chest, a thin blanket from her pack between the infant and her mail, but was indifferent to it. Sweat was something she didn't miss.

Poor humans.

On a lower level on the other side of the street, a row of sweating men bent low, shaping stones with axes much cruder than those she'd seen the Dwarves of the Duodenary Mountains use. Yet, farther up the street, a gnome in plaid spats and a businessman's suit with matching highlights was instructing a feathered and furred manitou in the use of a steam-driven lathe much smaller than anything she'd ever seen Glinfolgo work with back home.

Other than the occasional food vendor pushing carts emitting savory smells, nothing was for sale here. All deals, Rae'en imagined, had to be cut in the central bazaar. This was where people worked. Not where they sold their goods.

Captain Pallos walked next to her father, keeping up a one-sided conversation of inanities, while the guards walked around them in a moving rectangle. A few of Mason's citizens paused to notice the two Aern but most went quickly back to their work, exactly as might be expected of "The City that's Seen Everything."

"The Guild Leaders will greatly appreciate this, Kholster Bloodmane."

Rae'en wondered how long it would take Pallos to notice the way her father's ears flattened a bit more each time "Kholster Bloodmane" rolled off his tongue.

She didn't mind it so much, humans calling her father by that name. To many of the younger generation, it seemed only right that the names of the Armored should be entwined with that of their warsuits. Was it that her father and the others were reminded of the fact that they were not yet reunited with their warsuits? When they were together again, would it be okay then to refer to them that way? Rae'en was afraid to ask. Anything that made her father's ears flatten in anger was best avoided.

The grit-scuffing sound of walking the streets of Mason was high on her annoyance list at the moment. The sounds happened with each step, magnified by the guards walking with them. Cadence did it the worst, though, shuffling her feet as though she was looking for coin on the dirty streets. *No*, Rae'en thought, *not actually dirty. Gritty.* There seemed to be a thin layer of dust, dust and grit, over the entire city. Inescapable deposits of rock dust, grit, and sand pooled at street corners. She spotted two men in what she guessed were city uniforms, working to move the deposits into rolling bins and sweep down the streets, one using buckets of water to damp down the grit and dust, the other sweeping or scraping up what he could. Rae'en did not envy them their endless work.

A few paces behind her, Cadence took an uneasy step, breaking the sound of her steady shuffling.

"Bird squirt." Rae'en managed to catch the shoulder of Cadence's top as the human fell, ripping the garment at the neck but managing to turn a full-out fall into a gentle drop to the stones without dropping baby Caius.

"She's down," Rae'en called to her father. Caius (marvel of marvels) stayed asleep despite a thorough jostling.

"Now that she's out . . . ?" Pallos ventured, hand straying to his sword.

"She will be carried." Kholster's eyes narrowed, ears flattening completely against his head like a challenged wolf's or angry cat's. "And kept safe."

"Safe as bones," said the Bone Finder, who dropped down from a nearby balcony, startling both the guards and the sculptor in purple. A broad stripe of dust marked his black brigandine as if he'd been climbing around the rooftops and had to pull himself up and over a ledge, resting on his abdomen. Ignoring the guards, he pulled a pick-head axe from his back. The spiked poll-and-leather-wrapped bone-steel haft, the blued to near-black surface of the tool, identified the Aern as Teru to Rae'en as quickly as if his name had been scrawled across his chest.

Kholster's warpick dropped from his back as he turned to face Teru. He caught it in his left hand as it reached waist level and clanged pick head against axe head before the two of them smoothly returned their tools to their backs in a single, fluid motion.

A skull-shaped half-helm obscured Teru's features, but his strong jaw and dimpled chin led Rae'en to picture him with a handsome face.

"Kholster, Rae'en," Teru said with a nod, his voice deep and full with an underlying confidence which sent thoughts of mating through Rae'en's head that she sincerely hoped her Overwatches hadn't heard.

"Ossuarian," Rae'en answered formally.

Dropping to one knee, Teru slid one arm under Cadence's back and the other under her knees. He stood in one swift motion.

"I have the bones, Kholster."

Rae'en had never before imagined a situation in which she might like to be hamstrung and carried off the field of battle by a Bone Finder. But now . . . if that Bone Finder were Teru . . .

"Kholster Bloodmane," Captain Pallos began, "I must object."

"Must you?" Kholster bared his canines.

I hope Pallos doesn't mistake that for a grin, Rae'en thought to Kazan.

"Captain Pallos," Kholster hissed between clenched teeth, "I am attempting to remind myself that I have shirts older than you."

"I don't understand."

"I know." Kholster's ears ticked up, the first in a series of incremental upticks that brought them fully upright again. "She," he pointed to Cadence, "is under my protection to the extent that, when she fainted, a Bone Finder arrived to tend to her. Until my hundred hours of protection has ended, when you threaten her, you threaten me. I hate to repeat myself, but I hope you didn't intend that as a threat, Captain Pallos."

"I meant no offense," Pallos answered looking a bit green. "I thought—"

"I know what you thought." Kholster held the man's gaze until the human seemed to have calmed. Then his ears pricked up as though at some sound in the distance Rae'en hadn't caught, and he was on the move.

"This way, Teru." Kholster headed to a side street with a haunted look in his eyes. "I am summoned."

CHAPTER 31
THE HUNDRED-YEAR OATH

"Murderer!" A cracked leather and strangled cat voice cut the stale air above the noise of the bustling crowd, stopping Kholster as surely as a sledgehammer to the temple. City guards in green brigandine, having replaced Mason's contingent when they passed through the gate from Mason to Commerce, stared imploringly at Captain Pallos, seeking guidance. Even as she wanted to mock the guards for not knowing how to react in the developing situation, Rae'en caught herself watching Teru, hoping to glean some clue as to how she should respond.

Teru stood impassively, eyes on Kholster, waiting unabashedly to follow his lead. Would he drop Cadence if he needed to attack? What should she do with Caius? Would the babe be safe if she just put him down?

Not exactly halting their commerce, the bazaar crowds split like an ooze, hollowing out an area around the woman, creating a path toward her in a way Rae'en had never before seen. A glow lit the periphery of Kholster's pupils, but whatever the memory was, her father did not share it.

"My apologies, Kholster Bloodmane," Captain Pallos choked. "I'll have the guards—"

"No." He took one short, sharp breath, in through the nose, out through the mouth, and then Kholster was in motion, striding in that I-Am-Going-This-Direction-And-None-Shall-Dare-Oppose-Me way Rae'en couldn't imagine herself ever mastering. "I know this woman."

Parting without argument or orders, the guards relegated themselves to observers in whatever was about to unfold. A child in brightly colored cloth stumbled into Kholster's path as the adult he'd been following turned abruptly to stay clear of the Aern, a bag of candied corn kernels falling from his hands. Dropping into a low spin, Kholster caught both the bag and child in one smooth motion, leaving them righted in his wake without slowing his pace. The streams of vivid ribbon festooning the market snapped in a breeze which sprang to life and died between the final steps which brought Kholster to his destination.

Standing under the recently repainted sign of an apothecary, a wrinkled old thing, crook-backed, with long, matted hair an untamed mass of white shouted, "Murderer!" again, showing a mouth full of ivory dentures. Her pale robes clung tight to her wizened form in the heat, a black shawl hung around her shoulders like a badge of office.

"Iella," Kholster towered over her, peering into her fierce black eyes. "You summoned me?"

"You remember me, Murderer?" She shook with equal portions emotion and infirmity. "You know what you did?"

"I remember everything." Kholster nodded. He bent toward her. At the door of the apothecary behind the old woman, a mass of young children crowded, held back by two young women and a pot-bellied man.

"Gramma!" one of the boys shouted. "Run, Gramma!"

"Get him, Gramma!" bellowed the smallest of the girls, leaning on the display window of the apothecary, colored glass bottles shifting precariously as she jostled them aside to get a better view. "Stab him inna nose!"

"You have an oath in your eyes," Kholster said when the old woman did not speak again. "What did you promise you would do if we ever crossed paths again?"

"I swore I would spit in the face of my father's killer!" She rocked back as she spoke, hocked her best and spat, a coughing fit robbing her projectile of its force and sending the gob of saliva to the ground at Kholster's feet. Eyes wet, she began to try again, gums moving up and down as she attempted to conjure more ammunition.

"Here." Kholster knelt on the ground in front of her. "Try it now."

Face turning red with frustration the woman worked her jaws, but nothing came.

Only subconsciously aware before, the crowd grew curious, acknowledgment of what was taking place spreading through the market. One man in a gray tunic and breeches let loose a braying laugh, which Kholster cut off with a shout of "Mock this and die." No one else laughed.

"Get her some water," Kholster called over his shoulder, never taking his eyes from Iella's. Rae'en looked to see who would do what her father asked, starting when she saw Teru staring at her expectantly.

Rae'en fumbled for the canteen in her saddlebag.

"From the shop, Rae'en," Kholster corrected.

"Sir," Rae'en jogged briskly to apothecary, hushing Caius as the motion stirred him to petulant half-wakefulness.

Fear, the stink of it, hit Rae'en as she reached the door, but the woman in the shop met her two steps from the door with a clay cup of what smelled like tea. Taking the cup from the woman's trembling hands, Rae'en stammered, "I can pay you?"

"No," the woman said with the briefest of head shakes. Her eyes darted to the woman. Don't let him hurt her, those eyes begged.

"Thanks," was the only answer Rae'en had to give.

How on Barrone should I know what he's going to do? she thought to Kazan.

Struggling against Caius's flailing, Rae'en managed to get the cup to the woman with only a drop or two sloshed over the rim.

"Here." Rae'en held it out. "I think it's tea. The lady in the shop."

"Myra," the old woman snapped.

"Myra, then," Rae'en said. "She sent it out for you."

Only mildly defeated, Iella took the tea and sipped at it hesitantly, shaking so hard Rae'en feared the cup would break if the woman's fingers didn't give way first.

Somewhere in the bazaar, a donkey brayed. Wind snapped the ribbons overhead once more with sails filled by a wind that, again, died as soon as it had begun.

"Get her something to sit on."

Rae'en looked back at the shop, but a nearby rug merchant was already holding out his stool. Rae'en ran over to him, gratefully took the stool, and ran back, cooing to Caius with some success as he woke up the rest of the way but remaining quietly curious, not in a tantrum as Rae'en had worried he might.

Rae'en reached out to steady Iella as she sat but drew back her hand at a subtle shake of Kholster's head.

"You're his?" the aged woman squeaked as she settled in a series of painful near-collapses onto the stool.

"Yes."

"You know what he is?"

"He is Kholster, First of One Hundred, First Forged of the Aern, First Armored. He is my father and my kholster."

"You're proud of him."

Rae'en nodded even though it wasn't a question.

"If there is any justice in this world, one of you will have to watch the other die."

"You made an oath," Kholster prompted.

Iella jumped as if she'd sat down next to a deadly serpent and forgotten, only to be reminded by its hiss. She seemed to forget Rae'en's presence the moment she locked eyes with Kholster. Dropping her empty cup to the ground, she placed one hand on each of Kholster's shoulders. Rae'en wondered if she even noticed the way Kholster caught the cup and set it gently down safe and unbroken.

This time, the old crone didn't miss. Her spittle struck Kholster full in the face, a gob of it dripping down his forehead and into his unblinking eye.

Rae'en had seen the looks of triumph on the faces of the Elevens she'd kholstered in their first battle, the exultation in M'jynn's smile when his soul-bonded weapon was completed, and the pride in her own father's eyes both when she'd explained how she wanted to forge Testament and when it had worked. Rae'en had never seen anything like the look in Iella's watering eyes.

"There," Kholster said as the spittle continued down his face, dripping from his upper lip to the lip below, "do you have it in your mind? Is it locked there so you can never forget the fulfillment of your hundred-year oath?"

Iella nodded, suddenly uncertain. "Why did you kill him?" she choked. "My father. Why?"

"Because," Kholster said as he stood, making sure to give her time to shift her grip to the stool, "I am a monster."

"Will you kill me now?" She looked small and frail in his shadow, as if, oath fulfilled, she was diminished, an old wine skin into which no new wine would ever be poured lest it burst.

Giving her his back, Kholster headed toward the opposite side of the street, the crowd parting for him as he walked.

"Why?" The voice, now tired and trembling.

"Who can know why monsters do what they do?"

Rae'en kept watching to see when her father would wipe the spit from his face, but it dried there, untouched by all save gravity and the weather.

CHAPTER 32
NO SIGN OF THE ZAUR

King's Watch was as quiet as North Guard had been. Farther west along the coastline, situated near the tip of a small peninsula, the tower of King's Watch provided an excellent outpost from which the Eldrennai kept an eye on the Holsvenians to the northwest. The only substantive differences between the two watch posts in Wylant's eyes were the view and the cuisine.

Seated alone at a small table on the balcony outside the office's quarters, Wylant looked down at the brilliant blue shell of the broiled Nar Lobster on her plate and sighed.

"Sir?" Kam, the youngest member of her Lance, stepped out onto the balcony after a curt knock and paled when he saw the dead crustacean on her plate. "Great Aldo, is that . . . I mean . . . I've never seen you . . ."

"Eat meat?" She took a forkful of the tender flesh and teased it free of the shell, dipped it in drawn butter, and put it in her mouth. It tasted wonderful, but her appetite was still off. *Too much* jallek *root.*

"What do you think I crumbled up into your stew when that broken hand wasn't healing last moon?"

"That?" He pointed at the lobster.

"No, but it was meat."

"General!" His eyes widened.

"The only reason we stopped eating meat to begin with was so we'd have plenty to feed the Aern, Kam."

She took another bite. Not eating it would offend the tower's old caretaker, Hakkin. For a human, he had served long and well. *For a human, Wylant?* She chided herself as she caught the casual racism in her thoughts.

His post was always in good repair, his journals always well organized and up to date. His performance was exemplary regardless of race, and she knew that. So why had she qualified her appraisal? She didn't really know, and the pang of guilt she felt at that lack of self-knowledge drove her to keep her seat and continue eating.

Hakkin always remembered her eating habits and had something wonderful for her to eat. She couldn't shame him by turning her nose up at food just because worry was turning her stomach in knots and the continual use of *jallek* root left a constant bitter aftertaste in her mouth.

The food was excellent and it was a delicacy and she was going to eat it, by the gods. *Well, no, not by the gods*, she thought. *Never by the gods.*

"The Vaelsilyn," Kam began. *He is such an infant*, Wylant thought. Barely seventy and still so new to the service Wylant felt sure he'd snap to attention in his sleep if she walked past his billet in the middle of the night.

"Vael," Wylant corrected. "You even met one, Kam. Remember Malli?"

"Yes. Of course. Sorry, sir." Kam flushed at that. Yes. He would never forget his first Vael sighting. At his shoulder, the batwinged storm cloud that was his elemental familiar darkened as well, reflecting its master's emotions, if imperfectly. "The Vael representative has arrived safely in Port Ammond."

He held out a crystal. "A courier sent this."

"Activate it," she said around another mouthful.

She felt Kam touch the elements, wending a delicate combination of air magic into the blue crystal. An image in rich colors sprang to life, revealing Yavi, full grown in the thirteen years since Wylant had seen her, the Vael who, if it were at all possible, would wind up keeping the uneasy peace between the Aern and the Eldrennai and, given the yellow tint of her hair, the subtle curve of her mouth, and the narrowness of hip Wylant knew Kholster found so appealing . . . stood a fair chance of sharing her husband's bed. *Ex-husband*, she reminded herself.

"What do you think?" she asked Kam.

"Sir?"

"The Vael," Wylant pushed, "what do you think of her."

"She's quite shapely?"

"And is that what's important?"

"Sir?"

"Her physical attractiveness." It was almost cruel to make the young Lancer feel so trapped, but Kam had potential and Wylant wanted him to show her how much. "Is that the key to her success at Oot?"

"Oh, I see." Kam's eyebrows arched as he considered the Vael more closely. "No. That she's female is important, because her scent will have a calming effect on a male Aern, which will help her keep Kholster calm in the presence of the lackluster wit King Grivek is sending to represent the Eldrennai, but that alone . . ."

"It will help, but don't expect an Aern to be overpowered by the scent of some Flower Girl." Wylant winced at her own use of the racial slur, but she bulled on. "Even one as pretty as this one. It will help, but what else?"

Another burst of energy flowed from Kam as he enhanced the image, allowing it to grow to full size. "An unscored dental ridge," he tapped the image, "shows no desire to appease the Eldrennai with her appearance. A well-used and maintained heartbow slung over her shoulder. The Vael is obviously capable of taking care of herself in a fight. And there's something in her eyes. They are pretty, and compassionate, but also . . . clever."

"And?"

"I would think all those things would be important."

"You'd be correct."

"General?"

"Yes, Kam?"

"Permission to speak freely?"

"Of course."

"She looks a great deal like . . . you?"

Wylant's laugh was a rough bark. "That's not why I picked her out, but Kholster has a . . . a few specific types. She and I are one of those."

"You always pick them out?"

"No . . ." *Just when your prince has doomed his people.* She trailed off, took a sip of wine and started over. "In the past I've rejected two representatives and sent them back. One male and one female. He was too gentle, too doe-eyed. The other was a pretty enough girl, but she was vapid. She'd have run off with Kholster at the drop of a hat and agreed to anything he wanted, including your destruction."

"So . . . you've been sizing them up, doing a strategic assessment." Kam seemed impressed. "This isn't—"

"Some strange jealous ex-wife control issue?" she interrupted. "No, it isn't."

Wylant breathed a shallow sigh. Kam had good instincts. If Kholster didn't kill him, she might even be able to train him to lead a squad in another decade or so.

Wylant stood up.

"Tell the Lance to mount up," she said. *If I'm going to look as if I've taken leave of my senses*, she thought, *might as well drool on my tunic and foul my breeches, too.* "We're riding to Albren Pass. Now."

*

Wylant reined in her horse. The Sidearms reined in as well, the hoofbeats of their horses muffled by horseshoes the elderly mage Sargus had prepared using some sort of Artificer magic with which Wylant was wholly unfamiliar.

"If it helps," Sargus had said, having tried and failed to explain the intricacies of the Artifact Creation to her, "I don't understand your elemancy either."

And—in a way—it had helped. That hunchbacked mage might be Uled's get, but thank Aldo for the acolyte whose blood spared Sargus his father's madness.

Wylant removed her helmet and sniffed the chill air, hesitantly at first, then with increasing urgency, like a hound on the scent of its prey. Light from the noonday sun glared off her shaven head where the bone-steel studs in her ears (a wedding gift from Zhan) caught the light but did not flash in its gaze.

From their vantage point atop Hunter's Hill, Wylant expected to see the hustle and bustle of the watch city below. Instead, a massive oblong chasm yawned where the watchtower had once been, the city itself lay ruined at the bottom, and the only sound was that of the waves crashing against the cliffs beyond. A foul stench issued forth from the depths of the oblong trench, heavy and reptilian. Wylant sneezed, and her horse tossed its head but did not whinny.

Now I wish I'd been wrong about all of this, Wylant thought.

Peering into the hole from this distance revealed almost no detail, but the lack of bodies disturbed her. Wylant grunted softly. *We have to go in.*

"Sir," Kam asked in hushed tones. "Where is the town?"

"The Zaur tunneled under and collapsed it," Wylant replied, patting her horse's withers absently. "Can't you smell them?"

She drummed her gauntleted fingers on her saddle horn while she thought. "Ride back and report this to the king. Show yourself to no one. Even if you see someone in need of aid, ignore them. It could be a trap." Wylant raised a hand to her forehead. She couldn't help but feel that she was forgetting something. "If you are compromised, send up green lightning, as long a burst as you can, straight into the air. Go."

Kam gave a quick salute then galloped back along the way they'd ridden. *Good soldier*, Wylant thought. She watched him go and waited for a hundred count, scanning the horizon. Quiet, but not deathly so, the land lied to her and she resented it. The birds still twittered merrily, and farther away an irkanth yowled. *It can smell them, too.*

"A clan raid wouldn't have been this organized. It's a warlord," she whispered to herself, "but of which clan?" Wylant scratched at the slight point of her ear.

"Gzimoch Clan has dug ambush pits before," Mazik said, his voice unearthly and metallic, "but nothing this big."

"Xira Clan hired a mage to cast illusions for them once," Hira said peering down into the destruction; the red crystal where his elemental focus had replaced his left eye caught the light, reminding Wylant of a warsuit. "But," he said after a moment's study, "this is no illusion."

Roc dismounted, the wind tussling his curly hair as his bare metal feet settled onto the ground. "This," he said, wriggling his toes, "feels like a big tunnel. Really big. So long I can't feel the end of it. This is bad."

"I agree." Wylant trusted her instincts, and her gut told her that this was what Dienox had been hiding from her. Now that he was done toying with her senses, it was time to see how bad it was. She cursed the god of war under her breath.

"Sir?" asked Hira.

Wylant raised an eyebrow in his direction.

"Did you say something, sir? I thought . . ."

Wylant put her helmet back on and looked at her Sidearms. "We're going into that trench, Lancers, and then we're going into the Zaur tunnel that must be down there. We're going to find out where it goes, what it's hiding, and we are going to report back to the king in time for the army to respond to it." She drew Vax, currently a double-edged sword, utilitarian and nondescript except for an uneven blue tint to the steel.

Her soldiers were worried; Wylant could feel it. It had been too long since many of them had seen real action, and Frip and Frindo—only a hundred years or so older than Kam—had only fought in skirmishes against a few odd human raiders. Going into a Zaur tunnel, they knew they might not come out alive.

Isn't that always the way of it, though? Wylant held Vax overhead and willed it to change. The blade caught the sun, elongating into a heavy lance. Wylant pulled at her reins as the king's Lancers stared at Vax, Roc struggling to remount as quickly as possible.

Hira and Griv frowned at the weapon, making Wylant wonder what they, with their artifact eyes, saw when they looked at him.

"You know me; I am not one for speeches." Her voice was flat, sword-edged. "Success or death." She met their gazes, each in turn, and willed them to be the brave, strong knights she had trained them to be. "I've taught you everything I could. If you die, don't come whining to me about it." That drew a grim chuckle from them. They were good soldiers. "Now ride!"

As one they charged down Hunter's Hill toward the massive hole, raising a cloud of dust in their wake. There was no longer a need for stealth. The Zaur would feel the vibrations of eleven riders long before they heard them, even with Sargus's magical horseshoes.

The edge of the pit loomed before them, and they rushed past it without pause. At Wylant's signal she, Mazik, and Ponnod called on the element of air, hardening it beneath the hooves of their horses. Each mount accepted this without surprise. Roc's mount rode a few inches below the others, but Wylant chalked that up to being an Aeromancer short in Kam's absence . . . and Roc's geomancy talent was strong enough that it seemed the ground didn't like him to be too far from it.

The knights rode along a gently descending arc. Much of the rubble from the town had been pressed deep into the sides and bottom of the pit, giving it an almost intentional-seeming tiled appearance. Broad trenches curved along the pit's floor in what might have been a sinuous pattern. Near the bottom on the southeastern wall was a tunnel tall enough for three soldiers to stand on each other's shoulders and wide enough for her knights to ride four abreast. Remains of the watch town littered the base of the massive pit, but there were no signs of the Eldrennai and human townfolk who had lived there.

A sneezing fit came over Wylant, and her eyes began to water. She came to a stop near the fragmented base of the town's ruined central tower, pulled off her gauntlet, and reached into her saddlebag for a pouch of *jallek* root. She bit off a piece of the bitter black medicine and let it rest under her tongue. Wylant returned the pouch to her saddlebag, slid her gauntlet back on, and waited for the herb to take effect, angrily fighting back sneezes.

As soon as she could speak properly again, Wylant addressed her Lance, "Reminders. The Zaur may be resistant to your magic, but their surroundings aren't. Don't hit a Zaur with ice, hit the ground at its feet. Use magic to control the battlefield, to mold it to your advantage. Don't think about what you can't do. Concentrate on what you can do."

"*Ikai*," Wylant urged her horse slowly forward into the tunnel. Zaur stench, which had been bearable in the pit, grew stronger beneath the ground, forcing her knights to struggle against nausea. Even Wylant had never experienced such a strong concentration of the reptilian musk.

"Mazik." Wylant mimed waving away an odor.

Behind her, the knight chanted an incantation and made fluid gestures in the air. The stink lessened, replaced somewhat by the smell of the royal gardens.

"Good job, Mazik," heckled Roc. "Now it smells like lizards and roses."

"I'd like to see you do better, Lieutenant," Mazik growled. "Not all of us can be as humble as you and ride the air a few inches low . . . out of respect."

"That's enough," Wylant ordered, glad they couldn't see the look of amusement beneath her helm. She gave another command and each of her Lancers summoned a magic lantern, little wisps of flame hovering above them in the dark of the tunnel to light their way.

At her signal, they rode forward in search of Zaur. *If all goes well, we'll get a look at part of the Zaur force, kill a few, take their measure, and then make it out alive. If not . . .*

PART THREE
CALL TO WAR

"The Vaelsilyn, or Vael, as they now prefer, were created as little more than a breeding aid in my father's eyes. He used the Royal Hedge Rose as a base partially because those were at hand and also because he noticed that Aern universally appeared to enjoy the odor of those hardy orange blooms. No examples of the altered Vaelsilyn Rose Bush exist. According to the official records in the royal archive, this is due to the draining effect of producing Vael infants. Each plant bloomed only once, producing an average of eight viable offspring before wilting.

"Uled's private notes tell a different story. Each successive generation of blooms produced a proportionately larger number of Vael with the potential for what my grandfather called 'prodigious and alarming spiritual abilities.' By the fourth generation, the Vaelsilyn Rose ceased blooming at all, the leaves turning blue and the root structure altering to resemble a large tree rather than a bush.

"Alarmed by the transformed plant's similarity to the notorious Genna Tree, Uled states that he began poisoning the bushes after their first yield, not wishing to repeat something he described as his 'reptilian error.'"

An excerpt from *The Bloom of Life—A Study of the Vael* by Sargus

CHAPTER 33
BLOOD-RED MOON

Under a blood-red moon, the four Overwatches moved at a fast jog, their boots slapping like pounding hammers beating out a steady rhythm on the stone of the Guild Commerce Highway. Summer was fading fast, and each of the four young Aern had fun trying to render the mental map they held in their minds between them with the most accurate details. Rae'en might never notice the difference, but Kazan had taken the detail of the map Malmung had shown them as a challenge.

Rae'en? Kazan sent out. He'd expected to get back within range faster than this.

Any of you able to reach her yet? Joose thought. Three tokens, one representing each of the other three Overwatches, went gray, a visual "No" they'd learned early on but had started using again after one of Kholster Malmung's Overwatches, Lena, had reintroduced the topic.

"A kholster needs to be able to pay attention to what his own senses are telling him, too." Lena had explained. "Malmung doesn't mind a little conversation, but the reason he doesn't send his auditory input, the reason Kholster doesn't typically share his, is sound can be more confusing than visual information.

"A kholster or a soldier can have a map in the corner of her vision and know it isn't really there. It might cost them a small portion of their field of vision, but it expands their overall knowledge."

"Put phantom sounds in their ears," Joose had spoken up, "and you just confuse them."

"Or endanger them." Lena had granted Joose one of her rare smiles, revealing an upper canine only partially regrown next to its neighbor. "A twig snap heard on your end could make them turn the wrong way and react to it unnecessarily, or if you're close enough to hear it, too, they might react in the wrong direction or hear it from both sides and not know how to respond."

Don't you think we should have been back in range by now? Joose thought.

Three gold tokens flashed on the map.

Lena told me we might have to get closer to reacquire full contact than we were when we lost it, M'jynn thought.

When were you spending time alone with Lena? Arbokk asked.

Hey, the mating age is twenty-one, M'jynn thought back.

What does that have to do with Lena teaching you how to knit? Kazan thought. *Because that's what she told me you two were doing. She even showed me some of your work.*

She did?

I am your Prime Overwatch and, in your kholster's absence . . .

Kholster Rae'en, M'jynn thought as loud as he could, including the others in his broadcast, *can you hear me yet?!*

I think she's already in the Guild Cities, Kazan laughed. *Maybe when we hit the halfway mark.*

Are we there yet? M'jynn joked.

*

"No," Lieutenant Kreej hissed at his human charge, "we are not there yet." Sibilance bounced echoes of the susurrant statement around the stone tunnels through which the two traveled. With the added clack of his fore and hind claws on the stone and the scrape as they gripped the subtle concentric rings which ran the length of the underground passage, Kreej hoped the human would be cowed.

Maybe if he took the human's lantern away . . .

"How can you tell?" Randall Tyree gestured at the walls with the offending lantern, casting shadows down the passage and elongating Kreej's hunched shadow into a distorted shape Kreej hoped the human would find frightening. "It all looks the same."

Kreej's gray tongue flicked out, tasting the air as he ran along the passageway on all fours. No fear in the air. No hint of even a cold sweat. "I know."

It was, perhaps, not strictly within the scope of his orders to try to scare the human, but something about the creature was so off-putting. At first Kreej had liked the human, but after the first day . . . it was as if Tyree was hiding something. The human understood things it shouldn't, and that made Kreej want to put it off-balance.

Realizing he'd padded too far ahead, Kreej paused (again) to wait for the human and his slow two-legged gait. Kreej took advantage of the free semi-private moment to express the musk glands near the base of his tail along the floor of the tunnel. He didn't know how it would help anyone (where was a Zaur going to get lost in a well-marked tunnel system like this?), but it was standard procedure, so he did as he was expected and added his scent to that of the hundreds of Zaur who had traversed the tunnel ahead of him.

Would anyone know if he failed to follow procedure? He couldn't imagine Warlord Xastix or General Tsan checking either, but he'd seen plenty of unexpected weather on this assignment. And where had that train of thought come from? Who cared if procedure made sense or not? Kreej just cared about the opportunity for another name . . . a name he would choose for himself.

"Can you tell me where we are going yet?" Tyree said as his lantern picked out Kreej's procumbent form.

"It would be meaningless to you." Eyes canted up so they would flash in the lantern light. Kreej growled when the human smiled in return.

"Come on, Dimples." Tyree breathed heavily as he caught up with Kreej and then jogged past the Zaur. "We'll never get to wherever we're going with you dragging your butt."

"I was merely expressing my musk," Kreej snapped.

"Oh," Tyree coughed. "There's no 'merely' about your musk. I'm sure it's quite the hit with all the girls."

"Thank you."

"Anytime." Tyree laughed again, but Kreej could not tell why.

"Dryga." Kreej said after the human stopped to rest some hours later. Why the human insisted on unloading its pack, laying out soft cloth and padding on the floor, and activating the second (and smaller) of the two Dwarven lanterns he carried with him was a mystery to Kreej. It was all so unnecessary.

"What is Dryga?" Tyree asked as he stripped out of one perfectly good cloth covering and into another. Kreej looked down at the ground and contemplated breaking the smallest of the two lanterns. He had no intention of telling the human about Captain Dryga, wasn't certain why he'd said the captain's name at all.

"There's a Captain Dryga, isn't there?" Tyree smiled, the light catching in his pellucid eyes. How did the human keep such white teeth? "You can tell me. I'm supposed to be your ward and ally—a friend of the Zaur . . . right?"

"You are to advise him at the forward base." Kreej's head began to ache.

"How far forward?" Tyree shook his canteen. It was old and battered but also obviously of Dwarven make. "This canteen Uncle Japesh left me may keep the water situation under control, but I'm going to run out of food if we don't restock somewhere. I'm not a bad hunter, nor a good one either, but I can't hunt where there isn't any game."

"Another day until we reach a supply store and a guard station."

"More bug rations." Tyree's veneer of unflappability dimmed then brightened again. "That will be the fifth one. I may be a little off, but that means, unless you've suddenly started doing things differently, that we've covered around two hundred and forty miles. We've passed completely beyond the Eldren Plains haven't we?"

"No," Kreej lied.

"How did you manage that without the Eldrennai catching you out?"

"We work toward His secret purpose," Kreej hissed, rising up on his hind legs, tapping his chest with his foreclaws. "The scarbacks would have found us as they have in the past, but the scarbacks are gone. The Eldrennai cannot stand against the chosen of Secret and Shadow."

"Calm down." Captain Tyree held his arms wide. "I'm on your side, remember? To His secret purpose, Musky. Remember? Who got you guys the information you wanted? Who is going to advise Captain Dryga?"

"You did." Kreej dropped to all fours, clawing angrily at the back of his scales. "To His secret purpose."

Tyree smiled again, and Kreej felt simultaneously soothed and alarmed. Something was wrong with this ally, and Kreej did not like one scale of it.

*

I don't like this, Kholster thought at Vander.

Walking through the gates of this Guild City twisted an uncomfortable knot in Kholster's stomach. He'd never walked its tree-lined streets, but the looks in the eyes of the people working and training here unsettled him. They watched him with, for the most part, the same gaze some Elevens did. Unable to meet his gaze but unable to stop staring when his gaze moved past them. He saw awe and worship in their faces as they paused in their training on the various grounds and tiered buildings. . . . Some practicing archery, others with melee weapons or unarmed techniques.

The students and instructors at the open-air schools of Warfare crowded at the fences edging their practice areas. Indoor schools found the windows and doors thrown open as the occupants of those buildings leaned out of windows, over balcony railings, or filed out the doors to crowd the edges of the street.

Walking at an even pace toward the hexagonal building he did not want to enter, Kholster frowned, the facial expression generating scattered cheers and hoots of approval. He caught himself wishing that Teru were still with them carrying Cadence or that the conversation with Dean Sedric, at the Long Speaker's College, had taken longer and given him a better excuse for moving on without acceding to the Guild Masters' request for an audience.

"Your word is unimpeachable, Kholster," the sour-faced human had said. "If you say this drug-addled creature has promise then I will train her myself. We will get her off the god rock. And, as I have not yet awarded the Dean's Scholarship for the coming term, she will receive it." He'd waved away all protest. "I have awarded it in previous years for deeds less noteworthy than having impressed the being who conquered my order only to help rebuild, restore, and then relinquish control of it."

Kholster would have even found arguing with the Patron or Matron of the Harvester's Temple preferable to this "audience," but Torgrimm's followers helped anyone or anything which bore a soul, just as he'd known they would. They'd cooed over the child so much even Rae'en had no second thoughts about surrendering him to their care.

I feel like we're walking into an ambush, Kholster thought as the building loomed larger. An arena dedicated to Shidarva was one thing, but one dedicated to Dienox, fighting for fighting's sake. . . . How did the humans, with such short lives, justify this waste?

Even from this distance, Kholster could pick out the statues of Dienox (with flaming hair worked in bronze even though Nomi had long ago stolen those fiery tresses from the actual deity) wielding different weapons of war. Four stories high and granite, the thing made Kholster want to tear it apart, to leave no stone upon another, as he had done so long ago with the arena the Oathbreakers had built at the site of the Battle of As You Please.

"Can we?" Rae'en asked, reaching back for her warpick. "You know?" She nearly shook with pride at the adulation of the crowd.

The Guild Masters want you to meet them in Warfare at Dienox's Grand Arena? Whatever could seem suspect about that? Vander practically chortled.

"You want to brandish our weapons?" Kholster asked Rae'en while sending *Sarcasm does not become you* to Vander.

Sure it does, Vander thought back. *What doesn't become me is this weather.*

"Kholster?" Rae'en asked.

"If you want." Kholster unslung his warpick and, on Rae'en's signal, thrust it into the air above his head. What had been scattered applause and cheering broke into a torrent of sound.

Even Captain Pallos sported a wide grin.

"They love us!" Rae'en almost sparkled, doubled canines bared in as broad a grin as Kholster had ever seen on her face.

"The idea of us, perhaps." Kholster frowned at the Lane of Champions where twin wedges of polished obsidian stood, one on either side of the Champion's Entrance to the arena—immense iron doors through which only those acknowledged as Champions of the Arena could enter, lest they be honor-bound to compete in an exhibition bout . . . or worse . . . depending on the mood of the Guild Masters. To Vander, he sent *Weather?*

Sky is clear and the wind is fair, but the swells are getting higher and higher. Coal says he smells a hurricane.

Where are you exactly? Peering at the mental map generated by the Overwatches with the invasion fleet, Kholster growled, *Too small*, and let the map take up more of his field of vision, with enough of his surroundings still showing at the bottom that he could see to walk. He traced the fleet's course, from the Dwarven-Aernese Collective to Veynir, the most Aernese-friendly of the Nallish ports, then across the Queelayan Ocean to Kankt on Gromm's southern peninsula, where his Aern would have eaten their fill and taken on new supplies. Vander noted five of the Long Arms manning the *Dragon's Perch* had swapped out there, which Kholster didn't like, but which was in keeping with the contracts he'd taken out with the Long Speakers. Apparently being so close to a dragon for so long was alarming for humans.

Due to the delay caused by his own slower than expected pace, Vander had then cut back and sheltered at the Altan Islands, all that remained of the land once holy to Shidarva which had been sacrificed in Shidarva's bid to become ruler of the gods. In fair weather, the islands were a boon to sailors, but during the rainy season the islands had a tendency to flood so much they became almost completely submerged.

Before the small continent had broken up and sunk beneath the waves, the storm route had taken bad weather mostly into the Gromman side of the waters, but now . . . it could land anywhere . . . it could chase his fleet right to the Strait of Mioden and—

Isn't it a little early for hurricanes?

Yes. Not unheard of, though. Vander laughed bitterly. *Coal said we should wake him when we could see the storm wall, so he could take wing.*

You could make for Gromm or Castleguard. Kholster didn't like the idea of revealing his intention to invade before the initial attack, but he didn't want to have to send the Ossuarian warsuits marching underwater to retrieve the bones of his army either. Sure, the warsuits could breathe for the Armored Aern, and they were technically immortal; and even if something truly disastrous happened the warsuits could haul the bodies up to Gromm, bring the warsuits, all of them, buy enough cattle to fill the armor with blood, and allow the army to regenerate, but . . . what if too much had changed? Would the Aern be able to reunite with their warsuits after all this time, even under those circumstances? Besides, they'd likely lose his brother-in-law, the humans with them, and possibly even their dragon in the process. It wasn't a good solution.

And have the Eldrennai get word of sixty Aernese ships hauling a dragon with them? Vander sent, interrupting his thoughts. *I think if we push on, make for the Strait of Mioden, we can use the weather to our advantage and pass through hidden by the storm.*

Storm might turn north and hit Gromm, Kholster admitted. *Or go south and hit Castleguard or even Bridgeland.*

Right, Vander thought back. *It's not as if the gods have sent the storm to chase us. They're never done something like THAT before.*

Point taken. I was there, too. Show me the—

Do you mean to be fighting in the arena? Vander interrupted. *If not . . . No, never mind. You're through.*

"Through what?" Banishing the sea map, Kholster looked around to find himself standing in the midst of the Champion's Gate with Rae'en smiling, surrounded by a group of men and women in the various robes of their chosen guilds. He smelled saltwater and fish under a layer of blood and sweat.

A curse lay ready to deploy at the tip of his tongue, but it wasn't worth it. Cursing would let Rae'en know how disappointed he was that she'd led him into an arena fight when any blame ought to lay firmly with him. *He'd* allowed himself to be so distracted by the fleet's issues *he'd* missed what was right in front of him. *He'd* also forgotten how much youth could crave a battle.

But all of that was in the past. It could not be altered. So instead of growling at Rae'en or continuing to berate himself, Kholster bared his teeth.

"You wanted to see Aern fight?" He held out his arms and turned in a slow circle. "Here we are. What's it going to be?"

CHAPTER 34
BATTLE BEGINS

"Take this." Kholster held out his warpick, the sun highlighting the blood oak detail work on the weapon's head. The crowd, too far away to hear her father's voice, erupted into a cheer. Rae'en took one final look around the stadium, the tiers of people. What looked like thousands, tens of thousands, of boisterous blood-hungry humans, gnomes, Dwarves, and even a manitou or three, cheered, howled, and hooted from the stands. The manitou in particular stole her attention, bestial-looking shape-shifters each in a chimerical combination of animal parts, united to create truly unique and ever-changing forms.

"Were they all here just in case we said yes?" Rae'en dumbly took her father's warpick.

"No." Kholster scanned the crowd looking for Bone Finders. He spotted three but felt certain he'd missed one. They couldn't give him a battle map, like Overwatches, but as these particular Bone Finders were Armored, they could still relay him information via Bloodmane. "They have bouts daily. The single largest peacetime source of income for Warfare."

He sent Malmung an image of Rae'en's four Overwatches and got a map in response, showing them nearing Juchim.

Not quite halfway then. No use.

You could take Draekar's Overwatches, Vander thought at him.

No, Kholster frowned. *They're on duty. We should be fine.*

"Give me Testament," Kholster prompted.

"I fight better with Testament." Looking down, Rae'en balked at the feeling of Grudge in her hands again.

"True, but I smell seawater."

"What?"

"Your warpick," Kholster hissed through a smile.

"Fine," Rae'en shouted. "Gods!" Warpick unslung, she more threw than handed him the weapon.

It's going to be okay. Kholster's voice rang out in her head. He smiled at the crowd. *Clear your head and catch the scent of what is happening here.*

What IS happening here?

You volunteered us, didn't you?

Yes, but you're acting like this is more than a fight.

This is a campaign on multiple fronts. Normally they don't try to kill me until I'm in Bridgeland.

Kill you?

Yes.

Who?

Anyone who wants to prevent the Conjunction from taking place.

Who would want that?

Anyone who wants the Aern destroyed.

What?

Well, I often set out on day three hundred of a Conjunction Year and spend a few months with the Vael in The Parliament of Ages before going on to Oot. In preparation, the Vael send their representative on to Port Ammond and allow them to spend time with the Eldrennai. I don't know why the Oathbreakers think it necessary, but I don't meet the Vael representative until I see her at Oot on three hundred and ninety-seven. The Conjunction begins, and on day one of the next year, I leave Oot.

Rae'en did a little mental math. *It's already three hundred and seventy-two!*

Twenty-five days is still enough time to make the trip, but we'll have to be faster now. Your tour of Castleguard will wait until after the Conjunction, perhaps after the war. I still want you to see the Changing of the Gods on our way through, but—

A drum beat began from somewhere up toward the middle of the seats. Kholster spotted the drummers, pounding the hide-covered instruments with huge padded mallets, beating out a rhythm—a phrase in Zaurtol, the tail language of the reptilian Zaur—he hadn't heard in years.

Many thought it meant simply "Bloodmane," but it was actually a sentence: "Bloodmane is coming" or more literally "Red Irkanth Hunts."

"I wonder where they learned that?"

"Does it mean something?"

"To the Zaur," Kholster said, nodding, "it means me."

"How can a drum beat mean anything?"

"Ask the Zaur." All humor left Kholster's face as their opponents walked out into the staging area of the arena. Ten opponents. One for each month of the year. "We're fighting the past year's worth of champions."

"That's not so bad, right?" Rae'en looked back at him seeking something. Approval? Reassurance? Kholster couldn't tell, so he grabbed her arm to steady her as the ground began to shift underneath them.

"I knew I smelled saltwater."

More cheers rose up from the crowd as the floor receded in six equal plates, sliding under the stands, leaving nothing upon which the combatants could stand except for a central platform roughly five paces across where the floor plates had met and a series of six beams running from the edge of the arena to the central platform—each no wider than a handsbreadth. Kholster growled, already in motion.

*

Following Kholster's lead, Rae'en leapt from the edge of the rapidly shrinking platform onto the scant beam. She overbalanced herself, landing too low, not used to acrobatics, while holding Grudge in her hands. Blowing out a tense blast of breath, she hooked Grudge under the lip of the beam behind her back to keep herself from going into the water.

Rae'en saw the creatures before the gasp of the crowd announced them, feeling no matching sense of exhilaration.

I thought this wasn't a fight to the death, Kholster.

Perched on all fours next to her on the beam, Kholster pivoted and stood, arms extended for balance, feet toe to heel with one another. *One is encouraged not to fall in.*

Sleek black figures moved beneath the water, stripes of neon blue pulsing in circles highlighting their dead eyes and racing back along their spines and along their sharp fins.

What are they? Rae'en regained her balance, winding up facing away from the platform, toward the outside edge of the ring.

Sharks of some kind. Her father was engaged in a race for the middle platform with three of the more agile opponents: a gnome wielding curved daggers and no appreciable armor, a man with a length of weighted chain wrapped around his shoulders and upper arms, and a woman with noticeably pointed ears and features which suggested at least partial Eldrennai heritage or a slightly crystal-twisted birth carrying a quarterstaff.

What kind of shark glows? Rae'en followed after, close, but not too close.

I'm not sure. They taste the same. The woman with the quarterstaff broke into a run, and Kholster burst into a sprint. *See the lip around the edge of the arena?*

Yes. Rae'en answered.

Make for it. Circle them. Don't fall in.

Rae'en broke off and shifted direction awkwardly, bobbing and lurching in short jerks to keep her balance until she had it again. *If I do, I'll get a chance to see what shark tastes like—*

Try not to eat the outer skin.

Out of the corner of her eye, Rae'en saw Kholster meet the woman with the staff on the platform, but instead of engaging directly, the woman played for time, thrusting at Kholster and circling the platform. The ferrules at the end of the staff were a familiar pearlescent color, and Rae'en smirked.

Bone-steel AGAINST an Aern? Stupid.

Kholster twisted too far to one side, leaving an apparent opening, and the woman took it, sweeping the back of his knee with a satisfying crack that garnered surprised oohs from the crowd and scattered cheers and shouts. An even bigger cry went up when the staff wouldn't pull free of her father, the ring of bone-steel sticking to him as firmly as Testament clung to his back.

Why not eat the skin? Rae'en asked, keeping her balance as she moved toward the rim.

*

It has scales like little teeth. Kholster slid the leg to which the quarterstaff was attached back and planted it hard to see if his opponent would fight him for the staff. *I think Glin calls them denticles. Makes the dried skin a good wrap for a hilt, though.*

With a grunt the woman let go. Maybe she felt she'd done her best, or maybe she realized the futility of engaging an Aern who weighed more than forty stone in a tug-of-war. Kholster snatched up the staff in time to start it twirling as the next two opponents, those he mentally dubbed Chains and Daggers, made it onto the platform. Daggers circled left, and Chains circled right, twirling the chain ends in both hands.

Two of the other combatants, a lean, wiry woman with iron paws clenched in either hand, giving her the appearance of possessing metal claws sticking out past her knuckles, and a dour-looking bald human with an axe frogged at his waist, moved along the lip of the ring toward Rae'en.

I've never understood the idea of nonfatal combat with real weapons, Kholster thought at Vander.

I'm told they have a point system. Look for scorekeepers at the cardinal points, each with a Long Arm and a Long Speaker.

How does one score nonfatal points with a pair of iron paws?

Superficial cuts to vital areas. There should be a tent for Torgrimm's medics there somewhere. They'll float the injured out by Long Arm.

What about broken bones?

Frowned upon, but accepted. It'll be a new experience. Those are good, right? Vander thought.

Not always. Kholster growled and darted at Chains, throwing the quarterstaff in a slow spin that easily knocked the woman wielding the iron paws off the rim. She grunted in pain and surprise as she found herself suddenly flailing in saltwater.

*

Wylant brought her horse to a sliding stop, quiet settling across the tunnel.

"General?" Roc asked.

She answered with a palm in his direction, silencing any further inquiries. Above the riders, globes of mystic flame flickered, partially banishing the darkness, a vein of Dienoxin crystal running through the eastern wall, sending off irregular flashes of illumination in response. Wylant and her knights had already traveled farther than she thought likely, and the tunnel had not yet turned north as she expected it might. She grabbed a compass from her pack and frowned before putting it away. Southwest?

"Roc, do you feel that?" Pulling off her helmet, Wylant dismounted and put her ear to the ground. Something big was coming. Something unfamiliar.

Dust fell from the rock above her head, making the horses snort and whinny. Wylant clapped her helm back on and stood waiting on the near side of her mount, one hand firmly on the reins.

"What is it, sir?" Roc called over the rising rumble.

"Something new," Wylant answered softly.

"I can't tell if it's coming from behind or in front of us," Lieutenant Hira called out.

"It may be both." Wylant cursed briefly as she swung up into the saddle. "This is wrong; they aren't fighting like Zaur."

"Should we report back now?" Hira asked hopefully.

No, Wylant thought, *we will try to lure some of them out of the tunnel where we can see them properly first.* She opened her mouth to give a brusque order but found she couldn't. *No, we must fight them here.*

"I have to see them." Wylant shook her head. "I have to cross blades with them before we report back. Otherwise, what kind of intelligence do I have for King Grivek? We got scared in their tunnels and ran away?"

"No!" Her knights looked at her in shocked silence from behind their eye slits. Numbness flushed across her cheeks and back along her gums. *I. What? That's not what I . . .*

Wylant ripped off her helmet and threw it to the ground with a resounding clang. "We are the king's Royal Lancers!" she found herself shouting. "Are we afraid to die for our king?"

"No!" they answered as one.

"Are we afraid to die for our people?"

"No!" they answered once more.

"Lances!" she ordered. Ten mounted knights surged forward.

"Roc. Hira. Mazik. Form up with me." *This is what I trained you for*, she thought with satisfaction as each rider she named smoothly joined her, *even if I don't know exactly why in all the hells it has to go this way.* As the others fell into well-disciplined ranks of four and three behind them, each with his lance couched under his right arm, Wylant felt herself pulled toward battle as surely as if she had been pushed from behind.

*

Kholster accepted the hit he was sure Chains meant for him to dodge, the right-hand chain wrapping around his left arm as he grabbed it left-handed and jerked the human toward him. A quick palm to the chest knocked the wind from Chains—and broke the man's sternum from the sound of it. A second hit to the chest seemed too likely to kill, so Kholster delivered a kick to the stomach instead.

I wonder if that counts for points?

Coughing blood, the man held up his hands, and Kholster let him drop to his knees. As Kholster tugged the chain free, the Long Arms positioned near the scorekeepers at the cardinal points of the arena caught the human and jerkily floated his limp body up, away from the fighting, toward the tent of Torgrimm's medics . . . Kholster could see it located atop the northern rim of the arena. He swung the chain over his head as he dodged another flurry of kicks and punches from the woman.

What are the others doing? he thought at Vander.

The big one with the trident and the one with the broadsword are just standing in the staging area watching. Same for the woman with the trident. Uh . . . hold a moment . . . none of the Bone Finders saw where the other two went.

Kholster barely dodged an attack from the gnome, Daggers, who darted in low and cut at the back of Kholster's knees. Repositioning himself to keep an eye on the two heading for Rae'en as well as the two facing him . . . Kholster gave a quick scan of the ring and didn't see the two missing fighters either.

*

"Charge!" Wylant yelled and snapped the reins.

Her Lance surged down the tunnel, developing a distance between their three ranks. She reined in sharply as twelve eyeless, rock-hided beasts came into view, each bearing a Zaur armored in black metal plates. These were a threat, clearly, but not, Wylant thought, big enough to shake the tunnel. "What in Aldo's name?"

Each beast was shorter than a horse, with broad shoulders; a heavily muscled chest; and hardened protrusions along its shoulders, knees, forehead, and sides. A single long braid of hair trailed from what should have been their chins, but the beasts had no apparent mouths. Each leg ended with six long, thick splayed toes that gripped the floor of the tunnel. Both Eldrennai and Zaur came to a halt, considering their foes.

The leader of the Zaur, every bit as strange to Wylant as the mounts upon which he and his soldiers rode, was larger than his companions. Zigzag patterns of brilliant blue ran luminously through the black scales covering his body. Twin yellow eyes peered at her from beneath thick eye ridges on his wedge-shaped head. He looked right at Wylant, her bald head glinting in the magical light, and saluted before giving an order in harsh Tol.

At his command, the ranks of enemy riders surged forward, spreading up the walls and ceiling into a deadly ring of mounted Zaur wielding Skria, longer versions of the angular Skreel knives. Four ran along the floor and four along the ceiling, with two on each wall.

Thin steel chains ran between the Zaur riders and their mounts, hooking the rider's armor directly into the hard, stony hide. Seeing no reins, Wylant could only guess at how they were controlling the mounts. *Tail slaps, perhaps?*

"How are they doing that?" Roc growled.

Wylant's mind cleared suddenly, as if a fog were lifting from her thoughts. "Ice the ceiling and walls on my command," she ordered.

I've felt like this before, she thought, *just after I forged Vax. Almost as if*. . . but Wylant put the thought aside. There was no time for thought. She had her information; now she needed to live to get it to the king and the High Elementalist.

*

Rae'en fought back a laugh as the woman with the iron paws scrambled frantically for the ledge. The sharks paid her no heed, and Rae'en wondered if it was because she wasn't bleeding. Realizing she couldn't reach the lip and had no way to climb out, the woman shouted something about the water being below regulation depth and demanded to be pulled out by a Long Arm.

She treaded water briefly, waiting, then made for the prep area where there was more of a slant and it looked possible to walk up out of the water.

Axe kept his eyes on his hands, feeling his way along the ledge toward Rae'en, so Rae'en gave him her full attention as well.

It's three touches to beat him, right?

I never paid attention to points when I fought in the Oathbreaker Arena, Kholster thought back. *We fought to the death. This is more civilized.*

*

"Now!" Wylant shouted. Unified pulses of elemental magic filled the air with bitter cold. Ice crawled up the walls of the tunnel ahead of them, each knight covering a different arc with his spell. "It won't hurt the Zaur much, but it might break the ring of wall crawlers."

The four beasts on the ceiling lost their footing simultaneously as they struck the ice. They fell, six-toed feet scrabbling desperately for purchase on the slick surface. Three riders were crushed as they struck the tunnel floor, but the fourth managed to free itself at the last moment, rolling clear of its flailing mount.

On either side of the tunnel, the four wall-riding Zaur succeeded in getting their beasts safely down to the floor, but the creatures came to a stop, refusing to continue forward despite the angry thumping of their riders' tails against their backs.

Ha! It is *the tails.* "They steer with their tails! Chop 'em if you get a chance."

Wylant urged her line of Eldrennai riders forward, and they clashed violently with the oncoming Zaur. The Zaur mounts made no attempt to sidestep the Eldrennai horses, bulling headlong at them. Roc's and Hira's horses managed to avoid a direct collision, but each knight lost his lance, buried deep within the body of a mounted Zaur.

Vax took the leader through the shoulder, shifting into an axe to avoid sticking fast, widening the wound as it tore free moments before Wylant's horse struck the rock-hided Zaur mount. Wylant and Mazik both took hard, bone-splintering hits. The shouts and battle cries of Zaur, Eldrennai, and horses filled the tunnel.

Mazik caught himself with a hastily shouted blast of air, but Wylant struck the tunnel floor hard enough to spot her field of vision with sparks of light and start the cave spinning around her. Mazik placed himself between his general and the Zaur, evading a blow from the dismounted ceiling rider's

Skria. It struck at him from all fours, dashing past on the knight's left, circling back on the right. Mazik instinctively tried to knock the first attack away with a blast of conjured wind, and the Skria slid along his armor, but the second attack caught him along the mail reinforcements behind his left knee. The armor held, but the force of the blow drove him to the floor. Ducking under a blow from the Zaur warrior's tail, Mazik cursed and drew his longsword.

"Caught flat-footed like a novice," he hissed under his breath. He pivoted on his knee, swinging his sword in a swift deadly arc. "It's been so long since the last raid that I'd almost forgotten what it was like," Mazik's blade found purchase in the Zaur's temple as it turned for another pass, "to fight you!" Blood sprayed along the blade as it cut horizontally, catching the top corner of one eye and slicing straight through the middle of the other. The dead Zaur fell to the ground scratching and kicking at random, its tail lashing up and down.

*

Kholster dodged a sweep from the disarmed woman only to find himself open to attack from the gnome with the daggers who'd slid around to his left side. Accepting the glancing hit to his mail, Kholster whipped the chain around, catching the gnome in the throat and then releasing his hold on one side so the chain wrapped around the gnome's neck.

An exultant roar came from the crowd as the gnome went down, daggers forgotten, clutching his throat. Kholster grabbed for the daggers, but too slow. The woman snatched them both up and scampered away from him before he could react. Kholster transferred the name he'd given the gnome to the woman . . . name following the wielder of the weapons. *I'll show her as Daggers now . . .* not that Vander was generating a map in his field of vision upon which a correction would be made . . .

The jab I took, Kholster thought at Vander, *did that count as a point? You'd think they'd have the score posted somewhere.*

*

As Roc and Hira dispatched the floor-rider Mazik had wounded, the four Zaur wall-riders charged in, running back up the walls as they reached an area not covered by the summoned ice and clashing with the second rank of Eldrennai knights: Bakt, Dodan, Frip, and Tomas. The two wall-riding Zaur on one side brought their Skria down at right angles, killing Bakt and his mount in one motion. The wounded Zaur leader caught Dodan in the neck with his Skria, decapitating him. His lifeless body fell from his horse and was trampled by the rock beast. Two of the Zaur mounts with dead riders angled straight for Frip's horse, sending the knight hurtling through the air.

Tomas leveled his lance at the opposing Zaur's mount, striking it in the shoulder and splintering the weapon, then bringing his sword up and across, killing the rider. "Dienox!" he bellowed as the enemy rider's Skria cut halfway through his torso, stuck, and sent him tumbling to floor beneath the feet of the enemy beast.

*

Kholster felt daggers slide along his mail, grunted hard when the woman danced out of reach, but he continued unwrapping the chain from the gnome's neck. He was still breathing, but so shallowly Kholster feared permanent damage if his breath remained restricted. *Why haven't the Long Arms floated him out?*

Tell me when she goes for my back again, Kholster sent to Vander.

I'll try, but there's a little delay . . .

Do what you can do.

Bending over the gnome as if he were checking him for signs of life, Kholster waited for the signal.

*

Blocked, Roc and Hira fought their way through Zaur mounts with dead riders. Four on three, the surviving Zaur charged toward the last rank of Eldrennai knights: Griv, Frindo, and Ponnod. Abruptly, the Zaur leader slowed. He shouted an order, and the three riders dropped their Skria, unlatched themselves, drew their Skreel blades, and leapt from the back of their mounts toward the mounted Eldrennai. One pulled Griv from his horse and landed on the ground atop his prone form. Frindo caught his attacker with the tip of his lance, steering clear of the mount and continuing toward Roc and Hira.

Ponnod's attacker missed his mark and succeeded only in sideswiping Ponnod's mount, severing the harness. The Zaur struck the ground beneath the horse's feet before rolling miraculously clear of the hooves.

*

Now.

Kholster spun, catching Daggers by the right wrist, snapping it, forced the dagger out of her hand and elicited a sharp yelp of pain as he came up twisting the woman's wrist, thumbs against the back of her hands. She doubled over, and he delivered a knee to the stomach for good measure, before following it up with a punch to the temple.

She went down hard. Perhaps too hard.

Kholster was moving in to check her pulse when he heard the splash.

Rae'en's in the water, Vander thought at him.

*

More debris shook free of the roof, raining dust and dirt down on Wylant's bare head. The cacophonous roar of galloping beasts puzzled her. It was growing louder.

Wylant finally caught sight of the thing that had caused the tunnel to shake—a serpent larger than any she had ever seen—as it rounded a bend in the tunnel and bore down on her remaining Lancers. "Great . . ." she slurred, catching herself before swearing by Dienox, "Bloodmane!" The beast tore Frindo from the back of his horse, and Wylant watched as he vanished wordlessly into that tremendous maw.

"Withdraw!" Wylant yelled as clearly as she could manage. "Every knight, take flight; tell the king what you've seen!"

Ponnod's saddle slid sideways off of his horse, and, though the Eldrennai knight caught himself with a spell, the serpent snatched him out of the air.

*

Kholster locked eyes with Axe standing on the lip of the arena close to where Rae'en had been. He saw shock and surprise in Axe's eyes. If the man had been responsible he—

A shark has her, Vander sent. *On Teru's side.*

Where is Teru?!

But then he saw her, clutched in the middle by the shark's maw, trailing blood in the water. Why wasn't she thinking to him? A familiar warpick dropped past her, sinking like a stone.

She'd dropped Grudge.

*

Roc and Hira turned as one, Hira hardening the air beneath the hooves of their mounts with a spell. Passing as far from the remaining Zaur as they could, the two knights galloped down the tunnel, back toward the ruined watch town. "Mazik," Roc shouted, gesturing vaguely toward Frindo's horse. "Grab the general."

"Forget about the general and follow your orders!" Wylant bellowed. The Zaur leader and his one remaining mounted soldier slapped their tails down, urging their mounts down the tunnel after Roc and Hira. Wylant scrambled for Vax, relaxing slightly when the weapon's mottled blue hilt came within her grasp. Mazik helped her to her feet. "I ordered you out of here, Mazik."

*

Do you want Teru to— Vander almost asked.

No, she can get out of there. She needs to stop panicking.

But, Kholster— Vander thought back at him.

Would you jump in to save me?

Kholster watched Rae'en flail. He wanted more than anything to dive into that water, kill the sharks and . . . and it would teach her nothing.

If she is to be First, she must learn to control the panic, he reminded himself.

Rae'en? he thought at her. *Calm down. Kill the shark and eat it.*

*

Mazik stepped forward, parrying a blow from the Skreel knife of the last remaining Zaur. Even through the mental haze that accompanied her head wound, Wylant could tell he was smiling beneath his faceplate; the sound of it was in his voice even through the metallic distortion of his foci. "I'm disobeying orders, sir," he answered, slicing the Zaur almost in half diagonally with his blade. "If we live, you can have me flogged."

*

You can do this, Kholster thought at Rae'en. As he still held Testament, he knew she could hear him. He almost missed the two shadows sliding across the open ground.

So that's where the other two were, Vander thought at him. *Shadowpaths.*

"Followers of Kilke, if you attack me before my daughter is safe, I vow to kill and eat you both," Kholster snapped at the shadows.

Ignore the pain. Ignore the fear.

One of the other sharks swam toward her.

Just kill the shark. Use your hands. Use your teeth. It's doesn't matter how. Just kill it.

*

"You just may get that flogging," Wylant snarled at Mazik, who had stayed behind to, she supposed, rescue her. Her mind was clearing, but the head wound pulsed painfully in time with her heartbeat. "Try a lightning bolt."

He chanted softly, drawing a circle in the air with his sword, invoking Dienox and the goddess Gromma. Sparks arced along his blade as the spell's power grew. It might not have any effect, but Wylant had to know. Frip's unconscious form vanished between the serpent's jaws, and Wylant wondered how much the thing could possibly eat. Its gullet looked big enough to swallow a horse.

"It's just an animal," she whispered to herself. Mazik completed his spell and spat a bolt of blue lightning coursing along his blade to strike the giant serpent in the face. It hissed and shook its head from side to side, steam rising off its scaly hide, but it barely paused in its advance.

*

You won't drown. I still hold Testament. In the same way Bloodmane took the heat of Cadence's Long Fire, I can breathe for you. Kill the shark.

Kholster took in a deep breath of air, enough for two.

I can't see her, Kholster thought at Vander. *What's happening?*

*

"Any other ideas, General?" Mazik asked.

"You run while I go for the eyes." Wylant managed enough of a flight spell to hurl herself at the serpent, losing sight of Mazik as she pierced the monster's eye. Vax struck home as a long knife and Wylant willed him to lengthen, to grow, like a spike toward the brain. Vax had been forged like an Aernese weapon, his abilities proof against the spell-disrupting capabilities of the Zaur. The blade functioned just as well against whatever magic resistance this giant serpent might possess.

"You're just an animal," Wylant shouted. "Die already!"

*

Kholster spat a long stream of seawater out onto the floor of the arena, breathing in deep, breathing for two.

Do you need me to assist you? Bloodmane's voice echoed in Kholster's mind. **I can breathe for you while you breathe for her . . .**

*

The few remaining Zaur mounts scattered before the serpent as it hissed in pain, thrashing from floor to ceiling, desperate to rid itself of the stinging, stabbing elf who clung to its head. Wylant felt her shoulder blade crack, as well as a few ribs, pain lancing up her arm and across her chest, but she held on, willing Vax to grow longer, into a spear, a lance. Finally, Vax pierced the brain. Victory washed over her as she felt the serpent's throes go from a struggle for survival to a death rattle, and then she fell, striking the ground hard as consciousness gave way to darkness.

*

If you can't do it, Kholster thought at his daughter, *any other way, use the Arvash'ae. Your body knows how to do this. Your mind is getting in the way.*

Teru says it looks like she's fighting the Arvash'ae. She—

I'm sorry, Kholster thought at Rae'en, then to all Aern, he thought: *All Recall.*

As it did each time, the sharing of a memory stopped Aern in their tracks the world over. Those who were in danger, certainly one in the midst of a battle with a shark, gave over immediately to the Arvash'ae. He hoped Rae'en would come to forgive him for robbing her of such a hard-won victory.

The memory Kholster shared was a simple one, one that was very much on his mind . . . the one Vander had mentioned earlier, when the gods had sent storms against them. He, Vander, and the other Armored on the mission had drowned. The warsuits had walked them back to shore where the Bone Finders had stripped their bones, killed animals to fill the warsuits with enough blood to cover the bones, brought them back according to the agreement he'd made with Torgrimm so very long ago.

He hoped the Armored found the memory reassuring, but he also knew two Overwatches, three Bone Finders, and a certain young kholster knew the real reason he'd shared the memory at that very moment.

The crowd had gone wild when the first shark carcass had flown up onto the staging area. When Rae'en had followed it, still dragging a live shark behind her, they'd risen to their feet. Now that the memory was over, the Arvash'ae faded. She was safe.

Kholster ended the memory with perfunctory All Know words about the coming storm on the water, about how the fleet would make it through one way or another. Only when he was done did he finally turn to face his daughter. In her eyes he saw not the anger he'd expected, but gratitude and shame.

"Thank you," she mouthed. The remaining opponents held up their hands, backing at least one step away, signaling their surrender. The announcer called an end to the match and declared them the victors, but victory was hollow.

Kholster watched the way Rae'en eyed the water warily and dropped into it himself to retrieve Grudge. As he emerged at the staging area and returned Testament, Vander told him what he already knew.

You should have given her more time, she would have gotten it.

Well done, thought Bloodmane. **You saved her.**

She didn't need saving, Kholster thought back to Bloodmane. *Now she thinks she did.* To Vander, he thought only: *I know.*

CHAPTER 35
GUILD CITY GOOD-BYE

At seven hundred and one jun long, seven jun wide, the Great Junland Bridge stood as the largest construction in the entire world. Connecting the continents of Northern and Southern Barrone, the bridge had been there longer than Rae'en's father had been alive. Maybe Coal, the great gray dragon, remembered a time when the bridge hadn't been there. Maybe he had even seen it built, but to a young kholster who'd never traveled north of Khalvad before setting out for the Grand Conjunction, even after seeing all the Grand Bazaar and the grand highway, the Dwarf-made continent seemed impossible.

Nevertheless, there it stood and beyond it, past the South Gate, MidGate, and North Gate . . . Rae'en would set foot on the Northern continent at Castleguard. She would travel on to The Parliament of Ages and the Eldren Plains and finally Oot, the Place of Conjunction where she would see statues of the gods, statues that changed to match their current forms. She'd meet an Oathbreaker and a Vael. Even after all she'd already seen, it was hard to imagine.

"What kind of a name is Oot?" Rae'en had asked her father when he first said the name.

"You'd have to ask the sculptor's parents," he'd answered.

"What?"

"You'll see when you get there," Kholster had answered. "The Oathbreakers contracted the manitou artist, Oot, to create the statues of the gods there. He was supposed to get to name the work and that name was to be posted in grand fashion. They didn't like the name he chose and tried to bar him from the site, so he . . . signed his work rather prominently." Then Kholster had laughed. Rae'en loved the sound of her father's laughter, and she didn't hear it very often.

He looked so . . . sullen . . . now. Defeated.

My fault. I let him down. She shook off the thought and tried to focus on the journey.

Oot.

If all went well, she would spend the three days and three nights required by her father's promise then signal the beginning of the end of the Oathbreakers by killing and arvashing Prince Dolvek. She hoped Oathbreakers didn't taste like weasel. Rae'en let out a long sigh at the responsibility of it all, to be the first Aern other than Kholster to represent her people at the Conjunction. To be the last Aern to ever do so. Six hundred years of tradition would end with her.

And after her failure at the Arena. . . . She touched her chest, but the wounds were gone, leaving only faint yellowed bruises in their place. Rae'en closed her eyes and felt the water covering her face all over again, rushing into her lungs, the pressure of the shark's jaws and then—she snapped her eyes open and shook the memory away.

Around her, on the Barrony side of the South Gate, taverns, inns, and vendors of all types lined the roads, built up as close to the wall as the Dwarves would allow. South Gate loomed. High up, if she squinted, she could make out the line of cannon which rimmed the walls of the structure. Where the Dwarves at home in South Number Nine liked to carve and decorate their creations, mostly with images of Jun the Builder, the Junland Bridge's walls were smooth and seamless. The familiar visage of the Dwarven god loomed only at the gates. Staring at it sent a rush of fear through Rae'en, as if the walls were going to come tumbling down on her at any moment.

The massive great gate was up and open, a solid wedge of metal, ready to crash down and reduce any intruder to meat paste. In the past, when she'd heard others speak of the gate being a quarter jun deep, Rae'en had assumed they were exaggerating, but now . . .

It's going to eat me. She reached back to touch the haft of her warpick, heart fluttering in mild panic before she could recall that her Overwatches were very likely fine, just too far away to hear her. *I guess almost dying has me a little jumpy.* She left her hand on Testament for a moment, feeling the warmth of the weapon, and adjusted it slightly as if doing so had been the only reason she'd grabbed the hilt.

If only I were Armored, Rae'en thought longingly, *none of that would have happened.*

Or not the way it had happened. Kholster wouldn't have had to save her, and she wouldn't feel so alone in her mind. As one of the Armored, she could have transmitted her thoughts via her warsuit or even had the warsuit establish a direct connection, if not with Kazan and the others, then with Uncle Vander or . . . or any other Armored.

Whose scars are on your back, Rae'en? she chided herself. *Just keep tracking along as if everything is normal.*

To the east and west, the wall ran as far as she could see. That was too much to take in, so she looked back at the gate, then at the line of merchants and travelers and caravans waiting to have their cargo and papers examined.

Sheens of sweat coated the skin of the humans, though some ablated the effects of the summer sun with parasols. *What*, Rae'en wondered, *would it be like to be so affected by extremes of heat or cold for an entire lifetime?*

Dwarven customs agents and border guards manned five different entry lanes leading through to the gate itself. Rae'en knew each gate also had one hundred Aern, the symbolic guard Kholster assigned to show that invasions against the protected target would incur the ire of the Aern. Even so, she only spotted twenty.

"Five shifts," Kholster said, as if reading her mind. "What do you think of the gate itself?"

"It's like a trip hammer in a giant's smithy," she told her father. "Can it really come plummeting down and . . ."

"Faster than any racehorse could gallop through it." Kholster smiled, baring his doubled upper and lower canines. "I'm told it's modeled after the trip hammer in Jun's great forge, but if so, he's substantially larger than his statue at Oot, and it's supposed to be to life-size times five already. You'll see it at Castleguard, in case—" he clipped off the statement and redirected. "But when you see it at Oot, that one is . . . better."

Rae'en's grin seemed fit to split her cheeks at the thought of that. *I'm still going to represent my father at the Grand Conjunction!* She'd worried that after the Arena he wouldn't want her to take his place. Hearing him say it flooded her with such relief she couldn't quite put it into words.

She stared at her father, taking in his bone-steel chain armor, then down at her own, which matched his. She rubbed the little finger on her left hand, which had finally grown back. It itched, the nail wasn't as long as her others, and the skin felt tight, but it was finally whole. Which made her feel complete, too.

She couldn't tell exactly how the One Hundred felt about her warpick, but they seemed to like the sentiment. She didn't need to reach back and touch the weapon to feel its weight against her back, but she touched its haft again anyway, feeling the warmth of its nacreous crystal even through the pale leather grip. Kholster caught the motion and waved her hand down subtly. *I'm glad to have you uncovered*, she thought at the weapon. It didn't reply, but she felt it heard her at least. Testament had always been a silent weapon, though she knew other Aernese weapons had a voice. Rae'en tried not to let it bother her.

"That's twice now," Kholster chided softly. "You'll make the guardsmen nervous."

"And we do that enough just by standing here," she acknowledged. "Yes, sir."

The thirty armed guards the Unified Guild Masters of Barrony had assigned them after their "performance" in the Arena walked in a rectangle around Rae'en and her father. Rae'en found the stink of their fear mildly repellant but tried to remind herself that not everyone thought the Aernese ability to fight and kill and eat the enemy was a good thing. To them, eating any sentient being was thought of as monstrous . . . therefore she, like her father, with doubled canines and metal bones, with eyes that to humans were completely the wrong color . . . they probably thought she was some sort of monster, too.

"I don't know why they feel the need to escort us," Kholster whispered.

"Maybe they want to avoid additional deaths," Rae'en said with a smirk.

"But what if we get hungry?" Kholster winked at her.

Rae'en snorted. Kholster had warned her of the fickleness of human infatuation with Aern, of times when humans had thrown rotten food at him or hissed, but these humans merely watched in awe at their passing. Wondering how much the Arena fight had to do with that, too, she spotted a young boy standing on a tavern railing to get a better look. Rae'en wondered if she should wave or smile, but settled her gaze back on the huge gate.

"Break formation," one of the guards shouted, and the front line of guards broke ranks to allow the Aern to move forward without them. A small escort of Dwarven guards in plate armor waited just ahead to receive them. Unlike the Dwarves back home, the Junland Dwarves looked fleshier. Many had long beards and came in shades of tan and light gray rather than the more mineral-like tints to which Rae'en was accustomed.

"Less rock in their diets," Kholster whispered.

"Oh."

An Aern in a bone-steel breastplate and helm stood with them, both vestments marking him as an Aern who had earned the right to forge a warsuit but had yet to do so. With the Life Forge destroyed, he would never have the chance.

"Draekar!" Kholster moved forward to greet the Aern, the two of them brushing knuckles and baring their teeth.

"Kholster," the other Aern nodded. "And this must be Rae'en?" As he turned to her, his smile vanished and his eyes grew cold, waiting. Only with the clash of their weapons would their relative rank be decided.

Rae'en unslung her warpick in one smooth motion, bared her teeth and growled.

Draekar smiled broadly as Rae'en's warpick caught the light of the sun, refracting the light and rainbow patterns prism-like on the road. He reached over his shoulder, drawing forth his own warpick, its pearlescent surface darkened with a bluing technique Rae'en had seen often in warpicks forged by older Aern. It had fallen out of practice, younger Aern preferring to let the bone-like sheen of their weapons show undimmed or augmenting it with brighter colors for effect. A bronzed look seemed to be the fashion for most of her generation.

Eying Testament's deceptively fragile appearance, Draekar hesitated.

"Yours will break long before Testament does," Rae'en said impatiently.

"It looks like glass."

"The Dwarves call it bone crystal, though bone-steel glass is what it really is." Rae'en waited three breaths for Draekar to strike the head of his warpick against hers and, when he failed to do so, slammed Testament against Draekar's weapon—Calamity—instead, with a pealing ring like a crystal bell had been struck.

Draekar's eyes widened as Rae'en's mind touched his, the collision of two soul-bound weapons providing a temporary link not unlike that experienced between a kholster and Overwatch. Draekar, by Braekar out of Varriday, his full name came to her. If Draekar had been astonished by her weapon's fortitude, he was positively amazed to find himself on the kholstered rather than the kholstering end of their brief connection.

Reports, guard rotations, and local intelligence flooded her mind and was digested, becoming a part of her knowledge as naturally as water drained from a cup became one with her body. Without needing to think about the information in detail, it felt right to her, and she found herself commending Draekar on his service, until . . .

"Father," she reached out to touch Kholster's arm.

Kholster narrowed his gaze and touched Draekar's warpick with Grudge, at which point Rae'en found herself immediately on the kholstered end of the connection once more. Kholster himself now kholstering both of them, read her concern and Draekar's chagrin.

"That's a dangerous oath Ghamud has sworn," Kholster said finally.

An oath, Rae'en thought to herself. She'd felt a wrongness but could not quite place it, then her father was there in her mind, guiding her along the pathways of Draekar's connection to his men, through his Overwatches, the Infantry, and on to Ghamud himself.

"He swore to see the Life Forge remade and his kholster's warsuit forged at last?" Rae'en couldn't quite believe the other Aern's foolishness.

"It was a brash oath," Draekar answered.

"I hope he may live to see his oath redeemed in something other than death," Rae'en said as Kholster, having pointed her to the cause of her consternation, withdrew, expecting her to proceed.

"As do I, kholster Rae'en," Draekar answered.

"As do we all," Kholster put in. "To have his bones crumble and be redeemed by death . . . not every Foresworn has my daughter to redeem his bones as a Testament."

Rae'en shifted, looking past Draekar at the land beyond South Gate. A breeze swept along the tunnel carrying with it the scent of grass and rich fields; not a smell she associated with Dwarven construction.

"I heard there was some excitement at the Arena?" Draekar asked, following her gaze.

Why ask how something went, when you really mean "May I please see it?" Rae'en thought at her Overwatches.

Draekar eyed her expectantly.

"We won."

"Excellent." Frowning, Draekar slung his warpick back onto his back.

Kholster's expression remained frozen—unreadable. Rae'en tried to guess whether he was pleased with her decision not to share the memory.

On his best days, her father could be maddening in his refusal to comment on the decisions of those under his command. She knew why and tried to keep it in mind as it applied to her and those she kholstered: He was First of One Hundred. Faint praise could be misconstrued. An alternate point of view could be seen a condemnation. She would hear from him later, she felt sure, but here . . .

"Are we clear to proceed?" Kholster interrupted.

"Of course," Draekar answered.

"Kholster Rae'en," Kholster turned to her, and Rae'en knew she had missed something other than the oath. The feeling swelled up over her. *Was it something in one of Draekar's subordinates' free time? Another oath? A—* "At your discretion."

And then she understood. "You have done well, Draekar. I commend you and your hundred on their faithful service. I hope you will be pleased with your next rotation. Am I right," she reached out for the details of what Draekar had shared with her, the bare metal information which remained even after their warpicks parted, "in thinking you were hoping for Castleguard rather than home?"

Draekar's frown vanished. "Yes, kholster Rae'en."

"We'll see what we can do," she mimicked the even tone her father used when he didn't see why he couldn't arrange something but wanted all the facts first. It was a promising tone, but not a promise. "Carry on."

Twenty Aern saluted as Rae'en and her father entered the massive gate. She walked into its shadow trying not to compare it to her memories of the exhibition, of the water rising up around her, of sinking to the floor of the Arena with her lungs filling with water.

I am not being swallowed up, she told herself. And once she was in the tunnel itself, her body agreed and the momentary panic bled away. She had made her home in tunnels far smaller. Once inside this one, she marveled that she had ever let herself fear it.

CHAPTER 36
CROSSING THE BRIDGE

A loud metallic peal rang throughout the courtyard as Kholster head-butted the elderly Dwarf. Rae'en's eyes widened as she watched the Dwarf's eyes glaze over. She hoped he wasn't going to pass out. The other Dwarves standing nearby, guards of some kind she surmised, blanched but fought to control their expressions.

They wore heavy breastplates and helms. Each also bore a shield on his back and a sword scabbarded on his left side. She'd expected them to all have long beards and axes or mattocks—maybe a pickaxe or two—but only four of the seven guards had long beards. Two of the remaining guards had short jaw-hugging beards like the one her father often kept—and had nearly regrown—the last was smooth-shaven. An inner struggle played out in the eyes of those guards as they fought the urge to reach out and assist the older, unarmored Dwarf.

Rae'en had never seen a Dwarf dressed like him. He wore a sleeveless burgundy shirt with platinum buttons up the front, its thin collar folded up against his neck. His bare arms revealed intricate tattoos done in shades of purple, blue, and gold which seemed of some significance, but if they had ever borne a resemblance to the runic markings her uncle's people used, it was too distant for her to recognize. The thick leather belt at his waist seemed to have little to do with holding up the plaid pants he wore, though the oversized bone-steel buckle was worked with the same patterns as his arms, so maybe it served a similar purpose. The boots she recognized. The same thick-soled work boots worn by her uncle back home.

What a strange Dwarf, she thought to herself. *I wonder if he knows he's bleeding.*

Blood an only slightly darker red than a human's trickled across the lines on his forehead. Not the dark, almost black of Glinfolgo's miners, nor the near orange of Aern blood. Her uncle had once told her the color in blood came from the mineral traces within it, the red color of human blood from iron, the near black of mining Dwarves from the overabundance of the same, and an Aern's orange blood from the near-complete lack of it.

When she'd asked why there was such a difference, Glinfolgo had been unwilling to share. *Dwarves and their secrets . . .*

After crossing to the Dwarven side of the bridge, Rae'en and Kholster had walked out into an open expanse of land which hardly seemed any different than the countryside beyond the walls of the Guild City, except that the grass was more lush and the trees she could see to her far left and right were of a more uniform height and obviously well-tended and carefully trimmed. She hoped to catch sight of one of the famous Bridgeland trams which hauled cargo along the Western and Eastern walls, but they'd used the pedestrian South Gate, so all she could see was the occasional flutter of one of the Bridgeflies, the steam-driven dragonfly-shaped craft used to scout the walls and occasionally move troops or cargo rapidly from one gate to another.

Rae'en had hoped they might get to ride in one, but instead they'd come to a stop in a courtyard about fifty steps outside the South Gate tunnel, where statues of Jun (as an anvil) and Torgrimm (as a single twisted symbol of infinity wrought in metal) stood across from a representation of Aldo (as an open book). Arced stone benches formed a triangular arrangement around the fountain, and Rae'en wondered if the water was supposed to represent Queelay or if it was just water.

Up ahead, beyond the Dwarves and the fountain, loomed a village with squat-domed buildings all of wonderful white stone. Obelisks made of the same stone provided direction as the large central road upon which they had walked out of South Gate diverged. Looking back over her shoulder, Rae'en spotted more guards back along the wall and thought she spied a recessed stair from which additional guards probably stood ready to emerge.

On a normal day, Rae'en imagined the place busy with the hustle and bustle of visitors, constant traffic which their simple arrival had brought to a complete standstill—at least at this gate.

Maybe the increase in traffic before and after make up for it, she thought, *people wanting to spot the great "Kholster Bloodmane."* She grinned at the thought, then covered it up quickly as she caught the smooth-shaven guard frowning at her.

The elderly Dwarf swayed slightly and coughed, clearing his throat. A light breeze picked up as if by design, the air smelling sweet. It didn't smell of the sea like she'd expected; then again she guessed they were awfully high above the sea itself.

Was it two thousand hands high, she thought at Kazan, *or three thousand?*

The Dwarf shook his head as if to clear it, eyes brightening, then going dull again.

Of all the cultural "Prove you're really an Aern" tests Rae'en had encountered, only the Dwarves had chosen one which involved physical discomfort for both parties. So many humans wanted an Aern to cut himself to reveal the bone metal within and a good flow of the orange blood which seemed to so easily amaze them. Kholster narrowed his gaze, concern showing on his face when the Dwarf wobbled.

"Karl?" He put a steadying hand on the Dwarf's armored shoulder.

"I swear your skull gets harder with age," the Dwarf said, waving him away.

Of course our bones get harder with age, Rae'en thought to her absent Overwatches. *What does he think would happen? They'd get brittle?*

Of course, there was no answer. Rae'en wondered if the information would all be delivered to them in a rush once they were back within range or if they were just lost thoughts. She waited for her father to confirm Karl's suspicions, but he did not clarify, so she didn't either.

At her father's age, his bone-steel was notoriously hard to work with, requiring heat approaching draconic levels of intensity to melt and shape. Fortunately, Dwarves didn't require a full-force head butt, just enough to hear the sound of the Aern's skull ringing. That was one thing the bridge Dwarves had in common with the Dwarves back home: they loved the sound of ringing metal, bone-steel in particular.

Are they weaker than the Dwarves back home? she asked her Overwatches. *They look weaker.*

Karl steadied himself. His tanned skin was a near-human shade rather than the mineral hues of home. Karl's hair was odd, too . . . a light chestnut which reminded Rae'en of human hair. She wondered if it was flammable like human hair. And further pondered why no one ever picked that test for an Aern.

Hair inflammability. Surely it would be much more comfortable for everyone involved. *Maybe it's too easy to fake*, she thought, and it wasn't as if Aern hair wouldn't burn, it just took more heat than it did to burn human hair. Cadence had burned Kholster's hair off pretty easily . . . and probably there were alchemists who could do the same sort of thing.

Several spells too, she imagined.

Karl, the elderly Dwarf, swayed on his feet again, then, seeming to master himself at last, smoothed the front of his burgundy tunic, resting his hand on the broad bone-steel buckle which graced his thick leather belt and breathed a sigh of relief.

"Welcome to the Great Junland Bridge, Kholster of the Aern," The elder Dwarf announced. "You are our welcome guest . . . ah . . ." he stumbled over the word as if just remembering her, "You and your daughter are our welcome guests. I greet you . . . eh . . . both . . . on behalf of my fellow servants of Jun."

"Thank you, Foreman Karl," Kholster said as the two of them clasped forearms. "Your head is hard and your works are an honor to Jun. I come in peace to your people and seek passage to North Gate where I shall continue on to Oot that I might fulfill an oath there."

"We would not hinder you," Karl said with the air of someone reciting a script he knew well and considered important, but one he wanted to get out of the way so the real conversation could begin. "But if you would like to grace us with your presence for a time, there are many matters we would like to discuss and many inventions we would like to share."

"Kholster Rae'en?" Rae'en jumped at the unexpected transfer of command, heart quickening. Foreman Karl? FOREMAN Karl? Her father was handing her command in the midst of a conversation with the Dwarf responsible for kholstering the whole of the Junland Bridge! She wondered how many Dwarves made their homes there and how many humans, gnomes, and manitou besides called the bridge their home and, this Dwarf, therefore, their kholster.

Something mischievous glinted in the old Dwarf's eyes. He covered it well, but she'd spent too much time around mine Dwarves to miss the look even on a bridge Dwarf.

"I'm sure we could spare you a few days, Foreman Karl, if the matters you wish to discuss cannot wait for our return trip."

Karl's eyes lit up at the word "days."

"Of course," Rae'en continued, "we would need to prevail upon your hospitality and complete our journey across your fair domain underland."

Karl's expression darkened.

That old Dwarf wants to maximize the number of assassination attempts, Rae'en bristled inwardly. *Can you believe him?* she thought to her Overwatches.

"Underland?" Karl asked, stricken.

"As I'm sure you are aware, Foreman Karl," Rae'en said as diplomatically as she could manage, "it is the common practice for assassins funded by Castleguard, the Guild Cities, and various other nations to attempt to kill my father on his sojourn to Oot. Historically, Bridgeland has been the focus of such attacks, as the Aern are unlikely to invade Bridgeland because of our friendship. I'm told there is some small amount of gambling involved."

"Gambling, you say?" Karl blinked. "In my kingdom? Are you quite sure?"

Kholster snorted at that.

"Kholster doesn't mind," Rae'en bulled on, "a certain amount of it. After all, he is one of the Armored and cannot die unless he allows himself to do so. As a result, I'm told most of the betting now has to do with how many attempts there will be, how quickly the assassins will be dispatched, and how long the journey from South Gate to North Gate will take to be completed." Rae'en smiled brightly.

"It's all in good fun from our perspective, but I'm further informed most bets have an underland route nullifier. While we'd hate to break the game, only an underland route would allow us sufficient time to enjoy your Dwarven hospitality at this point."

Kholster leaned forward. "I know I, for one, am very interested in viewing some of the air-gardening techniques you've been using—"

"Of course. Of course." Karl nodded. "We'll make ample time for that on your return trip."

"But, Foreman," Rae'en jumped back in, "if the matters you have are truly urgent, the Aern would be loath to—"

"It can wait," Karl blustered. "No trouble at all. I have to look into this gambling business immediately. Would . . . would you and Kholster like an escort? I mean, if you're going to be attacked by these . . . assassins . . . in my domain, I—"

"We'll be fine, old friend." Kholster interrupted, putting a hand on Rae'en's shoulder.

Well done, his thoughts touched hers for an instant, and she repressed the urge to grin from ear to ear.

"It's settled then," Kholster continued. "You're sure it would it give no offense, Karl, if we waited to spend time together on my return trip?"

Karl sighed. "We Dwarves are patient and I know your task weighs on your mind. On your return then?"

"You have my intention."

"But not your oath?" Karl raised an eyebrow.

"Not this time, my friend, but I assure you the lack of my oath is no indication of my feelings toward you or your kingdom. We remain one people in peace and friendship as far as the Aern are concerned."

"The Dwarves feel the same." Karl nodded. "We are kin."

Kin that apparently think it's great fun to set you up for assassination and then watch, Rae'en grumbled to her Overwatches.

As they took their leave, Kholster unslung Grudge from his back and offered it to her. "Swap with me?"

It was a question, not a command, but she swapped weapons all the same, feeling guilty as she handed over Testament and felt Grudge's extra weight settle against her back. In her mind's eye she saw the weapon dropping through the seawater. *I will never drop it again.*

I'm told that Karl bet long, which means either the assassins are particularly impressive this year, or there's some new wrinkle he doesn't think I'll be able to get around too easily. Kholster's thoughts flowed into her mind. *Best to stay in easy communication range until we see what's going on.*

Yes, sir.

Shall we run or take it slow?

Aren't we in kind of a hurry now?

Haste would not be inappropriate.

Run, then. Rae'en breathed a sigh of relief. The desire to run through Bridgeland as quickly as possible and only pay real attention to it upon their return—when no one was trying to kill her—was what she craved.

Shall we make it something of a race then?

Done! Rae'en burst ahead of him as she answered. Behind her, Kholster laughed and the world felt right again.

CHAPTER 37
THE BRIDGE RACE

We'll need rules, Kholster sent Rae'en shortly after her head start.

Rules? Rae'en thought back at him.

Kholster waited until she was out of sight, glad to see her happy, hoping it was the first step in putting his mistake at the Arena behind them both. Once she was clear, he jogged back to the courtyard catching Foreman Karl and his guards at the top of the one of the recessed stairs leading into the Underbridge, where only Dwarves were allowed.

A guard tapped Foreman Karl, and he turned as Kholster approached.

"Forget something, old friend?"

Yes. Kholster thought back to Rae'en. *Rules. Otherwise it's only an endurance test.* To Karl, he said: "They can try to kill me, Karl, and it doesn't even chaff my skin, but her—"

"Kholster," Karl smiled broadly, arms wide. "This gambling and assassination, I'll admit I'd heard rumors, yes, but—"

Closing with the Foreman, Kholster chose to ignore the nearby guards moving as if to intercept him. Karl's surreptitious waving them off told Kholster all he needed to know, but he had to play it out. Sometimes other sentients insisted on seeing these social interactions through even when the outcome had already become heartshot certain.

So Kholster leaned in close to the elderly bridge Dwarf, keeping his voice light, eyes bright and smiling. Doubled canines peeking out like swords with only an inch of steel showing above the scabbard—a threat . . . but one that could be denied.

"I can't die, Karl." Kholster's words tumbled out. "But she can. She's just realized it herself, and I need to give her time to move past it."

And in a straight endurance test you'd automatically win, Rae'en thought back.

"Then shouldn't you let her get right back in the mine and swing the pick?" Karl firmly but gently pushed Kholster back, and Kholster let him.

"Maybe I'm the one who has to get used to it," Kholster said as he stepped back. *Probably. If this is going to be fun, it should also be fair*, he sent to Rae'en.

"What do you want me to do, I can't be everywhere at—"

"You think I don't know about your fly spies," Kholster scoffed, pointing directly at one of the minute bronze insects with its translucent wings, "or those scrying posts?" His gaze shifted, looking for one and not finding it right away. "I've ignored them in the past, but now I need you to use them to keep her safe."

"And if I don't?" Karl tucked his thumbs into his belt.

"I think you will."

"Are you threatening me?" The warmth in Karl's voice chilled but did not altogether vanish. His pupils widened.

Fair how? Rae'en asked.

You tell me, Kholster shot back.

"I shouldn't have to." Kholster spread his hands wide. "But . . . 'the Eye that spies on me, I shall pluck out.' It's not an oath, but it is a . . . firm opinion. A warning."

Well, I have to sleep for three— Rae'en's thoughts touched his mind, and Kholster liked the edge of bemusement which accompanied them.

Four.

Four, Rae'en admitted, *hours each day, so . . .*

"So you're putting me in charge of your daughter's protection or you . . . what? Attack? Declare war?"

"Will be exceedingly disappointed in you." Kholster let out a breath he hadn't realized he was holding. "Just keep an eye on her and let me know if she gets into any trouble . . . in time for me to do something about it or to decide to let her handle it." Kholster bowed low. "Please? One father to another?"

So we break for four hours every nineteen, Kholster thought at Rae'en.

"Ha!" Karl clapped him on the shoulder. "The day Kholster said, 'Please.' Very well. For that reason alone I'd have agreed."

This isn't the way to handle it, Vander thought. *This is for you and not for her.*

I know, Kholster answered as he turned to chase his daughter and make up some ground. *I know.*

*

As far as Rae'en could determine, the buildings of Bridgeland came in two varieties: the elegant well-constructed buildings owned or operated by Dwarves and the blocky ones. Dwarven construction could appear anywhere and in any shape, though she noticed that the bridge Dwarves seemed to incorporate more domes and spires than Uncle Glin's architects might have done. Some buildings ran directly up to and through the exterior walls of the bridge itself, particularly at the tram stations. Buildings built by other cultures tended to have shingled roofs or square construction, came within no more than one hundred paces of the wall, and seemed to try to reach as high as they could without being higher than the bridge walls.

Rae'en determined very quickly that regardless of the architect or homeowner, no one liked an Aern running across their roof.

Maybe it's the boots, she thought to her Overwatches. Even so, Rae'en wanted to be up on the wall proper, so she could look down at the vast expanse of sea. She knew she wouldn't catch a glimpse of the fleet, but that didn't stop her wanting to try. One part of her wanted to be out there with them, to see the look on Uncle Glin's face around all that water. Then again, another part of her didn't like the idea of being surrounded by water ever again.

So we break for four hours every nineteen, Kholster thought back at her. She'd half-wondered if he'd been attacked, he'd been quiet for so long. *Probably something to do with the fleet more likely*, she thought at her Overwatches.

Who keeps the time? she thought at her father. Still moving at a full run, she broke past the initial welcome area of the pedestrian portion of the Junland Bridge, the ornate tile giving way to smooth road with grass on either side. Rae'en let her course drift northeast off the road in hopes of seeing one of the commercial trams.

You tell me.

Bloodmane, she thought as she jumped a fence onto a plot of farmland. Dwarves and humans worked the field together harvesting red corn and some other plants. To her it was just cattle feed. *AND you have to pass along to me the correct time from Bloodmane as soon as reasonably possible given your current circumstances when I ask.*

In the distance, steam-powered monsters of brass and steel lurched through farmland, filling their metallic maws with produce from the fields. Overhead a dwarvenfly buzzed low, its bronze-colored body gleaming like molten metal in the sun. It swooped low enough for her to see the Dwarven pilot, then, having apparently identified her and judged it acceptable for her to be where she was, it flew higher, banking off to the west to continue its patrol.

Perhaps. Kholster answered. *We'll work out the exact wording of the oath, if we truly need one, to make sure it's fair and decent. For the keeping of the time, I agree to trust Bloodmane if he agrees to do it.*

Why wouldn't he? Rae'en puzzled that one over as she reached a stream of freshwater running through a stone trough at the edge of the farmland. She jumped it in a single bound, barely wondering at the deep drains she saw at its center.

I think he will be happy to help, Kholster thought, *but it will be a request, not an order.*

O-kay, Dad. He was getting so weird about Bloodmane lately. Weird about her, too. He didn't exactly say anything, but she felt it. If only she hadn't fallen off the cursed wall and into that water. She wanted to blame it on Grudge, but if Kholster hadn't forced her to exchange weapons, she would have drowned.

Or maybe not. Maybe I'd have just had quiet in my mind, not knowing if he saw me until the All Recall, when he decided my body could fight better without my mind in it. Or maybe I would not have fallen in the water at all. It hurt her head to think about it.

Any other rules? Kholster asked.

Huh? Speeding her pace as she approached the northeastern wall of the Junland Bridge, Rae'en felt that same queasiness in the pit of her stomach. It wasn't the mass of stone but the abrupt angle of it, jutting straight out of the ground on the other side of the tram tracks. *How can I even get up there?*

Jogging along the edge of the tram line, Rae'en watched as long flatbed cars on metal wheels hauled goods along the rails. Was it steam-driven? Magic? Either way the rhythmic clacking of the wheels on the rail reminded her of some of the group percussion rounds she practiced back home with her squad, all of them pounding their implements against the ground, relaying bits of stories or poems.

Workmen—Dwarves, humans, gnome, manitou, and even the occasional humanoid she'd never seen before and didn't have a proper name for—noted, but did not seem too concerned about, her passing. After all, they had Token Hundreds of Aern at the gates . . . they'd seen Aern before.

Do you have any other rules to suggest?

What other rules need there be, Kholster?

I've found in many competitions, Kholster thought, *it is fun to add an extra dimension to the task . . . to measure a nonphysical trait like creativity or time management. It helps—*

Even the hunting ground. Yes, I can track that. Time management. Creativity . . .

Do you have another rule to suggest?

You have to buy me a present? She thought it as she saw the sign for Midian and liked the idea immediately. Kholster was always a great gift giver, but with only a little notice . . . She smirked.

Ha! I'm not sure how that—he thought back.

—I mean we each have to buy the other a present . . . in Midian. Not something expensive. We set a price limit, but the present is judged on originality and thoughtfulness and is weighed into the final results by . . . Zhan?

I would agree to that. He was silent for a long stretch. She could almost feel the weight of him studying the game now, determining his strategy. *Is it allowable to make something?*

Ye-es. She answered after a similar time of deliberation. *But you can't start it until Midian and you can't leave Midian until it's finished and you still have to buy something—it can't be made only with what you may have stashed away in those saddlebags. I don't think I've ever even seen you open your left one.*

Pacing the train, Rae'en spotted an iron ladder leading up the side of the wall. She waited for the tram to pass, crossed carefully to the other side, and started climbing.

Do we consider the cost of anything brought with us if we use it as part of the item? Kholster asked.

Um . . . Rae'en thought about that as she climbed the fifty-foot (fifty-one, more likely—knowing Dwarves' love of primes) ladder. *I don't know . . . no. If you brought it with you, you can use it.*

Agreed. Kholster answered. *And when do we exchange gifts? At North Gate? In Castle Guard?*

At the Changing of the Gods in Castleguard, Rae'en decided.

Fine. Now about that oath . . .

*

Kholster enjoyed the idea of a race more than the actual race. By day two he'd reached Midian and used the bulk of his gift allotment to hire forge time. The look on the Dwarven smith's face when Kholster cut off both of his own middle fingers was equaled only by the horror on the smithy's face when Kholster chewed the meat off the bones to get at the bone metal. Eyes rolling up in his head, the smith fainted dead away.

That wasn't very nice, Vander thought.

I didn't eat the nails, Kholster thought back, *I don't know what he found so shocking.*

You didn't go with the little fingers?

No. I know you all think I'm crazy, but I feel like I lose far more hand strength that way. Kholster thought.

Or you could just do what I do and wait until you have enough discarded teeth.

Left arm. Right arm. Then repeat, I seem to recall.

That was to make my warsuit. We all did that. Vander sounded only slightly indignant.

Afraid Uled would change his mind about letting us use the Life Forge. Afraid he would understand too much about the warsuits.

What are you making? Vander asked.

You'll see soon enough. Kholster bent to his work. Melting down the silver he'd purchased was much easier than melting down his own bones. Only the Central Forge of Midian could be heated to a sufficient temperature. *How is the storm coming?*

It's time to wake Coal.

No outrunning it?

We tried. Irritation and weariness crept into the edges of Vander's thoughts, coming through loud and clear. *I'd swear the thing is following us.*

It probably is. Kholster cursed. *Wake the dragon then. I'll wait on deploying the warsuits. You may yet make it through intact.*

True.

Unable to do anything to help his troops out at sea, Kholster turned all his energy toward making Rae'en's gift.

An hour later, Kholster was pounding the resulting silver bone-steel alloy into a square wire. The Dwarven smithy had suggested a wire mill, but Kholster couldn't imagine it working properly. Besides, this was how he knew to do it, and six thousand years of habit doing things a certain way were hard to overcome.

You'll want to see this, Vander broke in. *Hear it, too.*

I've got time, Kholster thought. *Show me.*

*

"You thought I was going to flee?" Coal croaked, his voice an unhealthy rasp, steam hissing from his throat as he struggled to be heard over the howling of the wind. After months at sea the great wyrm's skin had gone a powdery gray, the only hints of flame visible in the dark of night when faint lines of orange and red played along his scales in a dying dance like embers in a fire pit. Under the pounding rain, the dragon looked pale, wet, quenched.

Vander stood at the edge of the *Dragon's Perch*, an enormous steel coracle topped by a flat platform. Five Long Arms took turns stabilizing it, but the real secret to its seaworthiness was, as far as Vander could determine, found in Dwarven rune magic.

"You did say to wake you so you could take flight," Vander shouted back, his hand clenching the abbreviated bow of the *Dragon's Perch*, rain pelting his skin hard enough that he wondered how the human Long Arms endured it without complaint. Their robes flapped madly about them despite the soaking they'd taken.

"Were I younger—" Coal erupted into a torrent of wheezing laughter. "Were I younger I would have charbroiled you for such impertinence, such lack of faith and vision. Get off my ship."

"I meant no—"

"I know when offense is and is not meant by an Aern, you bareheaded spy." Coal's eye lit up from within, and a bloom of red and orange leeched out to light his scales. "Get off my ship because it's going to sink when I take off."

Vander scrambled back into the rowboat he'd used to approach, a feat only possible in these chaotic seas with the assistance of the human Long Arms who now joined him in a rush. The Dwarven glass lenses one of the Long Arms wore in wire frames across his nose were ripped from the man's face, flying off into the storm to be brought back in pieces by the human's power.

Vander looked into the angry clouds, then back at the fleet. Not a stitch of canvas showed anywhere. As waves crashed over the side of the rowboat, he sincerely hoped the dragon's plan could keep them all from going to the bottom . . . although it would have been impossible to be any wetter, even standing in Queelay's court. The Armored would survive, but the humans and Glinfolgo . . . and all those guns and cannons . . .

Oars? He thought to his fellow Overwatches.

Three gold tokens flashed assent in his mind.

We're coming back. The dragon is going to do . . . something.

Vander gave the order, and three of the Long Arms latched onto the nearest ship with the strength of their minds, beginning to pull the vessel away from the *Dragon's Perch*.

Waves pitched the vessel maddeningly from side to side. At one point, Vander seemed certain he would be cast into the sea, but the Long Arms held him fast.

"Get some distance," bellowed the dragon, shifting from side to side, stretching his wings, each stretch punctuated by a series of deep, fast inhalations and sharp exhales. "I'll have to pull heat out of the water for many jun in all directions to kill it, and I don't want you stuck in the ice!"

"Ice?!" Vander yelled back. "What do you mean?"

"Everything in nature has its predator, Aern." Coal's chest swelled up, and he unleashed a huge gout of steam into the air as he spread his wings out to their fullest. "Gods, Humans, Dragons, even hurricanes!"

"What hunts weather?"

"Watch and see, Vander by Uled on the Life Forge, Second of One Hundred." Curling in on himself, gathering his strength, Coal sprang into the air. "Watch and see for the very last time on this plane of existence! See what it is to be a dragon!"

Off in the distance, beyond pounding waves and cascades of beating rain, the wall of the hurricane loomed, its funnel churning across the surface of the ocean. Overhead, the sky flashed blue, red, and green in a way Vander had never before experienced.

Great Torgrimm, Kholster thought

Vander was at a loss for words.

Coal rocketed at an angle, following the spin of the mighty storm. The dragon's skin began to change, a wave of black flowing out from the center of his mighty chest to the tips of his massive wings. All light left the surface of the beast. The air crackled and snapped, the sultry heat of the storm shifting to cold. Rain become hail, then a mixture of hail and snow as Coal whipped around the eye in tighter and tighter circles.

Lighting arced from the roiling storm clouds to the sea and across the clouds themselves along a horizontal plane.

How is he doing that? Kholster asked.

Vander didn't even know he'd made it back to the *Oathkeeper* until he felt himself lifted into the air by the combined might of the Long Arms and heard Glinfolgo's voice in his ear.

"He's absorbing the heat," Glinfolgo shouted, his voice elated even as he clung to the deck for dear life. "It's why his surface has gone completely black! What we're seeing is a massive display of heat absorption and energy exchange! A hurricane is heat converted to work . . . to power. It's driven by heat and the water cycle!"

"I don't understand."

"Dragons live on heat," Glinfolgo shouted. "I just hope he survives the cold."

"What cold?" Vander shouted. "The snow? Why is it snowing? Is Yhask attacking us as well?"

"Pulling out the heat creates the cold! It's simple thermo . . ." Glinfolgo's mouth snapped shut like a trap. "Just trust me! Have you ever seen ice form around the cooling pipes near the geothermal linkages back home?"

"Yes!"

"It's the same principle!"

Round and round the dragon went, the storm spewing lightning in all directions.

*

From his spot in the smithy, Kholster watched the impossible. He barely noticed the first assassin. Kholster killed him with a distracted blow to the throat on instinct alone, refusing to look away.

*

A sheer white line of ice and frost advanced along the slick black surface of Coal's hide. For one, two revolutions, the great wyrm trailed a cloud of snow and ice, then the funnel of the great storm seemed to collapse upwards, expanding as it blew out and up against the clouds that roofed the sky. Coal dropped down into the sea. Where he struck, the surface of the ocean froze as he vanished beneath it.

"We need to move!" Glinfolgo shouted. "Aern to the oars and row! Quick as you can."

"Wha—?" Vander started. "I don't. What?"

"To keep the hurricane from re-forming he'll have to steal the heat over a vast area," Glinfolgo shouted, "an area we don't want to be in. Be glad you listened to my committee when it came to building the ships. Why use sails alone when you have all this tireless muscle?"

Vander gave the order but stayed frozen watching the waves as they stopped moving. With the crackle, hiss, and snap of water transforming from liquid to solid at an astonishing rate, the sea began to freeze. A wall of pale green and white rippled across the paralyzed waves, radiating out from the point at which Coal, the great gray dragon, had plunged beneath them.

They stopped rowing an hour later. Aern and Dwarf stared back at the layer of oceanic ice. With a roar and a crack, the ice shattered upward, and out climbed the dragon, clawing his way onto the ice and then launching into flight. His skin blazed as if he were made of molten lava, and indeed, chunks of shed liquid rock dropped to the ice, melting through and tossing gouts of steam into the air.

As old scales dropped away, liquefied, Coal seemed to shrink slightly, revealing a layer of black scale chased with flame. Diminished, yet also much more lithe and serpentine, the dragon buzzed past Vander's flagship with a deep rumbling laugh.

"I will meet you on the Eldren Plains or in The Parliament of Ages," he cried, looping the ship.

"What? How?"

"I am quickened." Coal reversed course so quickly Vander's neck ached keeping pace with the adjustment. "This is my last state. Number now the years of my life upon a human's scale. A final blaze to burn bright and clear and sear my mark upon the world . . . and when my fire dims and cools, I shall burn no more."

"So the natural predator of dragons?" Vander yelled.

"Is Time," Coal bellowed the answer as he flew west. "And other dragons."

CHAPTER 38
MIDIAN

Rain reached Midian about the same time Rae'en did, the heavy drops of water coating the—she didn't know what to call it—sprawl? Even back at Darvan where the people lived in a cluster—buildings atop buildings, sharing walls, one neighbor's roof serving as another neighbor's floor, she had seen nothing like Midian.

It's almost like, she thought to Kazan, though she knew her Overwatches couldn't hear her, *Darvan and the Guild Cities were smashed together and reshuffled like a deck of cards.* Not that she'd seen a deck of cards before the Guild Cities. Back home, the Dwarves preferred to play games centered around runed tiles and nesting crystal pyramids. Tiles stacked on other tiles, and the three different sizes of pyramids each had different abilities based on size.

Midian's bones reminded her of a game Glinfolgo favored in which each player tried to get all three of his pyramids to the center of the arrangement of tiles to seize a central stack of tiles. Escape. Such a strange name for a game about getting to the center of things. If it was called escape, then why not start in the middle and move outward? One never knew with Dwarves.

Thoughts of the game drew her eyes to the middle of the city where, from her perch on the wall, she watched white plumes of steam trailing up from the Central Forge. Its massive middle chimney stuck up well beyond the height of the bridge walls. Most of Midian's buildings soared like that. Only the buildings closest to the bridge walls kept to the sub-wall height restriction seen along the rest of Bridgeland.

Architecturally, the construction in Midian appeared to have been started by Dwarves, many buildings rising as high as twenty stories. While the core of the buildings matched the Dwarven magnificence Rae'en had seen elsewhere on the great bridge with rounded spires and triangular wedges arcing up to immense heights, these were dotted with architecturally diverse additions jutting like barnacles from the buildings' original design.

She'd missed the sound of rain on stone. The sight of the city all wet and clean reminded her of the watch stations back homes, the way they glistened in the rain.

Of course, back home, the only flying beasts would have been birds or Coal. Rae'en fancied she could almost make out his figure far off to the west diving through the clouds and twirling through the air.

No dragons in Midian. Instead, the insectoid Issic-Gnoss could be seen flying through the steam-choked sky alongside the bronze dwarvenflies and the occasional winged manitou. To her left, a human with webbed membranes running from her hands to her feet jumped from the roof of a dark-gray building, gliding down to a lower structure while guards of mismatched race shouted after her to stop.

Rae'en found a rain-slick ladder and started her descent, marveling as she dropped lower and lower at the way the streets were even more crowded than the air. Horse-drawn carts shared the smooth, even streets with steam-driven horses, trams, and small carts pulled by humans, Issic-Gnoss, or the occasional being she could not identify.

At ground level, glowing signs flashed in the air announcing services on the walls of buildings.

More Dwarven rune magic? she thought at her Overwatches.

Bloodmane says it's Stopping Time, Kholster's voice said in her mind.

I just got to Midian, she thought back.

Remember you'll need to find an inn, Kholster advised. *They do not take kindly to street sleepers in Midian.*

Any suggestions?

I never sleep there. Too noisy. Too many thieves.

It's big. Rae'en looked back up at the wall, wondering if she might be safer climbing back up and rolling out her bedroll on the wall again.

It is.

Are . . . are you still here?

Yes, Kholster answered, *at the Central Forge.*

When did you get here? Rae'en passed by street vendors selling everything from soup with noodles, various charred, steamed, or raw things on sticks, to fragrant teas and breads. She bought two rats on a stick from a vendor who looked part rat him(or her?)self. One was glazed with a thin layer of salt, nuts, and honey, the other raw, sold by special arrangement with the vendor from a stash beneath the main compartment of his cart.

A few days ago.

A few? Rae'en thought back. Unlike human flesh, the rat's tasted better cooked than raw, but from the loud complaints her stomach was making, she was certain it would give her a very interesting yarp later.

Many of the lower floors of the buildings appeared to be occupied by shops and pubs, while upper floors, based on the children she spotted looking out of windows and laundry lines hanging between buildings, appeared to be occupied at least in some cases by living space.

A spider-like Issic-Gnoss tempted her with a small sack of fried, candied, and salted roaches. Though it seemed pleasantly crunchy when she relented and sampled one, she wasn't sure how they'd sit with the food she'd already eaten, so she tipped him (it?) and moved on.

Two hours of shopping later, she'd purchased and consumed a soup of spicy goat and mushrooms, as well as a bag of fried roaches from a different vendor. She'd also been sick into a bin filled with garbage. Unlike other places, the residents didn't seem to find her presence at all strange, and, in fact, the gnome selling the goat stew had sold her on it by telling her it was a favorite amongst the local scarbacks.

What she had not done was find a gift for her father. She looked, but nothing seemed like him. Buying her father an implement of combat was useless. If he wanted a weapon, he'd make it. He wouldn't eat cooked meat, so the idea of a rare food item didn't sound good enough . . . plus, she'd long suspected his sense of taste wasn't very good anyway.

She passed a store selling gnomish and Dwarven creations, but the only things she could afford under the agreed-upon budget were little more than curiosities. She didn't think Kholster would have much use for fake crickets which chirped back when you whistled at them or little bronze kittens that batted your finger when you stroked them.

Clothing was out of the question. Kholster expected clothes to last forever. Every Aern knew about the "incident with the shirts." Never mind the fact that the newest of the shirts in question had been ten years old.

Buying him a plant or a pet, even though she thought he would look cute with one of the mug-sized lizards she saw some citizens carrying around . . . there was also the chance that he might eat it. Even Rae'en wondered what they tasted like.

Finally, sleepier than she ever remembered being, Rae'en headed back to the ladder. It took longer than she thought it would. Several times, she got turned around, not able to see the wall, before she stopped and took the time to re-create a map in her head, retracing her steps. It was much easier to let her Overwatches do it, but she was a kholster. She could remember.

Halfway there, in the middle of a long line of street vendors, she saw . . .

The perfect gift.

She had it wrapped and stowed in her saddlebags quick as a neck snap without even haggling over the price.

*

"She's sleeping on the wall," the smith's voice called above the clanging of hammers and the loud whoosh of the Central Forge itself.

Kholster looked up, his pliers slick with blood from the most recent assassins. Seeing the Dwarf's reaction, Kholster shrugged.

"I've stayed in one place for too long." He bent the last link in the chain into a complete loop and smiled as he held up his gift. "It was convenient anyway. Soul bonding doesn't require blood after the first slaking, but the more you use, the easier it is. I've never understood exactly why."

He held out the loop of silvered bone-steel and its matching chain.

"Soul bonded?" The Dwarf's eyes widened. "You did that all here?"

"Only the ring is soul bonded." Kholster wiped them down with a cloth. "Every time it's different. This time, the piece of my soul that went into it was long and quick. Like a snake . . . or a ferret. Do you think it's because of the ring? The way we hammer it into wire?"

"I don't know." The Dwarf's eyes went down to the carnage.

Kholster's latest assassins had been a trio of crystal twists. A pile of dismembered parts lay scattered on the ground at Kholster's feet.

"Oh," Kholster noticed the Dwarf's discomfort. "They kept interrupting the engraving. Do you know how hard it is to get bone-steel engraving just right?"

"Yours?" The Dwarf shook his head. "Difficult."

"Did Karl tell you how many assassins his men have had to . . . divert . . . from Rae'en?"

"Only three."

"Did she notice?"

"We don't believe so."

"Good."

It's time to resume, Bloodmane intoned.

Kholster blew out a breath of air. He wanted to let her sleep, just delay things until he knew she'd had a full four hours. But that was not what he'd said he'd do so . . .

*

It's time to move.

Rae'en's eyes did not exactly snap open, but they did open . . . mostly.

Rae'en?

Yes, sir, she pushed herself up on her elbows, only half-surprised to find rain pouring down on her, soaking her bedroll. *Are you still in Midian?*

I'm getting ready to depart.

Then so am I, Rae'en forced herself the rest of the way up and began packing her sodden bedroll, wringing it as best she could, letting the water splash down onto the stone.

We can discontinue the race, Kholster offered. *If you like.*

Why? Rae'en started running along the wall, stumbled once from sheer exhaustion, got back up, and started running again. *Getting tired?*

Kholster's laugh rang out in Rae'en mind, and as happy as she was to know she'd amused him . . . she also wanted to strangle him . . . just a little.

CHAPTER 39
THE GARDEN OF DIVINITY

Stepping through the North Gate of the Junland Bridge felt like stepping backward in time. The cobblestone streets of Castleguard stank in a way that the inhabitants of the Guild Cities would have found offensive in the extreme. No dwarvenflies flew north of Bridgeland. No steam-driven horses trod its muck-encrusted streets.

It reminded Rae'en of certain areas of Gastony or Khalvad, but the people here were mostly light-skinned humans instead of the many shades of brown and tan closer to home . . . and . . .

Do they not have running water?

Many places don't, Kholster thought back.

But, this close to the Dwarves, surely—

Look at the gates. Kholster gestured past the Dwarven fortifications, up the winding path in the mountains to the human-built walls and towers where Castle Mioden sat like a suspicious golem glaring in baleful disapproval at its unwholesome neighbor. Rae'en recalled the Guild Cities' border with Bridgeland, which had no walls except for those the Dwarves themselves had erected. Castleguard's defenses treated the bridge continent as a threat of invasion, the walls of the city even trailing down to the seaport below. It did not look as though the people of Castleguard were friendly with their Dwarven neighbors.

She peered out across the ocean and smiled to think the fleet had lost only two ships to the ice—all the Aern rescued—and Uncle Glinfolgo was safe.

Once, the water would have tempted Rae'en even though she could barely swim in it because of her bones. She'd sailed around the Cape of Cavarous, with its massive cliffside caverns filled with the bat-winged Cavair, to fish and trade, but now that she'd been in a fight underwater . . . the idea was less appealing. She thought of Vander and the five thousand Armored . . . a journey of so many miles over sea . . . Rae'en wondered what that would be like.

Maybe Uncle Vander will share the memory, she thought at her Overwatches.

No Token Hundred had greeted them at the Castleguard border, only human men-at-arms in royal-blue brigandine backed by stone walls festooned with archers. There were nonhuman residents in Castleguard, but none were allowed to join the guard or be a knight in Mioden's service.

Is the castle named after the king or—?

I believe the current monarch is Mioden the Twenty-Seventh, if that answers your question.

Why are the humans all so pale?

It must be their diet, Kholster thought with a mental shrug. *I don't know. Humans come in lots of different shades. They all taste the same.*

Drizzling rain clung to the mountains, wreathing them in mist, even covering the streets in a layer of fog. The guards said nothing to them as they passed deeper into the city, as if being an Aern was all that was needed to allow them to wander wherever they wanted. Rae'en spotted other travelers being stopped to have papers they carried stamped or marked.

Kholster kept them moving, past drab little shops and mirthless inns. Rae'en had seen beggars before, but the ones in Castleguard all seemed to be maimed in some way, some missing limbs, others missing eyes or tongues.

Veterans probably, Kholster explained. *They don't treat them the way we do. If they can't fix them, they cast them aside. And Castleguard is perennially at war with Gromm, so there is rarely a shortage. I'm sure it makes Dienox happy.*

Moving up the mountain toward the castle proper brought cleaner streets and shops of more unique nature and higher standard.

There are some wonderful caverns and gardens, even a museum I'd like to show you when we have more time, Kholster sent. *They have a preserved Gromman Mount.*

Rae'en had always wanted to see one of the plant steeds of the Gromman Plainsriders, but she guessed it would have to wait.

"How much time do we have left?" Rae'en unslung Grudge and offered it back to her father.

"Twelve days." Kholster raised an eyebrow but accepted the warpick and returned Testament to her.

"Can we still make it?"

"It's just under nine hundred jun to Oot." Kholster settled Grudge on his back, and Rae'en wondered if he noticed that she moved in unison with him, returning Testament to her back with the same one-armed careless sling. Her shoulders, aching from days of near-constant travel, flared with pain when the warpick snapped into place on her back, but it felt good to be whole again.

"We will have to keep a steady pace, like we did in Bridgeland." Kholster patted her on the shoulder.

She smiled, but inwardly her heart sank. Did her father's muscles not ache as hers did? Fiery lances of protest shot through her thighs, calves, and the bottoms of her feet with each step. Even her back and arms hurt. At any moment she was sure she'd start trembling and not be able to stop, but . . . *is Kholster hiding it?*

Probably not, she answered her own question. She wondered if age would grant her that boon as well, or if that was a benefit only afforded the Armored.

"The Garden of Divinity." Kholster nodded toward Castle Mioden, "is on the far side of the castle."

"Then we can find out who won the Bridge Race." Rae'en perked up, patting the saddlebag containing her gift.

"I win either way, you know." He looked at her askance.

"How do you plot that course?" Rae'en smirked.

"Simple." They walked together under a bridge lined with soldiers. "If I win, I am victorious, and if you win, my troops have seized victory, and, as Kholster, I am therefore . . . ?"

"Victorious." She laughed. "Very funny."

*

They reached the Garden of Divinity a few hours before noon, and Kholster guided his daughter through the manicured garden surrounding the likenesses of the gods on a scale which Rae'en felt had to be about twice life-size. After all, the statue of Kilke was roughly twice the size of her father, roughly thirty-six hands, and what god would need to be larger than Kholster?

Worked in white marble, some of the gods looked diminished, while others seemed well suited to such a pale palette. The statues were arranged in half circles, six on one side, six on the other, with Shidarva standing where Kilke once stood, at the head of the design, one half-circle on her left, the other on her right. A tremendous fountain in the middle sent up synchronized lances of water into the air.

Kilke, with his two horned heads on either side of the central stump he'd lost in some long-ago cosmic coup, leered at her with one head, the other tilted toward Nomi, the once-mortal woman who'd stolen Dienox's flaming hair as he slept in a postcoital daze, becoming the goddess of fire. Xalistan, the hunter, appearing as a snarling wolf (also horned)—*these male gods love their horns*, Rae'en thought to her Overwatches, partly out of habit and partly out of hope that they could hear her even when she couldn't hear them—his teeth bared at the outstretched hand of Queelay, who appeared to have playfully dampened his fur.

Yhask, god of the wind, ignored them both, glaring hatefully across the fountain at the figure of Dienox in full plate armor who—

"Is he pouting?" Rae'en prodded Kholster.

"I'd say he's angry that Coal killed his hurricane." He studied Yhask, running his hand between the layers of statue; the wispy rings of Yhask's elemental form did not quite touch, some hovering over others with a magic Rae'en's father clearly found interesting. "Yhask, I would imagine, is angry that Dienox didn't believe it would all be for nought, but look at his eyes."

At a second glance, Rae'en saw triumph layered amidst the disdain, revealed by a scarce turning up of the lip and crinkle at the edges of Yhask's eyes.

"He got something out of Dienox," Rae'en said, "Yhask still isn't thrilled about it, but it's a consolation."

"I agree."

Kholster tipped his head to the statue of Aldo, who, despite his appearance as an Oathbreaker in voluminous robes, was reading a book. Rae'en started as Kholster stopped at the base of Shidarva's statue and yarped up a wet mass of hair and bones on the statue's feet.

One of the few stalwart pilgrims milling about the garden with them opened his mouth to protest, thought better of it, and waited for Kholster to pass before reaching down to clear the pellet away.

"Don't touch it," Kholster snapped as he stopped before Sedvinia, the weeping goddess of sadness and joy. Trembling with indecision, the wrinkled pilgrim looked to Rae'en, but she shook her head.

"Just leave it until we go," she advised.

Not watching to see what the pilgrim decided, Rae'en moved ahead to join her father as he passed the Bone Queen's statue. Kilke's mono-headed sister (the only goddess with horns) stood with regal bearing, her beauty both wonderful and terrible. She wore corsetry the same way Dienox wore his plate mail, as armor, and seemed lost in conversation with Jun, who stood to her right and past Jun to Gromma, goddess of growth and decay, her hair filled with brambles, her clothing a collection of furs and pelts sewn together with barbaric pride.

"Again?!" Rae'en put her hand to her mouth in mock dismay as her father moved on to Dienox and yarped a second, larger pellet on his feet. "You all empty now?"

"I was saving it up." Kholster chuckled.

Dienox's statue was frozen in mid-argument with the Harvester. The god of war's lips curled back, and his accusing finger pointed at Torgrimm's bone plate.

To Torgrimm, Kholster bowed low.

"Find one you like?" Rae'en quipped around a yawn.

"Yes," Kholster sat down on the statue's foot, resting his back against the deity's shins. "I liked him better before he felt the need to wear the plate armor."

"Why?" Rae'en settled down next to her father.

"Because I don't understand why he needs it and it scares me a little to think he might."

*

Somewhere between pondering his remark and opening her mouth to ask about her present, Rae'en fell asleep slumping against Kholster's shoulder.

She's tired, Bloodmane and Vander sent in unison.

This is one of those moments, Kholster thought back at them both, his eyes watering, *where I have to wonder: will this ever happen again?*

Probably not, Vander thought back. *Enjoy it.*

I don't understand, Bloodmane intoned.

Kholster tried to open his senses more completely to his warsuit, but nothing happened. Bloodmane could see through his eyes, relay his orders, even share other sensory data with Kholster, but not the other way around. Kholster closed his eyes, and for the first time in centuries, he closed them to what Bloodmane saw and stared instead at the inside of his own eyelids, the way the light shone through them as a vague orange haze.

He stayed that way until his tears stopped, wiping them carefully away with his hands before opening his eyes again, first his inner eyes, which saw what Bloodmane saw—the cursed exhibition hall, and secondly, his physical eyes. He wrapped his arms around Rae'en, held her, and slept.

The Changing of the Gods did not wake them.

CHAPTER 40
A PARTING OF WAYS

"I can't believe you won." Rae'en smiled down at her ring. Kholster had forged it perfectly. She held it out by the silvered bone-steel chain her father had crafted to go with it and marveled at the way the inscription caught the light. On the outer ring, Kholster had wrought a stylized representation of his scars, but on the inside, he had engraved: Daughter, of you I am proud.

"I can't believe we slept through the Changing of the Gods," Kholster countered. "We'd best not wait until midnight."

"I know. I know." The sun didn't shine so bright in Castleguard, but Kholster was wearing the smoked-glass lenses she'd bought him, their circular lenses held in place by wire frames the color of silver, so she hoped he liked her gift. Rae'en waited for him to ask to take her Testament away and hand her his Grudge, but Kholster never asked for her weapon again.

"You can do this." He pushed the smoked lenses back up on his nose, smiling like an Eleven at first kill, so pleased with the way she looked at him when he wore them. She didn't have the heart to tell him he looked silly, especially since it was only partially true. The truth was he looked different and dangerous in a way she couldn't explain. His whole attitude changed, not toward her but toward the space around him. It reminded her of the way Irka moved when he showed a female around his gallery—confident and masculine—but was not the way a daughter imagined her father.

"I kept you too close on the trip, but you didn't need it. I apologize."

She loved him for that, more than she'd ever thought possible, responding with a hug made only slightly awkward by their clinking mail shirts. As his arms enfolded her, she could not imagine a safer place in all reality. Those arms, she imagined, would be safe even if they'd been standing in the midst of a cataclysmic battle instead of the road leading down out of the mountains.

"With the ring, you can reach out to me if you want and I will hear you. The connection will only be one way, but I doubt you'll need it unless you want to send me details about the Conjunction."

"You aren't coming with me?" she asked his shoulder.

"You kholster it. Do you need reinforcements?"

"I get to pick?" She stepped back and eyed him quizzically, head tilted, ears askance.

"I don't see why not." He looked off into the heart of the forest. She was sure he saw something in the distance amongst the pines and firs with evergreen leaves and the blood oaks which, unlike other broad-leafed trees, refused to surrender their red leaves even during the end of autumn. It, whatever had his attention, wasn't in the forest, and he didn't see it with his eyes. Was it a memory? It didn't seem to be Vander. When Vander thought to Kholster, the corners of her father's lips tilted up in a phantom smile. Nor was it Bloodmane; these days his communications pulled her father's cheeks tight and furrowed his brow. "One day you will make all of the decisions."

He looked . . . wistful?

"Once this war is over." Kholster looked back at her, and she suddenly wished he would take off the smoked lenses. "When you're ready, the One Hundred and I feel it is time for a Freeborn to kholster the Aern."

"But surely one of the more experienced." Rae'en took an involuntary step back. "One of the Armored."

"They want a Freeborn, one of my children. You could," he looked back at something trammeled by the path they had taken or back to the past itself—which, Rae'en could not know, "wake one of the others, my unawakened, perhaps but . . ."

"Unawakened?" She threw up her hands. "Children? How many unawakened do you have?"

"Ask Zhan when you're First."

"Why didn't you—"

"They were born before As You Please."

"Oh."

"Someday, they must be awakened, but you have another sibling I must see to first."

"An Unawakened?"

"Mostly." He looked down at his gloved hands.

"Mostly?"

"Yes." A tear rolled down his cheek, and she was suddenly glad for the smoked glass which stood between her and her father's crying eyes. "So. I asked you a question." He sniffed once and his demeanor changed, hardened. "Do you want me to come with you to Oot, to be your Overwatch, or would you prefer to kholster this alone?"

"Where will you go?" She tucked the ring, together with its chain, into her left saddlebag.

"If you don't need me?" He looked off into the forest, gazing northwest. Again a sad smile touched his lips. "I might like to see Kari again, to see where Irka grew up."

"Go." She kissed him on the cheek. "I can kholster this. It's just three days and nights camping."

"You've only five days to get there."

She rolled her eyes. "Maybe I'd better get going then."

He let her go.

*

Rae'en unslung her warpick, spinning it overhead in a tight orbit. Light sparkled along the weapon's crystal head, tossing rainbows overhead even though, at an hour before dawn, the forest was still dark.

Rae'en remembered well the day she'd completed the warpick and had brought it before her father.

"My warpick, Kholster."

Kholster had taken the warpick, given it a few test swings, and then frowned as he examined the haft.

"It is a fine weapon, Rae'en, but it has no spirit. You are not one with it."

"I know . . ." Rae'en had frowned. "It's stubborn. I can feel part of myself reaching out, touching the weapon, but it won't take root."

"I remember before the Sundering," Kholster had said, running his thumb along the central blade, giving a satisfied smile as the blade bit into his flesh, "when Crimmar was still among us. He made a bow with which he wanted to become one. He worked on it for days, tried everything he could to make Flitter take in his spirit. It was the same way with his warsuit and with his first warpick."

"Did it work?" Rae'en had asked.

"In the end. All it needed was encouragement!" As Kholster had spoken the final word, he'd swung Testament over his head and down toward the cavern floor.

"No!" Rae'en had reached for the weapon to snatch it from her father's grasp, to protect it. Now she suspected he'd had no intention of smashing it, but then, it had been so clear he meant to break it. A low rumble, deep within Rae'en's chest, had risen up and out. Time had slowed, and an irkanth of pure spirit had torn free of her body, lunging into the weapon. Mortal irkanths have light-brown fur, but this one had been the color of spring grass. Her father had shortened his blow, swinging Testament in an arc a mere hairsbreadth from the stone below and tossing it up and over to Rae'en.

"Yours is a reluctant spirit," Kholster had told her. "Like Crimmar's, it was loath to make such a strong connection, but once made . . ."

"It is unbreakable," Rae'en whispered to herself.

She had seen the spirit within Testament that one time, but now, running through The Parliament of Ages, whipping it through the air, she felt it and wished she could hear him roar. Grudge cried out like a hawk in battle from time to time, but Testament remained silent, reluctant. Kholster had said if she ever faced the Zaur, it—

Testament roared inside her mind, bringing her to a quick stop, Testament at the ready.

Um . . .

Rae'en crept through the forest in the half-light of dawn. Around her, birds woke and the forest prepared for a new day. The dew dampened her boots, but she spared it no thought.

Is that? Guys, I think I feel something. A vibration.

Rae'en pushed her hand gently into the cool soil, eyes closed in concentration.

I swear, she thought at her absent Overwatches, *I'm not imagining . . .*

Did she hear something at the edge of her mind, too? A muffled shout? Or did she miss them so much she was imagining voices in her head?

Kazan? M'jynn?

Ignoring the inner thrill at receiving even such a distant mental murmur, focusing on the vibrations, Rae'en lay her head against the sod.

There it is, she sent. *Skritch-scratch. Thum. Brum. Thum. Brum. Testament roared, and in the silence after I heard . . .*

Rae'en stood up sharply, arms akimbo, long red braid dangling over her right shoulder. *The real question is whether that is digging or someone traveling through an underground tunnel.*

Rae'en chased the phantom vibration, darting from tree to tree, treading as lightly and quickly as she could. *This would be so much easier if Uncle Glin were here.* She tried not just to bring back all the things her uncle had ever taught her about danger signs in a mine but also to apply them to the current situation. Back home, huge steam-driven fans endlessly turned, forcing fresh air throughout the deepest of tunnels. She still knew how to recognize black damp (air that was too bad to breathe) and ways to safely test for fire damp (air that was dangerously flammable), but she hadn't needed to ever really use the counter-insurgency training in how to detect an enemy tunneling into her territory before, not since the Mining Kingdoms all joined together under one democratically elected Foreman. That was before her dad's time, before the Underminer Wars were ended by the arrival of the Aern . . . she didn't even know if there were any Rock Dogs left in the world, but if there were, they stayed away from the Dwarven-Aernese Collective.

Unslinging Testament from her back, she began to alternately pound the ground and scan the terrain for any spot that might naturally conceal a hole or air vent or . . .

Whud. Whud. Whud.

There's definitely a big hollow space under here. Somewhere, but kind of deep down. I—

Rae'en spied a lump of banded gneiss. It wasn't that such a rock couldn't be found in the middle of a forest, but there was something "placed" about it. It wasn't poking out of the ground, it . . .

She walked a wide arc until she could see the way it abutted a large tree. A dead tree.

"It's an air vent," she whispered smugly as she approached it at a crouch. "But who could be tunneling under The Parliament of Ages? The Vael would have shaped the earth, not dug into it . . ."

The rough, banded surface—a sequence of grays and browns—would have spoken volumes to Uncle Glinfolgo. She pictured him licking the rock and making some deeply insightful pronouncement like: "They live in the mountains, born of foreign stone." He would close his eyes and point far off toward the Sri'Zauran Mountains, his face blank and motionless as if hewn from the rock the Dwarves so loved. "The foreign stone," he would say, "is that way, miles and miles of it, mountains that Jun has long since abandoned."

Bird squirt! She'd just been joking, but . . . there couldn't be Zaur here, could there?

*

Kholster smelled Zaur in the forest. A salty, lizard scent—like fish and Oathbreaker mingled together—lingered low, clinging to the short, broad blades of violet-tinted myr grass. His muscles tightened, body taut, eyes closed, senses straining.

Where are you?

Sunlight broke through the boughs of the ancient oaks overhead, playing along his brow, highlighting his close-cropped red hair that had been bleached almost blond during the long trip from South Number Nine to The Parliament of Ages. A familiar wolfish expression spread across his lips, half-grin, half-snarl, revealing not only the doubled upper and lower canines but the slightly enlarged, almost saw-like, first molar.

There are Zaur here, he thought at Vander, scratching absently at the flaking skin at his pointed ear tips. It took a great deal of sun to give an Aern sunburn, but Kholster supposed close to a hundred days above ground traveling all day each day counted.

A scouting party? Vander asked.

This far south of the Eldren Plains, it could hardly be more than that.

Even though a century had passed since he'd last ventured through The Parliament of Ages, the forest belonging to the Vael, Kholster thrilled at its sounds and smells. The myr grass underfoot released an acrid odor as it crushed beneath his boots with a lack of stealth his trainers would have beaten him for when he was still a slave all those millennia ago.

As much as Kholster wished otherwise, the forest was no longer truly his home. Each time he returned, it took longer for his senses to become used to the primal world from which he had been exiled. He, like all his people, had embraced his new life on the sea and under the ground. As a result, his tread was heavy, not as heavy as when his people had stalked clad in their warsuits, sheathed in their metal skins, their true skins, but heavy enough for the Zaur to feel the vibrations if he wasn't careful.

He hadn't seen a Zaur scouting party in five centuries, not since a chance encounter years before while trading at Port Na'Shie with the humans in northern Zaliz. To discover them now, so close to the Conjunction, was both curious and exhilarating. Since their last warlord's death, the Zaur had shown little evidence of organized leadership. They stayed close to their tunnels and burrowed deeper into the cracks and crevices of the Sri'Zauran Mountains to the north. They were the humans' and Oathbreakers' problems.

He felt vague pang of guilt that Rae'en hadn't stumbled across them herself and gotten a chance at them.

Then why am I tracking them, he asked himself, *and why am I so excited?*

Because, Vander laughed, *killing Zaur is why we were forged in the first place.*

A flash of memory stained Kholster's thoughts. In his mind's eyes, a wizened Oathkeeper, his robes drenched in the bright-orange iron-deficient blood of the Aern, screamed at him. A reptilian creature writhed on a stone table, chained in place. "You! Will! Eat!"

Kholster had indeed eaten . . . had been compelled to do so. . . . He'd never understood all the screaming, the beatings . . . the other cruelties. Why not simply order him in a calm clear voice?

Ah, well. To his surprise, the Zaur had tasted good.

Putting the memory of his creator out of his head, Kholster circled the central oak to where the scent was the strongest and found the still-damp mark where a Zaur—a scout, he assumed—had voided itself. Definitely Zaur.

Kholster crouched down, outlining the tracks with his fingers. Zaur moved on all fours, and Kholster knew the signs intimately, even though he had grown unaccustomed to tracking prey overland. He eyed the markings in the soil, noting the sign of the hind feet—four front claws and one center back claw on each pad—and the indentation which ran along the middle, made by the belly and the tail bumping the ground as the Zaur ran. The forepaws were set wider, leaving not claw holes but knuckle marks in the dirt. Two thin lines to the outsides proved that his quarry was armed with twin Skreel knives.

Kholster fancied that he could almost make out the tongue trail. Warpick slung on his back, Kholster ran after the Zaur. He ran silently, careful to break step, letting each footfall land on the softest earth. Within the space of an hour, he spotted them in a clearing.

Do you see it? Kholster asked Vander.

I see what you see.

One of the scouting party flattened itself prone, flicking its tongue along the ground, and Kholster froze. Like snakes, the Zaur weren't known for their hearing, but they sensed vibrations well enough, especially when they lashed the ground with their dull gray tongues. Kholster waited until the scout's tongue flicked out over the grass, then he stamped his feet on forest floor and, reversing his grip on his warpick, struck the ground with it in a pattern he hadn't used since the last war.

Kholster spoke Tol passably, but he had never been good with the language of vibrations and tail slaps Zaur used to supplement their verbal speech. He did know one phrase well. He tapped the message out with his warpick and watched to see what the Zaur would do.

<<Bloodmane is coming.>>

The lead Zaur grabbed one of the others, forcing his head toward the ground. Kholster stilled himself again, grinning wickedly from his vantage point between the trees. Years of tracking over rocky terrain or underground might have dulled his skills for the forests of his old home, but not so much so that he couldn't outwit a few Zaur. He waited until the other Zaur looked like it was about to rise and then moved forward, using the loping, skip-like run the Aern had developed in the wars to ensure the Zaur knew who was coming for them, to repeat that same phrase with every few steps.

Bloodmane is coming. If only that were true.

*

After only a little digging, Rae'en managed to widen the air shaft enough to lean in and get a look. Holding onto the withered roots of the tree, she slid down far enough to look both ways. The root snapped, dropping her unceremoniously into the tunnel proper.

In the tunnel, Rae'en found traces of blood.

Whatever it is, in the dark our blood looks the same. Something had put up quite a fight, but this was where whatever or whoever it was had been taken down. A lance pinned a Zaur corpse to the tunnel wall.

Rae'en tugged the weapon free of the wall, bringing the dead Zaur down with it. The sight of shredded muscle, covered thickly with clotting blood, pulled at Rae'en's senses. Her stomach grumbled hungrily. *Now is not the time for the Arvash'ae*, she told herself.

Perhaps only discernible due to the nearness of the Arvash'ae, Rae'en caught other scents beneath the reptilian pall. A human maybe? And some other smell. Like the half-blood in the Arena. An Oathbreaker?

Zaur never take prisoners, she thought to her Overwatches. "So where are the bodies?"

Teeth gritted, Rae'en skipped over the body of another dead Zaur. Rough gashes around the reptilian throat of the Zaur corpse showed that the creature had been garroted with a length of chain. A gentle breeze carried the earthy scent of sweat and blood through the underground passage. Rae'en's nostrils flared; a low growl slipping past her lips.

The Arvash'ae. Early. She snarled, her mouth watering. Something about the reptilian scents was more appetizing than the most succulent cuts of beef. *I should have been fine for at least another three days. Back to the vent.* She forced herself to turn, teeth clenched, hands tightening around Testament's haft to keep them from shaking.

She took one step and then another, heading back the way she came as she fumbled in her saddlebag for the soul-bonded ring on its fine chain. *Out. Out. Out. Report this to Kholster. Out. Out. Out.*

As her fingers searched her saddlebag in vain, she heard the first hiss.

"Scarback?" said a voice. "In my tunnels."

There were more of them than she wanted to see, but having turned away from the air vent, she could not bring herself to turn back toward it.

Just as her questing fingers closed on a loop of the ring's fine chain, Rae'en's amber pupils widened slowly, inexorably, as the Arvash'ae began to take hold. Forgetting all thought of finding the ring, making a report, Rae'en charged.

*

Kholster dashed into the clearing, roaring like an irkanth. One of the Zaur rose up on its hind legs, lifted its crossbow, and fired a quarrel at him. The bolt went through his right shoulder, the tip poking out through the skin on the other side. Orange blood rushed from the wound, and a barking laugh tore free of Kholster's throat.

"What are you doing in my forest, little lizards?" he hissed at the scouts in their own sibilant yet guttural language.

"Death to the scarback," snarled the one that had fired the quarrel. It dropped its crossbow, drew its Skreel blade and charged on all fours. "Tear its brood father's scars from its back!"

"These are not my father's scars," Kholster answered, tensing.

Skreel blades, Kholster mused. *How long since we've seen one of those?*

Nostalgia can still cut your nose off, Vander shot back.

Skreel blades of the Zaur were made for slashing, with the blade extending out from the bottom of the fist and then cutting back at a right angle almost to the elbow of an average Zaur.

I hate those things.

That's because you're no good with them, Vander thought. *Caz likes them. Maybe you should bring him back a pair?*

"For Warlord Xastix!" The others leveled their crossbows, shouted, and fired, but Kholster was no longer there.

Leg muscles stronger than any Zaur's propelled the Aern into the air, and as he landed the sharp end of his warpick caught the Zaur leader a piercing blow to the head, driving deep into his temple. Kholster pivoted, lifting the impaled Zaur into the air, then slammed his victim into two of its comrades, pinning all three to the ground.

Kholster's amber pupils dilated widely, almost totally obscuring the jade irises. With the first kill, Kholster felt the thrill of battle come upon him, washing the pain from his shoulder and stirring his inborn urge to kill. Some of the younger Aern called it the rashiel, a half-step between normalcy and the Arvash'ae. Kholster just thought of it as the hunger for the kill.

His field of vision expanded by thirty degrees on both sides, and all his senses sharpened. He missed the comforting weight of his warsuit, the familiar grip of his first warpick, Hunger, and the sound of his brother Aern fighting, but the battlefield was still home, even more so than any other home he'd ever known.

Kholster jerked Grudge free of the dead Zaur and kicked one of its trapped companions in the mouth as the Zaur tried to strike him. The remaining Zaur dropped to all fours and rushed him with their angular Skreel blades. Kholster laughed out loud in delight.

"I've missed this!" Turning to his attackers, Kholster felt two blades rake across his mail, sending yellow-white sparks into the air. One of the Zaur opened a long slash in Kholster's forearm, a thin line of orange welling up and running down to his wrist and onto the bone-colored leather which wrapped the haft of his warpick.

I'm getting sloppy.

No. You're playing with them, Vander sent back in reply. *You've missed them, too.*

I wonder if they still taste the same.

I hardly think they come in different flavors now, came Vander's answering thought.

Continuing his spin, Kholster skimmed the ground with his weapon and caught the fourth Zaur in the chest with his gleaming warpick, its wicked beak punching straight through the reptile's splint armor, where it stuck fast. He released the haft and flipped over the Zaur as the lizard collapsed. Twisting through the air, Kholster landed crouched and ready to pounce, facing the other four Zaur.

*

Rae'en's vision narrowed, a sliver of black creeping in around the edge of her irises, eyes locked onto the Zaur watching her. She knew there was something she was supposed to do other than kill Zaur, but even after pushing herself part of the way back, she couldn't think what it could have been.

With the tunnel curving to the left and then sharply to the right around a deposit of hard-to-work Jun stone, Rae'en knew to expect an ambush. She leapt high and swung Testament low, striking a waiting Zaur in the skull. An unconscious Oathbreaker female with blood on the chain binding her wrists was surrounded by ten Zaur. Two of the lizards, larger than the others, stared at Rae'en with luminous orange eyes. Their bright-yellow scales were dotted with a black diamond-shaped pattern. Armorless except for thick bands of steel on their lower legs and forearms, both strange Zaur charged her on all fours.

Five other Zaur fired crossbows over the heads of their charging companions. Rae'en tucked and rolled, avoiding all but one of the bolts. The lucky bolt struck high into her upper thigh. The pain would have dropped an Eldrennai to the ground; balanced on the edge of the Arvash'ae, Rae'en stumbled but did not fall. Shifting her weight to her uninjured leg, the Aernese warrior swung Testament in a deadly defensive arc, rotating with the weapon, using its weight as counterbalance.

One yellow-scaled Zaur attempted to dart under it, but Testament's forespike sank deep into its side, killing it instantly. The unexpected contact sent Rae'en into the cave wall, tearing her weapon from her grasp. Testament pulsed with warm yellow-green light, and the scream of the dying Zaur was eclipsed only by the triumphant sound of Testament's irkanth roar. Rae'en's heart soared.

Three smaller, ruddy-brown Zaur slithered along the tunnel floor toward Rae'en, Skreel blades clicking wildly against the cavern floor. Both died sizzling, horrible deaths, screeching in pain as bolts of violaceous energy struck them from the Oathbreaker's position. Rae'en tore the crossbow bolt out her thigh and impaled the third approaching Zaur neatly through the eye with it.

As five Zaur with crossbows threw down their weapons and drew blades, the surviving yellow-scaled Zaur charged toward the Oathbreaker. She spat two more bolts of sizzling fury. One soared high above her attacker and the second scarcely missed. Hissing furiously, the unusually agile Zaur leapt upon the still-prone figure, following with twin blows to the Oathbreaker's head. His five remaining companions held back, unwilling to engage the Aern.

"What now, scarback?" the yellow-scaled Zaur asked haughtily.

Rae'en shouted incoherently. The more thinking part of her tried to force its way back to the fore, but she was into the Arvash'ae far too deeply to pull free without eating her fill.

Rae'en clamped her jaws shut and tried not to heed the call of the warm meat of the Zaur corpse lying next to her. Her belly yowled in protest. Aern and Zaur looked simultaneously toward where Testament lay.

"That the warlord wants you alive is all that spares you," the Zaur said savagely.

Both scrabbled for the weapon; the yellow-scaled Zaur reached it first, but Rae'en landed on his back, her fingers over his claws, and sank her teeth into his neck. The two archers, having reloaded, opened fire again. Rae'en released her grip on Testament, grabbing the Zaur by the shoulders instead and using his body as a shield.

Oh no! Blood ran from his neck wound into her mouth. *I think I just—*

The world narrowed to a single thing, the Arvash'ae, as her jaws closed, tearing a mouthful of muscle and scales from the dying Zaur's neck. Focused as she was on the glorious ripping, tearing, and chewing of fresh meat to fill her stomach, she barely felt the blows raining down upon her from the four remaining Zaur.

*

"Do something useful before you die," Kholster hissed at the Zaur again in their own tongue. "Where is this Xastix?"

Expecting no answer and not waiting for one, he grabbed a fallen Zaur's blade and tested its weight in his right hand. Skreel blades were built exclusively for slashing strikes. Zaur warriors tried to close with their opponents, to slash with their blades, and, more importantly, to bite with their fangs. Some used spears or strange serpentine axes, but most seemed to favor the Skreel because it gave them the freedom to remain quadrupedal.

Not to be outdone, Kholster rolled forward at his foes, his right arm extended with the Skreel blade facing out. He brought it down like an ax on the neck of one of the prone Zaur as it tried to struggle out from under its fallen comrade. The blade shattered when it hit the ground, but Kholster managed to parry a quick succession of blows with the hilt before springing to his feet and dropping the hilt and the scant inch of remaining blade to the forest floor.

Arms spread wide, he beckoned to the remaining Zaur, who hissed at him in unison.

Zhan says you're just trying to show off.

You're relaying this, Vander?

Should I not?

The thought of his army of exiles watching their kholster battle the enemy the Aern were created to oppose made him swell with pride. *No, it's fine. Share it all.*

Sound and everything?

It's fine.

Color bleached from his vision, the scents of Zaur forest and myr grass muted as Bloodmane shared his senses with the other exiles. Burning stabs of pain announced the joining of his sensation to theirs, and he felt the presence of others in his mind, riding alongside him. *This*, he thought, *must be what it feels like for the warsuits to be always connected.*

A sea of voiceless emotion surrounded him, a wordless connection, weaker than the one he felt during a shared memory or a full-scale announcement.

I, of course, would have been able to convey color and scent without degrading my own perceptions, Vander chuckled.

If I were an Overwatch, and you my kholster, Kholster sent, *then I would taunt you in a similar fashion.*

Good-natured laughter echoed through the link accompanied by an overwhelming sensation of mirth from the rest of the exiles in response to the oldest debate many of them had ever known. Kholster fought the joy and focused on the task at hand. Aern would take killing Zaur over jokes any day.

“Go away, scarback,” hissed the one on the right.

“We are here for the softskins: the weeds and the magic slingers, not for you,” spat the one he’d kicked in the maw. It stood, rising up on its hind legs, and ran a careful finger over ruined fangs. Black blood trickled down its claw; it yowled in pain and sprinted off.

“Three to one.” Kholster grinned. “Tell me where I can find this Xastix and I’ll let you little lizards scurry back home.”

“We’ll take your head to him when we cut it from your dead body!” shouted a Zaur. Without any distinguishing scale markings, these Zaur all looked alike to Kholster.

Charging as one, the three Zaur lunged at him, and Kholster leapt up and over them, kicking the center one on the back of the head as they passed beneath him. While they were still turning to face him, he wrenched his warpick free of the fallen Zaur’s chest and swung it in a wide circle, leaning back slightly against its weight.

“Come on!” he shouted.

Separating, the Zaur moved to surround Kholster, just as he had known they would. With incredible speed, he stopped his turn and tossed the warpick end-over-end at the Zaur he faced, rushing after the spinning weapon as it flew. Grudge caught the surprised Zaur in the face and let loose a hawk-like battle screech, striking the reptile dead as it rose to meet Kholster. Grudge enjoyed the fight almost as much as Kholster, and her excitement in the combat gave her voice. Dark blood sprayed from the wound, covering the Aern as he snagged the weapon’s grip and wicking along the painstakingly etched blood oak leaves on the head of weapon, bringing out the detail work in bold contrast.

Faster than its cohort, the Zaur on his left side cut a deep gash in the Aern’s nearer leg, dropping Kholster to one knee and leaving him momentarily exposed to a slash from the Zaur on his right. If the Zaur had struck lower, its Skreel might have connected, but the reptile swung for the base of Kholster’s neck and he ducked under it, seized the Zaur’s outstretched paw and pivoted on his good knee, sending the helpless Zaur into its companion.

The two went down in a pile of seething, angry scales. Kholster lost his balance from the maneuver and fell onto his back, hard, barely maintaining his grip on Grudge. He felt the head of the crossbow bolt in his right shoulder strike a tree root and rolled his eyes in exasperation. It was stuck fast.

That’s what you get for trying to impress the troops, Vander chided.

Think you would do better? Kholster asked.

I can take charge if you want.

Kholster's barking laughter rang out. *Just keep watching.*

Reaching up with his left hand, Kholster grabbed the shaft and tried to break it off. The bolt, made of some exotic metal he didn't recognize, bent instead of breaking. Kholster swore.

Let me know when you get to the impressive part, Vander sent again.

You'll know it when you see it, Kholster sent.

Dragging the warpick and the dead Zaur on the end of it to him, Kholster tried to work the weapon free but couldn't get sufficient leverage with only one hand. He swore again as the last two Zaur regained their composure and began their advance. With no other choice, Kholster drew up his knees, tucked in his chin, and thrust with all his might into a backward summersault. The bolt still gripped firm into the root, but the bent shaft pulled through and out of his shoulder with a disturbing metallic twang. Kholster landed gracelessly on his backside, then threw himself to his feet, reaching for Grudge.

The two Zaur froze in their tracks, turned, and ran.

"Never run from an Aern," Kholster chortled, charging after them into the forest, the cadence of his steps still declaring over and over again <<Bloodmane is coming.>>

It's actually not a bad move, Vander thought at him. *It's been a long time since you were truly one with The Parliament of Ages.*

Kholster didn't answer, his mind given over to the thrill of the hunt which Uled had forged into him. He didn't like to be grateful for anything his maker had done, but he did enjoy the hunt almost as much as he enjoyed the taste of Zaur.

Are they quicker than they used to be? Kholster asked as the two Zaur split off in separate directions, crossed paths with one another again, then split up once more, confusing his senses and making it hard to track both Zaur.

You're slower, Vander shot back, *and that pattern they're running is one you aren't used to without an Overwatch's map.*

No, Kholster thought, *they know this terrain better than they should.* They weren't running blindly; they purposefully led him across terrain which slowed him down.

They're running a scent trail set up to elude pursuit and set up an—

Kholster missed the broken-fanged Zaur until the last moment. Twenty arms shy of catching the two fleeing Zaur, Kholster sensed the incoming attack and managed to block the Skreel blade with Grudge's haft. "Ambush," he chuckled. "Almost."

"I have never fought your kind before, scarback," his opponent hissed. "You are a true warrior. I doubt the others will fare as well."

Kholster slapped the Skreel aside with his warpick and caught the Zaur by the throat. "The others?" His mind raced. The Zaur had said they were here for the softskins: the weeds and the magic slingers.

"Is your warlord trying to stop the Conjunction, lizard?" Kholster growled.

"When scarback's rage," the Zaur hissed, "brings him for war / Then Aldo's prophecy will spur / the quick defeat of Aern and weed / serving Kilke's secret need."

"I respect Aldo, lizard. I do, but those are merely words in the wind to me. The Aern are not slaves to prophecy."

"To His secret purpose," the Zaur rasped. "To His secret purpose."

Kholster swore under his breath, and the Zaur spit blood in his face. With a quick exchange of blows, Kholster ended it, the Zaur falling lifeless at his feet. Kholster wiped the blood from his warpick and smiled as he saw a nearby blood oak.

You got all that? he asked along his link. With the fight over, the connection with his people tapered off, color seeping back into his vision.

Maker! Bloodmane shouted in his mind at the same time Vander shouted, *Kholster!*

What?

The two spoke over each other so much that, at first, he couldn't make out what they were saying. Something about Malmung and Kazan and . . . Rae'en.

One at a time, he shouted at the two of them. *Vander, speak!*

Malmung sent word via—an image of Malmung's warsuit hit Kholster's mind—Kazan, M'jynn, Joose, and Arbokk were almost within range of Rae'en when she thought: "Oh no! I think I just—" and then she stopped sending.

Kholster abandoned pursuit of the escaping Zaur, stopping as swiftly as a bull struck dead in in mid-charge by a war maul.

Did she send anything else before that?

Kazan says he thought she'd found some sort of tunnel and she thought something about blood being the same color in the dark and Zaur not taking any prisoners.

"Zaur take no prisoners," Kholster whispered. Blood seemed to congeal in his veins. For a being who was not bothered by the elements, Kholster felt as if he might freeze solid and never move again. Chest tight, he clutched the mail over his heart. "If she is dead, then I will kill every single—"

Zhan! He sent, cutting off his oath. *How close are your nearest Bone Finders?*

I sent them on ahead to Fort Sunder to reunite with their warsuits. Once you reached The Parliament of Ages, I—

Rae'en has encountered the Zaur and stopped transmitting. Are her—

I'm checking, Zhan sent back. *She's not sending at all?*

Not according to her Overwatches—they say they were almost within range for full contact.

I can't touch her mind, Kholster. I can only sense her bones . . . approximate distance and direction. The closer I am, the more information I can glean, the more precise I can be—

I know all that, Kholster snapped, *but is she—*

Her bones are in motion. I can't tell you where exactly; it doesn't work like that, but we can—

FIND. THEM.

If she is still alive, that would be a violation of our purpose, First Bones, but with her status undetermined, I can act under the presumption that she is dead and her bones need to be retrieved. You will have to tell me very explicitly, or I cannot act lest I be Foresworn. What do you want me to do?

I want, Kholster stared blindly at the blood oak tree which had made him smile only moments before. Hands tightening around Grudge's haft, he swung the implement, Grudge's forespike biting deep into wood. Releasing the haft he stepped away from the warpick and fought back a roar.

I want you to bring back the bones of my daughter, Zhan. The Armored Bone Finders are temporarily relieved of all other duties . . . except Caz. If Rae'en is still alive you will have my thanks and my apologies for what will then, with the benefit of hindsight, be viewed as an extreme overreaction and a misuse of the Ossuary's limited resources.

And do you have any further—

Break. Kholster tore Grudge free of the tree and struck it again. *No.* And again. *Oaths.* With the fourth blow Grudge screeched like an eagle diving for prey . . . and with a resounding crack, the tree came down.

The Ossuarian, Zhan thought formally, *sees no reason to deny the kholster of the Aernese army this request.*

Kholster stared at the felled tree and shook his head in disgust, not just for killing the tree out of rage and frustration but at what his oaths required of him next. He wanted nothing more than to turn back and look for Rae'en. Alive or dead, he didn't know, but he needed to know. If she was dead . . .

Are you going to join up with the Bone Finders, Vander thought, *or—*

The Conjunction is upon us; I have sworn an oath, Kholster thought grimly, *and the representative I dispatched to keep it has been delayed.*

Kholster turned, breaking into a run. *Show me roughly where I—*

A map appeared at the corner of his vision displaying his estimated position and the suggested route to Oot.

If the Zaur are trying to stop the Conjunction, Vander thought, *the other representatives might need assistance.*

I swore to be there. Nothing more. Kholster thought bitterly. *Let them die.*

CHAPTER 41
AGE-OLD ENEMIES

Sneaking down the hallway of the royal palace in Port Ammond, Yavi spotted Gloomy. Gloomy wasn't his real name, but it was what Yavi had come to call Prince Dolvek in her head. She had always known there were physical differences between her people and his, but she hadn't expected them to make such a big difference. Vael tried to focus on the being inside the flesh, not the flesh itself, but the Oathbreakers, Dolvek, in particular, couldn't see past it. As a result, Yavi had taken it upon herself to catalogue the differences in hopes of understanding the Oathbreaker's point of view even if it was, well . . . stupid.

Gloomy, like most Eldrennai, stood a hand and a fist taller than Yavi, and where her ears were long and pointed, his showed a more subdued, rounded point, almost like a human's ears. Smaller ears probably explained why it was so easy for her to sneak up on him. Gloomy had teeth instead of dental ridges. His hair was fine, like silken thread, not thick like hers. Her spring skin—she tried not to think about what it meant for her to have kept both her head petals and soft skin this late into Fall when heading to spend an extended period with an Aern—was very similar to his, still soft, smooth, and supple, not yet coarse and dark as it thickened at winter. Yavi still couldn't understand why it made such a huge difference.

All Eldrennai possessed a certain preoccupation with their own thoughts, which, in Yavi's opinion, made Dolvek's people rather stuffy. Vael had no such problem. Forging a life in the wild, far from the dead cities, her people lived life with an exuberance and freedom she wished she could explain to Dolvek.

Unable to convey this fierce pioneer spirit to him, she settled for sneaking up behind him and making him spill his tea.

"Good morning!" she said sharply as she passed behind his chair in the Great Hall. As was becoming usual, he dropped his teacup entirely and reached for his sword before he realized that he'd been "Vaeled" again. Yavi loved that phrase.

"Fair morning to you as well," he said gruffly, wiping ineffectually with a silk handkerchief at the green tea on his blue velvet doublet. His long black hair fell partially in his eyes, and she grinned back at him from beneath her samir.

One of the serving women, Tasha, stifled a giggle and winked at her. That was another difference: Eldrennai dressed much too formally. Even the human serving woman wore a lace-trimmed formal gown. Yavi had tried to wear one of those contraptions to a dinner held for her by the Eldrennai, and the results had been quite scandalous.

Worn backwards, the dresses were much more comfortable, but far too revealing for the prudish Eldrennai. *I mean honestly*, she thought to herself, *they're just nipples. We only have them because the Oathbreakers like them so much. Why are they so afraid to see them? And why were they so scandalized by her pants? Was it that they didn't know she had legs or that they wished she were shaped like a bell, carried around by tiny roots, like the cilia of a caterpillar?*

From that point on Yavi had worn her doeskin leathers, and no one had suggested she do otherwise. Yavi wondered briefly how an Eldrennai would react to the sight of a Vael sunning herself, then blinked it away with a cold shiver as she realized she didn't really want to think about it.

Fetching her own plate, a thin ceramic dish bordered with enameled roses chased with silver, she went right into the kitchens and served herself several slices of toast. She hesitated at the eggs and the thickly sliced bacon, then looked to the cook for confirmation that the food was safe.

"Don't you worry, dear," the large matronly human cook said. "I sent my Jason out this morning to find wild quail eggs, and that bacon is from the same boar our Howard killed yesterday. All properly hunted and pleasing to the Huntsman."

"My thanks to you, Emma!" Grinning, Yavi helped herself to two soft-boiled quail eggs and three large slices of the savory boar bacon. "And to Jason and Howard."

"I," Emma hesitated, "had Felix bring in some of his good potting soil too, if you have a craving . . . ?"

"No, but thank you." Yavi shook her head. "I might sneak back in for some, but it distresses the prince. I don't know why. There are good minerals in there."

Emma laughed. "It'll be here, Princess."

Tasha steered Yavi out of the kitchen with a gentle tap—backs of her fingers only—against Yavi's waist and gestured to a seat across from the prince.

As Yavi sat down, Grivek, king of the Eldrennai, came into the Hall. Far more severe than his son, Dolvek's father scared the yarp (not that Vael yarped or had any need to rid themselves of bodily waste, but Queen Kari had assured her that was the new Aern word for their equivalent of defecation) out of Yavi every time he walked into the room. His eyes had seen the passage of millennia and found fault with most of it.

"Our human scouts sighted an Aern male traveling north toward Oot," Grivek said as he walked up to the table. "Reports from Silver Leaf claim the Vaelsilyn spotted a female Aern traveling alone two days back."

"Either one is good news," said Dolvek. "So the Grudgebearers really are sending . . . someone." He paused, noticing the displeasure on his father's face and the amusement on Yavi's.

"Kholster gave his word, son," Grivek said. "Barrone itself would have to break in half and be scattered into the ether before he or his representative would fail to arrive for the Conjunction."

"I'm sorry, Father, but you must admit they have held a grudge against us for centuries. The Eldrennai have offered reparations, generous reparations, over and over again and have been rebuffed . . ."

With a scowl and a slight movement of his fingers, Grivek sent a bolt of green flame at his son's plate, disintegrating the fragile china. Impressed by the prince's reaction (barely a flinch), Yavi retreated hastily beneath the table, taking her plate, the small pot of butter, the honey, and the jam with her. Taking a brief moment to adjust the tablecloth so she could spot any further pyrotechnics, Yavi removed her samir.

Howard picks great boars, she thought as she bit into a piece of bacon.

Queen Kari had not mentioned this particular aspect of Oathbreaker dining, but Yavi had gotten used to it after the sixth broken dish. Much more fun than the plays, recitals, and art showings they continuously tried to engage her interest in.

If they'd only have a real duel . . .

"We created them and then enslaved them!" Grivek shouted. "We made them fight our battles for seven thousand years. Just slightly longer than the service we forced upon the Vaelsilyn. They fought the Zaur for us, not to mention the humans, the dragons, and the Ghaiattri."

There was a whoosh as he lifted himself into the air. Yavi feared for the chandelier but not enough to say anything or interrupt her breakfast. Instead, she began to slather honey, jams, and butter onto pieces of toast.

"We would have been slaughtered without them, but when they asked for their freedom we refused. At the slightest sign of discontent, my father punished them." Grivek's eyes unfocused and in that instant he seemed to see something horrible from the past, which haunted him. "Brutally."

"Debts long paid, Father." Dolvek's palm slapped the table. "We now owe them nothing!"

And away he goes, thought Yavi just before Dolvek took to the air as well.

"Don't owe them?" Grivek snarled from somewhere near the ceiling. "When the world crystal was shattered, it was Kholster himself who led the combined task force to rescue the pieces and hide them so they could not be threatened again. He saved our entire plane of existence and we still called him slave. And you say we don't owe them. Gods! Is it any wonder he . . . they . . . rebelled?"

On the "rebelled" Yavi heard another gout of flame and the tinkling crystals of the jostled chandelier. Yavi braced for a crash, and when it didn't come, decided to try a quail egg, her eyes closing raptly as the perfectly cooked yolk burst on her tongue.

"Apologists like you need to stop playing the weeping woman about the past, Father."

Maybe if I drilled a little hole in the table I could see better. She peeked out from behind the table's edge, a jam-covered piece of toast sticking out of the corner of her mouth. And why "weeping woman"? Were human women or Eldrennai females more prone to tears for some reason of which Yavi was unaware?

"The Aern need to move past these exaggerated horrors of an over-dramatized apocryphal past." Dolvek floated next to the chandelier facing his royal father, a war of emotion displayed plainly on his face, fury fighting against duty and propriety. "And I am not the only one who thinks so!"

"They happened," Grivek said, his voice firm.

Yavi suspected that if they ate more meat, the Oathbreakers as a whole would be less irritable. She brandished a strip of crispy bacon in her hand as if she might charge into the fray and save them with it, but she couldn't bring herself to waste good bacon on an Oathbreaker.

"My memory may not be as clear as an Aern's, but I trust that my son does not mean to imply that his father the king is a liar." Grivek gestured angrily at his son, sparks sizzling at the tip of his accusing finger. "Just because the Vaelsilyn saw fit to forgive us, to make peace with us, doesn't mean . . ." The king's voice trailed off as he noticed Yavi under the table.

"Great Aldo," he sighed. "What have we done?" Landing in a kneel at the table's edge, he peered beneath the rich dark wood. "Please forgive me." From this perspective, he looked less severe, almost grandfatherly. Yavi decided she liked him after all. A little.

"The green fire bolt was prettier than the purple one yesterday." Yavi smiled at Grivek. "But I think the blue from the night before was best. I've been wondering though . . . can you do pink? Oh, and we use the word

'Vael' now. Just say it like you're saying 'Vaelsilyn' and when you get to the 's,' stop."

Grivek chuckled despite himself. "If only the Aern were as amused by our tempers as your people," he said softly.

"Your crazy great-great-great grand evil created us to be amiable." Yavi handed him her plate and crawled out from under the table, taking her seat once more. "Besides, Your Majesty," Yavi said sparklingly, "I never get to see flashy magic at home unless it's being used on shadebeasts or irkanth. Though you're right; my mother said that at the last Conjunction Kholster almost left because of what the Eldrennai representative said."

"According to the history books," Dolvek protested, "it was Aernese pride that caused the Sundering. All Bloodmane had to do was kiss the king's sword and swear fealty, and instead he murdered him!"

Grivek shot an angry glance at his son, who winced. "It was more complicated than that, Dolvek. And why would an Oathbound slave need to swear loyalty to his master. Half the points you and your fellow ideologues propose make no sense at all." The king sounded tired, as if this were an argument he had with his son over and over again. "King Zillek—my father—could have dealt with things differently. We are all very thankful to the . . . Vael for helping us survive."

"Without your people," Dolvek simpered at Yavi, whose samir lay on the bench next to her plate, "all three races would have died out long ago . . ."

"Fallen into darkness," Grivek cut him off. "Aldo said all three races would fall into darkness if the Conjunction failed to take place. There is a difference."

"I bet Kholster would prefer to take his chances with prophecy," Yavi said in a whisper, picturing not the Aern her mother had described but Bloodmane, Kholster's armor, with a warpick in its gauntlets. She remembered the armor's gentle touch on her cheek. *Here where you are safest.* Convince Kholster to come back in another hundred years. Pollination optional.

Grivek nodded, favoring Yavi with a tender smile. "Only the Vael could convince him to agree to come, and he has done so personally each century not because he fears what will happen if he does not but because of a promise." He let out a long breath. "In a small way, we are lucky that the Aern share our immortality. I'm not sure any other Aern would come, unless Kholster gave the order."

"Then why don't you go, Father, if you like this butcher so much?" Dolvek asked.

"I doubt he would tolerate my presence. I was the one who exiled his people after he killed my father, and . . . Rivvek has scars on—" King Grivek winced at whatever he had been about to say, swallowed the words like bitter medicine, and continued. "I was the one who insisted they leave their armor and weapons behind. I had no way of knowing at the time that the Aern had wrought life into their armor. It was the Aern's most closely guarded secret, though it seems Uled suspected it." Grivek looked at Yavi, who raised an eyebrow.

"You were taught that Uled went mad after creating your kind? Driven mad by the one flaw in his last masterwork, your people?" Grivek shook his head. "He was no longer King Zillek's court Artificer, and it's true he was unhinged. Which is one reason I never paid much attention to his scribbling from the years afterward; it all seemed too much like Dwarven rune magic to me." Grivek said that last bit quickly and with what sounded to Yavi like a hint of regret. "If I had known, things might have been different."

"Okay, so thanks for breakfast." On that uncomfortable note, Yavi popped the last egg into her mouth and replaced her samir. "I'm heading to Oot this morning."

Flustered, Dolvek bit his lip, head cocked to one side. "The time of the Conjunction is near." Yavi said the words in unison with him, even getting the emphasis on "is" to match. Dolvek's frustration grew in proportion to the twinkle in her eyes.

"I've already gathered my things," she said. Darting out into the hall she grabbed up her pack from beside the door outside the dining room. Snatching her bow out from under a china cabinet and her quiver from the top of a display case, Yavi walked past him ready for traveling: pack on her back, her quiver over one shoulder and her bow on the other. "Come along, will you? We mustn't be all day."

*

As they traveled, Dolvek expounded on their destination, but Yavi paid him little heed. She knew all about it, could not wait to see it, for Oot was one of the few spots on Barrone where mortals could see statues of the gods as they actually appeared. Or perhaps, as they chose to appear. One such location, the Great Temple of Shidarva, had sunk beneath the waves with Alt in the last Demon War. Now, the one most people visited was in Castleguard. Yavi wanted to see it too someday.

Oot was special, though, and the excitement of seeing it for the first time put an extra spring in her step the farther they got from Port Ammond.

Where the monument on Pilgrim's Hill was made of a white marble impervious to harm, Oot's construction was blacker than obsidian. Near Oot, the forest gave way to three separate black paths, one for each race of the Conjunction, approaching the statue of Shidarva. The goddess of justice and retribution's statue had not always been in that position, according to Dolvek. Once the god Kilke had stood at the entrance, his three heads tilted at a haughty angle, resplendent in his role as king of the gods.

Shidarva's statue now held a curved blue sword in its left hand, dangling at its side; her right hand held a scale with a dagger on one side and a shield on the other. Kari had told her daughter that when she saw the statue, Shidarva had been holding Kilke's disembodied head, and when she'd seen it, she had wanted to run from it or warn the goddess, because the head's eyes still seemed alive, its expression twisted toward Shidarva in a mask of hate.

Yavi imagined Shidarva could take care of herself, but she still wanted to see the statues. After all, it wasn't bad luck to visit Oot during a Conjunction. Visiting it at any other time was said to incur the wrath of the gods. As the expression went: "On Pilgrim's Hill, the gods smile still, but blackest Oot shows their dispute."

"You believe that drivel?" Dolvek asked, puzzling Yavi until she realized that she had spoken the old expression aloud.

"Well, my mother has been to the Garden of Divinity," Yavi said defensively, "and she said that the gods' statues all faced toward a fountain and that they were all smiling, even Kilke's disembodied head."

"Perhaps the Garden of Divinity is a fake, then," Dolvek allowed. "Everyone knows that Jun has been angry with the other gods since time immemorial, facing away from them completely. If my people were allowed to go there, then perhaps we could study it for ourselves."

"But the kings of Castleguard have always sided with the Aern on that one, I know. I know," Yavi said gently. "You can't even hire Long Speakers anymore and I'm sorry, but the Vael have nothing to do with that."

"You're right," Dolvek answered softly. "Please forgive my manners."

"Maybe you should try being polite to Kholster when you see him," Yavi offered, "Try asking him nicely if he might allow a few of the Eldrennai, the ones born after the Sundering, to visit the south?"

Dolvek did not answer, and Yavi let the silence hang between them as they walked on along the extension of the White Road. At one time the Eldrennai had wanted to build a grand road to Oot, surround it with walls, and guard it. Fortunately they had asked the Vael's opinion about it before they actually began construction, and the Vael had pointed out that if they proceeded as planned, the Aernese representative would not set foot on it. Instead, they had built an extension of the Big Road that stopped five miles short of the obelisk and had then ceded the borderland on which the obelisk stood to the Vael. Over the years, the forest had reclaimed the land, running almost up to the coastline.

As they entered the forest, Yavi felt a profound sense of homecoming. As if The Parliament of Ages had missed her almost as much as she'd missed it. But The Parliament was disturbed here, ill at ease. Yavi strained her senses, listening for a trace of what caused the disturbance, but Dolvek interrupted again, distracting her.

"This is idiotic," Dolvek started. "We have to hike for five miles through the forest because some Grudgebearer refuses to set foot on Eldrennai land."

"Mother says they only like it when Dwarves call them that," Yavi chided. "From them it's a compliment; from your people it's an insult."

Dolvek threw up his hands in disgust. "Aldo forbid we should insult the Butcher of the Sundering. He single-handedly killed more than five hundred Eldrennai that day, Yavi. He shed our blood in the Halls of Judgment! Even without him in it, his armor killed two of my guards. You saw it! They are barbarians! His warpick was so drenched in our blood that it is permanently stained. If your people hadn't interceded, he would have wiped us all out."

"I suppose you think he was overreacting to the whole thousands of years of slavery thing," Yavi muttered, more to annoy Dolvek than really to argue. One thing the Vael knew was that arguing with the Eldrennai was useless. In many ways they were more stubborn than the Aern.

As they came closer to Oot, a strange, almost fishy smell assailed Yavi's nose, and she noticed that the animal noises in the forest had gone silent. As it became more distinct, the odor seemed less and less like fish. It was too earthy for that, almost reptilian. Her nose twitched, and she held up a hand.

"Shush," Yavi whispered. "I smell something up ahead."

Dolvek stopped and cupped a hand to his ear. "I don't hear anything," he replied, also in a low voice.

Scrambling up a tree without answering, Yavi saw the obelisk of Oot in the distance. Ninety hands tall, it towered over the surrounding representations of the gods. The statue of Shidarva loomed at the conjunction of the three black paths. Her hair sparkled with bright-blue shidarvite crystal. Yavi knew the eyes, could she see them, would match, shining forth from the goddess's grim and disapproving countenance.

Milling about the base of Shidarva's statue were creatures the young Vael had never seen outside of scrolls but recognized instantly. Seven Zaur crawled across the site, gray tongues flicking out over the stone, their scales as black as the stone upon which they stood. Each wore splint armor and carried two strangely angled long knives and a heavy crossbow. They moved on all fours, sometimes rearing up on their hind legs to peer about. One, smaller than the others, lay flat on the stone and let its long gray forked tongue flick across the ground before gesturing to the woods in Yavi's general direction.

"Dolvek," she hissed, darting down the tree as quickly as she could manage. "Dolvek! It's the Zaur!"

CHAPTER 42
BOW AND BLADE

Kholster watched from the shadows. Seven Zaur weren't enough to guarantee a kill. They might get the job done, but Zaur preferred overwhelming numerical advantage on the order of twenty to one.

Maybe if they didn't send their youngest into battle first, they wouldn't need such an advantage, Vander sent.

Kholster ignored the old debate. The Zaur fought the way they fought, preserving the Named among them, treating the Nameless as fodder.

There was a Named here, Kholster thought back, *but he departed, leaving these seven. Can't you smell it? The scent is far too strong for just these.*

I wonder where it went? Vander thought back.

Kholster frowned but sent no response.

Are you going to help them? Bloodmane asked.

Have you heard anything about Rae'en?

Not yet. They haven't reached—

Not even the Vael? Vander cut in.

Look at her heartbow; the Vael doesn't need my help.

Yavi and Dolvek backed slowly away from the obelisk and the Zaur scouts that stood at its base. Kholster could only guess it was the material of which the monument itself was composed which prevented the Zaur, even with their inferior hearing, from sensing the vibrations of the Oathbreaker's approach. Sounds were dampened by the monuments, giving even raised voices a muffled effect.

"We should go get reinforcements from Port Ammond," Yavi said as she thumped the Oathbreaker's shoulder. "We might do fine against these seven, but what if there are more? Zaur like to fight in large numbers, right? There should be more."

"There aren't more," Dolvek whispered back. "A larger force couldn't have made it through from the mountains without getting spotted by patrols. I can see how seven could have gotten past your people, but not . . ."

"My people!" Yavi winced and lowered her voice. "My people didn't miss them. Oathbreakers are the ones who use mystic artifice to patrol their borders. These could come through Rin'Saen Gorge, or even through the pass at Albren. Unless the few nonmagical patrols you have were paying more attention than they usually do, an army of Zaur could get through!"

Dolvek shook his head and drew his glittering longsword, the blade erupting in mystic blue flame. "If you want to get reinforcements, go. I shall rid the world of these Zaur personally."

With that, he ran toward the Place of Conjunction, flaming sword in his right hand and a conjured shield of ice on his left arm.

This one's not worth saving, Kholster sent to Bloodmane from his spot in trees.

But he's a prince.

Royalty doesn't season the meat.

"Of all the pompous . . ." Yavi fumed quietly. "Magic doesn't work against the Zaur! Did they forget to mention that in your training?" She shook her head.

Even in the heat of battle, he's running up the Eldrennai path, Vander scoffed.

"I just hope Kholster gets here soon," Yavi muttered. "If not, I'll have to save Gloomy's hide myself."

Kholster felt a tinge of guilt and unslung his warpick. *I'll intercede if she needs me.*

Good, Bloodmane answered.

The young Vael stopped talking and concentrated on her connection to the forest. Kholster had seen it often, the way a Vael spread out her arms, fingers splayed, even the long ears flexing out in an arc reaching, stretching for the forest. Muttering a quiet prayer to Xalistan, god of the hunt, Yavi readied her bow and ran in a wide arc to attack the Zaur's flank.

Kholster admired the bow. He could no more grow such a weapon from a living tree than a Vael could forge a soul-bound weapon, but he respected the craftsmanship that went into creating a Vaelish heartbow. It was hard enough for some Aern to convince their own souls to bond with a forged implement; he could not imagine how the Vael cajoled nature spirits, or in rarer cases, a sliver of the spirit of the forest itself, to abide within their bows.

She'll be fine. Even so, Kholster lowered his warpick and moved closer . . . just in case.

*

For the life of her, Yavi couldn't understand what Dolvek was thinking. Noiselessly gliding through the forest, Yavi paused at the edge of the clearing and blanched as the Zaur crossed swords with Dolvek. He clearly wasn't used to fighting opponents like these, and it showed in his sword work. The Zaur darted about like quicksilver, striking with their angular blades.

Taking careful aim, Yavi nocked an arrow, drew it back, and fired. The first arrow thunked against a Zaur's left vambrace. Yavi fired again, and the second shot struck home, piercing one of the Zaur at the base of its skull and sending it crashing to the ground, rolling and twitching like a dying snake.

Dolvek swung at the Zaur in front of him, inflicting a deep cut to the Zaur's right shoulder, but as the fiery blade touched the creature's skin, the sword's flame flickered and went out. Ignoring his misfortune, Dolvek blocked two blows from a Skreel blade with his ice shield, only to watch, mouth agape, as the shield began to crack.

He probably wouldn't believe a berry was poisonous until he'd eaten three of them.

Dolvek soldiered on, the thin core of steel worked into his longsword gave him something to work with even without the layer of flame and crystal, but the shield would soon be completely useless. Moving around him in a circle, the Zaur lashed out at him with their Skreel. Dolvek didn't notice when the first Zaur Yavi killed went down, but he did hear the cry of pain when her next arrow took a Zaur to his right through the arm.

It shrieked, black blood running down the injured limb, a shriek that was echoed by Dolvek when one of the Skreel blades found its mark and cut through his crystal armor, shattering his right vambrace. Maintaining the grip on his longsword was the perhaps the most difficult thing he had ever done, but he smiled when he slashed the throat of one of his attackers.

Two of the Zaur broke off and ran for Yavi. As one, the other three rushed Dolvek and grappled him to the ground. Something stung the back of his hand, and the sword dropped out of it. Pain shot up from his wrist to his elbow, and he realized that one of the Zaur had bitten him. He could already feel the arm going numb.

"Run for reinforcements!" he yelled at the top of his lungs. "Don't let them get you, Yavi! Get out of here!"

*

Yavi fired at one of the two Zaur charging her position; her arrow struck it in the eye. The point drove deep into its brain, and the creature only took two more steps before falling dead on the ground. The second Zaur kept coming, running in a low, tucked position and zigzagging as it came.

Nocking an arrow, Yavi held her shot, aiming as long as she could. She would only get one shot before the Zaur would be upon her. Taking two quick breaths, she let go the arrow between them and cursed as the creature nimbly dodged.

Yavi drew her long knife, whispered a spell, and hoped that the breeze spirits would respond quickly.

The Zaur closed with her, delivering two rapid slashes with its blade. Yavi parried the strikes with equal parts luck and skill.

"C'mon," she said in a singsong voice. "Please? It'll be fu-un!" Around her, the wind slowly picked up, a cooling zephyr from the Bay of Balsiph. It began as a small breeze but grew in strength with each passing second. Continuing its strikes, the Zaur darted in to attack, but Yavi felt two ethereal hands grasp her under the arms and jerk her into the air.

"You are marveficent!" Yavi cheered. "Fabtacular!"

"Come back here, little bud!" The Zaur rose on its hind legs and hissed at her. "We have your mate."

"Not mine," Yavi sheathed her long knife and drew her bow, firing with less grace than usual, her hair petals flapping in her face. The first arrow went wide, thudding into the ground, but the second struck her opponent in the neck.

A series of grunted curses in Eldrennaic brought Yavi's attention back to Dolvek. The prince struggled, facing the three remaining Zaur, and—to Yavi's amazement—appeared to have disabled one.

One of the last two opened its maw to bite. Dolvek reached into its mouth and grabbed its serpentine tongue. The other Zaur sank its teeth into the prince's shoulder, but Dolvek refused to let go.

Letting her spell fade, Yavi dropped lithely to the ground, mouthing a quick thanks to the wind spirit before loosing another arrow. Dark blood gushed from the throat of the Zaur biting Dolvek's shoulder. It fell dead, and the prince rolled atop the remaining one, continuing to pull at its tongue. Dolvek's face seemed transformed before Yavi's eyes from the arrogant scholar who played at swords and magic to the beginnings of some new barbaric thing, mouth opened in an unintelligible cry of aggression. With a wet, tearing sound, the Zaur's tongue came free.

Dolvek rolled to one side, kicking the choking lizard off of him. Yavi quickly finished it with a shot from her heartbow.

"That was utterly revolting," Yavi said, walking over to him. "And why didn't you fly?"

Dolvek's blood ran from numerous shallow cuts, his crystal armor covered in weblike cracks and jagged holes where chunks had broken away.

Three separate bite marks, one on his shoulder and two on his arm, had already begun to swell and turn red. Yavi thought she remembered something about Zaur poison only being fatal during their mating season; the rest of the year the fast-working venom acted only as a paralytic agent. Purple lines lanced away from the bites, following the veins. "That can't be good."

"It will only paralyze me." Dolvek tried to get back up but fell onto his back instead with a groan.

"And you know for certain that this isn't the Zaur mating season?" Yavi asked.

"You can tell by their bellies." Dolvek propped himself ineffectually on an elbow. "According to Sargus, their underside turns purple, and they emit a very distinctive scent."

Yavi looked over the one that had gnawed at the prince's shoulder, nudging it onto its back with her boot. A faint purple blotch darkened the center of its stomach. It smelled different than the others too, reptilian, but coppery and bitter. "I'm going to call this a bad sign."

"Depends on your point of view," growled a deep voice behind her.

Yavi fitted another arrow as she turned, releasing it in surprise. The newcomer, an Aern wearing smoked lenses, bone-steel mail, and carrying a warpick, took the arrow in the chest. He reached up and pulled the arrow free, with no more sign of anger or pain than a raised eyebrow. "That sort of greeting, I'd expect from the Oathbreaker."

"Bloodmane," Yavi gasped.

"My warsuit; not me. I'm Kholster," he handed her back the arrow heedless of the near-orange blood that stained its tip, "but you already knew that."

"You have to help Dolvek," Yavi said. "He was . . ."

"Bitten by a Zaur in rut." Kholster circled the fallen Eldrennai twice before kneeling to examine his wounds. "Pulled its tongue out. Almost impressive."

Dolvek blinked furiously, trying, Yavi thought, to focus on Kholster. After a few moments of trying, the prince coughed once and slumped to the ground, unconscious.

"He'll be dead by morning." Kholster spat on the prince and sat down, his back against the central obelisk, warpick resting across his knees.

"You can't help him?" Yavi asked.

"Won't." Kholster closed his eyes, a smile crashing against the edge of his lips and dying there, unsuccessful.

"What?" Yavi demanded. "Why not?"

"I want him dead. He's an Oathbreaker." His eyes flicked open. The amber pupils glowed dimly. "I want them all dead."

"Is it something I can do?" Yavi took a few steps closer, kneeling down in front of Kholster.

"A cure for Zaur venom is our birthright, but no Aern would lift a finger to help an Eldrennai, much less this one . . ." He let the rest of his explanation die on his lips and shook his head before continuing. "If you want to help the Eldrennai, you should go back to Ammond and tell Grivek his son is dying. Tell him to send out the eldest one," he gestured absently, "Rivvek. No. Wait. He's one of mine now. Tell the old king to come himself. If he's lucky, he'll die before his child. That's what parents want. I'll be here when you get back. I might even leave them something to bury. Do you think I should eat him now or wait for the poison to kill him first?"

That someone could hate another people so much was almost beyond Yavi. She stared at the Aern, half-hoping it was some cruel jest but knowing it wasn't.

"One of yours?" Yavi asked.

"Aiannai. My own scars, for that one." Kholster's eyes narrowed. "It's not that surprising to have found a few hundred Eldrennai who weren't really Oathbreakers."

"Explain that," Yavi ordered.

"If I have to explain it," Kholster said softly, "then it has no meaning."

CHAPTER 43
FIGURES IN THE CLOUDS

Kilke chuckled at Kholster's words, scratching absentmindedly at the stump between his two remaining heads, the sound of blue talons on his deeply purple flesh like a tiger rending a burlap sack. Peering unseen into Kholster's angry gaze, Kilke's eyes thrummed with a subtle silver glow, casting strange shadows on his brow.

Those same shadows occasionally withdrew from his face completely as if needing to be refreshed by the chimerical garb of living shadow he wore. Then, suddenly, he was clad in full plate wrought of blackest pitch covering every inch of him, even going so far as to encase the massive horns adorning his two remaining heads, the next moment, the plate gave way to voluminous hooded robes.

"Are you sure I can't choose him as my champion, Torgrimm?"

Kilke knew the answer already, but goading the Harvester of Souls was one of the dark god's favorite hobbies.

"You know the answer, Kilke." Torgrimm materialized next to the god of secrets and shadows, clad in bone armor reminiscent of an Aernese warsuit.

"Still wearing the warsuit?" Kilke's laughed boomed. "Decided to give Dienox a good thumping, or did my sister ask you to play dress-up?"

Ignore the bait like a good little god and spell out the rules again, Kilke thought. *You know you want to do it.*

Kilke had memorized the speech. It was the same every Conjunction. Kilke would ask if he could make Kholster his champion. Torgrimm would say, "Other than myself and my wife Minapsis, any deity may choose a mortal soul as champion, but it must be one I have delivered into a being and that in time I shall collect and deliver to her . . ." He would pause, wave his hand to the statue of his goddess wife standing beside him, ". . . safe keeping. The first One Hundred Aern may not be chosen. Their souls are the creation of the Eldrennai wizard, Uled. I am not required to collect them nor am I required to accept them as candidates in the competition."

Kilke waited. The speech did not come.

The Harvester? Up to something? How interesting.

"No lecture?" Dressed in plain brown robes with a golden book tucked under his arm, Aldo appeared in the air above his statue, choosing to appear as a noble Eldrennai rather than sport the empty-socketed visage which Kilke knew to be his more true self.

"None." Torgrimm shook his head. "You have chosen to play games with the souls of mortals once again. Another grand game. I merely hope the souls of those involved will not suffer too greatly. Whenever you all do this, I have to reincarnate half of the players."

"Calm yourself, Harvester," said a golden-haired goddess. Sunlight and starshine radiated from beneath her eyelids, the eyes themselves unseen.

"I am quite calm, Shidarva."

"Majesty." Kilke bowed. *Usurper!* he thought, struggling to mask his hatred of her. He longed to cleave her head from her neck and cast it down to the ruins of Alt for the fish to worship—if Queelay would allow such a thing.

"I see Dienox's new champion has been laid low," Shidarva said, stepping past him.

"He should have sided with me." Kilke turned to speak directly to Aldo, giving Shidarva his back. "Dienox spent all that time cloaking the Zaur from the Eldrennai and the Vael to make sure the war was large enough . . . I will never understand the desire for a drawn-out victory."

"So you've chosen a Zaur as champion? This Xastix, perhaps?" Shidarva asked.

"Aldo knows my choice, as required." Kilke brought the talons of his right hand together in a point, the shadows wrapping around them to form gauntlets, resting against his lips. "I have no desire to ruin the surprise when you meet them."

"Them? If you have broken the rules—" Shidarva began, but her voice was cut off by a roar. Xalistan, lord of the hunt, master of wilderness, emerged from the clearing's edge, tossing back his massive irkanth head in a second roar, his tremendous leathery wings spread wide in a threatening display.

"I may quake with fear eventually," Kilke yawned. "I wasn't ready. Try a third time."

Xalistan bared his leonine teeth, an expression Kilke met with an indolent smirk.

"No one is cheating," Aldo said with all the emotion of a bored schoolmarm. "I would know."

You should know, Kilke thought. *In the past, I would have gone so far as to be sure you would know. But do you? Do you really? It would be almost worth it to test you.*

"What did you do to him?" Dienox appeared in a burst of flame, soaking wet and smelling of the sea. He crouched over Dolvek with a snarl. "Get up, fool!"

*

Dolvek could hear many voices arguing over his body. Words slid through his head with little impact as he flowed in and out of consciousness. He had an impression of Yavi arguing passionately with the Grudgebearer. Warmth flooded him. *She's fighting for me.*

"Kholster, please," Yavi laid the back of her hand against his shoulder. "Compared to you he is just a child. If you won't help him yourself then surely you can help me to help him."

"If I must," the Grudgebearer said slowly. "I will tell you how to make the antidote to the Zaur poison, but you must make it yourself, and you must promise . . ." Other voices rose up, obscuring the Grudgebearer's next words.

"Ha! He's going to help him. I still have a chance!" one voice shouted over the murmurs of the others.

"Perhaps you will at that, Dienox," said an oily-sounding voice, "but you can't rely on the Aern to rescue him every time he . . ."

"On the contrary," interrupted a cold, distant voice. "The Aern are reliable to a fault. If the Eldrennai manage to enlist their aid . . ."

" . . . All right," a soft, warm voice said. "Will these risaberries do?"

"Yes, Yavi," Kholster answered. "Crush them with the helva root. You want to blend them gently until they're very purple, but if the mixture is too dark you'll have to start over."

"How dark is too dark?"

"Stop. Let me see what you have. You want it a few shades darker than that, but not . . ."

The words of the Aern drained away to silence, once more replaced by other, more insistent, voices. Strange beings appeared at the edges of Dolvek's perception. One of them stood in better focus than the rest, an Aern in bone armor. He crossed to stand directly over the feverish Eldrennai and said nothing, but Dolvek knew him instantly.

"Are you going to collect him, Torgrimm?" asked a scholarly voice. "Is it time?"

"Lord Torgrimm," Dolvek muttered weakly. "Harvester of Souls."

"He'll either die here or take the first hammer blow of his forging," Torgrimm answered, his eyes locked with Dolvek's. "It is not up to me, I simply collect them: the fulfilled, the unlucky, the unwilling."

"Unwilling?" asked someone impatiently.

"Yes," Torgrimm continued. The Harvester bent low, his breath surprisingly cool on Dolvek's fevered brow. "The fulfilled are those who die having accomplished all that they meant to do. Some are old, some are young. But they welcome my embrace. They miss their world, but they are ready for me to take them to the next one."

Hot jagged pain lanced through Dolvek's entire body and he screamed.

"It's hurting him." Yavi's voice echoed in the distance.

"There is a final ingredient," Kholster said, sounding to Dolvek as though he were somewhere deep beneath the ground. "Without it, the antidote is a poison more deadly than the venom itself." Or perhaps it was simply that Dolvek now seemed to soar above them. A man in bronze armor coalesced next to him. Other figures sprang in focus as well, a woman, regal and dressed in white, a two-headed monster, a human girl with flaming hair . . .

"I can see them," Dolvek gasped. "I can see the gods!"

"The unlucky are many," Torgrimm continued, bending even lower so that his weight bore down on the prince's chest. "The murdered, those who die in accidents . . . they had no choice in their own deaths. When I come for them, they are bewildered and confused. It is different for the unwilling."

All of the gods faded away, except for the Harvester. His callused hand, warmer and more comforting than Dolvek had expected, touched the Eldrennai's forehead, and the god seemed to apply gentle pressure. As the pressure increased, Dolvek felt himself propelled downward, back into his pain-wracked body. Yavi's and Kholster's outlines returned and snapped into sudden definition, though he could still see the form of the Harvester bending over him.

Do you want to come with me now? Torgrimm's eyes asked him.

"No."

Very well, an eyeblink seemed to say.

Yavi shook her head as Kholster offered a knife to the Vaelsilyn. "I can't," she protested, pressing her knuckles against his wrist, pushing the knife away without entrapping his arm. *She is in awe of him*, Dolvek thought, his mind drifting. *Why can't she treat me that way?* "A Vael would never . . ."

"It is the only way that he can live," the other said firmly. "The blood of an Aern is the final ingredient. I will shed none for an Eldrennai, but for the Vael, I will offer it gladly; you have simply to collect it."

"No!" Dolvek protested weakly, "I will not . . . I cannot allow myself to be . . ." His skin grew paler and his breath more ragged. The thought of being saved with the blood of a Grudgebearer was unacceptable.

The Harvester of Souls leaned closer to Dolvek's face, the god's mouth almost touching his lips. As Torgrimm spoke, Dolvek felt himself begin to lose hold of his own body. "The unwilling come to me full of emotions: hate, fear, loathing, despair. They try to lecture me, to protest that it was not fair, to blame anyone but themselves."

Torgrimm sneered at Dolvek as if he were a loathsome thing. "The unwilling die because they are not willing to live. They whine and mewl, but their deaths are on their own hands, not mine. I kill no one. I deliver. I collect." Torgrimm rose in one motion as Yavi took the knife from Kholster. As she drew it free, Dolvek saw Kholster tighten his grip on the blade, causing it to slash his palm.

Drops of orange blood fell from the wound, hot and scalding on Dolvek's cheek, bitter and peppery in his mouth.

"There," exclaimed a distant voice. "Aern's blood. The antidote is complete! Was it soon enough, Torgrimm?"

"That is not up to me, Dienox," Torgrimm said acidly. "As I've explained before, I do not choose. I could, but I have never done so. I collect only upon death. I am never late, but neither am I early."

"I want to live," Dolvek whispered.

You have not stopped living, the god's gentle voice echoed in Dolvek's mind.

Hovering over his prone form, Yavi looked into the young elf's eyes, then back to Kholster. "Will he live?"

"Not if we're lucky," the Aern answered dryly. "A warrior has to fight to survive. The only fighting blood in this one is what he just swallowed." He clenched his fist again over Dolvek's face, and one last orange droplet struck the prince's cheek.

Darkness crept in around the edges and his vision began to fade, but Dolvek fought, raging voicelessly against the Zaur, against Kholster, and most of all against that part of himself which thought it would all be easier if he simply gave up and went with Torgrimm to the next life.

"Not yet," he murmured feverishly as he drifted from semiconsciousness into healing slumber. It was not a restful sleep, nor did he dream. He had no time for dreams. Dolvek had accepted the first hammer blow of his forging; he was too busy fighting.

CHAPTER 44
THE THREE RACES OF ELVES

Yavi watched as Kholster slammed together two fist-sized blocks of obsidian, each carved with sharply chiseled runes. When they met, the stones merged and the runes blazed red. Kholster set the combined block on the ground near the fallen Eldrennai and sighed.

"That will keep him warm."

Yavi felt the heat from the stone even where she stood, several feet away. "Is that a Dwarven Hearth Stone?" she asked.

Kholster smiled broadly, revealing his doubled canines. Combined with the light of the Hearth Stone it lent a demonic cast to his features. "No," he answered softly. Yavi marveled at how gentle his voice sounded, so different from the cold, angry tones he had used when helping her make the antidote for the Zaur venom. "It's an Aernese Hearth Stone, but yes, Dwarves made it."

He pointed to the top of the glowing Stone. "A Dwarven Hearth Stone would have an indentation on top."

"What for?" asked Yavi, coming closer to inspect the Stone.

"To deactivate it. It would cool and then separate."

"So Aernese Hearth Stones are only good for one use?"

"No. We pick them up and pull them apart to turn them off," he answered, miming the action with his hands.

"That sounds painful," Yavi said, blanching at the thought.

"It can be," Kholster said glibly, then chuckled. "To be honest, most of us just use our warpicks." He lifted his and swung it in a careful arc. As its tip struck the exact center of the Hearth Stone, a small line appeared and the blocks began to separate. Withdrawing the tip before the two stones completely parted, Kholster slung the weapon on his back once more. "It's an excellent test of precision and muscle control."

"I can see that," Yavi acknowledged. "What about Dolvek? Will he live?"

Kholster walked over to Dolvek's prone form, crouched to inspect the wound on his shoulder, and then dug his fingers sharply into it, eliciting a loud groan from the slumbering Eldrennai.

"It seems likely," Kholster told her. "It's hard for me to care." He showed Yavi his palm where she had cut him. The wound was already closed; only a thin orange line marked the cut, and as she watched even that faded to match the surrounding bronze skin. "Eldrennai heal too slowly for me to be sure, but if he can feel pain and react to it, then he might recover." He shrugged. "If not, you can always get a replacement from Port Ammond."

"Don't be so callous," Yavi admonished. "I could have been dead without him."

"No," Kholster disagreed. "I would have interfered if you'd been alone."

Yavi glared at him, then turned away and walked to one of the ancient *ehmar* trees. Its leaves were broad and round, and from beneath its bark the tree spirit peeked out at the three humanoids.

"How long did he stand there?" Yavi asked. "Did you see him, *Ehmar-ama*?"

A round, fat head pushed out from beneath the bark. "See?" it asked. "I see him, that one, many times, Pretty One, but for how long which time? Too many times is he here, that one. Always arguing and fighting, but never with fire. Heats rocks, that one. Puts out fire, that one. Never brings it."

"Thank you," Yavi said politely, then she stomped her foot and looked petulantly at Kholster. "It doesn't know."

"Then why don't you ask me again?" Kholster asked as he walked past the obelisk and the statues of the gods, out onto the pier. Formed from the same material as the obelisk, it extended out into the water of the Bay of Balsiph. On the end of the pier, the same words floated, written in all the known tongues of Barrone, including some which were no longer recognized. On Kholster's back, the spirit within his warpick flowed up its hilt and perched on his shoulder like a bird of prey. The same bright orange as Kholster's blood, the spirit watched Yavi with amber-colored eyes. It looked away from her and shrieked angrily at the obelisk. Kholster laughed.

"She doesn't like this place. This stone. It looks like obsidian, but no one knows what it really is. Grudge doesn't like it, because she can't cut through it."

"She?" Yavi asked.

"You're a Vael. I know you can see her," Kholster explained. "I've only seen Grudge once. When the metal cooled, as I finished wrapping her haft, she flew out of me, a beautiful, angry hawk, and sank into the weapon. Then I knew she was complete. When my mind is quiet, I can feel her. When I fight, I sometimes hear her battle cry."

Yavi ran her hand along the smooth surface of the obelisk as she listened. It rose up into the sky and out along the ground, a seamless mass of black. Fifteen hands wide and ninety hands high, the obelisk was ringed with inscriptions in every language. Careful golden letters and runes, not carved but floating just below the surface, spoke cryptically to its purpose: "Welcome to Oot."

Yavi followed the Aern from the base of the obelisk out along the pier. "She's beautiful," Yavi said softly as she closed with Kholster. She felt self-conscious standing next to him, resisted the urge to lean against him. Vael were made for the Aern. Yavi had heard that over and over growing up, but she'd never felt it, not before meeting one.

"Thank you, daughter of Kari." Kholster pointed to the sun, setting in the distance, and walked back to the obelisk. His hand touched its black surface above the Aernese translation. "I, Kholster, First of One Hundred, of the Exiled Army, once slave, now free, greet you in good faith."

"What?" she asked. Her eyes widened, and she joined him at the obelisk. It was the ceremony! She looked at Dolvek's prone form. Kholster was starting the ceremony early. Could he do that?

"I . . . I am Yavi, daughter of Kari, princess of The Parliament of Ages and Guardian of the Rule of Leaf. Your ancestral home awaits you should you wish to return to it. You and all your kind are welcome here. You have long been missed."

Kholster removed his smoked-glass lenses, revealing eyes that were black where they might otherwise have been white, just as Yavi's mother had said. His irises were pale jade in color, his pupils amber, a startling contrast to the blackness surrounding them. "I speak for the Aern. We will gladly return to the forest with you to dwell together with the Vael, to teach and be taught. We do, however, have one condition."

"And what might that be?" Yavi asked sadly. She had been warned Kholster always responded the same way.

"Do the Oathbreakers yet live? Have their towers tumbled? Has their lifeblood poured out upon their beloved plains?"

"The Eldrennai dwindle, but they live. Their borders shrink, but their towers stand tall," Yavi said softly.

Kholster's eyes flicked to the left as if he saw something she didn't and was enraged or heartbroken, she couldn't tell which, only that behind it loomed a wall of hatred and slaughter so great she could not encompass it all. "Then the Grudge we bear is borne still, and we regret that we cannot return. We, most of us, will dwell upon the blue forest of the sea and in the lush caverns far to the south with our brothers, the Dwarves. The Vael may visit us whenever they will, and we will make for them a welcome place at our table."

Kholster cast a hate-filled glance at Dolvek. The injured prince's chest rose and fell slightly as though he barely drew breath. There was no way he could answer.

"You can't expect him to go through the ritual," Yavi protested. "He's been injured."

"His oath to break," Kholster said dismissively.

"No, it was the Zaur's fault," she argued.

"I've never seen a battle involving an Eldrennai that was not the fault of an Eldrennai, but if you tell me it is not so . . . that you were ambushed . . ."

"Are you quite finished?" Dolvek coughed weakly.

Yavi thought she spied a look of admiration cross Kholster's face, but it quickly vanished.

"The ritual, you high-born, stump-eared maggot," Kholster chided. "Invite us to your lands."

"Will you . . . come . . . in peace to the El . . . to the Eldren Plains?" Dolvek gasped through a fit of coughing.

Kholster waited until Dolvek caught his breath before responding. "No, only to destroy them."

Dolvek opened his mouth to reply, erupting instead into an even more painful-sounding hacking cough. Yavi felt Kholster press a waterskin into her hand. She gave him a perilous look of anger but took it and helped Dolvek swallow a few sips. The water seemed to help.

"Will you sit in peace at our table?" Dolvek gasped out.

"Only in celebration of your doom," Kholster answered.

"We understand of old the ill will you bear us. We created your people and the Vaelsilyn as slaves, forgetting the most basic tenet of our people, that life is sacred and that no thinking being can be owned by another. If there is some reparation we could make, some way we can make amends, please tell me and I will carry it back to the Council of Elements." Dolvek uttered his memorized words as quickly as possible and then grabbed for the waterskin.

Kholster waited patiently for him to finish drinking and then took the empty skin from Yavi. "There is."

Yavi gasped. This was not the usual response. Kholster continued, "Seven times I have come here." He pounded his fist against his chest. "I, who still remember the touch of the Eldrennai lash, have come here to this place each and every time my presence has been requested." He shook his head. "For centuries I have had to look into the face of an Eldrennai, a so-called noble prince, each of whom seemed to feel the Aern should still be in the thrall of their former masters."

"Let it go," Dolvek sneered.

Kholster snorted. "My words are like seeds sown on salted earth. You reject my offer before it is even made. So be it. You should have listened to Wylant, you are all of you doomed."

"What?"

Kholster closed his eyes tiredly, replacing his smoked-glass lenses, and turned to Yavi. "You are the most beautiful female I have ever seen, and I have walked the face of Barrone for more than seven thousand years. You know that the Aern do not lie. So, with whatever great ill comes to pass from the breaking of this pact, know that your people have but to call and we will come in force to help you. Should you need to flee your forest, come to the sea or to our caves and we will make you welcome. Life to you and yours," Kholster turned on his leather-booted heel and strode toward the water.

"Good riddance," croaked Dolvek through gritted teeth.

Sighing, Yavi rubbed her eyes. It was exactly as her grandmother had said it would be. "The Eldrennai never fail to argue with the Aern," her gran had told her. "It will be up to you to keep the peace. There has yet to be a peaceful resolution to anything between those two that the Vael didn't carefully nurture and bring to pass."

Remembering her gran, Yavi held up her hands and shouted, "Wait!"

Kholster stopped, listening, but did not turn.

"You must stay," she said gently. "All three of us are needed here. Three, one of each race, for three days. That is all that is required to keep the trust."

"Forget the trust," Kholster told her, tossing the words back over his shoulder. "Think instead about the Zaur on your borders. I killed more of them in the forest; scouts, just like the ones you fought here. There is a new warlord. His name is Xastix."

Dolvek let his head fall back to the ground, but Yavi simply stared. "How do you know that?" she questioned, following him out onto the pier.

"I interrogated one of the scouts." Kholster folded his arms, still presenting his back to both Yavi and Dolvek. "Xastix wanted to stop the Grand Conjunction, to keep it from taking place. Then, I think he plans to attack."

Yavi touched his shoulder with the back of her hand, a uniquely Vaelsilyn touch, intended to calm but not to restrain. "Do you know when?"

"He'll likely give his scouts two or three days to report back," Kholster said thoughtfully, turning to gaze past her toward the sinking sun. "Then he'll take another day or so to rally his troops, get them moving. I worried about the number of Zaur here, though. There should have been more."

"And a Named one," she agreed.

He looked down at her again, pointing with such precision as he spoke that Yavi was certain he knew instinctively where the cities lay, despite his long absence. "He'll probably hit Stone Watch or Albren. They'll attack the Eldrennai first, giving the Vael time to prepare a defense or . . ." He stroked Yavi's cheek along the edge of her samir gently with his fingertips, his voice dropping to a more intimate level, too quiet for Dolvek to hear. "The Vael can come with me, retreat south toward Castleguard. It would not take long for reinforcements to arrive."

"No," Yavi told him. "We couldn't."

"Once the reinforcements get here," he continued in his normal tone, almost ignoring her words, "we can push back into The Parliament of Ages, ensure its safety, and head northeast into the Eldren Plains to drive the Zaur out and reclaim our homeland."

"What of my people?" scoffed Dolvek, setting off another fit of coughing.

"You'll be dead by the time we return," Kholster snarled. "We'll build a monument to you, of course. It can tell how the Eldrennai redeemed themselves with their final sacrifice . . . how they protected the homeland of the Vael and the Aern with their last breaths," he continued sarcastically. "Don't worry, stump ears, I'll make sure it's fit for a king."

CHAPTER 45
UNLIKELY ALLIES

King Grivek entered the Aern exhibit his son had built and dismissed his guards. Bloodstains still marred the rich carpet, and the whole chamber stank of death. The slender crown of crystal and steel he wore upon his brow seemed to press down on him as he walked. His face was young, but his movements revealed his age. It was all so very tiring. Shards of crystal crunched under his boots with each step as he walked across the room and stood before the armor of General Bloodmane.

Phantom voices of advisors, both living and dead, haunted his thoughts. He hadn't asked anyone's permission, nor had he asked their opinions. They had been with him so long he knew what many of them would tell him anyway.

"It's rash and unwise," Barthus would say.

Ghijik would have asked for money and suggested "a simple but exhaustive oracular analysis of the possible outcomes."

If Braert had survived the Sundering, then Grivek would have asked for his thoughts on the subject, but like so many good beings on all three sides, Braert had been struck down in fury and hatred, in the chaos of the rebellion. Lastly there was Wylant.

He owed his crown and the lives of all his people to Wylant, but he knew what she would say. She would advise a path of bloodshed. The Sundering had broken something in Wylant . . . since that time, she'd grown harder, colder. She was still a brilliant tactician, but there was an inner glow, a lust for life that had vanished. The only blonde in a dark-haired race, her golden tresses had marked her as blessed by the gods, yet since that time she had shaved her head regularly, letting not even the barest hint of stubble show. Maybe Wylant could come up with another miracle to defeat the Aern, but Grivek thought too much blood had been shed already.

"You're weak, boy!" He imagined his father's outraged voice, strong and unwavering, but also quite wrong. "You should have killed them all, the ungrateful savages! How dare they raise their hands against us? We created them! We are their gods!"

In his splendid robes, King Grivek approached the center of the chamber and stared at the homunculus, the unborn Aern. In the remains of their cases, ten warsuits of the surviving first One Hundred Aern glared at him, unmoving but possessed of an intelligence beyond even what he had come to suspect.

He spread his arms in a gesture of peace before addressing the armor. It wouldn't do to have them strike him down in an attempt to protect a comrade who was in no danger.

"I'm not going to hurt him," he said in Aernese. "Bloodmane, Falcon's Claw, Heart Taker, Eyes of Vengeance, all of you . . . I want you to know that."

He approached Bloodmane and bowed his head, placing the scroll on the floor before him. Grivek removed his crown and set it on the pedestal next to Hunger, General Kholster's ancient weapon. Words slid from his grasp beneath the armor's crystalline gaze. What could he say to make them understand what he was trying to do? They were intelligent; Yavi said Bloodmane had spoken to her with eloquence. Their spirits were battered and angry, but they were good spirits with noble minds, not the mindless implements of war his father had thought them to be.

"I . . . I was wrong, and I'm sorry. My father was wrong. We didn't understand, have never understood. We thought we were gods, but though immortal, we are not divine." He fumbled with his cloak self-consciously and reached for words with his left hand as if they might succumb to his searching and materialize in his grasp.

"None of the past can be undone, but I can put one thing right." He gestured to the homunculus, still sleeping, unliving, yet, as Yavi had assured him, with a spirit attached to it for all these thousands of years, waiting to be born.

"Your brother can be awakened." He met the eyes of each suit as he spoke. *Great Aldo, let them see my sincerity*, he silently prayed. "I didn't know enough to know that he had a soul . . . that he was waiting for the words of life. I thought . . . In my ignorance, I thought he was a thing, a physical prototype . . . until the coming of Yavi, daughter of Kari, a princess among the Vael. After much searching, I have found the scroll in the archives amongst Uled's writings. I don't want to offend you further by reading it myself."

Swabbing his brow absentmindedly with the edge of his sleeve, Grivek realized that he was sweating. "No magic should be required. Just the correct words . . . so I was hoping you would read them. Then you would know I'm not . . . not trying to be a god . . . just trying to . . . make things right."

Crystal eyes inset in the helmet resembling a roaring irkanth lit up from within, and Grivek took two steps backward. He'd managed to get their attention.

"This?" whispered a metallic voice. "The words are on this paper?" Bloodmane stooped to pick up the scroll and held it in front of Grivek.

"Where it says 'Rite of Creation,'" Grivek answered.

"Are there others?" the voice asked.

"Other scrolls?" asked Grivek.

Bloodmane stepped out of its shattered display, crystal crunching beneath its boots. "Other sleeping ones."

"No. Or, rather, I think not. I'll look. No, that's not the whole truth. Yes, I will look, but we'll know soonest if I have Sargus look," Grivek assured the massive metal warsuit. "If there are any other sleeping ones I . . . we . . . will find them and bring them to you."

For four long minutes that felt like hours, the armor stood and watched him. Grivek's gaze flitted from warsuit to warsuit as their eyes flickered brightly in no discernable pattern. Were they communicating? Could they somehow speak with one another telepathically?

He remembered seeing the Aern in battle, before the Sundering, their uncanny coordination and wordless combat. Even in the Battle of As You Please, a demonstration he'd been forced to attend as a child, the Aern had moved in a silent ballet of death. That had to be it! But if it were true, great Aldo, what if the armor was still in contact with the Aern? What if Kholster knew that Grivek's son, whom he'd sent to the Conjunction, had broken the treaty by moving their weapons and armor?

Ten sets of crystalline eyes flickered brightly, and then Bloodmane spoke. "Why are you doing this?" it asked.

"Because someone has to do something," he answered. "Someone has to step forward and do more than offer empty platitudes once every century. And who else is there, but me? I am the king." He closed his eyes briefly and sighed. "I was there."

"Yes, I remember," the armor said softly, then snapped out an order. "Send soldiers to Oot. Send a physician with them."

"Why? What has happened?"

"Do not question me, Eldrennai king."

Eldrennai? Not Oathbreaker? Grivek struggled to hold his tongue.

"Send scouts, real scouts, not mystic constructs, to check the Watches. There are Zaur within your borders. We must know how many there are and how soon they can attack." The armor rested a cold gauntlet on his shoulder. "We must do this if we are to save your land, Eldrennai king."

"I will do as you say," Grivek stammered. "It will be done at once. Thank you."

"Do not thank me," the empty armor told him. It pointed at the plaque beneath its empty pedestal. "I am Bloodmane, armor of Kholster, but I am not Kholster. I can forgive you. Perhaps it is because I lack blood to boil. Perhaps it is that I have no heart to ache, but I believe you are worth forgiving."

"But surely," Grivek said imploringly. "You could speak to them, explain to them."

"That you have convinced me and my fellow warsuits is useless unless you can convince the core of us, our soldiers, our makers, our rightful occupants. We are tools, the implements of war. What our creators will, we do. An axe has no loyalty to a tree. If an axe is turned by the woodsman against the very tree from which its haft was hewn, will it not cut as deeply? If it feels sympathy for the wood, to whom does it protest? It is merely an axe. So it is for me and mine, Eldrennai king."

"I understand," the elf king sighed, then glanced toward the unborn Aern. "I will leave you to perform the ritual in private."

Once the doors were closed behind him, Grivek and his royal guard stood listening at the entrance. Their hearing was not as good as the Vael's or the Aern's. Eldrennai senses were scarcely better than a human's. Grivek could not make out the words Bloodmane spoke, but the cadence sounded right.

Jolsit, captain of the guards, stared at his king, confusion clear upon his face. "Your Majesty?"

"How many squadrons of Crystal Knights have you formed? Was it four?" Grivek stepped away from the large doors. "Tell me it was more than that."

"Six, your Majesty. Seven if we count your royal guard."

"Do they still have metal armor?" Grivek asked.

"They do, Majesty," the captain admitted, "but they wear it in exercises only as punishment. Though Wylant and her Lance always wear metal."

"Is she still in North Guard?"

"She has taken her Lance to Albren Pass, but I know she intends to press on to Stone Guard . . ."

"Excellent." King Grivek laughed bitterly as he left the museum. He walked quickly, nearly running. It would normally have amused him, watching his guards trying to maintain decorum while matching his pace, but this was no time for frivolity. "Ready them all, my royal guard included. They are to pack their crystal armor but wear their plate and mail. Each troop is to head to the watch towers. We are going to physically check our borders. Gods, what I wouldn't give for a handful of Long Speakers right now."

"Of course, sire, but may I ask . . ."

"You may not; there is no time!" Grivek insisted. The king looked mad in the moonlight; with his crown abandoned at Bloodmane's feet, his ebony locks were in disarray. "Muster our forces. Ready every human and every elf who can wield a weapon. Send a runner to the Tower of Elementals and wake the High Elementalist. Tell Hasimak I want his best students, except Sargus, practicing all the spells they know that have worked on the Zaur in the past."

"The Zaur, sire?" Jolsit gasped.

"Bloodmane says we are being invaded by the Zaur, and I have no reason to doubt it." Grivek paused and looked up at his mighty castle. "Tell Sargus to meet me in my study. I have a research project that cannot wait."

He fought back the urge to vomit and closed his eyes. Sargus would be pleased to do research, even though Grivek could hardly spare such a talented Artificer now, deformed and twisted though he was. Wylant would feel vindicated, but he couldn't imagine that she would be happy. She would be more likely to share his concern. If he could not find a way to make peace with Kholster, none of it would matter. They could win the fight with the Zaur and still be crushed by the Aern.

PART FOUR
TRUE CONJUNCTION

"Breeding and Bloodline. It may one day be said that those two concepts, or the pursuit of them, were the final downfall of the Eldrennai. Is there a living being who can claim otherwise? Why, other than a need to control and shape bloodlines, would King Zillek have ordered the creation of a new species of slave for the Aern to breed with instead of granting permission to pursue the actualization of female Aern? A breeding between a male and a female Aern would have (and did when female Aern eventually came into existence) allowed the creation of new bloodlines.

"One wonders how Uled controlled the births of the Aern and the Vael to prevent female Aern and male Vael from coming into being for as long as he did. I have searched his notes thoroughly, and while numerous diary entries pertain to his worry of losing control over the breeding program, he is mute on the subject of attaining this control.

"Many have supposed that Uled realized early on that an Eldrennai female, having once carried an Aernese offspring, would become barren, but my research does not support such a claim. Did he consider such things unimportant, or did Uled, in his characteristic desire to place experimentation over research, simply not care?"

An excerpt from *Uled: Savior or Destroyer* by Sargus

CHAPTER 46
CHAINS OF THE ZAUR

Xasti'Kaur, Wylant thought, *the Shadow Road. Well, at least I know what they call it.*

She hung on a wall of cold, damp stone clad in her bloodied arming coat and trousers; the many ties which secured her plate mail to the arming coat had been thoughtlessly slashed rather than properly untied, which meant even if she could get free and find her armor, it would be of limited utility. Wylant pulled at the steel manacles which held her wrists, arms spread, high above her head with similar restraints binding her at the ankles, waist, and neck. Most annoying of all was the leather bit they'd forced into her mouth and secured to the wall behind her with some sort of ring apparatus she couldn't see very well. From the way its touch burned, the leather had to be Zaur hide, which meant her magic wouldn't pierce it.

Zaur don't keep prisoners. She blinked away the useless thought and focused on the things she could control, the problems she might be able to solve. *Zaur have never dug tunnels this far or this quietly either. Something has changed, something vital.*

Along the side of the massive chamber, to her right, three Zaur workers had just finished bolting an identical set of restraints to the wall and were moving on to add a third. Wylant wondered what the space had originally been intended for: a barracks, a mess hall?

Certainly not a prison.

She narrowed her eyes, examining the ceiling. A large central vent dominated it with smaller vents at the five corners of the room. *They're holding me in a kitchen?* The implication was not pleasant.

Twenty ruddy-scaled Zaur crouched on all fours around their commander, Skreel blades at the ready.

Sri'Zaur, she thought. *That's part of the change, this new species of Zaur.*

Their commander, a massive Sri'Zaur named Dryga, paced in front of the prisoner, examining her first from a quadrupedal stance, then rising up on his hind legs for the second pass. A sinuous pattern of transverse blue and black scales covered his body, arcing dramatically over the creature's piercing yellow eyes. Wylant remembered him from the tunnel.

Thoughts of the tunnel and the fight within brought visions of the dead to her eyes, hardening her heart into a lump of impotent rage. Struggling to control her emotions, she clamped down hard on the leather bit in her mouth and reminded herself of the useful data. There was no sign of Mazik. He might have escaped. Roc and Hira seemed to have escaped. All was not lost. The king would be warned.

Would he have enough intelligence to understand the scope of this Zaur incursion? Yes, she thought, even if only Kam had reached him. . . . Sargus could likely deduce what the king needed to know, just from what happened at North Watch.

Ever defiant, she raised her shaven head and sneered. *Even if I die*, she thought, *they'll be ready for you now.*

Dryga gestured to a length of mottled blue-black metal wrapped around her right arm from her armpit to where the shackles covered her wrist. "Your weapon refuses to be removed," he said in unaccented Eldrennai. His voice was surprisingly cultured, similar to the scholars in the Tower of Elementals. Hearing it from reptilian lips filled Wylant with revulsion.

<<You can pretend not to know Zaurtol if you like, kholster Wylant,>> Dryga tapped out on the ground behind him, <<but I'm not going to unblock your mouth . . . Thunder Speaker.>>

<<You should see the devotion I inspire in my knights,>> Wylant tapped out on the stone behind her. Vax was cutting painfully into her skin, but she understood why, even if she didn't want to think about it. *It's fine*, she thought at the weapon, *Calm down. Loosen your grip. I won't let them take you.*

"Your accent is interesting, your cadence hard to follow, but I can understand most of it. Perhaps if you would allow yourself to be disarmed I could make you more comfortable," Dryga gestured to a heavy metal door being fitted into the room's single entrance. "Once the door has been properly secured I would happily allow you greater freedom to move about. Your mouth would still need to be bound to prevent magical attempts at escape, but . . ."

<<Let me go and I'll fight you for it,>> she tapped weakly. Her tongue felt partially numb, the left side of her face puffy and strange. Even her vision was still ever so slightly unfocused. *A concussion*, she thought. *Worse, the cursed* jallek *root is wearing off.*

"I have no doubt that you would, but to fight, even injured, a female that single-handedly slew a Zaurruk would be quite foolish." He spoke in Eldrennaic, while tapping simultaneously in Zaurtol. *What kind of mind could do so . . . so easily?*

<<A Zaurruk? You mean that giant snake? I'll remember that for my report to King Grivek after I escape.>> Wylant ran her tongue experimen-

tally across her teeth as best she could. Her left back molar ached but seemed to be intact. <<If I kill a second one do I get a prize?>>

"Likely your freedom, I should think," the Sri'Zaur answered, "but you will not be provided with the opportunity."

<<Coward,>> Wylant tapped.

"You are used to dealing with our less pragmatic kin, kholster Wylant." Dryga laughed—a series of cough-like barks. "Your opinion of me is of no consequence. I will be judged by He Who Plots in Darkness, not by any warmblood, however valiant she may be."

<<What do you want with me? Zaur don't keep prisoners.>>

"The warlord requires blood from each of the three races involved in the Conjunction," the Zaur captain answered. "In your condition, you may or may not have noticed the new cut on your thigh. Beyond that, he wants you alive, so alive you shall remain. Your capture was divine providence. For both of us. Now we lack only the blood of one of the flower girls."

"And an Aern." Wylant managed a defiant sneer. "Good luck catching Kholster, lizard. He's the only Aern you'll find anywhere near the Eldren Plains."

"Capturing Kholster Bloodmane," Dryga said, walking casually to the doorway behind the waiting Zaur warriors, "might indeed have proved too great a task for my scouts. I would send no less than a hundred Sri'Zaur to capture such an infamous warrior." His tail slapped the ground, and four new guards carried a bound and gagged Aernese female into the room. "He Who Plots in Darkness has provided us with another option."

The Aern's clothes were in blood-spattered tatters, and her mail had been stripped from her, leaving her clad only in torn jeans and the abbreviated top female Aern wore to accommodate the nudity taboos of other races. The garment covered her breasts, clinging to her skin only by small bits of sewn-in bone-steel, so the pattern of patrimonial scars lay revealed on her back. Wylant's eyes widened at that design. They were the same scars she wore on her own back and had hand-stitched to the back of all her clothing.

Kholster's daughter? I have to get her out of here. He can't lose another one; I won't have it.

Wylant masked her surprise but felt certain Dryga noticed something. <<Who is she?>>

"The daughter of Bloodmane," he responded. "Surely you recognize her scars as easily as did I." The guard fastened the young Aern into a set of the newly installed restraints.

Why would Kholster bring his daughter to the Grand Conjunction? Wylant asked herself. *To learn something? To show by example? To show her what? The face of her enemy?*

No, no, he could accomplish that anywhere north of the Great Bridge. To prepare her to take his place in the Grand Conjunction? Maybe . . . maybe more than that. What would Kholster plan for his life after the destruction of the Eldrennai? Was this daughter to take his place as First? Was that why he'd chosen her, a Freeborn daughter, to come with him?

Reining in her emotions, she focused on the present. Maybe if she could keep Kholster's daughter alive, she could bargain with him, at least buy the Eldrennai more time . . . roll their destruction back . . .

<<He'll kill you,>> Wylant tapped, stalling for time to think. With the *jallek* root's anti-hystemic effect almost gone, the itching, swelling, and general yechness made it hard to think.

"After the warlord has the blood he needs, we will trade her to the scarbacks in return for their non-interference in the war."

Okay, they were already planning on letting her live. A rescue then. She wouldn't ransom Kholster's daughter to him; she couldn't do that again, but he'd be more willing to negotiate after his daughter was safe.

A guard sidled up to Dryga and hissed something low.

Dryga's tail slapped the floor in a complex pattern that wasn't Zaurtol before his attention returned to Wylant. He ran his tongue along the floor, nodded as if he'd gotten the information he wanted, and then rose up on his hind legs. "Our high cavern brothers do not comprehend the value of captives," he said. "But that is neither tongue nor tail, is it? We were discussing the removal of your weapon. My soldiers say that it changes shape on command, a marvelous gift for Warlord Xastix. I would prefer not to be forced to remove your arm to obtain it for him."

<<I couldn't give him up if I wanted to,>> Wylant told him. Vax snaked up her arm, across her shoulders and beneath her neck manacle, like a harness. Its fear cut into their connection like an ice pick. Though she had sensed the weapon's feelings on rare occasions before, the thrill of victory, warmth, and contentment when she cleaned or sharpened him, Wylant had never felt anything as palpable as the blade's current distress.

"Interesting." Dryga ran a claw-tipped finger over thin red welts Vax had left on her arm and shoulder. His scaly touch brushed the metal harness into which Vax had twisted itself. Like a drowning man clutching his rescuer, Vax constricted about Wylant's throat, cutting off her air, his edge cutting into her skin.

Stop, Vax, she ordered. Vax did not heed her command until Dryga drew back his hand.

"If the weapon starts to do something useful, kill her," he ordered the guards. "We can always obtain another Eldrennai."

Dryga swept out of the makeshift prison, leaving Wylant and her fellow captives with their guards. The cold manacles that bound the Eldrennai general did not interest her; she knew she could not break them. *If we're lucky, Vax*, she thought to her blade, *I won't need to.*

So this is Rae'en, Wylant squinted at her husband's (ex-husband's) daughter thoughtfully. *I never thought I'd see you in person, my dear. Please excuse the shackles.*

In slumber, Rae'en looked remarkably like her father. Both of them slept like little children, comfortable under all circumstances, with all the hardness of the warrior within cast aside. Congealed blood clinging to her lips, chin, and throat broke the illusion.

The Arvash'ae, Wylant assumed, adding one more note to her mental stash. *Did they use it against her or did her youth betray her?*

Strong and secure, the chains that bound Wylant would have held any humanoid on Barrone . . . except an Aern. The bolts, set too shallowly in the stone, were too thin to hold an Aern and needed to be counter-sunk.

Wylant sighed; another bit of knowledge she'd gained during the Sundering: if you can't make peace with an Aern, it's much easier to kill it than to keep it. Wylant would have bound the girl wrist to wrist and elbow to elbow, hooking the wrist cuffs to a chain so that the Aern's hands wrapped around her own throat. Once the Aern's knees and ankles had been bound, Wylant would have buried her up to her neck, "planted," as the Eldrennai called it. Since one couldn't rely on magic to bind an Aern, planting was one of the few remaining options if you needed to keep one alive.

So Rae'en is how we'll get out of these bonds; now, how to escape Xasti'Kaur once we do . . . Wylant shut her eyes, ignoring Rae'en and the twenty Zaur standing guard . . . and plotted.

CHAPTER 47
HARVESTER OF SOULS

"I am not pleased," Torgrimm's voice rang out.

Dienox ignored the Harvester. The god of war continued, instead, to kneel in the cold stone tunnels of Xasti'Kaur watching his former champion; unseen.

The clitter-clack of Torgrimm's bone armor as he approached solicited not so much as a backward glance from the war god. Dienox's golden armor, dark and unpolished, reflected its wearer's foul mood.

"Dienox!" Torgrimm unslung his bone warpick. If Dienox noticed the weapon's similarity to Kholster's Grudge, he made no mention of it.

"I wish that we could pick the same champion twice." Dienox pushed himself up to his feet. "Wylant did such a good job."

"Once was enough to destroy her life." Torgrimm drew closer. "Your victory, not to mention your direct interference, cost the woman her child and her husband. An argument could be made that it also cost her soul."

"I won." Dienox smiled smugly. "That's all that matters, though she did look better with hair. Still, it's pleasing to know she takes her devotion to me so seriously now . . . to shave it all and match me. Too bad it was only a side game. If everyone had been involved, I'd have the dragons back." Dienox clapped his armored hand on the bony ridge of Torgrimm's chest plate. Dienox's lips curved into a frown as he noticed the warpick. "Why are you armed?"

"You touched two of their minds," Torgrimm said, avoiding the question. "You made Wylant toss her helmet aside, and then you pushed Rae'en into the Arvash'ae early. Neither is your Justicar."

"And more times than that. What of it?" Dienox straightened. A battered iron shield forged to resemble a snarling dragon appeared in the war god's left hand. In his right hand, an iron greatsword manifested, its fuller resembling a dragon as well. "You might as well know I 'influenced' the human captain as well. Minor infractions. At worst it will cost them their lives. Call for an accounting; I'll pay the penalty Aldo demands, but it's not enough to get me ejected from the game. As far as I know, no one has laid claim to them. They aren't anyone's chosen champions."

Torgrimm swung his warpick. "You disgust me!"

Dienox took the blow on his shield, rolling back in obvious surprise as the bone blade sheered through the metal, cleaving the shield in twain.

"Have you lost your mind, Harvester?" Dienox crouched low on the balls of his feet. "I am the essence of combat! You can't defeat me."

"No. You are merely war. You have allowed yourself to sink lower than any other deity, abandoning your dual nature. I am eldest, Dienox. When you think back to your earliest memory, whose face do you see?" Torgrimm's warpick cut toward the war god. Dienox sprung over the weapon, seizing it by the haft with both hands.

"Your face, Harvester, and if I acted far enough outside the rules, I suppose nothing could save me from you. If I'd committed such a crime, you wouldn't be talking to me now. I would already have gone to . . . where do gods go when they die, Torgrimm?"

"To the Artificer." Torgrimm rammed his bone helm into Dienox's forehead, but the war god only laughed.

"Tell me what's really bothering you, Torgrimm. You can't be worried about three souls. Is it Minapsis? I counseled you against marrying Kilke's sister. I've always thought Shidarva more your type . . . or a perhaps a mortal lady? Is that it? You fancy one of these?"

Dienox gestured at the prisoners.

"Take one," Dienox laughed. "Take them both. Have your fun. I won't tell anyone."

"You disgust me," Torgrimm spat. "That's the problem with all of you. You spend so much time in pursuit of your own needs, your own entertainments, you've forgotten how to be gods. You act just like mortals!" He pointed at the captives.

"By me, not this again!" Dienox let go of the warpick and shoved it away. "I know that you're close to them, Harvester. But you must stop this. You need perspective."

"I'm not the one who had a portion of his powers stolen by one of them," Torgrimm muttered.

"True," Dienox picked up the pieces of his shield, fitting them back together, metal flowing into metal until the shield was whole again. "She was worth it though."

Between them both, two forms appeared.

"We're in trouble now," Dienox said in mock fright.

Aldo and Shidarva stared at the two gods. "What is the meaning of this?" Shidarva asked.

"Just because you're the new ruler of the gods, Shidarva, doesn't mean you have to get a nit up your nethers over every little thing." Dienox pushed Aldo out of his way and stood directly before the goddess of justice and retribution. "Torgrimm and I had a . . . disagreement. It's nothing to worry your regalness about."

"Is this true, Soul Warden?" Shidarva asked Torgrimm.

"Ask Aldo," Torgrimm snarled.

"I have heard from Aldo, but I would prefer to hear the truth from your lips as well."

Torgrimm's body vanished, replaced by a radiant symbol of infinity. "That is the problem that faces us, lady." His voice was deeper and more resonant, less emotional. "Gods should not have lips. In the past when we appeared to mortals, we put on mortal seemings at Kilke's suggestion. He said that it would put them more at ease. That it did, but now it has gone too far."

"Now we occupy ourselves with mundane enjoyments. We eat and drink and make merry as they do. We squabble like the mortals placed in our care. Dienox can no longer assume his true form. Neither can Gromma, Xalistan, or even Aldo."

Shidarva transformed as well, from a beautiful but sad female Eldrennai in long, blue robes . . . into a stylized balance with a dagger suspended from the left side and a shield from the right. "That is not true of all of us."

"But it was true during the last game," Torgrimm countered. "In the last round, when you were on the verge of defeat, I recall how distraught you were when you could not resume your divine aspect."

"And I regained my center . . ."

"Yes, and so should we all," Torgrimm intoned. "Even now, can you see the web of destiny if you look? Can you observe the tatters these games have wrought?"

"None who played have been able to do that since the first game, Torgrimm," Shidarva answered.

"It is in tatters!" Torgrimm shouted. "You do not hear the cries of those souls that should have been delivered and were not because of your games! I can. I do."

"That's a lie," Dienox roared. "You're being melodramatic."

"Am I?" Torgrimm asked, resuming his mortal seeming. "Ask Aldo if I lie. Or can even he see that far beyond the games you play? Do any of you have room left for the laws of reality?"

Aldo, in his gnome-like aspect, gazed at the ground with empty sockets. Reaching into the folds of his robes, he withdrew his box of eyes, selected two glowing gold ones and inserted them into his sockets. When he was done, he cleared his throat and stared up at his fellow gods. He looked Shidarva in the eye but could not meet Torgrimm's gaze. "I . . . It is true that my knowledge has narrowed considerably, but I feel that this is a natural thing, the will of the Artificer."

"Even you have been corrupted." Torgrimm knelt, touching Aldo's cheek and looking into his eyes. "I'm planning something. Something to put an end to these games you all play with mortals. I know you know that, but do you know what it is I plan?"

"I . . . have my theories." Aldo looked away.

"The god of knowledge with whom I stood side by side at the dawn of this creation would have known." Torgrimm stood, taking a step back. "When I put his soul inside the embodiment the Artificer fashioned for him, he shone with divinity, with a knowledge and intelligence so keen that I had seen its like only in the presence of the Artificer alone. Now, when I look upon you, I see a gnome playing god."

"Now see here, Torgrimm!" Aldo's face flushed red with anger. "I will not have you address me in such a . . ."

"I'm entering the game," Torgrimm interrupted.

"You can't," Dienox objected.

"Torgrimm," Shidarva began tactfully. "I know how hard it is to watch and not be able to play, but you know that the rules forbid . . ."

Aldo remained silent, the light of his eyes shifting from gold to silver, brows furrowed.

"There is a way," Torgrimm said softly. "Aldo knows there is. It's merely unthinkable to most of you."

"How is it possible, Aldo?" Dienox grabbed the other deity by his robe, shaking him violently.

"I cannot say," Aldo answered as understanding dawned. "Or perhaps 'am not required to reveal' would be a more apt choice of words."

"You know the identity of the champion I am allowed?" Torgrimm asked, ignoring the other gods' protests.

"I do," nodded Aldo, "but not how you plan to get him on the board."

"That's not fair!" Dienox bellowed. "He could reap the souls of the other champions before their time and . . ."

Aldo touched Torgrimm's breastplate nervously. "If you fail . . ."

"Then it will be the end of everything."

"If you succeed . . ."

"It will be the end of everything as it is now."

"That person is not yet eligible."

"If you could see the web of destiny," Torgrimm chided, "then you would know he soon will be. The battle will come. Many will die, a hero will fall, and then what is fair enough for Kilke and Dienox will be fair enough for me."

"Be careful, my friend," Aldo began.

"I want Dienox punished."

"You what?" Dienox bellowed. He brandished his sword, stepping toward the Harvester, but Shidarva stepped between them, two scimitars limned in a cerulean blaze appearing in each hand. "He tells tales against me, Shidarva!"

"You have never before—" Aldo began.

"He has done enough." Torgrimm's voice was calm but firm, a whisper that roared. "I wish to mulct him in a tangible fashion . . . I demand an amercement paid not to me but to the mortals he has offended."

"Torgrimm—" Shidarva frowned.

"I demand it under the rules of your own game," Torgrimm's voice dropped even lower, "or are you not the goddess of justice and retribution? Do you no longer obey rules?"

Blue-edged blades whipped about, ahead of the goddess herself, they shattered when they touched Torgrimm's bone plate armor, and Shidarva cried out in pain.

"What?" she hissed.

"I am the Sower and the Reaper, and my course is completely right and good and just. When those conditions are met—"

"No one may oppose you," she completed. "You are correct. I apologize. What fine . . . what amercement do you suggest?"

"As a former champion, Wylant was to be free of his influence. He has controlled her three times I know about in the last decade alone and has admitted to more."

"She was going to kill herself," Dienox objected.

"As would have been her right," Torgrimm sighed. "Though had you never interfered with her at all, I doubt she would have found herself with such feelings of guilt and loss and hopelessness."

"I gave her glory!"

"No." Torgrimm seemed to grow larger, even as his shoulders turned in and his head drooped down. "She gave you victory. You gave her nothing but blonde hair and a runny nose in exchange."

"What do you want from me?" Dienox growled. "To set her free and slay her captors, to—"

"I revere mortals, foolish god. I want no such thing—"

"Leave her alone," Aldo coughed. "He wants you to withdraw your . . . ahem . . . blessings . . . all of them . . . and then to leave her alone forever." He took out one of his eyes, rubbed it on his robes, and popped it back in. "Right?"

"That is what you want?" Shidarva asked.

"It is all I ever want," Torgrimm said, holding up his palms, "for all mortals to live their lives as they choose to live them, to do their best, and that when we do help them, it is because they ask and even then . . . sparingly."

"Done," Dienox pouted. He held out his hand, and a sliver of divine essence slid free of Wylant's soul. The only outward signs were a subtle darkening of her eyebrows and easing of her breath.

"Thank you." Torgrimm faded from the Shadow Road, reappearing where the web of destiny, as clear to him as the day he was forged, shone around him. Human souls flared briefly within the weblike strands, bright but fleeting. The souls of the Dwarves burned with less intensity, a steady flame, rarely changing, slow to start and slow to blink out. More dazzling were the souls of the elves, burning erratically—in one instant scarcely an ember, a raging inferno the next—but ceaselessly. Wisps of webbing blew free at the corners.

In the center yawned one ragged tear, chasm-like. Souls poured into it and vanished, others flared into existence where they were destined to arrive, then sparked out in the absence of the strands that should have sustained them. Torgrimm sent his essence out along that part of the web like a spider, mending it as best he could, catching the fading souls and storing them in caches of cocoon-like divinity until he could find a place to slip them back in, find them a place where their presence would not disrupt the flow of birth and death.

"Once," Torgrimm bemoaned, "all of us worked together and the web was always whole." Now, most of his fellow gods appeared only at the periphery of the web, striking blindly, spewing webbing without care, heedless of the pattern they could no longer perceive.

There was only one other presence which moved with intent across the web, a presence Torgrimm knew well. It cut strands that should have been preserved, working to widen the holes. Torgrimm peered across the web at Kilke, god of secrets and shadow, and snarled.

Leaving the web of destiny, he returned to the realm of the gods, shifting beyond that to the realm of souls. He stood at the bone gates, gazing on the one hand into paradise and the other into punishment.

"Husband?" Minapsis appeared moments later, clad in red silk. Torgrimm knew he loved her more than she loved him, but that was only because to be what she was, the goddess of reward and punishment, required a certain detachment. Her eyebrows furrowed. The gauzy film of a shredded soul hung from one of her crown-like horns. "I was in the middle of—"

"May I ask a favor?" Torgrimm looked into her eyes and hoped she would agree. If his plan was to go forward, there was one last preparation which needed to be made.

CHAPTER 48
CAPTIVE

"What did I do to get chained up with an Oathbreaker?" Rae'en asked, spitting out the remains of her gag. Her mouth tasted like a lizard had relieved itself, or perhaps a small animal had died in there.

She narrowed her eyes at her fellow captive. "I am Rae'en, by Kholster out of Helg."

I think that's Wylant, she thought at Kazan, trying to send him the image. *She looks like bird squirt.*

Rae'en examined the woman's bonds, the Zaur-leather bit in her mouth and nodded. *Thunder Speaker; that would fit.*

"You're Wylant, aren't you?"

The Eldrennai . . . no, Aiannai, Rae'en corrected herself, nodded.

Rae'en glared at the twenty Zaur guards. Surely Wylant and she could take twenty of the cursed lizards if they worked together.

"I'll tell you when," Rae'en blurted in Aernese, incrementally increasing the pressure she was exerting against her manacles. Disguising it as an angry attempt to grab at Wylant.

Did they know she was Aiannai, not Eldrennai? Or did they expect Rae'en to occupy herself trying to kill her? Rae'en pulled again, taking the measure of the chain binding her to the wall. It felt strong, but there was enough give to the bolt to convince her she could break free if she had sufficient time—and if there weren't twenty Zaur soldiers staring at her from across the room.

"Stop talking," one of the guards ordered sternly.

"Or what?" Rae'en snarled. "You'll kill me? Beat me unconscious? I'm an Aernese warrior, you belly-crawling reptile!"

"I'll use acid to flay the scars from your back."

Rae'en worked her tongue at the scale between her canines as she thought that over. Would that even work? She didn't think so. Maybe Ghaiattri flame would do it, but she was pretty sure if teeth came to bone she could strip the skin from her back and the scars would be whole once it grew back. But did she want the Zaur to think the threat worked? Let him think he could control her with it?

The scale finally worked free and she spat it on the ground. Low and ready, the Zaur edged toward her, reptilian eyes glaring up at her inscrutably.

"Well?"

Rae'en made an open-handed gesture of agreement and nodded curtly.

Wylant made a rude noise, the cousin of a donkey's bray and laugh, accentuating the sound with a vulgar Aernese gesture: little finger folded in, her other fingers and thumb waggling. It was a gesture older Aern used to gently tease children and one Rae'en had seen a lot while making her chain mail. Puzzlement gave way to comprehension when Wylant cut her eyes to the guards.

Rae'en knew it was gentle chiding, almost warm and affectionate, but the Zaur didn't know that. She lunged at Wylant several times in quick succession, growling like an animal.

"Stop teasing the Aern," the guard ordered again. "Or I will cut off one of your paw digits . . . from one of your hind paws. You'd hate that, wouldn't you, biped? Perhaps I should do that anyway and feed the bits to the Aern."

Twisting her head as far left as she could, Rae'en looked on in amusement as Wylant responded with the same defeated gesture and nod Rae'en had used to signify her own acquiescence. Wylant met her gaze imperiously, eliciting a snarl from Rae'en.

By Torgrimm, was this woman really Wylant? In the paintings Rae'en had seen, Wylant had been blonde. This Eldrennai, or Aiannai, had dark, almost black, eyebrows. Had she shaved her head and dyed her eyebrows black to pass as a rank-and-file Oathbreaker?

Hours passed, each refusing to be the first to look away, drawing the guards into their staring match, keeping their attention focused away from Rae'en's subtle movements.

Rae'en's neck muscles began to burn, but by then her head was clear and all signs of injury from her battle with the Zaur were gone, healed, thanks to the marvelous physical superiority imbued in the Aern by their creator. Rae'en concentrated on the muscles in her neck, relaxing each one individually. Vander would have been impressed. She rarely found much use for meditation back home in South Number Nine, preferring to spend time with Kholster or her Overwatches learning the daily needs of the army.

They would rise early; the entire army, soldiers and noncombatants alike, would line up in the great hall of the forge masters for the morning workout. Many Dwarves would come to watch them, lining the underground terraces and balconies. Some did their best to keep pace with the Aern, managing it in the beginning but nearly always giving up toward the end of the exercise.

Officially, every Aern was part of the Aernese Armed Forces, but in truth, in truth . . .

A spasm went through Wylant's neck, and she almost looked away. This had to be torture for her, Rae'en realized. As beloved as the Aiannai was by the Aern, she didn't have their fortitude. The wounds from some recent battle still covered her body. Bruises. Lacerations . . . not all of them looked like Zaur work to Rae'en.

Realizing she couldn't keep up anymore, Wylant gave in to the pain, loosing a single bit-muffled scream, letting her body writhe in the agony she surely felt.

Smiling slightly at Wylant's past-the-mark performance, Rae'en incrementally increased the tension she was applying to the chains that bound her arms, simultaneously flattening the soles of her feet against the wall behind her. She pushed off the wall, shifting her weight upward, putting pressure against one side of the metal band which bound her waist.

I have to get her out of here, she thought at her Overwatches. *She needs medical attention.*

CHAPTER 49

NEVER TRUST A PIRATE

Randall Tyree awoke to what he was sure must be the sounds of battle. The slightly acrid smell of metal filled his nostrils. A great weight pulled his head forward and down. Irrationally, he felt certain that one of the Zaur had put a bucket on his head as some kind of sick prank. Which, if he was honest with himself, would have been an improvement . . . something . . . anything to break the monotony. He'd already found the money he was to be paid, stolen it, and put it back a hundred times or more.

He'd even been caught twice, but Dryga didn't seem to care in the least: where did Tyree think he was going to escape to and past how many guards and wasn't he an ally anyway?

"Bird squirt." Tyree reached up to pull the imaginary bucket off only to cough up a mass of whitish pus into the metal basin next to his bunk. Pain sloshed randomly through his brain, clouding his thoughts.

I guess this is yet another Zauran delicacy that disagrees with me, he realized slowly.

Where was Kreej? Tyree looked around his "room" and didn't spy the Zaur. At least he was someone to talk to.

"Kreej?"

No answer.

Tyree lay on the small bunk, the dim illumination from one of his Dwarven lanterns casting a soft glow over the stacks of books, small desk, and wall hooks upon which his three sets of clothes hung that were all there was to the small quarters in which he'd been billeted.

"But none of the other gals are lucky enough to have a door that locks," he said mockishly to himself. "Now if only they'd installed it on the correct side . . ."

<<The scarback and the stump ear are causing trouble,>> Kreej's tail thumps rattled from the stone.

Aern? Tyree stood quickly, relieved to find his head spinning only a little, and darted as carefully as possible from room to room to catch the best vibrations.

<<Leave it for now,>> someone thumped back. Tyree guessed it was Dryga. <<We have the blood we need from them. Once I get it to Warlord Xastix, he will give orders on what we should do with the prisoners and the human.>>

Prisoners, Tyree rubbed his arms and legs to get the blood flowing. *And the human.*

"I don't think I like the sound of 'And the human.'" He took a drink from Uncle Japesh's canteen, a disreputable-looking, battered thing that refilled itself at least once a day, even in the tunnels of the Zaur. Tyree rinsed the taste of roundtrip bug out of his mouth. Then, he sliced the top bit off of the twig he used for cleaning his teeth and went about getting ready for his day. Quite possibly his last day in the prison. They'd taken his weapons, true, but they'd left him his pack. Did they really think "And the human" was so stupid as to not have a few tricks up his sleeves? He slipped on a pair of innocent-looking steel bracelets and pulled his lock picks out of their leather casing. Silly lizards really weren't used to keeping prisoners.

And the human.

Nope, not a good sign at all.

Time to go.

As he reached through the bars to pick the lock on his door for the umpteenth time, Tyree ran over his mental map of the tunnels. One human pirate couldn't fight his way out of here, but one human pirate and an Aern . . . ?

"Don't pass wind and tell me you were whistling, Dryga," Tyree muttered under his breath.

*

Randall Tyree trod along the underground passage cursing himself and fingering his steel bracelets as he approached a guard he recognized. Of course, they'd increased security with an Aern and an Eldrennai down here.

Tyree mentally traced the image of the maze that filled his mind.

"You've walked far enough, human," a Zaur hissed. "You're near a restricted area."

"Restricted? Aw, don't tell me I'm going to be cooped up on the same route every time I want to go for a walk, Fifth H, because I'm going to be here for the long haul."

"Nevertheless, here is where you must turn around." The fifth hatching of Majita's third brood walked forward to place a restraining claw on Tyree's arm.

"This is where you're holding the Aern and the Eldrennai, right?" Tyree whispered with a conspiratorial air. "I heard you've got two females in their smallclothes. You've got to let me see them. I may not see another woman for a long time."

"No."

Slipping out from under the guard's claw, Tyree felt the tip tear his sleeve. "I won't even say anything. I'll just peek in from the hallway. What could it hurt?" *This will never work*, Tyree thought. *It's a lizard. You can't charm a lizard this quick.* He tossed the guard his most disingenuous grin. "Trust me." *Trust me.*

A sensation not unlike a fingernail on skin slid up Tyree's spine. He held the smile, let his eyes twinkle. *Trust me!*

"I don't know why." The guard made a gurgling rumble in the back of its throat. "And it's against my better judgment." *TRUST ME!* "But I do trust you, Captain. If Lieutenant Kreej or Captain Dryga catches you . . ."

"I'll tell them that you left me safe and sound in my quarters and I snuck out again on my own," Tyree assured him.

"Very well." The Zaur nodded, twitching its tail in a matching motion before dropping to all fours. "I'm going to get my meal ration. I'll expect you to be back in your room when I return."

Tyree saluted the Zaur, touching his fist to his own chest twice. "You're a real gem, Fifth H. I can't believe they haven't named you yet."

With careful treads to minimize the vibrations as he walked, Tyree slipped past a partially installed door affixed at the entrance of a room that he guessed was a former dining hall. A mass of Zaur were partially visible to the left of the doorway guarding two highly unlikely prisoners.

The Eldrennai he recognized. "Wylant," he muttered her name in an unconscious whisper. He'd had to steer clear of her when he'd been arranging his deal for the census data. If he helped rescue her, the reward could be nearly as large as the payment he'd been promised by the Zaur, and he wouldn't have to waste the time stealing it before they left. For that matter, his knowledge of the tunnel system would buy him no small reward by itself.

At the mention of Wylant's name, the Aern's eyes flicked open and found him crouching in the shadows. Gods, she was beautiful, as though Shidarva herself had fashioned a Vael out of Aern flesh. Even chained, she looked dangerous, defiant. Tyree held a finger to his lips.

"I'm here to help you," he whispered so softly that he couldn't hear his own words, but from the look on the girl's face, she heard him well enough. *Those Aernese ears*, he thought to himself.

"How many guards?" he whispered again. The Aern blinked the number to him, in slow, natural-looking blinks, and Tyree was suddenly glad he hadn't eaten any breakfast. Twenty guards. In what could only be recognition of his dismay, the Aern laughed.

"It offends me that you think twenty of you are enough to guard an Aern, lizard," she spat at the nearest guard.

"Silence or I will get the acid," one of the guards warned.

"If I had my warpick you wouldn't be able to make such a threat!"

"Last chance," the guard said.

She snapped her mouth closed, then bared her doubled canines at him but remained silent. Tyree winked at her before continuing down the tunnel. Once clear of the impromptu detention cell, Tyree straightened up, walking with confidence and purpose. No matter what culture he was dealing with, Tyree adhered to an old adage: look like you're supposed to be doing what you're doing, and fewer people will question it. A single Zaur stood watch in front of the armory, pacing on all fours. "How many guards do you need in the middle of an underground fortress?" Tyree murmured.

"What was that?" the guard asked. Tyree walked directly up to him, a little too close, hands clasped behind his back. The daggers in his left and rights hands were the only weapons he'd managed to slip by the Zaur; long, thin, and needle-like, they had been a gift from Captain Hananka. When not in use, they curled around his wrist, looking for all the world like two innocuous metal bracelets.

"Hey, listen, I'm all turned around here, pal. Could you tell me which way back to the main mess?" Tyree watched for it, the momentary relaxation. *That's right, lizard. I'm just a stupid mammal, lost in the tunnels. No threat here.*

Raising his foreleg to point out directions, the guard was completely unprepared for human treachery. Diving over the outstretched limb, Tyree plunged one dagger into the base of the reptile's spine to paralyze the tail. A second blow, lightning quick and precise as a jeweler cutting a diamond, drove the other dagger into the Zaur sentry's neck. "Sorry about this," Tyree told the dying Zaur, "but your boss should have paid me on delivery as agreed and let me go."

Tyree knelt over the guard, removing the armory key from around its neck, quite pleased with himself. The key fit nicely in the lock and turned without protest. Well-oiled and maintained, the hinges didn't even creak as the door swung toward him to reveal another guard, larger than the first, with blue scales bearing a pattern of concentric amber rings.

"Get a healer, quick!" Tyree called out.

Nictating membranes flicked over the Sri'Zaur's black eyes. "Human scum!"

"I'm not an idiot!" Tyree spat. "I knew that you'd be in here. That's why I opened the door. I found him this way and you were the closest Zaur that could help . . ."

The Sri'Zaur drew its Skreel blade, dropping to all fours. "You killed him, human! Now I'm going to kill you."

"Can't win every hand," Tyree said amicably. He darted backwards into the hall, dropping his daggers so that he would have both hands free. As the Sri'Zaur charged, Tyree slammed him in the metal door: once, twice, three times until the Sri'Zaur went limp. "See? I told you . . . you can't win every hand."

"While I, on the other hand . . ." Stepping over his second victim and retrieving his daggers, Tyree entered the room. He spied the Aern's weapon immediately. It was the only warpick, along with one saddlebag containing a pair of strange-looking tubular weapons, a small bag of round metal balls, an Aernese Hearth Stone, a Dwarven canteen, and a small leather horn with stopper.

Spying the horn together with the round balls, he realized what he'd found and made the sign of the Foursquare in front of himself, just in case.

He'd only once seen them fired, when Hananka was captured by the Dwarves, but they were powerful and loud, spewing bits of metal propelled by a Dwarven concoction—a powder that exploded when lit. Tyree grabbed the small leather horn with the curious nozzle. He tipped a tiny amount of the contents out onto the table and smiled at the mysterious purple-gray powder. Yep, Dwarven junpowder.

"I'm not stealing the juns and junpowder," he said aloud, "just taking them back to the Aern. I assume they're hers."

A proclamation, Tyree thought certain to be unnecessary, but one could never be too careful when it came to Dwarves . . . or gods. You never knew when they might be watching. The contents of the other saddlebag lay scattered about the floor of the armory as if the Zaur had been rifling through it. Quickly shoving things back into the bag, he grabbed cloths, a sharp knife, and an odd assortment of traveling gear. He grabbed the chain shirt resting with the plate armor and dumped it in as well.

For moment he could have sworn he saw a ring on a chain, but when he reached for it, his mind went fuzzy.

I'm not carrying that or the plate mail, he thought to himself. Had someone else said that first?

Warpick. The Aern would want her warpick. He snatched it up. Wasting little time, the captain threw both reptilian bodies into the crate and secured the warpick and the saddlebags.

In his mind, the Hearth Stone and the junpowder swirled together to form a plan. It was crazy, dangerous, and likely overkill. Maybe that was why he liked the idea so much.

"Old Dwarven saying: If it wants loving, send Vael. If it wants killing, send Aern." Tyree surveyed the armory with a critical eye, looking for anything else, but he had everything he needed. His plan might even work. "But if it wants deceiving, send humans."

CHAPTER 50
ILL MET BY BOOMLIGHT

Rae'en pretended to stretch, using the movement to apply an incremental increase in pressure to the shackles binding her arms. Placing her palms flat against the wall behind her, the Aern used the leverage to force her waist against the restraint about her middle.

"Be still, scarback," snapped one of her reptilian captors.

"I'm stretching," she objected.

"Stop stretching or I get the acid."

"I don't believe it will work."

Zaur fangs flashed as scattered chuckles erupted from the guards. "Hear that, scale brothers? She doesn't think it will work."

Wylant made an obscene noise.

She looks horrible, Rae'en thought at Kazan. *At least that rash around her mouth seems to be going away and her eyes look a little less puffy. Did they spit venom in her eyes or something?*

If the man who had gestured from the hallway came back, they would need as much of a distraction as they could get. As if in answer to her unspoken wish, the human appeared in the entryway, sweat beading on his brow. As he propped her weapon against the wall nearest him, Testament called to her, so close. He held a bulging leather gunpowder pouch against his cheek, concentrating on it. Large coarse threads marked the upper seam of the pouch as if it had been slit open, had an object inserted, and then been sewn shut.

Holding up four fingers, the human met her gaze, folding the fingers down one by one, counting down. The last finger bent inward, making a fist, and he stepped into the room. Rae'en screamed as loudly as she could, a wild, piercing thing tearing at her throat: the best distraction she could manage. The human, as yet unnoticed by the guards, hurled the powder bag into the rear of the pack.

He snatched up Testament with both hands and heaved it in her direction. Grabbing for their weapons, the guards did not seem to know which threat required the more immediate response.

Rae'en would have laughed if she had not been busy breaking her bonds. She pulled hard on her right hand manacle, loosened by her constant straining, ripping the bolt out of the wall entirely. She caught Testament awkwardly by the head of the warpick, then jerked her left hand free as well.

Four guards rushed toward the human, who responded by dropping to his knees and covering his ears.

"I surrender," he shouted. "Cover your ears, ladies!" No sooner had the words left his lips than the loudest explosion Rae'en had ever heard tore through the mass of guards. The force of the blast ripped Testament from her grip and snapped her head back against the stone wall. For the Zaur, the results were even more dramatic. Six Zaur were on fire, the rest charred, battered, or knocked down, and one had a Hearth Stone embedded in his shoulder.

Rae'en watched dumbly as the human made a snapping motion with his wrists. The steel bracelets he wore unrolled into long, thin daggers with which he dispatched the closest surviving Zaur.

"I'm Captain Randall Tyree," the human said. "You don't mind escaping a little early, do you?" Rae'en could hear nothing but a loud ringing in her ears and was forced to read his lips.

"You're a maniac!" Rae'en shouted. "Wylant and I had it sorted. What kind of a rescue do you call that?"

"A successful one," Tyree said cheerfully. "After all, any rescue you can walk away from . . ." He stabbed a Zaur that was beginning to rise.

Several of them scrabbled to their feet, clutching their Skreel blades. Rae'en cleared her head and concentrated on pulling herself free. The long yet inadequate bolts pulled out of the wall one by one, the final bolt clattering to the floor next to her warpick. Rae'en's dilated eyes took in the entire scene, the dead, the living, and her fellow prisoners. Tossing Testament and catching it in a better grip, she whirled madly, plunging the warpick into one Zaur after another, accepting their slashing cuts without thought or pain. This is what the Aern had been made for, to fight Zaur.

Having previously fought them only while also trying to fight against the Arvash'ae, Rae'en experienced for the first time was it meant to be doing what she had been born to do. Unlike any fighting she'd experienced before, this was pure joy, meaning, purpose—fulfillment. The ringing in her ears faded, replaced by the sound of combat. A single Zaur slipped past her guard, pretending to be dead until she stepped over him, then sank its fangs into the exposed flesh of her ankle, stabbing its Skreel blade toward her inner thigh.

When the blade did not strike home, Rae'en was surprised. A mottled blue spear, thrown by Wylant, had pierced the attacking Zaur with such force the tip penetrated the thick, bony ridge above the Zaur's eyes and continued through its lower jaw into the floor beneath.

Captain Tyree removed his shirt, revealing a muscular chest, well defined and bearing its own share of scars. He draped the fabric around her shoulders, hands gliding along her breasts as he fastened the middle button. Had he done that on purpose? "Can you get the Eldrennai loose?" His words were soft, his cheek next to Rae'en's.

"I can," Rae'en answered.

Crossing to the Aiannai, she ripped the bit free.

"*Jallek* root," Wylant coughed as soon as her bit was removed. Her allergies hadn't come back, but they were sure to do so soon.

"I found some of the Aern's things in the armory," the human said, "but I don't know if there's any of that."

"My saddlebags? Where?" asked Rae'en.

"In the hall."

Rae'en dashed out to grab them; when she came back, she was wearing her chain-mail shirt, and her saddlebags were belted back into place.

"We'd better get moving before all the Zaur in this wretched hole come barreling . . . in . . ."

Her voice trailed away as she fixated on the spear Wylant had thrown, now slithering rapidly across the room like a snake. It coiled itself around Wylant's leg and climbed up to her hands, where the weapon transformed into a pair of thick shears, the metal remaining the same mottled blue.

"Meet Vax." Smiling at Rae'en's confusion, Wylant watched as Vax, curled around her forearm for leverage, begin to cut through her chains. As the last bolt parted, the Eldrennai dropped to the floor in a defensive crouch, the shears shifting yet again, this time into a sword. "Shall we go?"

Tyree patted Rae'en's shoulder. "Let's get stepping, sugar bosom."

"Sugar bosom?" Rae'en's brain disconnected. "You . . . I . . . Wha?"

"I know the way out." Tyree smiled broadly. "Even though you could have both freed yourselves, you've got to admit that last part is handy."

Echoes of Zaur voices raised in shouts of dismay, anger, and alarm found their way to Rae'en's ears. "You know the way?" she asked.

"Trust me." The human winked at her. "How are we ever going to be married if I don't get you out of here?"

"Married?"

"I like him." Wylant moved past them to check the hall. "And the good thing about humans is if you decide you don't like being married to one, they only live a hundred years or so, and then you can find a new one."

Rae'en dug through her saddlebags, looking for the ring her father had given her, but it wasn't there.

"Did you see a ring?"

"No." Tyree shook his head. "But the Zaur were packing things up to send to their warlord. Something that small . . . maybe they sent it on ahead?"

"It was soul-bonded to my father," Rae'en growled. "We could have sent him word."

"You can tell him you're safe in person." Wylant pulled Tyree toward the hall. "Which way?"

"This way." Tyree immediately led them in the direction from which the shouting seemed loudest. *Were they fighting someone else?*

"Are you sure?" Rae'en asked.

Tyree simply smirked. "Trust me."

Rae'en absolutely did not, but Wylant followed the human and Rae'en followed her.

CHAPTER 51
HOMECOMING

You're relaying all this?

Of course, Vander sent.

Yes, Maker, came Bloodmane's unnecessary reply, **the Armored are watching.**

Resisting the urge to let his fingers curl his hands into fists, Kholster took in his surroundings slowly. What he saw brought on a flood of mixed emotions as he reentered the city of Port Ammond for the first time in six hundred years. Home. Through him, they were all home, but it was as if he'd returned from a long campaign only to find the barracks infested with vermin.

On either side of Kholster, a contingent of guards maintained a polite distance, their gazes turning to him as often as they scanned for other dangers. Behind twelve mounted knights Dolvek was carried on a palanquin with a healer tending assiduously to his wounds.

Maybe the Vael didn't mix the antidote right, Vander thought to him. *He could still die . . .*

Not with my blood in him, Kholster scoffed.

The healer, a worried old Oathbreaker in flowing white robes with Sedvinia's features tattooed over his own, waved his hands over the prince. Sedvinia's likeness, so similar to her twin Shidarva's, shed tears as her tattooed eyes opened and the soft aura of her magic flickered up and down the prince's body. Kholster sniffed disdainfully, and one of the youngest guards reflexively dropped a hand to his sword.

A rabbit, Vander warned.

Amused, Kholster growled at the guard, feigning a charge.

"Leave him alone, Kholster," Yavi disapproved.

"No more taunting stump ears?" He laughed bitterly, turning his amber and jade eyes in her direction. Kholster waved at the dark-haired guard. The young Oathbreaker's ears had darkened noticeably in embarrassment and his lips were pale. "You didn't wet yourself, did you, boy?"

Perhaps . . . Bloodmane let the transmission trail away.

Perhaps? Kholster thought back, keeping an eye on the guard's hand, which was straying dangerously close to the hilt of his sword.

"No, I didn't, scarback."

"Good for you, stump ears." Kholster grinned, baring his doubled canines. "You going to draw that sword?"

Any word?

Not yet, Kholster. They just found an entrance to the tunnels and engaged the Zaur. As soon as Zhan knows anything—

Fine.

"Kholster," Yavi said more sternly. "Please."

"I only asked a question." Kholster spread his arms wide in invitation. The young soldier cast a pleading look in the direction of his commander, but the officer was at the front, with the knights.

"I'm exactly what you fear me to be, stain," Kholster continued. "You've seen the passage of what, two, three hundred years?"

The guard nodded. Captain Fahn's shadow stretched across the ground between them. The captain watched the exchange from horseback as he rode back down the line.

"Is everything all right here?" he asked Kholster.

"Nice to see you again, Fahn," Kholster answered. "I was just trying to entice your young guardsman here into drawing his weapon so I could kill him with it."

Fahn bore the haunted expression Kholster associated with other veterans of the Sundering. It was the same look he'd seen in the eyes of his own troops who'd waited years to make new tools afterward, the soldiers who hunted too much and spoke too little. Fahn cleared his throat.

"Please, Kholster. The guards are here for your own safety and . . ."

"Liar!" roared Kholster, taking two quick steps toward the mounted Oathbreaker. "They are here because you fear me. Do not pretend I need protection from you."

"Please, sir," Fahn stammered. "A little decorum . . . is it really too much to ask?"

"It is," the Aern hissed, spittle landing on Fahn's saddle and lower legs. "Keep your soldiers away from me, for their protection, because if any one of their blades clears its sheath, if any of you lying, untrustworthy, oath-breaking wastes of life so much as lays a finger on me to help me up the stairs or catch me should I stumble, I will send them to meet the Harvester and they can complain to him."

Fahn looked at the palanquin and then back to his men, resignation in his eyes. "Sergeant, break your men up into groups of two. Send them ahead to clear the streets. I want all the shutters closed. No one is to look out of any windows facing the street."

"Yes, sir." The soldiers began to separate into groups, and Yavi rolled her eyes.

"Do you really have to be that way?" she asked. "These aren't the same people you fought against."

"Some of them are," Kholster replied. "Captain Fahn over there was a foot soldier during the Sundering. He has a Litany. You recite it, and I'll fill in the details." He waited a beat. "No? I recognize some of the rank and file as well. Most of all, I recognize the loathing. I'm a blemish on their honor, a mistake."

Yavi folded her arms beneath her breasts. "I just can't take you anywhere, can I?"

That's cheating, Vander sent. *She's—*

I know what she's doing.

Captain Fahn gave the remaining soldiers the order to advance. Two guards remained at the rear, and two knights rode in front of the palanquin, but the others had gone on.

Ammond was still a beautiful city, but much had changed. Kholster wasn't sure why the changes took him by surprise, but they did. The Tower of Elementals had once possessed four globes of magic spinning in circles at the apex of its central tower. The globes had represented the eternal cycles of air, fire, earth, and water. In their places there were now stone images, each depicting a humanoid embodiment of an element.

It was nearing dawn, but there were no cook fires burning in the central barracks; no scent of chirrum-smoked venison drifted on the wind. Instead, the air smelled like horse manure and garbage. By dusklight, the city seemed dead and lifeless. The strains of some far-off tavern song or another carried in the night; it was sung not by the raucous voices of Aern but by humans instead.

Kholster noticed Yavi adjusting her samir and spat on the ground.

"Hey, I like this samir. It doesn't bother me at all," Yavi protested. "It's kind of an honor to wear it. My mother wore this samir."

"And your grandmother," Kholster answered. "I know. I was there. I recognize it."

"Is that the fabled Aernese superiority, I hear?" Yavi snapped. "Surely you're not looking down your noses at the mortal Vael?"

"This was a mistake," he said angrily. "You have my apologies. I will await you at Oot." The Aern turned away from the gates and walked toward the forest. *To hells with Oot and the Grand Conjunction! I came. I met. Oath fulfilled. I'm going to see what the hells is keeping Zhan. I'll find Rae'en myself.* Kholster still wasn't certain how he'd let the Vael talk him into coming to Port Ammond at all. He should have held his ground and insisted that they treat the Eldrennai prince, Dolvid, Dolvan, Dolvek, whatever his name was, at Oot.

Vander, I want you to—

"Kholster, wait," called Yavi.

Kholster had almost begun to turn when one of the two guards walking at the rear stepped into his path, a hand on his sword hilt. "Stop right there, Bloodmane. The Vaelsilyn said to wait."

"So she did," Kholster snarled. Faster than the soldier could react, Kholster buried Grudge in the guard's chest and snatched the soldier's sword with his left hand. "And as it so happens, I was going to do so, but she is not my kholster. I am not subject to your laws. And my name is not Bloodmane. It's Kholster."

"You scarbacked murderer!" The other guard drew his sword.

Kholster jerked Grudge free of the knight's chest and parried a blow with the sword in his left hand. The knights from the front of the column signaled the bearers to lower the prince's palanquin, and Captain Fahn sat astride his horse, openmouthed and unsure.

Show them this, Kholster told Bloodmane as he spun to face the other soldiers.

Maker, please, Bloodmane sent back, **they're only—**

Only what? Kholster sent back. *Only slavers? Only stump-eared fools who shouldn't even walk this planet, much less the land my kith and kin shed blood for? Only the people I hate most? Only what, Bloodmane? WHAT?!*

Kholster felt the Arvash'ae rising up inside him and he welcomed it. *Yes*, he thought to himself, *me against the city. They'll kill me eventually, but my army will kill every last Eldrennai. The Bone Finders will find my bones. Death will be a welcome rest for me. Unlike . . .*

". . . Rae'en," he hissed.

Kholster turned toward Fahn with a growl, rolling his head to stretch his neck muscles. Perhaps thinking he saw an opening, the guard swung at Kholster's back, grimacing when Kholster batted his blade away with a swift swipe of Grudge, shattering the blade.

"Stop!" shouted Yavi. Her samir slipped down around her neck as she shouted, head petals falling in front of her eyes. "All of you, just stop it! You're acting like children. Deadly, scary, heavily armed children, but still children!"

Kholster's Arvash'ae bled off without ever getting started. Nothing could stop a raging Aern more quickly than a Vael. His anger picked back up when he saw the lustful looks on the faces of the Eldrennai. As if reading his mind, Yavi tugged her samir back into place, her hands shaking.

Kholster, Bloodmane's voice echoed in his mind. **I have something to tell you.**

Ye-es? he thought back to the armor. Oathbreaker glances flickered back and forth, catching the lantern light.

I told the Eldrennai about the Zaur.

Of course you did. Kholster slung his warpick up onto his right shoulder, ignoring the flecks of blood spattering his cheek and back.

I should have asked you for guidance, I know, but I acted alone and . . .

Did you tell them anything else? Kholster thought back icily.

No, they don't know about the army and they don't know we can speak together.

"Why?" Kholster said aloud to Yavi and thought back to Bloodmane. The young Vael's samir moved gently with her breath. In that moment, she reminded him of Wylant, fiery and beautiful. He closed his eyes and saw through Bloodmane's. It was the same empty chamber, but the unborn Aern no longer stood at the center of the room.

The Eldrennai king came and asked me to listen to him. He offered me a scroll with the words of life on them. You should listen to him. I was there at the Sundering. I was with you when you fought. He is a different being now.

Aren't we all? Kholster's world spiraled out of control. Yavi was speaking to him, but he was too engrossed by what Bloodmane was telling him to give her his attention.

Very different. Changed. Stricken. The guilt he feels is palpable, Kholster.

Guilty? He's guilty? Kholster thought angrily. *Well, I guess we might as well go home then and tell all the other exiles that the Eldrennai are different now. Nothing left to avenge; they feel guilty! We can all be Foresworn and let the blacks of our eyes go white, while our bones crumble and our teeth fall out leaving empty holes in gray gums that will never be filled, because the mighty Eldrennai after thousands of years have finally grown a conscience.*

I think he wants to return us to you, to give us all back to our rightful occupants. If he returned us, couldn't that satisfy your Oath? Is there room for mercy?

I have none left. Kholster sat down in the street. *It died with Rae'en.* He dropped the guardsman's sword and unslung his warpick, letting Grudge rest across his knees. Yavi continued speaking to him, but her voice, soft and gentle, fell upon deaf ears. The moment—the sudden feeling of confusion—was identical to the feelings which had coursed through him on Freedom Day.

Kholster dove deep into the memory hoping to find the sudden clarity he'd found then.

Under Eldrennai rule, every victory earned new rewards for the Aern. Sometimes that had been a new barracks, or a rarer ingredient for weapons or armor, or a new training area. Near the end, they had even been granted two days leave each month. At each victory celebration, King Zillek would award them something as a sign of his thanks.

On Freedom Day, at the end of the Demon War, Kholster remembered kneeling at King Zillek's feet, listening to his speech. Zillek had been fond of speeches. He had praised them for pushing the Ghaiattri back into the demon world. He had acknowledged the brave Aern who had died to accomplish it, the loss of Aern who had at the end advanced Armorless into the void as part of a last desperate gamble to take the Ghaiattri by surprise and close the gate from the Ghaiattri side. He had named them the Lost Command, had ordered a monument built at Fort Sunder in their honor, and then he had offered the Aern anything.

Kholster would always remember it. "Anything, sire?"

"Yes," the king had boasted. "Nothing is too good for my brave army."

The Eldrennai king had offered *anything* . . . and Kholster suspected the king was Oathbound to provide it. As a soldier who had been a slave for millennia, whose people had been tortured and killed for sport by kings this one never even knew . . . what else could he do but ask.

"So what is it to be?" Zillek had patted him on the head affably. "A new barracks? More Vaelsilyn? Perhaps you'd like your own keep near Albren Pass or Stone Watch, a better staging area for defense against the Zaur?"

"Freedom," Kholster had whispered.

"What?" The king had recoiled as if Kholster had transformed into a Zaur. "Don't be absurd," Zillek had said, as if he were speaking to a naughty pet. "I like the idea of the keep. I'll give you the keep and send some more Vaelsilyn out there with you. Good. Now that's settled. Kiss my sword."

In that moment, Kholster had felt the chains of magic binding him to his king fail. A tightness he'd never lived without fell away, and the breath he took next was the first he'd ever taken that truly tasted good.

A direct order from an Eldrennai superior had always brought instant submission from the Aern; part of the enchantment which had been bound into them from creation, but no longer. In denying them their freedom, ironically, Zillek had granted it. Kholster had been, for the first time in his long life, free to act as he chose.

Staring into the eyes of his king, Kholster saw his own realization echoed there. Next, he had done the only thing he knew how to do. Without any thought or plan, he had reached out with his right hand and grabbed the king's sword. Forged of enchanted steel, the blade should have sliced through his gauntlets and into his fingers, but it hadn't. It had shattered like glass, just from Kholster's desires: for revenge, for freedom, and to be something more than an exceptionally well-trained beast of war.

As he had hoped and planned through long years since the Battle of As You Please, Kholster had struck out with Hunger, burying its spike deep in Zillek's skull.

No.

Peering into Yavi's green eyes, Kholster came back to the present and saw himself reflected within. Blood from the fallen guard ran down from Grudge's hooked head, and dark stains ran up his arm.

"Kholster, are you all right?" Bloodmane and Yavi asked him in unison.

"You will never understand, Yavi," Kholster said softly. "I see that now. Or maybe I'm the problem. Maybe I am the only one who still . . ."

No. I'm not. Bloodmane, he transmitted mentally, *Please send word to the fleet. Tell them the invasion begins in three days. The Zaur will likely attack from the south, and we will come from the east as planned. We will crush the Oathbreakers between the two armies and then fight the Zaur.*

Yes . . . Master, Bloodmane thought back.

Master. Kholster's blood chilled at that.

I am not your MASTER! If you don't want to do it. . . . Overwhelming loss filled Kholster as he communicated with the armor, a piece of himself as changed as the Port Ammond to which he had returned. *Then don't. Rise up. Fight for the Eldrennai if you want. Let their king wear you if you must, but do not call me Master! You are not my slave. You are a part of me. If you want to be separate, then so be it, but I have sworn an oath. I set the conditions upon which I would return and kill them all. They brought this on themselves. I pledged to see them dead and I keep my oaths.*

Must it be so? the armor asked.

Kholster did not answer.

He wiped the blood from his hands, smearing it across his jeans in a long, semi-clotted streak. Bittersweet, the scent of the blood oaks in bloom wafted over him on the chill night breeze, mixing with the aromatic hint of roses from the royal gardens. Yavi was still speaking in gentle tones, part conciliation and the rest subtle rebuke. Even one hundred years ago, perhaps, he might have fallen in love with her, but now she was too young and too naive for him.

". . . and so that's just what I'm trying to say, you know, that none of us really understand how it feels to carry the weight tied to your heart, but . . ."

Kholster pushed himself upright, Grudge hanging loosely in his right hand. The maneuver brought him cheek to cheek with Yavi, the Eldrennai blood on his face leaving a thin red smear along her samir. Startled, she skipped back a step and the guardsmen reached for their blades.

"You have until three dawns have passed. I . . . or my representative . . . will uphold the Grand Conjunction the Eldrennai care so much about, delayed though it may be," Kholster spat out. "One. Last. Time. Then our truce is ended."

"But," Yavi began.

"Prophecy or no prophecy," Kholster bulled on. "By my own life and the lives of those who died still in Eldrennai bondage, I so swear, there will be war between the Aern and the Eldrennai until every last one of them is dead or . . . until I am."

Yavi turned away. It was too late, and she seemed to know it.

Maker, Bloodmane began. **Kholster. Please.**

No, Kholster thought back at the armor. *If you want to stop me, Bloodmane, words won't do it. Kill me, then refuse to accept my bones. My oath allows the Aern to stop if I'm dead. I leave this plane of existence or they do.*

To Kholster's left, the healer knelt over the fallen guardsman. His eyes found the Aern's and they stabbed at him with their accusations. "He's dead. My magic should have been able to heal him, but . . ."

An eagle's cry sounded from the warpick in the general's right hand. "He was wounded by the grudge I bear, healer. No magic could save him, only strong medicine and a stronger will. He had neither," Kholster replied wearily. "Let's get Prince Stump Ears to the palace before you lose another patient."

The healer nodded, and the procession moved on.

CHAPTER 52
CLOSE QUARTERS

Dolvek's personal suite had been hastily rearranged to accommodate his two new guests. Though Yavi'd had her own set of rooms during her recent stay, all agreed that the Conjunction necessitated a certain proximity. The prince sat out on the balcony, attempting to perform his daily exercises and frustrating the ministrations of his attendant healer. Yavi found him quite entertaining. She made another circuit around the spacious quarters.

The suite was larger than one person could possibly actually need. Three doors led off to adjoining rooms: one to the prince's bedroom, another to a private guest room, the other to the prince's washroom. A steel door stood ajar, open to the hallway, its spell-seal currently disengaged. Yavi watched a small, bored spirit, the embodiment of the magic within the spell-seal, mimicking the prince from its perch atop the large bolt that could be brought across the door.

A new suit of crystal armor already hung on a mannequin set in what Yavi privately thought was a small shrine to Dolvek's military prowess. Weapons of steel, crystal, and other more exotic material hung in neat rows on the wall. Above the armor, a mystic rendition of the prince in full armor glowed brightly, sneering down at her.

Prince Dolvek's small military library occupied one corner of the room and held Kholster's interest to the exclusion of all else. He sat in the prince's reading chair, a map spread out on the desk before him, looking back and forth from it to the book he was reading. His warpick lay propped against his thigh for, she assumed, easy access in case a horde of Zaur managed to climb the battlements and storm the balcony.

How could her mother have ever been attracted to this Aern? A certain charm, a very primal charm, did exist there, but it was overbalanced by a hatred that confounded Yavi. "You're reading an updated record of public works?" she asked.

He nodded. "For the invasion. It will be much easier to capture the city or reclaim it from the Zaur if I know what changes have been made."

"He's reading what?" Dolvek stormed in from outside, his healer protesting ineffectually. "How dare you? You sit here, in my home, enjoying my hospitality and . . ."

Kholster shut the book with a loud pop. "I think," he said as he stood and walked to a bookshelf, "I will make this," reshelved the book firmly enough to rock the shelf, "my son's art studio," and turned, arms crossed, to the prince, "when I capture this place. He may never visit, but it will be nice to have one waiting for him all the same."

"Do you have to threaten him every five minutes?" Yavi asked. Their bickering never seemed to end for long.

"I only speak to him when spoken to, Yavi. Is it my fault he refuses to keep his mouth shut?"

Yavi saw Prince Dolvek begin to open his mouth and spoke first to cut him off. "How is Irka? Any new sibs?" Kholster's broad grin took her by surprise. *He looks like any other parent when he thinks of his son*, she mused.

"He has a sister, alive, I hope." His chest puffed up with obvious pride then deflated as some dark thought banished the light.

"You hope?"

"The Zaur take no prisoners. She went missing, apparently among Zaur. I had intended her to take my place at Oot."

"You'd feel it if something happened to her, though. Right?"

"I like to think I would."

"Tell me about her."

It was on his lips to say no, she could almost see the words in outline on his breath, but he relented.

"She's something special. Females are rare among my people; each one is a treasure, and not just because of their scarcity. . . . They are a triumph over the Eldrennai—it was intended by our creator that all Aern be male. When she was ready I intended to make her First."

"First?" Yavi asked.

"To bestow upon her my rank. More so than your half-brother, Irka, Rae'en has what it takes to kholster my people, and she was Freeborn. Don't think that means she'll be easy on you." He pointed at Prince Dolvek. "You had best hope that matters are settled between our peoples before she becomes First. You'll be torn apart like a hunter who's stumbled across a mad irkanth defending her cubs. When . . . one day the Aern no longer need me, I will surrender my spirit to her and give her my strength, knowledge, all that I am, and she will truly be First. It's a process usually reserved for Incarna, but Torgrimm has allowed male Hundreds to bequeath themselves to their female offspring before. It's why there are nineteen female Hundreds now. He will grant me the same favor."

"Aernese tale spinning!" Dolvek spat.

"See it so," Kholster quipped. "Live long enough and see it so."

King Grivek stood in the open doorway, a shadow across his face. "It's true, I'm afraid," he said without entering. "I've seen it happen. It's why the Aern don't worship any gods, because their souls do not leave Barrone." He stepped inside and closed the door gently behind him, leaning against it. Yavi felt the tension between Grivek and Kholster so strongly that it appeared to her eyes a spirit in potential, a powerful thing she could have unleashed with her magic. But it would be a wild and untamable creature, beyond her control. The spell-seal spirit sensed it too and hid behind its lock.

The king held his hands out to Kholster palms down and fingers splayed, a gesture of respect as old as the Aern—one that the Aern had been forced to offer their Eldrennai masters. "Kholster, I bid you welcome . . ."

"Spare them," Kholster snapped. Confused, the king began to speak again, but Kholster interrupted him. "Your words, Eldrennai king, and your empty gestures. Do not break them on my battlements. They can neither take the castle nor storm the gates . . . so spare them; they are ill spent on me."

"At least let me thank you for saving my son."

"I did not save him." Kholster's voice dropped in volume until it was barely perceptible. "If you must thank someone, your gratitude belongs to Yavi."

Yavi's cheeks darkened. "No, Kholster," she protested. "I could have never tracked how to help him without you. The antidote wouldn't have worked without your . . ."

"Do not shame me further." Kholster stepped close to her, his body pressed against hers. She flinched, expecting him to grab her arms, but his hands remained at his sides. His words hissed into her ear, tiny impassioned whispers. "What you did with the information I gave you, with what you took, for good or for ill, is on your ears, not mine. Please understand that."

Dolvek drew his sword, dumping the attendant healer onto his rump. "Get away from her!"

"You think I would hurt her?" Kholster laughed, taking a step back from Yavi. "Me, with whom she is safest? She should have let you die and spared your father the grief of yet another half-wit son."

"I can take care of myself, Prince Dolvek." Even as she spoke, Yavi was struck by Kholster's choice of words, so similar to the words Bloodmane had spoken when they met in the museum: *He will think that you are in danger*, the armor had scoffed, *here where you are safest.*

"Of course, I didn't mean to imply . . ." The prince's voice softened.

"You didn't mean, you didn't understand, you didn't think," Kholster berated. "You are all the same. You only mean something if it works. You only accept responsibility for a gambit if it succeeds. Any failings should be forgiven you, because the high holy Eldrennai always have the best intentions!"

"Could you please not shout like that right over me?" Yavi held her hands to her ears.

"My apology is yours, Yavi," Kholster responded instantly. "I let him get beneath my armor." The backs of his fingertips touched her cheek, soft and feather-like, a phantom touch. *Gromma*, she thought, *you'd think he was a Vael, no grabbing, no confining movements. Even when he stood against me, he didn't grasp; he left me free to escape. I think I know what Mother saw in him after all.*

"And my forgiveness is yours, Kholster; just keep it down to an irkanth's roar."

Kholster nodded. Yavi waited for someone else to say something, but they all stood in the silence, glaring at one another. Dolvek sheathed his sword grudgingly but showed no sign of returning to his exercises.

"Do you have to wear that in the house?" Yavi tapped the center of her forehead then flicked the finger outward, an expression of noncomprehension.

"As long as the Aern is here," Dolvek said defensively, "and it's a castle, not a . . ."

"Put it away," Grivek said acidly.

The prince complied by drawing his sword and hurling it at the wall, where the blade stuck point first. Yavi and Kholster remained silent. The king stood quietly too, but his silence seemed born of embarrassment, rather than the hatred between Kholster and Dolvek.

"Have you heard back from your scouts, Oathbreaker?" The Aern returned to his seat at Dolvek's desk.

"From three of them," Grivek answered. "The South Watch is safe, as is Forest Watch. My Lancers also checked in on Silverleaf and Porthost as they traveled the White Road."

"And the third watch city?" Kholster asked.

Grivek looked down, his emotions unreadable. "The North Watch tower is gone. Wylant led her Lancers down into a tunnel they found in its place. I have not heard more than that which young Kam brought with him."

"Wylant will be fine," Kholster snorted, leaning back in the chair and propping his boots up on the desk. "She's just decided to engage the enemy. You'll hear back from her when the fighting's over."

When he spoke of Wylant, Yavi thought she heard fondness, almost affection, in his voice. *I must be hearing things*, she told herself.

"I hope that is true." King Grivek looked away.

"The North Watch is gone?" Dolvek demanded. "When did this happen?"

"While you were sleeping." Kholster drummed his fingers thoughtfully on the bone-steel rings of his mail shirt. "I'm impressed they've decided to use tunnels. They've dug pits before, but to tunnel under a Watch and take it from below . . . Warlord Xastix must be a cunning reptile indeed."

"Kholster," Grivek began. "Since you're here, perhaps you would give us the benefit of your military advice?"

"I suggest you build a tremendous bonfire and burn yourselves on it." Kholster put a hand casually on the haft of his warpick. "Why ask me? Why not ask your dear friend Bloodmane? He seems sympathetic enough to your cause."

"Great Aldo," King Grivek sighed. To Yavi, it seemed his spirit flickered and dimmed. She offered him a hand for support, but he waved it away. "So you do know."

"I knew before I came, Eldrennai king." Kholster slid his boots off the desk, his heels leaving a faint scuff on the finish. "When your idiot son dared speak down to my wife, when he questioned whether or not I could even read. More than thirteen years ago he implied that I was not 'a specter of death looming in the shadows and waiting to destroy' you all. That's exactly what I was. More than thirteen years ago, Dolvek shattered our truce, and yet here I am, fulfilling my part of the bargain, keeping my oaths. I said that I or my representative would return in one hundred years for the next Grand Conjunction." He stood, brought Grudge up in an arc and slammed it down, reducing the desk to splinters. "And here I am." He pointed at Grivek with his warpick, and it let loose the angry cry of a bird of prey. "As promised. My other oaths will be kept as well."

"Kholster, I know what we have done to your people. I recall your oath, and yet it is my hope . . ." Grivek began cautiously.

"Do not beg from him, Father," Dolvek interrupted. "If our truce is no more, then he is an enemy of the Eldrennai. I say we put him to death."

Kholster grinned at the prince, as if daring him to try.

"Be silent, Dolvek," roared the king, "or blood or no blood, son or no son, I will put *you* to death! You don't have the barest inkling of what is at stake here. If the Aern come for us, they will destroy us. If we do not have the Aern's help, the Zaur will destroy us. How many Zaur do you think there are in the mountains? How many of them do you think are trained from birth as warriors?" He reached out to put a hand on Dolvek's shoulder, but his son turned away.

"You are a coward, Father, just like Rivvek." Dolvek walked back to the balcony doors, his attendant doing his best to stay out of the way. "You bow down to the Aern like we owe them our lives," he snarled. "So we enslaved them? We freed them as well. We created them! Wylant could have wiped them out at the Sundering, but you stayed her hand. We let them go. We owe them nothing else! Price paid."

"He's such a nice bowel movement," Kholster told Yavi, stepping over the splinters of the desk. "Aren't you glad you decided to preserve him?"

"And you accuse us of hatred?" Dolvek shouted from the balcony. "What did we do that was so terrible? I've read the histories and nothing seems . . ."

"The Battle of As You Please," Kholster said softly.

"More tale spinning," Dolvek laughed. "Everyone knows that did *not* happen."

"It happened," said King Grivek dully.

"Oh, please," Dolvek protested. "Maybe something like it happened, but . . .

"It happened just as the Aern say it did," Grivek continued, almost emotionlessly. "I have never heard it told falsely, except by Eldrennai."

Yavi held up her hand. "Um, right, just so that I'm tracking you all . . . what is the Battle of Azupleez? I don't even know where that is."

"As. You. Please," Kholster corrected. "The Battle of As You Please. There are other reasons. Being used as breeding stock. Being forced by magic to follow orders, being treated as property instead of as allies . . ." He shook his head. "Not allowing my direct descendants to forge warsuits and join the ranks of the Armored. I can forgive many things, but I cannot forgive the Battle of As You Please."

CHAPTER 53
THE BATTLE OF AS YOU PLEASE

Grudgebearer, Vael, and Eldrennai stood in the prince's chambers. Yavi sat down on an overstuffed sofa, and Dolvek's father sat next to her. Both of them looked on with rapt attention as Kholster deliberately removed his bone-steel mail. Seeing the Aern bare to the waist increased the prince's ill temper, but he shepherded his words carefully. Anything he said at this point would only make Yavi more likely to side with the lying Grudgebearer. What was the Aern trying to prove by wearing mail without a gambeson? As if he were actually that hardened.

The prince leaned against the sofa reluctantly, watching Kholster as he drew a bone-steel chain bearing little charms and ornaments—also bone-steel—from his pack, attaching them reverently to his warpick until the chain-wrapped weapon resembled an awkward percussion instrument.

"These are the bones of my children, a single chain or charm from each of the slain. The links from sons. The charms from my daughters."

Yavi made a surprised noise and covered her mouth with both hands, but Kholster did not look at her. He turned away from them, revealing his broad, muscular back. Dolvek had expected it to be covered in battle scars but instead found the tan skin of Kholster's back oddly smooth except for the scars, identifying lineage, borne by all Aern. A wedge as long as Kholster's index finger angled inward along each shoulder blade, and a vertical thumb-width line marred the flesh along his spine. The last scar was at the small of his back. It was a diamond shape, each flat side of the diamond bearing two matching lines parallel to it.

Kholster flexed, and the marks whitened.

"These are not my father's scars." Kholster pounded his warpick on the floor rhythmically, speaking in a singsong voice, calm but pregnant with emotion. "I have no father. I am of the One Hundred, the First, held by no womb, without mother."

The jingling beat of the warpick and the cadence of Kholster's words reminded Dolvek of an entertainer who had once come to them from the far-off land of Khalvad, but the Aern's performance was neither whimsical nor erotic. It was somber and rebellious.

"When you hear these chains and charms, tremble, for you hear my children and they are born slayers. Rae'en of Helg: my heart; Irka of Kari: my peaceful son—my Incarna. They are my only Freeborn children, for I took no wife for five centuries, to honor the memory of my sons and daughters who died in a battle against no enemy. To them I was no father but Kholster only, yet they bore my scars and were my offspring. Of their mothers I know not."

Drawn in despite himself, Dolvek involuntarily flinched back when Kholster spun around, warpick extended but still bent low, bouncing on the balls of his feet.

"Know me, that you know my tale is true. Told with words of one who saw and did, told at the edge of the Arvash'ae," he said as his amber pupils expanded and lit from within, the jade of his iris all but banishing the black of his sclera, "that no lies can be spoken and memory cannot fail." He drew a ragged breath and released it from his nostrils. Steam did not flow out with it, but Dolvek had expected that it might.

"I was there at As You Please, for I am now, have always been, the kholster of my people. Three weeks after we defeated the Zaur at North Watch, drove them back to their mountains, back beneath the rock, that was the day of As You Please. Seven hundred and two sons I lost that day, and daughters three. Each bore their father's scars.

"Zillek was angry. Zillek, the Leash Holder king; Zillek, the liar, the betrayer. Pray for him you who hear; pray that the Oathkeeper souls stay world-bound, that we never enter into the place beyond that holds his soul."

"Laying it on a bit thick, isn't he?" Dolvek whispered to Yavi.

"Hush," she replied.

Dolvek walked back to the balcony doors. This was all really just a sham, wasn't it? Kholster was just doing what all Aern did, playing up "legendary" misdeeds that happened thousands of years ago. Why was his father buying into this Grudgebearer nonsense? If the Zaur were really attacking, then Dolvek and Grivek should both be reviewing defense plans, not listening to overblown fireside chants. His father was acting as if, in the face of the Grudgebearer's overly dramatic declaration outside, a Zaur invasion was the least of their worries.

"In those days each great victory won a tribute from the king. Zillek, the king, the Leash Holder king, his highness pronounced it upon us, a gift, a boon, not of our choosing: more Vaelsilyn sent to the soldiers' beds, new quarters for sleeping, better grounds for training or practice. We were spell-sworn in those days, bound to obey, bound to answer, enslaved souls, but free of mind. The king offered a boon of my own devising, a gift, my own to name. The Leash Holder king had guests from afar; he'd impress with magnanimous grace. The boon that I asked angered Zillek the king, and he gave us the Battle of As You Please."

"See," Dolvek called from the doorway. "He admits that whatever happened they brought it on themselves." The others hissed at him to be quiet, and he complied. It had been a halfhearted protest in any event. His real problem with Kholster's tale was that it didn't ring false. That troubled him.

"I might have asked for freedom, but that concept—freedom—lay yet beyond my understanding. I asked that we be allowed to choose our own mates, to breed only when we wished to do so. Oh, the anger I saw in his eyes when he said just three words: As You Please. It was clear in his bearing, the set of his jaw as his guests laughed and jeered at his plight . . . King Zillek, the king, the Leash Holder king would a reckoning devise to punish my crime.

"The histories tell of As You Please as a day when great heroes were born, sacrifices made, the kingdom preserved in the end. The Oathbreakers say the Aern fought that day humans in costume, disguised as Aern. But hear now the truth of As You Please, the words of a slave now freed, how the Oathbreaker king, just to punish his slaves, brought his entire army to its knees. The king, he divided us up for a game, half to watch and the others to play. We divided again at the Leash Holder's whim, putting eldest and youngest at bay."

Yavi flinched and looked questioningly at Dolvek, who shook his head. "It's a lie. I mean, it's so obviously a lie. Who would do that? Zillek was a great king, not some petty lunatic! Father, tell her!" His father did not answer, and Yavi rose from the couch, putting distance between herself and the king.

"I pled with the king and begged him pronounce some other way to atone." Kholster's gaze went back and forth between the three listeners—Yavi, Dolvek, and Grivek—as he continued, making eye contact with each in turn, contact that was broken only by the movements of his dance. Even so, Dolvek felt that the Aern was staring only at him, accusing him of acts that had happened before he'd even been conceived. "He laughed in my face, did the Eldrennai king, and commanded me lead the attack. 'Your pleasure you've had,' he spat with a laugh, 'but the pleasure had here will be mine.'

"He constructed a box overlooking the field, a seat for each royal and guest. Then on that day he commanded his slaves, Oathbound with no choice but obey: 'Each side will to the death fight the other, but the rules of the battle will change as you go. When one from the box shall call out a rule, his voice you must obey. Each new rule ends the former, but yet you will fight. You'll shout "As You Please," and quick as a wink, you'll apply each new rule to each other.'"

Dolvek's attendant stood open-mouthed, but the prince ignored him. He needed fresh air. The atmosphere even at the entrance to his suite from the balcony was unbelievably oppressive. *Even if it is all true, it doesn't mean anything*, Dolvek fumed. *It's ancient history. Half those elves are dead now. The Aern give us no credit for freeing the Vaelsilyn or for ceding three-fourths of the kingdom to them as reparation for any crimes, real or imagined.*

Unceasing, the tempo of the song never varied, and Kholster continued tirelessly, dancing erratically in a series of moves reminiscent of Aernese fighting techniques.

"On one foot we slaughtered our sons and our daughters, hoping in vain it would cease, but the Leash Holder king who'd imagined this thing had no intention of early relief. They took turns in the box shouting 'dance,' 'sing,' or 'swear' and lower commands at their beasts. We fought out that way for most of a day, and at last we had won—and lost too. Ten thousand Aern fought that battle of pride, and one-tenth of that number survived. It was then that I knew a day would come, soon or perhaps far away, when the Leash Holder king or his brat of a prince would ask my choice of a boon for my Aern. On Freedom Day, As You Please would seem but a brawl, and I'd deprive the good king of his head first of all." Kholster ended with one final smack of his warpick against the floor.

Inside, someone sobbed bitterly. *A Vaelsilyn couldn't be expected to hear such things without being overwhelmed*, Dolvek told himself. He wasted no time heading in to comfort her, but she was dry-eyed, helping Kholster with his shirt.

"What?" he asked aloud. "Father, you weren't even there, you can't help what Grandfather did."

The king looked away; he could not bear to look at him.

"Act only forward," Kholster sighed.

"What?" Dolvek demanded.

"It's the command your father gave as I tried to save my eldest daughter." Kholster's voice fell cold and hard on Dolvek's ears, but his eyes remained locked with the Vael's. "She was behind me. I couldn't save her, and I couldn't let my other children kill me because I'd been ordered to fight as hard as I could, to fight to the death." Kholster's eyes cut toward the Eldrennai and blazed with feeling.

"Of my sons that died at As You Please, I killed three hundred and seventy-six with my own warpick. Of the daughters I lost that day, two of the three died at my hand. I tore Jhilla's throat out with my own teeth because we'd been ordered to fight like literal animals when she came against me in battle."

Dolvek opened his mouth to deny it, but the words dried up in his throat.

"Bloodmane," Kholster continued, "can forgive your crimes. It doesn't feel the things fleshly beings feel. It does not yearn for a lover or mourn for a child. It does not know what it is like to be used as a stud to produce more brave fighting Aern. It is alive, and it should be no one's slave, but it cannot burn as we do. It cannot hate." His gaze softened as it returned to Yavi, and his hand came up to gently stroke her cheek. "Or love—as fiercely."

"All right . . . all right," Dolvek agreed. "But what do you expect us to do? We can't bring back the people you lost or undo what our ancestors did. How could we begin to make it up to you, even if we wanted to?"

"Kill every Eldrennai who was alive then," Kholster answered flatly. He fastened the belt around his waist and shrugged his mail into place. "Kill them all, let the survivors, those who never held the leash swear allegiance to the Vael and the Aern, and I will come to their aid.

Divide the survivors into groups. Let them ask to bear our scars, and those we accept will become Aiannai. The Eldrennai will be dead, and my oath will be fulfilled."

"The people would never agree to it," Dolvek protested. "Some, apologists like Rivvek and his crowd, yes, but the rest . . . Father could possibly convince them to relocate, to cede all our remaining lands to the Vaelsilyn, but what you're asking . . . it isn't going to happen."

"A few would," answered Kholster, catching up his warpick. "But for the majority, there is no mutually acceptable solution." His footsteps sounded harshly on the flagstones as he moved to the interior door. Dolvek tensed; the danger in the air suddenly became almost palpable.

Something had changed in the Aern, and it was not for the Eldrennai's good. Kholster slammed the spell-seal home, locking the door from within as behind the prince sounds of combat rang out from the courtyard. Dolvek spun, rushing to the balcony to see below him armored figures, forming up in ranks by company, gathering in rows outside the palace. The guards attacked them, but the intruders did not strike back. Each held in its gauntlets an Aernese warpick. The prince's mouth went dry as he watched them pour into the streets, some covered in dust, others with remnants of storage containers still hanging around their necks. Five-thousand-strong, the Aernese warsuits had risen.

CHAPTER 54
PEACEMAKER

"You have to call them off, Kholster." The lithe Vael interposed herself between the Aern and the Eldrennai royals. Standing with his back to the door he'd just locked, Kholster leaned down and kissed her, his lips and hers separated only by a bit of kidskin leather. On the edge of recoiling, Yavi surrendered when his arms did not enfold her.

Hands clasped firmly behind his back, eyes open, not out of distrust but rather complete trust, nose to nose, Kholster let her see his spirit, his intentions, fully. The lids of their eyes closed simultaneously, as they both, heads tilting slightly, continued the kiss, lips pressing together, but apart. Yavi reached up to remove her samir, heart pounding and mind lost in the wanton whirl of a thousand mental images of her and Kholster moving together.

This was what her mother had warned her about. Vael were made for Aern; the yearning curled her toes and tore the breath from her lungs. A new potential spirit hung between the two of them, a child, a boy child, beautiful and strong, just like his father. The decision not to join with Kholster, not to make that child right now, was actual physical pain.

"Do you see now?" he asked her when she pulled reluctantly away. "Do you understand?"

Yavi wasn't sure of much in that moment, but she did know that the warsuits had forgiven the Eldrennai, wanted to work with them again, and that it was killing Kholster, literally fraying his spirit with internal conflict.

"Get away from her!" Dolvek's sword, ripped from the wall, flashed, matching his own anger. A bolt of lightning arced down the blade and struck the side of Kholster's face.

The blow that would have killed a Vael knocked Kholster's head back with the force of a strong right hook. A trickle of bright-orange blood flowed from a small cut on his cheek, and he smiled coldly. "It takes great skill to use just enough magic to create a mundane bolt, one to which I am not completely immune. Well done. You want to play games with me, stump ears? To play the hero?"

Yavi and Grivek both shouted for the two to stop, Yavi beseeching Kholster and the king imploring his own son.

"He's an invader, Father." Dolvek hurled another bolt, this one directly into Kholster's chest, evoking dancing sparks across his bone-steel mail.

"I am not some young pup for whom your magic holds danger. I am First!" Kholster's fist caught the prince under the chin, tossing him onto his back; blood trailed from a gash in his lower lip, and the sparkling crystal sword tumbled to the floor.

"The suits aren't attacking," Yavi shouted. "They've risen to help you."

"You lie," Dolvek snarled, grasping for his sword. His voice cut off mid-word when Kholster lifted him into the air by his throat. Gurgling, the prince thrashed out with an ice spell. Gooseflesh rose on Kholster's exposed skin, the breath from his lips steaming from the cold.

"Liar?" The Aern shook him roughly. "Apologize to her now, Oath-breaker! Beg her forgiveness! Beg!"

Her ears ringing, Yavi closed with the angry Aern. "Kholster, let him go, please." Yavi placed her knuckles against the small of his back, pressing slightly more firmly than usual to be felt through his mail. The gesture implied gentle restraint. The Eldrennai would not have recognized it, Yavi knew, but Kholster responded instantly, releasing the prince and shoving him away in one fluid motion.

"As you please." Amber pupils surrounded by jade irises, within the pools of black that were Kholster's eyes, contracted as his gaze lingered on the prince, daring the much younger elf to retaliate. Dolvek caught himself with a conjured flight spell, landing gracefully on his feet.

"She tells the truth," Grivek called from the balcony. Yavi hadn't noticed him move; he appeared to simply have been standing there all along. "They are lining up in formation along the old Lane of Review."

"Stand down at once," Grivek shouted to his troops below, effortlessly summoning the wind to amplify his words. "The warsuits are offering us their assistance. I repeat, stand down and stand clear of them. Let no one provoke them further."

"You could have said something," Yavi rebuked.

Kholster's eyes softened again. "I had no need. You were here." The knuckle of his middle finger glided with butterfly-like tenderness up her brow from between her eyes to her hairline and back again—another Vael touch. "There is an old saying about the curse of the Vael. It describes your people as all things the Eldrennai desire and all things the Aern need."

As they walked out to join the king on the balcony, Kholster's disdain for Dolvek and his sad hatred for Grivek shone more clearly than ever. To Yavi, it seemed that Kholster pitied the monarch but, despite his own feelings, could not forgive him. Yavi wondered if that lack of forgiveness was a trait built into the Aern and if that one mistake might yet cost all the Eldrennai their lives.

Grander than she had envisioned, the Aernese warsuits stood in two hundred ranks, twenty-five deep, weapons held at the ready, absolutely silent. "They have decided to help you," Kholster told the king, "until the Conjunction is completed."

"Bloodmane told you this?" Grivek asked.

"He didn't have to tell me."

"And then?"

"Then they will . . ."

"Rejoin their masters and kill us all," Dolvek croaked, rubbing his throat.

"Not masters," Yavi corrected quickly so Kholster need not do so. "They are a part of each other. The hand is not enslaved to the brain; it is a part of the whole."

Guards pounded on the door. "Your Majesty?"

"All is well." Grivek crossed to the door and threw back the spell-seal to allow them inside.

"We must travel back to Oot," Kholster said to the other two, "and complete our time together. I suggest we start again, to ensure that your prophecy is fulfilled and my word is not broken."

"Nothing says we have to stay at Oot, Grudgebearer, only meet there," the prince muttered.

Kholster opened his mouth, but King Grivek interrupted. "Thank you for your willingness to begin again, Kholster. Perhaps you would stay the night here, inspect the warsuits?"

"Huhn," Kholster coughed. "Do not seek to overstretch my patience or my generosity, Oathbreaker king. Very well." He bit his lower lip, two upper canines peeking out from one side as he stroked his beard with a thumb. "I will stay here tonight, conferring with Bloodmane, and tomorrow, examining your museum and, should you allow it, the old armory. I will depart for Oot with the second dawn and return to my own purposes once your Grand Conjunction is complete. You have the best part of five days to make use of the warsuits' aid."

"Thank you," Grivek uttered in palpable relief, offering his hand for Kholster to press knuckles.

Spurning the offered hand, Kholster pushed past the assembled guards. "Kill as many Zaur as you can, Oathbreaker. It will save me the effort of slaying them myself."

After Kholster left, Grivek seized the hilt of Dolvek's crystal blade, surprising both Yavi and the prince when he straightened his arm, the tip of the sword resting above his son's heart. "He was giving us more time. Open your eyes! It is possible that we can use this reprieve to push back the Zaur and further our cause with the warsuits."

"Further our cause with the warsuits? Father, you're mad. They are just tools."

"So I once thought of the Aern, my son. So my father thought. And I'm assured of your intelligence to such a degree that I am confident we both see that way of thinking as the delusion it was."

"He's right." Yavi flopped down on the couch. "I've spoken with them. They are as sentient and reasonable as you or I. Well, a bit more than you, Prince." She stuck out the tip of her tongue beneath her samir. No one saw it, but it made her feel better.

"But surely, a flesh-and-blood creature would be more suited to . . ."

"That's why I'm placing you as second-in-command," Grivek interrupted his son.

Great Aldo, not him, Yavi thought.

"Thank you, Father, you won't . . ."

". . . under Bloodmane. I will go to the . . . to Oot with Kholster and Yavi for the Grand Conjunction."

"There may be some dissension," Dolvek said frankly.

"And you will make sure our troops are won over, that they heed every hollow intonation which issues forth from that remarkable suit of armor."

Dolvek closed his eyes, swaying as if he might faint. "And if I can't?"

"Execute them," the king answered grimly. "Bloodmane may be our only chance to drive back the Zaur without Wylant's leadership. Only one being on this orb has more experience fighting the Zaur than General Bloodmane and that is the being who forged him. Kholster has given us five days to defeat the Zaur. It will be hard, but not impossible, if our people do exactly as the warsuits command. Though they are but armor, they have, after all, done it before."

Grivek left the room in silence. Yavi crept out after him. She had no interest in watching the temper tantrum she was sure would soon take place.

CHAPTER 55
EMPTY WORDS

Nothing about the mission was going as planned. The long rows of Aernese warsuits, standing aboveground in the open sunlight, heartened Kholster, until he considered their desire to help the Eldrennai. Bloodmane stood at the far end of the group with the nine other suits who had been placed on display in Prince Dolvek's Aern exhibit. Kholster's keen ears picked up the sound of protesting Oathbreakers, residents and business owners arguing with the knights about being confined to their homes. King Grivek clearly did not want a fight to spring up on his doorstep.

Kholster, eyes forward, walked the entire length of the arrayed force. A chant began as he started, and by the time he reached Bloodmane, it was deafening. "Kholster! Khol-ster! Khol-ster!" Light flickered within the crystal eyes of the warsuits of the One Hundred, a sign his Armored were conversing mentally with their chanting creations. Kholster assumed his Aern were trying to silence the army, but the troops were too excited. It had never happened under his leadership, but after their millennia in captivity, Kholster was inclined to let them yell.

"Maker," Bloodmane's hollow voice greeted Kholster. The voice was strange to Kholster, so empty compared to the words he felt in his head when he conversed with the armor.

"Kholster Bloodmane," Kholster replied with a nod, a gesture of equality.

"I am not a kholster."

"Yes." Kholster placed his hand on the armor's spaulder and sparks flashed around his fingertips, the contact burning him. An Artificer might have used long words to explain what was happening, how their souls, once part of the same being, had over time become incompatible. Kholster needed only one word: betrayal.

Bloodmane had sided with the enemy, and in doing so, the touch of the armor, which had once been soothing and pleasurable, had become pain and loss. Unnatural and unholy as it was, Kholster could not bring himself to hate the armor that had once been one with him. He pressed his hand down despite the pain. "You are. You became one when you sided with the Oathbreakers. Your army is there." He raised his chin to indicate the ranked warsuits. "They were once a part of my army, but no more."

"But you are Kholster Bloodmane, I . . ."

"Wrong!" Kholster's voice was a shout. Grinding his teeth together, the Aern bridled his anger and removed his still-sizzling hand from the armor. "We were Kholster Bloodmane, together. Now you are kholster Bloodmane, the new kholster Bloodmane, and I am merely Kholster and my soldiers are the Aern. Though the Ossuarians and their warsuits are one, my army is not. My army fights without its mighty armor of old. Even the humans know that."

"Don't do this." Bloodmane held out its empty gauntlets in supplication.

"Do not lay this at my feet, kholster," Kholster continued, holding his scorched hand up to the armor's crystal eyes. "I did not change. You changed! I stand here now only because I said we would be together again, and I keep my word. Keeping my word is what I am! I am an Aern, an Oath-keeper, a Grudgebearer! And this," he raised Grudge high over his head before slamming it down, burying it point first in the white marble street, "is my Grudge!"

Long strands of violet energy surged between Grudge, Hunger, and Bloodmane, violently forcing the armor and its weapon away from Kholster and his. Silence swept over the assembled warsuits, their crystal eyes flashing with accelerating rapidity.

"You changed," Kholster whispered, his voice filled with a pain that was far from physical. "You forgave. You let go of your hatred for the Oathbreakers."

"They changed too." This time the voice came from Eyes of Vengeance, Vander's armor.

"They did not change!" Kholster protested with a voice so loud it reverberated within the metal bodies of the armor nearest him. "They merely no longer have the ability to treat us as they once did because we," he waved a hand to indicate both himself and the armor, "took it away from them."

His voice softened but still carried to all the warsuits. "You were there, all of you. Of course they seem different. They no longer have slaves. They have servants. They pay humans to do their dirty work. But I have stared into their hearts, and I see no reason for forgiveness." Both his voice and his eyes hardened as he ripped Grudge from the marble, shouldering it once more. "Deaths cannot be undone! For the wrongs they committed there can be no atonement."

"They will give us back to you," Bloodmane told him almost pleadingly. "I spoke to the Eldrennai king."

"They offer what they cannot give." Kholster's head dropped, the sun beating down on him, glinting off his mail. "They offer me my warpick, my warsuit, my old friend, but it no longer exists. In its place, there is only you, a new people, a people once made by the Aern but no longer one with the Aern. A good people. A proud people."

"We will do whatever you wish," Bloodmane countered. "If you want us to kill the Eldrennai, we will do it. We are implements of war."

Kholster laughed dryly. "Clearly not. You are more. The Aern are weapons. You wish to be shields. I don't know how it happened, but it did. I will not forge you into something you are not, nor will I enslave my own creation."

"Maker, please." Bloodmane stepped closer to Kholster, but the Aern warded him off with a hand.

"Not maker. You've remade yourselves. Become more than we made you. You are your own makers." He almost spat the final word. "I am Kholster, First of One Hundred . . ." again his voice softened, "and I ask you, kholster Bloodmane, to limit your army's aid to the Oathbreakers to the end of the Grand Conjunction."

The response was instant and unanimous. "We agree."

"At that point, my army intends to invade the Eldren Plains, to kill all the Eldrennai, and retake our homeland," Kholster warned. "Fight against us, aid us, or ignore us. The choice is yours to make."

"I understand. We will help you, if you will let us." Bloodmane stood strong and tall. Kholster wondered if this was what it was like for others to stare up at him thousands of years ago, when he was younger and the world made sense . . . when he stood inside his own skin, his warsuit, born of his spirit . . . and belonged.

"Why?"

"By helping the Eldrennai now, we are merely killing Zaur. It has been many years since we last saw battle; we long for it. It was to fight the Zaur that we were forged. The desire to fight them was worked into us all."

Kholster saw Rae'en's gift to him from the race across the Junland Bridge: his smoked-glass spectacles lying on the ground, unsure of when he had dropped them. He put them on, staring at Bloodmane through the darkened lenses. "That doesn't answer my question."

"We will never fight the Aern. Always, we will come to your aid. Together or apart, our place in battle is with the Aern."

After no more response than a simple nod, Kholster saluted the armor and turned to leave. As he made the long walk past the assembled warsuits a second time, there was no chanting, but in every company there was at least one suit of armor that reached out to him tentatively, as one might reach after a loved one who is going away on a long journey.

Grivek stood waiting for him at the long stair leading down from the royal tower. "I will be taking my son's place at the Grand Conjunction, if you will allow it," Grivek told him.

"Good," Kholster told him. "It's always better for a father to die before his children. When the meeting at Oot is done, that favor, at the very least, I hope I can grant you."

Once inside the tower, alone in the shadow of the entryway, Kholster knelt down, his head in his hands, and wept. It was not the first time he had ever cried, but he thought he could count the number without taking off his boots.

Kholster. Bloodmane's voice echoed in his mind. **I have never led an army before, not without you.**

I will help you, Kholster thought back. *Guide you, teach you; you may ask me anything. Connected as we are, I will be with you no matter where you go. Which reminds me . . . what of the unborn Aern? Did you wake him?*

The Eldrennai are caring for him, Kholster. Bloodmane sounded embarrassed. **He is alive, but he neither blinks nor speaks. He does not respond in any way to anything. They think that it might be trauma induced by his long time of waiting.**

They will tell you if he responds?

I left Call to Battle watching over him as well.

Kholster wiped his eyes and slumped against the wall in exhaustion. *Five more days*, he told himself, *and all of this waiting will be over. I will wipe out the Eldrennai, and perhaps, in time, our armor will be one with us again.*

CHAPTER 56
ROLE REVERSAL

Dolvek's raised voice echoed from a planning chamber in the central mess hall where the assembled leadership of the Eldrennai military and the College of Elementalists had convened to discuss the matter at hand. "We should charge through the tunnels and assault the main force." The prince stabbed his finger at a point on the mystic battle map spread across the table.

Your boyfriend is an idiot, Kholster spoke in Bloodmane's mind.

Not exactly. Bloodmane loomed behind the prince without audible comment, preferring to grant Dolvek time to demonstrate to those in attendance what the armor felt King Grivek should have recognized long before: the prince had a sound tactical mind, but his arrogance blinded him. He had been spoiled and for far too long. "My cavalry can lead the assault . . ."

That's an excellent plan. Let the Crystal Knights lead the charge, Kholster thought gleefully to the armor. *They are the most battle-ready units the Eldrennai have available, and if they charge down those tunnels like overeager children after a treat, they will be shattered, scattered, and completely undone.*

My thought was to locate as many of the tunnels as possible and collapse them, Bloodmane countered to Kholster. **The Geomancers can ride with Lancers to the six known access points and seal them, except for the northern tunnel.**

You think the northern tunnel overextends them? Kholster thought.

Bloodmane felt a burst of pride from his maker as the Aern considered the idea. The armor wondered briefly if Kholster knew Bloodmane could feel his emotions even when he didn't give them voice.

I do.

Not a bad plan, Kholster agreed. *How are you planning on making that work within your timetable?*

There is only one way I can think of to make it work, Bloodmane continued. **If the College will consent to allow access to the Port Gates in the Tower of Elementals, we could deploy seven Eldre . . . Oathbreaker teams through the gates.**

Those cowards? Kholsters thoughts brimmed with disdain. *They won't want to risk the possibility of a Ghaiattri coming through one of the ports while it's open.*

There is no other option. Bloodmane wished there was one. **Unless you . . . ?**

I'll evaluate your plans, old friend, but don't expect me to help you help them any more than that.

So you do see another way?

Tell me more about your plan.

Bloodmane squelched the desire to ask more of Kholster. **We'd have to use the Port Gates sparingly. I would station fifty warsuits in the chamber, and we would only access one gate at a time.**

You should be able to accomplish, Kholster sent, *six or seven transports before the Ghaiattri become an insurmountable problem, but you're still looking at definite small-group contact.*

No more than one or two, Kholster.

It only takes two. A single Ghaiattri your combined forces can handle, but not without paying a price for it, a price that might impact my troops if the Ghaiattri use soul fire, which you know they will. If two come through . . . just two . . .

It would be a new Demon War, Bloodmane replied. **Two will not come through**, he added confidently. **I will not allow it. I will then send one thousand warsuits down the northern tunnel. Once they have progressed sufficiently, we will seal that tunnel as well.**

And if I take casualties from a fight at which my Aern are not even present?

I . . . Bloodmane had not considered that. **Do you wish to order me not to—**

I'm not giving you any orders at all. Kholster's thoughts seemed strained. There was something in his tone. *I just want you to know that if I lose Aern in this, with my own warsuit helping the Oathbreakers. . . . It's on your helm.*

Kholster, I—

Your helm. Now, what of the other forces? Kholster asked.

Half of the force will remain to defend Port Ammond. I am dispatching two thousand warsuits to the Vael territories to reinforce their own defenses in case the Zaur plan to assault them as well. We must assume the Zaur have numerical superiority.

The Zaur always have numerical superiority, Kholster transmitted. *It's a good plan. Once those tunnels are closed, will the sealing groups spread out in search of other tunnels?*

Yes, I'm also dispatching Crystal Knights and Aeromancers as air patrols to spot suspicious activity.

The Crystal Knights won't like being used as scouts. Kholster sounded pleased at that.

They would like being dead less, the armor retorted.

"Have you been listening to a thing I've been saying?" In the room, Prince Dolvek's face was flushed with red.

"No," Bloodmane admitted easily. The irkanth-head helmet turned, taking in the room, meeting one by one the gazes of all present, crystal eye to organic. "I can see by the faces of those assembled that it is a bad plan. I expected nothing from you, honored prince, but a plan rife with glamorous conflict and needless deaths. You are a fool, and if the assembled did not sense it before, they know it now."

Jolsit, the captain of the guard, and Hasimak, High Elementalist of the College, were the only two who managed not to look relieved. Bloodmane raised his arm, pointing a gauntlet finger at each of them in turn. "Jolsit, you are my new second-in-command. I am relieving Prince Dolvek of his leadership responsibilities and rank. He has much to learn, and he will learn it as your aide."

"I will not!" Dolvek smashed his fist into the table.

"Failure to follow the orders of your commanding officer is a serious offense." Bloodmane spoke passionlessly. "I believe it can be punishable by summary execution in times of war." The armor reached back of its shoulder and gripped Hunger's haft.

Dolvek nodded, his black bangs falling in his face. He managed a "Sir, yes, sir," but it came out choking and weak. No one in the room laughed, but Kholster's amusement was evident from a chuckle that Bloodmane heard clearly.

"Hasimak," the armor continued, "are there any mages left who have the ability to activate the Port Gates?"

All heads turned to face the wizened Elementalist. Hasimak was one of the few Eldrennai Bloodmane had ever encountered who actually looked old. Faint lines showed on skin that had been smooth for millennia; his black hair was streaked with white and gray. The voice that left his lips was musical and concise, sounding younger by far than the aged exterior would have suggested. "Three, counting myself. I always maintain a minimum of three, but not to open the gates. I train them in case one should open so that the memory of how to force them closed will remain. Of course all recruits receive some basic training, but nothing I would consider completely reliable. It is forbidden to open the gates."

"Then you will all die." Bloodmane lowered his gauntlet, thrumming the fingers on the table in an approximation of the tell-me-I'm-wrong stance Kholster had often employed in similar situations across the wars the two had fought together.

Eight Eldrennai bored holes into Hasimak with their gazes. Hasimak's eyes locked with the armor's crystal eyes, but warsuits do not blink. "Could you tell me why we need to use them? If I understood that the gain outweighed the risk . . ."

"Of course, High Elementalist. This is what I have in mind . . ." Reluctant initially, the gathered commanders began to nod their heads as he explained.

They had questions. Bloodmane had expected questions, but what he had been unprepared for was the immediate acceptance of his own role as general. He had seen these looks before. He remembered them from previous wars, in some cases on the exact same faces. Jolsit made the same insightful, refining queries he'd made in the distant past. The Elementalists had the same concerns as always. The only thing lacking was the comfort of his bearer, enfolded safely within his metal casing, warming him from within, providing guidance.

He remembered the sight of Kholster's burning flesh, as their spirits collided and rejected one another. Bloodmane had hoped that spending time with the Eldrennai, seeing the infighting, the prejudice, would change him back to the way he had been, make him hate them irredeemably once again, but it did not. They could change, were changing, had changed. All they required was assistance in completing their transformation, rooting out the final threads of stupidity and misinformation.

If only Kholster could change too, then Bloodmane would not have to fight those he now protected once the Conjunction was complete. Bloodmane watched the Eldrennai in the room, all confident, sure they had a chance, and wondered what they would think if they realized that in a handful of days he and his warsuits would turn against them, crush them beneath their metallic heels and wipe them from Barrone like an unsightly growth. Such, the armor told himself, is war, and he tried to think of it no more.

"Kholster?" Jolsit asked. His face looked pained.

"Yes?" Bloodmane asked.

"Isn't that a waste of . . . ah . . . war material? You and your fellow warsuits are powerful, but even in an enclosed space, one thousand are unlikely to hold against the many thousands of Zaur that surely inhabit the tunnels."

"We will only need to hold them back long enough to get Geomancers into the correct position to expose the central cavern to the air. The presence of warsuits will ensure the largest number of Zaur militia are present when this happens."

"And then?"

"Live long and see your answer," Bloodmane said mysteriously.

This, Kholster sent, *I suppose, is the point where you ask if you can enlist the aid of my friend . . . the dragon?*

About that . . . Bloodmane replied. The plan could work without the dragon, it could, but the losses for the warsuits would be dreadful. Bloodmane thought of Coal, the great gray dragon and hoped against hope he could convince Kholster to lend him Coal's aid.

CHAPTER 57
WAR STORIES

"Commander Jolsit," Dolvek said brusquely, as he entered his superior's quarters. A fraction of the size of Dolvek's own rooms, the older Eldrennai's living space was sparse in decoration. His bed, a small desk, and a chair took up most of the room. Weapons hung from a rack bracketed to the wall over a large, plain metal trunk. Two armor racks stood next to it. Jolsit looked up from his position kneeling over the open trunk.

He wore a suit of curious-looking armor, dark orange, nearly brown, like the dead leaves of winter. It resembled plate armor, but the vambraces, greaves, and sabatons looked more like bone than metal, while the rest of the armor seemed likely to have been fashioned from individual scales fused together. The helm, which rested on the floor near Jolsit's knee, struck Dolvek as equally bizarre, like a great horned skull had been emptied of its gruesome contents, polished, and refitted as a helm.

"Ghastly, isn't it?" The commander stood, gesturing to his armor and then the helm. "From the Demon Wars." As he crossed to the bed, Jolsit appeared to flicker a hand or two to the left or right with each step. "It's made from a Ghaiattri primus, one of their elite infantry. In the last years of the war, Kholster had them made for the Eldrennai who fought with him at Keirryn's Peak."

"To close the last open Port Gate," said Dolvek, hoping he didn't sound too awestruck. "And retake the final shard of the World Crystal." He hadn't realized Jolsit was . . . quite that old.

Jolsit nodded. "It's magic-resistant but doesn't hamper the wearer's spells, and it's as strong as enchanted steel. It holds up against the eccentricities that disable crystal armor when fighting against the Zaur, too."

"It's magnificent."

"It's unnatural." Jolsit sighed. "When you wear it, the walls between this world and the Demon World grow thin to your eyes, and you see things . . . sources of magic glow. Smells come over wrong, and you can't help but feel like the armor's going to reanimate and eat you. It's physically comfortable, though, lighter than it has a right to be, and it makes sense to wear it if we're going anywhere near a Port Gate—open or closed."

Dolvek nodded. "General Bloodmane says that he and his warsuits are ready."

Jolsit picked up his helm. "Let's not keep the general waiting."

The two walked in silence along deserted streets that were usually filled with traffic, humans heading to and from their various jobs, harbor traffic, soldiers doing their turn on city patrol. The patrol was still running, but now people were keeping to themselves, or, rather, they were collectively avoiding the royal tower.

"They're afraid," Jolsit said, as if reading Dolvek's thoughts. "For two days, the Aernese warsuits have walked the streets. Word has gotten around about Kholster and the guard he killed. People are worried. And scared."

"We can beat the Aern."

"No," Jolsit told him flatly. "We can't."

"Wylant beat them at the Sundering," Dolvek argued.

"We were lucky; she was a monster, and there is no longer a Life Forge to shatter," Jolsit said. Outside the Tower of Elementals, the Eldrennai soldier touched its smooth surface, reciting his rank and a prearranged code. White stone melted away, revealing an open passage into which the two Eldrennai stepped. "Flight gave our Aeromancers an advantage, as it did the Crystal Knights, but the rank and file cannot use spells so effectively for long. If we fought them now, without their armor, then our archers would give us an additional edge, but if I know Bloodmane . . . um . . . Kholster, I mean . . . the Armored will keep coming after us even if it takes a thousand years to win. They don't really die, you know. You stuff their bones back in their armor, add blood, and poof . . . instant Aern."

Dolvek mulled that over in silence.

"It was the right move, destroying the Life Forge," Jolsit said reservedly. "A particularly hard move, but the right one. Even after millions of them died, the surviving five thousand Aern marched on. Then, Wylant had the Crystal Knights raid the crèches of the unborn Aern, steal the unawakened lumps of metal. She threatened to destroy them, too. Melt them down. Kholster acted like he was proud of her. Each monstrous act she took made him bloom with praise.

"Near the end we tried surrendering, but they wouldn't accept our surrender. Kholster gave the order to advance. You could feel the tension; everyone knew we were standing at the final Port Gate, as the saying goes, but . . . Aldo knows I'll remember it to the last day. . . . We were saved by a little scullery slave, Merri. She floated down from the tower, still holding her mop and bucket. She was a beautiful little thing, the guards used to pass her around . . ." Jolsit's voice trailed off in sudden embarrassment.

Dolvek opened his mouth to say something about that, to make an excuse, but he couldn't find one.

"That tiny wisp of nothing walked up to Kholster, put a hand on his chest, and said, 'Please stop.'" Jolsit continued, "Once the rest of them saw that it had worked, the other servants came running; they stood between us and the Aern. Kholster looked down at Merri—she was short, even for a Vael." There was a slight hiss at the end of "Vael," as if Jolsit had nearly said "Vaelsilyn" but caught himself.

"He got down on one knee so that he could look at her face-to-face. To this day, I've no idea exactly what she said, but they whispered to each other, and she laughed." He smiled reminiscently and shook his head. "And took their unawakened children and left in peace. Grivek and Kholster were in talks for two weeks after that, but we all knew Merri had negotiated the truce out there on the Lane of Review."

Jolsit paused as if clearing his head.

There was no more talking on the way to the Port Chamber; both Eldrennai walked with only their thoughts for company. Prince Dolvek had only been inside the chamber once, and even then it was only to be shown what a Port Gate looked like, how to close one, and which markings to hack away after it was closed so that it could never be opened again. Every Eldrennai who took basic elementalism lessons learned that much, and Hasimak taught the class himself. If you couldn't learn to close a Port Gate, then the elemancers forbade you from practicing any kind of magic. Even the Artificers had to know how.

It looked as cavernous and foreboding as Dolvek remembered. Thirteen Gates stood at the top of thirteen raised platforms, spaced evenly around the circular chamber. At the center of the chamber, the master gate lay crumbled, broken as it had been when Kholster and his troops charged back through it with the stolen shard of the World Crystal. Dolvek had never believed the story, but now, standing next to a knight clad in armor made from the remains of a Ghaiattri, looking out at the fifty warsuits standing in the chamber, having met Kholster, having seen him fight, Dolvek began to believe all kinds of new things.

Bloodmane stood before the shattered Port Gate and demonstrated to the warsuits the most reliable way to seal a Port Gate if the only magic you possessed was a hardened warpick.

"Kholster Bloodmane," Jolsit called.

"You are here," Bloodmane answered in his throatless voice. "We can begin. Thank you for wearing the demon armor, Jolsit. Tell us which Port Gate looks safest."

CHAPTER 58
A HATE THAT BURNS FOREVER

Kholster sat slumped against the obelisk at Oot, gazing out over the obsidian pier toward the water. He was supposed to have begun an invasion by now. Port Ammond should have been in flames, and the Eldrennai should have been hiding at one of the Watches trying to rally their defenses. Bloodmane and he should have been reunited, not unable to work as one because of the armor's desire to forgive the enemy. And Rae'en should be alive, at his side, and taking the reins of command from him. *Where did it all go wrong?*

*

Teru and Whaar moved through the tunnels, one pair of fifty Armored Ossuarians reunited with their armor, hacking their way through Zaur with purpose. Zaur swarmed them from all sides, a writhing mass of scales, teeth, and claws. Teru's warsuit, Bonestripper, ran thick with Zaur blood, a clump of ragged flesh clung to the tip of one of the small, sharp horns mounted over the eye slits of his skull-inspired helm.

Whaar's warsuit, No Escape, covered in a similar gore, clove a Zaur's forepaw from its wrist with the axe-like blade which ran from the crown of its knobby brow to the base of its helm. Striking out with his sword, No Surrender, Whaar pinned a Zaur to the tunnel wall with a thrust through the throat as Teru split two Zaur in unequal halves with Last Kiss, his double-bladed axe.

"She's still moving," Teru called.

"First Bones has metal here." Whaar whirled Last Kiss in arcs of death. "We find one then the other."

"And don't report back until we have both," Teru completed. "I remember Zhan's orders."

*

Grivek remained wisely silent, sitting motionlessly in meditation at the end of the pier. Yavi, on the other hand, was not so obliging.

She paced around and around the obelisk, wanting to speak. Kholster knew she wanted to say something because every third or fourth revolution, she would pause, look at him, lips slightly parted, and then continue pacing. He wondered absently if it could be called pacing, as the movement was circular rather than a back-and forth-repetition. Circling, perhaps?

Closing his eyes again to check on Bloodmane's progress at the Port Gates, he noted things were going well. There had been one close call, but four groups had made it away already, and he had confidence in Bloodmane and all the warsuits, whether they were his or belonged merely to themselves.

"Why did you kiss me?" Yavi asked on her sixty-eighth orbit.

"Because I love you," Kholster answered easily, his eyes still closed.

"What?" Her eyes widened. She obviously had not expected that response, which was fair since he hadn't been aware he was going to say that until the words had escaped him. She had so much to learn. He could feel her desire to respond, but he made no move toward her. The Vael did not like to be grabbed or cornered. They did not like pursuit.

"I did not know what else to do," Kholster answered, finally looking up at her. "We are both physically mature. When an Aern and a Vael are in proximity for an extended period of time, it tends to happen."

"What do you mean it tends to happen? You hardly even know me," she demanded.

"That generally comes later."

"I could never . . . you, I . . ." Yavi began orbiting the obelisk again, but Kholster remained still, quiet. He wasn't being fair to her, he knew. She'd never been sought after by an Aern. The best way to woo a Vael involved knowing when to be still, when to be . . . passive.

"Shall I start dinner?" he asked.

"Are you going to eat any?" she countered.

"No." He closed his eyes and watched Bloodmane push a demon back into the Port Gate, only to be thrown back as a Ghaiattri forced its way forward. Grudge slid into Kholster's hand. "Ghaiattri," he muttered.

"How many?" Grivek shouted from the pier, moving closer.

"Just one so far, but the gate is still open."

"Why don't they close it?" Grivek demanded.

"They're trying." Kholster rose to his feet.

*

Rae'en, Wylant, and Tyree burst out of the tunnel system through an air vent much like the one through which Rae'en had entered. She gasped in a breath and looked at the sky; there were barely enough stars still visible for her to gauge the location of Oot.

"This way." She took off at a run.

"Keep up, or go your own way," Wylant clapped Tyree on the back. "Your choice."

Calling on the wind, she rose on a wave of magic and shot off after Rae'en.

"You have got," Tyree said between pants, "to be kidding me."

*

Port Gates were basically eight-foot-tall doorways with crystal double doors. To close it properly, a mage had to shut the doors and perform a short ritual. To Kholster, the ritual seemed too long. Two warsuits were trying to force the doors closed, but the Ghaiattri was lodged between them, halfway in and halfway out.

"A second Ghaiattri is heading toward the gate." Kholster recognized Jolsit's voice. He'd thought to wear the demon armor. *Smart boy.*

Let it past so they can close the gate, then kill the one you let through, Kholster suggested to his armor. One Ghaiattri could not create a Wild Gate, but two could.

Bloodmane charged up the steps, ducked under the Ghaiattri's sword-like claws and grabbed it by the horns. "Let it pass, then shut the gate!"

"What's happening?" asked Yavi.

"They've let one in so they can close the gate," Kholster answered.

Bloodmane pulled the Ghaiattri through, and the gate slammed shut. The door buckled like an elephant had struck it from the other side, but Hasimak dashed for the gate and sealed it.

"Well?" asked Grivek.

"They're fighting the Ghaiattri now."

Kholster had not been present when the Ghaiattri had forced the Port Gates at the start of the Demon War, but he remembered the surviving Elementalist's description. He claimed the door had been sealed, but the Ghaiattri had forced their way through after it closed. It was that very gate Kholster had later destroyed. When the gate had been forced from within, the doors had changed from blue to purple, then shifted to gold. It was happening again.

Bloodmane, have Eyes of Vengeance, White Light, and Death Knell destroy the gate that Ghaiattri came through! They're forcing it!

Kholster felt the message slip wordlessly along the network of warsuits to Eyes of Vengeance. Eyes of Vengeance, Vander's armor, could do it. The warsuit raised its mighty warpick, Scorn. Scorn's haft was shorter than that of Grudge or Hunger, with a broader wedge-shaped head, splitting into two curved spikes at the poll.

Scorn struck the apex of the Port Gate, opening a rent in the stone but not shattering it. White Light and Death Knell struck the right and left sides, once, twice. Hasimak screamed for them to stop, his cries cut short as the door sprung open.

*

Dryga cursed the scarbacks as he rolled free of his mount, the canteen containing the Eldrennai's blood and the one containing the Aern's blood jostling in a mesh bag strapped to his back. A pair of Armored Aern, Bone Finders from the look of them, struggled to free themselves from where Dryga's steed had pinned them to the wall.

"Kill them, Kreej." Dryga tossed one of his two Skreel blades to the wounded Zaur accompanying them. "Make it back to the base alive, and I'll petition for a second name for you.

"To His secret purpose," Kreej hissed.

Dryga ran, vanishing in the dark of the tunnels.

Kreej eyed the Bone Finders in their warsuits, gripped his borrowed Skreel blade tightly, and ran the other way. No name was worth that.

*

"I can't get there in time." Kholster opened his eyes. Grivek and Yavi were wide-eyed, panicked.

"What's happening?" Yavi placed her hand on his shoulder; the touch distracted him.

Closing his eyes once more, Kholster watched the second Ghaiattri try to push through. Eyes of Vengeance struck the gate a third time, and the top of the gate crumbled into the yawning yellow light from the open portal.

When the gate collapses, it will try to suck everything into it until the runes are destroyed, Kholster transmitted. *You must destroy them in the correct order, or they won't break.*

Do you remember the order? Bloodmane was panicking. The warsuits never panicked.

Yes. Kholster pictured the symbols one by one in the order in which they needed to be destroyed. *Calm down. I remember everything.*

In the center of the chamber, Bloodmane grappled with the Ghaiattri, the armor's metal gauntlets glowing red-hot as a nimbus of lightning flowed over him. Scale Fist, a warsuit with a helm like a three-faced Zaur, battered the beast with its warpick. Darting in and out with perfect synchronization, the warsuits rotated through, hammering the Ghaiattri with blow after blow, but the beast did not bleed, would never bleed, not as mortal creatures do.

Reinforce the broken gate, Kholster ordered, wincing at the sudden matching heat in his palms.

Ten suits broke away from the fight, knocking mages out of their way. Confusion reigned among the Elementalists; Hasimak screeched uselessly, imploring the warsuits to stop destroying the gates. Kholster laughed out loud when he saw the flat of Jolsit's blade strike the old Eldrennai from behind, knocking him unconscious.

"I need every mancer to concentrate on holding the other gates closed," shouted Jolsit. "They'll try coming through them soon. Dolvek, you have training; help them."

Twelve mages looked at the prince with the same shock Kholster felt as Dolvek shouted clear and appropriate orders. "Twelve Gates. Twelve of you. I want one of you at the base of each set of stairs, holding those gates closed. From the base, you should still be close enough to affect the gate but far enough away that if it blows we won't lose you. Go!" The mages ran to their positions as Dolvek ran toward the center of the room.

Jolsit charged the incoming second Ghaiattri, screaming, "Move!" The armor parted, and the knight clad in demon armor tackled the stunned Ghaiattri back into the portal. Eyes of Vengeance caught the flying Oathbreaker by his ankle, pulling him back into the room just as Death Knell destroyed the final rune.

*

"I hope you don't mind," Wylant bellowed as she snatched Rae'en up off the ground, pulling them both up, over the treetops.

"But how?" Rae'en gasped.

"You're immune to magic," Wylant laughed. "But I'm not holding you up with magic. I'm holding ME up with magic. I'll swing you around onto my back, and you hold on."

The speed almost took Rae'en's breath away. The view succeeded. They rocketed over a canopy of green, the sunrise breaking over the horizon, blinding in its dazzling hues. Sweat, blood, and forest smells filled Rae'en nostrils, and she let loose an involuntary whoop.

*

"They closed the gate." Kholster smiled up at his companions. If they noticed the pain in his voice, they didn't let on. "I never would have thought Jolsit had it in him. He tackled the Ghaiattri back into the Demon World. It was too surprised to react." The flesh on his palms was blistering, the searing pain creeping slowly up his forearm. He clasped his hands behind his back. It was nothing he wanted the Vael to get upset about. He'd had worse.

"We will long remember him," Grivek said, his head bowed.

"I should think you will," Kholster crowed. "Eyes of Vengeance caught him and pulled him back out again. He—" In mid-gloat, Kholster abruptly stopped speaking.

"Are you all right?" Yavi asked.

"No." The pain spread. Wisps of smoke trailed off of his skin as the heat encompassed his arms then moved outward, leaving tissue bubbling in its wake. Lungs burning, Kholster gasped for breath, steam pouring out of his open mouth before his skin ignited.

He did not scream, but in his mind, Bloodmane did. His vision blurring, Kholster ran for the water. Grudge fell from his back, hitting the black surface of the pier with a loud clack. Ignoring it, Kholster ran on, stripping off his mail, the pier vanishing from beneath him as he stepped wrong, tripped, and fell into the water below. Darkness closed in as his eyes boiled in their sockets. The last thing he heard before the water enveloped him was Rae'en's voice, distant but clear.

"Kholster!" she shouted. "Father, I'm—"

He would have laughed if he could have drawn in breath to do it.

Kill the Ghaiattri already, Bloodmane! Kholster shouted along their link.

I'm trying, Maker. He's very tenacious.

In the water, the pain subsided, sensation drifting away. The fight continued in the Tower of Elementals, but it seemed distant. Bloodmane's surface glowed red-hot, his gauntlets white, before the Ghaiattri finally fell, spitting lightning and magic as it died.

Kholster, Bloodmane called urgently. **Are you alive?**

You did well, Kholster thought softly. It was not Kholster's first time to be burned by soul fire, but he'd never been burned so badly. Bloodmane had never allowed it. Maybe, having gone so long without being worn, the warsuit had forgotten what it was like to consider the fleshly worries of a wearer.

What have I done?

You beat the Ghaiattri, held it back . . . prevented another Demon War . . . did enough of your troops get through?

Only four groups, but they can reach all six sites between them with only a slight timetable adjustment, Maker. Bloodmane's voice echoed. **How bad is it? Can you heal it? Show me your wounds. Kholster!**

There were more words. Some belonged to Vander, some to Bloodmane, but they all dissolved into unintelligible burbling as Kholster's bones sank down, down, down, and his soul pulled free of them. Jerked like a taut cord toward his warsuit, his soul soared toward its anchor. He had lost bodies before, his soul taking refuge with Bloodmane inside the massive warsuit until his bones could be reclaimed, stripped, cleaned, and interred within Bloodmane. Vander usually did the honors, filling the armor with blood and immersing his bones. Cow blood. Enemy blood. It didn't matter. Just so long as it was blood.

It was so much calmer to be free of the flesh.

Kholster saw the core of his warsuit in the approaching fog of the spirit world and understood the problem moments before he struck this splinter of his own soul, which had, over the centuries, grown into its own compete self, a self who cared for him deeply but whose wants, dreams, and desires were now separate from his own.

Souls are not supposed to feel pain, but when Kholster struck the core of his warsuit, it was as if he'd fallen from a cliff top and landed on solid granite.

Pain.

Shock.

And lastly heat. Bloodmane's spirit reached out to him attempting to embrace him, to shelter him, but where the armor touched his soul, Kholster burned.

CHAPTER 59
IN DEATH ALL OATHS

All know. Rae'en is First of One Hundred. If you don't hear me again, Rae'en . . . Is . . . First.

Kholster fell through a web of flashing lights. At its edges mad spiders chewed through the moorings as if to destroy the webs, while a single spider worked to repair it. He fell through the center, landing on a plane of endless gray. All pain had left him and he stood renewed, feeling stronger than he had ever felt.

He did not see the Aern in bone armor before his gauntleted hand was on Kholster's shoulder. But Kholster recognized the gauntlet.

"I was burning as my soul collided with Bloodmane's." He shook free of the gauntleted hand, turning to face the armored figure. "You pushed us apart."

The being in bone armor nodded.

"Where is this?"

"I can't replicate your thoughts of the afterlife, Kholster." Kholster recognized the gentle voice of Torgrimm at once. "You never gave it any thought at all."

"Torgrimm," Kholster mouthed. "Am I dead?"

"That decision is yours alone. I am not required to collect you." The Harvester's voice was calm and reassuring. "Are you not an Aern? Firstborn of One Hundred? Fatherless? Motherless? Held by no womb? Is that not how you describe yourself?"

"You don't sound as imposing as I'd expected."

"No more so than when last we spoke. No soul has anything to fear from me," Torgrimm replied. "I hold them when they are small and newly formed. I put them into the right body when it is time. And when they must leave, I take them safely to the next step on their journey."

"All things die." Kholster felt his arms grow heavy, as if leaden weights had been attached to them, sunk into the skin with tiny hooks. But with the weight came a feeling of connection as if he were only now sensing other secondary connections between his soul and the world of flesh.

"And life continues," Torgrimm completed the quote. "Book of Torgrimm, chapter one, verse one. End of book."

"It's a short book."

"I'm a simple god."

"If I'm not dying, then why are you here?" Kholster tried to move but couldn't, as if the mass of new connections had webbed him into one spot. "This doesn't feel like a strip and dip."

"Oh, you'd have to reconcile with Bloodmane for that. Or you could destroy him, retake the warsuit for your spirit, and when you are reborn, leave a new . . . more compatible splinter of yourself within." Torgrimm said, "He is strong, but you are stronger and have the strength of all the Aern to empower your spirit should you call upon them. You were made first. Even without the warsuit, your body will heal eventually if you choose to live."

"If I choose to live?" Kholster echoed, making the statement into a question.

"Or you can die. If you choose to die, I'll do what you wish with your spirit, spread it amongst your people or transfer it to your Incarna."

"No. Rae'en, not Irka, if it comes to that, but no. No dying," Kholster growled. "I have oaths to keep."

"The choice is yours to make," Torgrimm said with a knowing smile.

"Why are we still talking then?"

"Because," the god said gently, "I have a favor to ask . . . and, in death, all oaths are redeemed."

CHAPTER 60
MY FATHER, MY KHOLSTER

Her father was not dead. He could not be dead. He could never die, never stay dead. For six thousand years or more, as long as there had been Aern, Kholster had been there to lead them. Rae'en crouched on the end of the obsidian pier staring into the dark water, her clothes soaked and briny from multiple dives.

Testament lay on her left, Grudge to her right. Her mail and saddlebags lay where she'd dropped them in her initial dive to find her father.

You have to be down there somewhere.

Out on the water, a family of red mallards, crepuscular by nature and native to the bay, swam in formation, ducklings darting in and out amongst the crimson bay grass looking for glow minnows and spark carp. Instinct told the mother duck to keep the others in line, when to check on her little ones, how to protect them from predators.

Where is my instinct?

Kholster, Bloodmane's hollow voice called as if from across a wide valley. **Kholster Rae'en? We are ready to begin the battle. I know there could be no worse time, but may I know now whether I may ask the assistance of Coal?**

"Shut up! Shut up! Shut up!" she hissed aloud and mentally. Bloodmane could not be in her thoughts. Could not be. Could never be.

A lone Bone Finder, Caz, wearing Silencer, strode toward her, his warsuit's armored feet fell like hammer blows upon the stone announcing his arrival, even if she hadn't been alerted to it by the map in her mind.

"He's gone, Rae'en." Silencer, rather than Caz himself, whispered. "His bones are gone, too. We do not know how, but he is gone."

She rose gracefully, water from her last dive still drying on her skin. Tyree moved to stop her, but the attempt was half-hearted. "You've been diving for most of a day, you can't keep—"

"He's down there," she snapped, the anger in her eyes frightening him into silence. "I can swim deeper."

"I know you don't like the idea," Tyree told her, "but you have to consider the possibility that he has passed on."

"No," she snarled. "I do not! His soul has not come to the Aern. We would have felt it! His knowledge, his essence would have come among us; I would be able to feel him! Kholster would be a part of each of us, or he would have passed his *spirit* on to me. He cannot have passed to Irka, or Irka would hear Bloodmane and I would not, therefore my father is not dead!"

"*Irka?*" Tyree questioned, pursing his lips together.

"My brother Irka," Rae'en answered, "is our father's Incarna." It was clear that he did not understand. "The First One Hundred . . ." she broke off. This was not a human thing; he could not possibly know or be expected to know. "This time I'm not coming back without Kholster," Rae'en barked, her jaws snapping like an angry dog's. His kindness irked her even more.

The Vael, Yavi, had been able to coax one of the water spirits, talk to it. Kholster had been in the water one heartbeat, and in the next . . .

Find him, she berated herself. *You are the only one who can. He is Aern, and only Aern can help him. He is of the One Hundred! He cannot just die. He's down there somewhere gone to metal maybe, like the old days, waiting to rust if I don't find him!*

She broke the water, vanishing beneath the waves even as her pupils widened, the Arvash'ae waited at the edge of mind to take her over. Would it make her dive deeper? She'd dived for hours into the bay, looking for her father's body, with no luck.

I will not return without Kholster! The phrase became a mantra in her mind. He was not here.

Kholster Rae'en.

She let herself drop, swam to speed her descent.

I'm so sorry.

He had to be here! He had to be. Casting about frantically, Rae'en found no sign of her father.

Please talk to me.

But she knew she wouldn't find him. Deep down she knew Caz would have already sunk like a stone to the bottom to retrieve his bones if her father were truly down here. Her feet touched the bay bottom, and she screamed out all of her air . . . or tried to.

Please.

Rae'en screamed again and again, bubbles rushing up to the surface. *I can't drown.*

You are Armored.

How dare you breathe for me?!

In her mind's eye, she looked at the map of Oot, at her father's warpick, an opalescent mark against the black of the pier. Grudge. A Grudge she knew he would lay down only in death. Bubbles drifted up toward the surface. She closed her eyes.

And saw through Bloodmane's, saw the broken Port Gates, saw Oathbreakers and warsuits standing tired and exhausted.

"Did you find the First of One Hundred?"

Surprised to truly inhale air rather than water. Rae'en opened her eyes to see Wylant standing next to her, a look of pain in the Aiannai's eyes as raw as the one Rae'en felt in her own. Walls of blue water rose up on either side of the Eldrennai, a wedge of air shoved forcefully into the bay by the Aeromancer. Wylant held out her hand.

"He's not . . ."

"That's not what I asked, Rae'en by Kholster out of Helg. Kholster is gone. In his place, he appointed a new kholster, a new First of One Hundred." Wylant drew back her hand with a sneer. "A leader, a kholster must push aside her fears, her pain, and serve her people even if duty is the last thing she wants to think about, even if she is overwhelmed. Such is what it is to be kholster, to be First of One Hundred. Kholster would have arranged for such a person to take his place, would have allowed himself to die under no other circumstance. Did you find her? Was she down here?"

A confused bay crab scuttled past Wylant's boot. Bass and a few minnows flopped breathlessly in the mud closer to the pier. Spurning assistance, kholster Rae'en pushed herself to her feet.

All know, Rae'en thought, *I am kholster Rae'en, First of One Hundred. I do not know what happened to my father, but one thing I assure you. His scars are on my back.*

"I see that you did," Wylant said with a smirk, adding in a whisper, "don't feel bad, kholster Rae'en. A few hundred years ago, I would have done the same thing. He's a hard Aern to lose."

Wylant summoned the wind, pulling herself up and kholster Rae'en out of the wedge to land safely on the pier above. The Aeromancer let the water flow back into place, the level of the bay returning slowly to normal.

Tyree, looking particularly dashing in clothes provided by the Eldrennai, leaned over the edge of the pier to offer his hand. The frilly lace at the cuffs of his sleeves took confidence to pull off successfully, but Tyree was one human with confidence in full supply. She accepted his proffered assistance, measuring his strength as he struggled to pull her out.

Grivek had retreated, fretting back and forth at the head of the pier, and the maddening swish of his fine silk robes made it hard to concentrate.

Wylant laid a hand on his shoulder, and he stopped with a self-conscious apology. Roc was the only other Eldrennai present now. Hira had left to take news to Port Ammond and establish a perimeter around Oot, leaving the other two Eldrennai serving purportedly as added security, but the underlying assertion that they were really Grivek's bodyguards rang through loud and clear.

Kholster Rae'en, Bloodmane thought at her, **I need a decision.**

"Fine," she said aloud. "Tell Vander . . ." Letting out a long breath, Rae'en pushed back the anger which had begun to reassert itself; a familiar headache took its place. She was kholster. She would tell Vander.

Unc . . . Vander, she thought, *let the blasted warsuits borrow Coal if he's amenable and only if*, she continued internally, *Coal will still consent to provide air cover to us in our upcoming fight against the Eldrennai.*

I'll tell them, Vander answered, *of course, but you could always tell Bloodmane yourself.*

I don't think Bloodmane would like to hear the things I'd like to say right now. Do you?

Vander didn't answer that one.

Any word from Kazan, M'jynn, Joose, and Arbokk?

Malmung says they've stopped in Castleguard to view the Changing of the Gods, before they head back home.

Back home?

Well . . . given your new status—

Have them watch the Changing of the Gods and then get their butts up here, Rae'en sent. *I may be First, but they're still my Overwatches.*

Vander didn't reply to that one either. Rae'en wondered if he thought she was making mistakes or just knew it wasn't the time to argue with her. Either way, she was glad for the silence.

CHAPTER 61
HONOR THY MAKER

"Are . . . are you all right, kholster?"

Bloodmane started when he realized the young Elementalist meant to address him. He remained where he was, gazing into the maw-like opening in the ground that had once been North Watch. So much death. Not more than he'd seen, but he found it disconcerting to enjoy watching the waves crashing below the cliffs. He felt the tragedy of those lost lives should have spoiled it, but the waves didn't care. Queelay's water ignored the destruction wrought by the Zaur. The unpleasant business at hand was beyond their notice. A Vael would have been able to see the elemental spirits at play in the water.

Emotions he hadn't been created to feel weighed heavily on the mighty warsuit's mind.

I was forged to fight and crush the Zaur. I want to do so, but when the Zaur are destroyed. . . . He glanced over his shoulder, eyeing the Eldrennai lieutenant. What was his name?

The lieutenant, the youngest of six Eldrennai Geomancers, stood at the edge of the White Road shifting nervously from foot to foot. Still loathe to come any closer to the warsuits than necessary, all of the six save this one kept to themselves, a huddle of idly whispering children, more suited to playing with stickswords than going to war.

Kholster, how do you keep track, he began mentally, but Kholster was not there. It didn't matter anyway; he remembered the Eldrennai's name now.

"I am well-maintained and in good repair, Lieutenant Hiln. Just communing with the . . . just communing."

"Did you get permission to use the dragon?" Hiln asked eagerly. They all wanted to know about the dragon. Bloodmane shivered, the vibration rattling through his plates. The Eldrennai would see more of the dragon than they wanted with kholster Rae'en in command.

He could feel her hate, for him and for the Eldrennai. One of those two hatreds he shared. How odd that self-loathing could allow him to do for Rae'en what he had failed to do for his maker. She had never tried to don him, but he felt that she could, sensed it.

United in disgust, he thought at Eyes of Vengeance.

We are imperfect, Eyes of Vengeance replied. **All of us.**

"Kholster . . . Rae'en granted me permission to enlist Coal's aid." Bloodmane nearly stumbled over the word "Kholster." "He should be here in a matter of hours."

"And then we fight?" Hiln asked eagerly.

"No."

"No?"

"No." Raising a gauntlet, the animated armor gestured to his fellow warsuits, one thousand of them, each standing empty and motionless in predetermined ranks, waiting for battle. "My brothers and I will attack. You and your fellow Geomancers will stand guard here."

"Why? Sir, we could fight too. I've practiced all my life for . . ."

"Because those are your orders," Bloodmane interrupted. "Give us two hours and then begin collapsing the tunnels behind us. Death Knell will stay with you to maintain communications throughout the battle."

"But what if you need to get out?"

Bloodmane hefted Hunger, his master's . . . his maker's . . . no, the warpick was now his own, the bright sun glinting off cold metal. The weapon unleashed a primordial screech. "We do not breathe, Lieutenant. If we need to get out, we will dig."

Laughter from the other warsuits echoed in Bloodmane's mind, unheard by the Eldrennai. They were one, each suit linked to the others and to their makers, their Incarna, or in Bloodmane's case, to his maker's daughter.

He still did not fully understand how it had worked. Kholster had been torn free of his body, his soul rocketing toward Bloodmane like a tripped snare. He'd felt Kholster's presence, felt the pain, the conflict.

I'm killing him, he'd thought. *How do I stop? How do I help him? If I die will that . . . ?*

And then . . .

Something had moved between them like a shadow, and for a stretch of time, Bloodmane had been alone. No maker at the edge of his thoughts, just a sensation of impending . . . what? Doom? Despair? Hope? He still couldn't define it. His connection to the other warsuits had grown dim, fading, and then . . .

"Will you protect my daughter?"

Of course. He'd answered, hearing Kholster's voice but not feeling him.

"I will not bind you against your will. I can free you completely, let you live connected only to the other warsuits . . . if you wish it."

Please don't leave me maker-less.

"I want Rae'en to be First."

I know. I know and agree. Where are you?

"Bloodmane, you are the most that I can leave her."

Then . . . then you are dead. Bloodmane had been silent for a while. *I should be with you in death!*

"No, you should not."

How are you talking to me?

"Look through the eyes of kholster Rae'en at midnight and you will understand. I am repaying a debt owed by all Aern. Rae'en must kholster . . . lead the army. If she is one with you, if you say she is First, there will be no question. Vander will ask Eyes of Vengeance, and Eyes of Vengeance will defer to you."

Of course, Kholster, but debt—what debt?

"A matter of the soul. Protect my daughter, old friend. Defeat the Zaur."

And the Eldrennai?

"That is up to Rae'en," Kholster had whispered. "I am no longer First. I put down my Grudge at the edge of the Bay of Balsiph. Whether or not Rae'en takes it up again is her decision."

Bloodmane? Eyes of Vengeance thought at him. **They are staring at you.**

Mindful of the eyes now upon him, Bloodmane lowered Hunger. "You know your places," he shouted to the assembled armor and Eldrennai. "You know your tasks." He pointed to the Eldrennai. "Your king has bid you follow my commands." His gauntlet moved to indicate the warsuits. "You were forged by Aern! By true warriors. Honor your makers! Make them proud." Bloodmane raised Hunger once again, high into the air, bringing it back down upon the stone with a loud clang. "Charge!"

Feeling too light, like empty shells without their rightful occupants, Bloodmane's army ran toward battle for the first time in centuries. Instinctively falling into an old rhythm, their metal boots stomped out the one phrase in Zaurtol known by every Aernese warrior: <<Bloodmane is coming.>>

This was not to be a surprise attack; Bloodmane's strategy relied on the Zaur having time to gather in the central corridor. Small stones and earth fell from the ceiling, shaken loose by the vibration of their charge. Bloodmane suspected that it would be an hour or more before they hit significant resistance.

Eyes of Vengeance, report, he transmitted along the link that bound all the armor together.

The Port Gates are still secure. I recommend maintaining a crew of two warsuits per Port Gate in case the Ghaiattri try to break through again.

Good plan. Execute it.

And . . . Kholster? Bloodmane was used to the other armors being candid with him, especially Eyes of Vengeance. Vander was Kholster's War Master, had been for millennia. The two warsuits were fast friends, just as their makers were.

What is it, Eyes?

Commander Jolsit says that when he went through the portal, to tackle the Ghaiattri back through, he saw statues.

What sort of statues?

He said they looked like Aern, Bloodmane. Statues of Aern, wrought in some kind of metal. He thought perhaps . . . bone-steel.

Did any of the orphaned warsuits feel their makers? Bloodmane asked, assuming Eyes of Vengeance would have already made a few quiet inquiries.

Soultaker says he felt something, but he couldn't be certain. I didn't ask anyone else.

The news shocked Bloodmane so strongly that he almost came to a stop. **But Soultaker is Vodayr's armor! He is of the Lost Command!**

I have asked Soultaker to keep it to himself for now, but I promised him we would look into it.

We will. Have you told Vander?

Not yet, Eyes of Vengeance admitted guiltily.

Let us keep this a matter of metal for a bit then, Bloodmane requested. **There is nothing they can do about it right now. Have the Watches reported in?**

Our Geomancers have located a tunnel near West Watch, ten jun southeast of Rin'Saen Gorge. They say Zaur are still working inside it.

Bloodmane could picture them in his mind's eye, lizards digging in the dark. The reports sent in by Wylant and the others warned of new foes: giant serpents called Zaurruks, half-blind stone mounts called Hratta . . . the armor could not wait to kill a Zaurruk.

Fortune of Battle reports, Eyes of Vengeance continued, **that there is no sign of Zaur incursion at Stone Watch. His team has scouted the mountainside and is going to head south across country past Fort Sunder, Fair Hollow, and Saerhi Village to see if it can find any sign of them. They left the soldiers at Stone Watch on high alert.**

Good. Bloodmane signaled a halt as they approached what he assumed was the aftermath of Wylant's underground battle. The dead lay where they had fallen.

Remove the Eldrennai remains that they may be properly interred, Bloodmane ordered. He stepped out of the way, picking up a discarded helmet, turning it over in his gauntlets.

South Watch and Forest Watch have both reported in as well, sir, Eyes of Vengeance droned on. **No sign of tunneling in or around either Watch. Blue Tongue will take his group along the White Road toward Waeren, joining the Geomancers with Backbreaker at West Watch.**

And Skinner's force at South Watch?

I was going to send Skinner to Porthost, to check Kevari Pass, General. I'm concerned that we haven't found the main tunnel from the Zaur territory. What if it's too deep for the Geomancers to locate it?

Then we'll find the passage when we invade the central complex. Bloodmane touched Wylant's helm fondly. He remembered it well, forged in the same fires on the same mighty Life Forge upon which he and his fellow warsuits had been created. But it was not alive, because she was not, could never be, a true Aern. A pity.

Have you spoken more to kholster Rae'en about the human's knowledge of the tunnel? Eyes of Vengeance asked abruptly. **Vander instructs me to make the inquiry.**

I haven't asked again. She's very upset right now, with the loss of . . .

We need more information if Jolsit's Elementalists are to meet us at the correct location, Bloodmane. You know that.

Bloodmane did know it. **You stand in one spot for six hundred years and the world changes very little, Eyes. And yet, when you step out of that spot, the world changes so quickly you can scarcely follow.**

I know.

"We will be one again," Bloodmane said aloud, "reunited with our makers."

"May it come to pass," Ambush, the warsuit running next to him, called out.

"Live long and see it so, my friend," Bloodmane replied. "Live long and see it so."

CHAPTER 62
CHANGING OF THE GODS

"May I?" Grivek gestured at a space on the pier next to Rae'en.

"You have a few days of life left," Rae'en said without looking at him. "Sit wherever you want."

She looked up at the stars instead, wondering what it would be like to walk among them. Wondering if her father could do that now, wherever he was. Cold air blew in off the water, and Rae'en realized she only knew it was cold because of the way Grivek shivered. Armored. She shook her head. Armored without a new Life Forge.

"I'm sorry about your father."

Rae'en did not kill him, but only because she felt honor-bound to start the Conjunction over again if she did so. Kholster had said it would be done, so she would do it. Oath redeemed in death or not.

"What do you want, stump ears?"

"If all oaths are redeemed in death," Grivek began, "I was wondering."

"Do not tell me you're hunting up that trail." Rae'en looked at him askance.

Grivek looked over his shoulder at the others. Wylant stood to one side near the cluster of blue, red, and green tents the Oathbreakers had pitched. Apparently the king couldn't be expected to sleep on the ground like an Aern or a Vael. Four of Wylant's Lance had arrived in the afternoon to regroup. Wylant saw the king's imploring gaze and held up her hands rebuffing any plea.

The Vael knelt at the base of Xalistan's statue, eyes closed, praying or meditating.

"We all know Kholster was looking for a way out of this war," Grivek started.

"You will all die," Rae'en said, looking back at the water. "All the Eldrennai die."

"All things die, kholster Rae'en," Grivek offered. "Perhaps if we could come to some—"

"You ALL die!" Rae'en leapt to her feet, looking down at the wizened Oathbreaker.

We will still invade the Eldrennai? Bloodmane asked. **In death all oaths are redeemed, so now . . .**

Whose scars are on my back, Makerslayer? Rae'en thought scathingly. *You killed my father so that you could defeat the Ghaiattri and fight the Zaur. Therefore, we will fight them. But he died because of the Oathbreakers. So. They. All. Will. Die.*

I understand, Bloodmane responded curtly.

Tyree looked over from where he was conversing with Zhan but did not interfere other than to give a wave when Rae'en's gaze fell on him.

Wylant flew to the pier, with one magic-enhanced leap.

"Daughter of Kholster," King Grivek began, but Wylant held him back.

It's almost midnight, Bloodmane interrupted.

What?

Kholster said we should watch the Changing of the Gods.

Father said that? When?

Before.

"Everybody shut up, I have to watch something." Rae'en turned. *How long until midnight?*

Now.

*

When do they do it? M'jynn crouched on the lip of the central fountain eyeing Aldo's statue. In the dark, golden light flowed from the pale eyes of the god of knowledge's likeness warring in the night with candles from the gathered humans, each praying to their chosen deity.

Kazan held up a cup of warm beef broth one of the Harvester's worshippers had handed him as they moved among the faithful providing warm soup to the devout. He blew carefully on his, mimicking the actions of the humans. Apparently blowing on the soup was part of the ritual.

Can we drink that? Arbokk asked, staring down at his own, standing at his side of the fountain.

I already drank mine, Joose thought back. *Tastes like hot wet meat and salt. I'd ask for another cup, but I already heard one of the females tell a little male it was rude to ask for seconds.*

You can have mine, Kazan chuckled. Did a little broth matter? How could Joose think about such things when they'd just been told the First intended to keep them as her Overwatches. Kazan was walking around the fountain to hand his cup to Joose when it started.

Shidarva moved first, slowly shifting positions, first to a defiant pose, arms on her hip, legs akimbo and then her mouth dropped open in . . . shock? Kazan darted back to his position. They'd all taken up position at what would be the cardinal points of the fountain so they could render a complete view of the Changing of the Gods here, since kholster Rae'en had missed it her last time through.

*

Kholster hovered in the realm between worlds, watching and remembering.

"I have never interfered," Torgrimm had told him. "But I have been convicted by the idea that things must change. I will force you to do nothing. I am deity and it is not my place. You, however, are not of the Artificer's will. If you were to take a portion of my aspect then you could do what I cannot."

"Then give it to me and let it be done with," Kholster had mouthed.

"You must fight me for it," Torgrimm had answered, "and I cannot give you any quarter, or I will violate my own oaths. I am not a god of war, but I am still a god. You will have to truly fight me."

"You're the only god I like, Torgrimm." Kholster had frowned. "Are you sure this is what you want? There is only one way I can think of that—"

"If you will, then do it."

The black vanished from Kholster's eyes, banished by the jade, amber pupils blazing.

Kholster roared, and Torgrimm, for the first time in his existence, knew terror.

*

"Why are they all doing that?" Rae'en asked Wylant as the statues of the gods turned, jaws agape, eyes focused on the pier.

"I don't know." Wylant, once more attired in her customary embroidered Aiannai doublet drew Vax, her weapon, in the shape of a longsword. "Something's wrong."

Tyree burst from his tent, holding his head. "Can't you hear that?" He dropped to his knees, eyes closed, face red, teeth clenched.

The wind picked up, swirling leaves around the central obelisk, the words on it flowing free and glowing white. Lightning cracked in new clouds overhead, and ball lightning arced back and forth in blues and purples, illuminating the night in pyrotechnic fury.

Unslinging Testament, Rae'en walked cautiously toward the end of the pier only to see a giant obsidian hand thrust up out of the water and grip the end of the pier.

A second hand joined the first, got purchase, and, as if kicking against something out of sight, a new statue hurled itself out of the depths, lurching over Rae'en, landing atop on the central obelisk, then leaping like an irkanth onto the statue of the Harvester.

"Dad?"

*

Screams echoed through the Garden of Divinity as the humans fled. Spilled soup and tin cups littered the ground. Only the bravest pilgrims and four Overwatches kept their positions as a new statue, one that had burst from the ground, ripped the helm from the head of the statue of Torgrimm and tore chunks out of the statue with its teeth.

I don't think Torgrimm was quite expecting that, Joose sent.

*

Without hesitation, Kholster had lunged to his feet, swinging at the death god, his fist crashing in under the helmet, breaking Torgrimm's nose and sending gouts of divine blood pouring down his mock-Aernese face. Two more solid shots kept the god off-balance while Kholster stripped the warpick from him with raw, skinless fingers, blood blossoming from his many wounds as he used the warpick to pry the helmet off of the dazed deity.

"I didn't expect it to be such a short—"

Kholster had cut off the sentence by tearing a chunk out of the death god's cheek.

Torgrimm had never felt pain before, not physical pain, and he reacted by trying to push Kholster away from him. Using the warpick like an oyster knife, Kholster stripped the chest plate from Torgrimm and cast it aside as he continued to bite and tear and chew.

*

White marble blood spouted from the throat of the Harvester's statue as it went limp and collapsed. Kholster's statue worked at the Harvester's bone warsuit, stripping it to expose the flesh.

"Kholster! Khol-ster!" the four young Overwatches found themselves chanting. Joose had been the one to start it, but Kazan didn't know that it mattered. *We have a god now* was the thought rushing through his brain. *One all our own.* He felt the Arvash'ae rising and pushed it back, not wanting to miss a moment.

Many of Torgrimm's followers sank to their knees wailing as others launched themselves at the two statues as if they could somehow force them apart.

*

Rae'en smiled from ear to ear, looking for matching expressions of joy on the faces of the others present, but she did not find them. Even the Bone Finders, though not horrified like Grivek and the Vael, were reserved, thoughtful. Only Wylant seemed to be having something even close to the emotions Rae'en was experiencing, but her smile was more of a smirk.

Rae'en growled at the statue of Minapsis as she stepped free of her base, walking with unhurried steps toward her husband's statue.

*

Kholster, in the throes of the Arvash'ae, took little notice of the horned goddess, sparing her only enough attention to track her movements should she attack. He tore at Torgrimm's belly, looking up as he chewed to keep track of his surroundings. The meat was sustenance, nothing more.

Minapsis raised her arms, and two mist-like shapes rocketed from her hands. They coalesced into human figures on either side of Kholster, their hands on his shoulders.

"That's enough, Grudger," Marcus Conwrath whispered.

"You Hunderts always were mean as frost," Japesh swore.

Kholster bit at Conwrath, but his jaws closed on nothing.

"No flesh here, friend," Conwrath laughed. "You killed me years ago."

"Ha!" Japesh slapped his mist-like hands together. "Got drunk. Fell off balcony. Oi win!"

Kholster snapped at Japesh, too, with the same result.

"See?" Japesh laughed. "Mean as frost."

"Is frost mean?" Kholster asked slowly, coming back to himself, pupils shrinking, black returning to his eyes.

"If it weren't mean, it wouldn't bite, would it?"

"You would laugh less were I not protecting you, Japesh, son of Wayne." Minapsis crossed her arms. "Are you yourself again, Kholster?"

He nodded, looking down at the blood, at Torgrimm's gory form.

"Then get away from my idiotic husband before I show you what the Horned Queen can do." With a gesture, Torgrimm became mist as well, flowing into her arms where he re-formed, armorless, clothed in simple farmer's garb.

"That," Minapsis nodded at the scattered scraps of broken warsuit, "is yours, Reaper. I might suggest you use Jun's forge to repair it, if I cared a jot. Which I don't. I must attend the Sower. Try not to eat anyone else while I'm gone."

CHAPTER 63
WHERE LIES THE HARVESTER

In the halls of the gods, Dienox roared. Waves of sound echoed through the chamber, reverberating off of the ancient architecture. The other gods paid him little attention. Most of them had spent eons dealing with the war god's tantrums. Kilke impressed himself by successfully holding back his laughter. In his true form, Dienox had once been quite frightening, but in the form of an Eldrennai clad in gleaming crystal armor, the god of war was far less impressive.

Dienox's unnaturally blond hair (and wasn't it sad to see the war god pretending the loss of his flaming locks no longer bothered him?) flared out as he swung his new crystal battle-axe in angry arcs, hewing large chunks of marble from the pristine walls of the Above. "Where is he?" Dienox bellowed again. It was not the first time he'd done so, but Aldo still did not . . . or would not, answer.

Kilke eyed them both, trying with all his godly reason to peer through Aldo's unreadable countenance and discern the secrets hidden within. Before losing his center head, Kilke's power over secrets and shadow would have granted him an inkling of the truths Aldo concealed, but without it, the effort resulted in a palpable ache behind the dark god's eyes and a renewed itch on the stub of a neck between his two remaining heads.

"I need not tell you, Lord Dienox," Aldo answered flatly, grasping the Book of All Knowledge tightly. It remained firmly shut, its bindings securely fastened.

"Been studying?" Kilke purred. *I bet it won't even open for him anymore.* "Trying to find him yourself?"

"The Harvester's whereabouts are necessarily concealed as a result," Aldo said, clearing his throat, "of the rules of the game."

Dienox hurled his axe into the domed ceiling, its sharp blade penetrating to the haft. A long crack opened and wended down the wall, cutting across where the war god's symbol was inscribed. His fist tightened around Aldo's slender throat. "If you do not tell me if Torgrimm lives or not, Aldo, so help me I will . . ."

"Unhand him," rang the clear, pure voice of justice. Erupting from the wall, Shidarva appeared in symbolic form, a glowing balance with a shield on one side and a blade on the other. Light searing his eyes, Kilke was forced to look away, but when his eyesight returned, Shidarva, as a human woman in a blue dress, had Aldo safely ensconced at her side.

"Shidarva, Aldo, I'm sorry," Dienox began. "But . . . but it seems to me that it must be against the rules to conceal oneself during the game after it has already begun! He just entered it! And we all saw what happened at Oot. Is he dead or not?"

"He should be here shortly," Minapsis announced, storming into the room. Her silk garments were in disarray, her hair, usually immaculately arranged about her crown-like horns, was equally disheveled. "I assure you he's quite well. Vigorous in his health, I may add."

Kilke liked the way his sister held back more than she knew, the way she hoarded knowledge, valued secrets. She had always impressed him, with the lone exception of her choice in husbands. He had urged her to marry Dienox or Xalistan. What they lacked in brains could certainly be compensated for in strength and power. Jun could have been used to build great weapons or inventions, but Torgrimm . . .

"I apologize for my delay," Torgrimm called as he entered the room, Nomi on his arm.

"So you don't mind explaining?" Torgrimm said to Nomi.

"I'll peek in and show him the ropes," Nomi said, vanishing in a swirl of flame.

The image bothered Kilke, but he could not immediately pinpoint what disturbed him. Torgrimm still chose to appear as a stern-faced Aern, and Nomi seemed the same as before. Had he dallied with the once-mortal goddess? Surely not. As Harvester, Torgrimm was certain to have a fondness for any mortal soul which had become divine. He had an unhealthy protectiveness of all souls, even the blackest and most cruel, but no, Kilke would surely have felt such a secret. It was subtle.

"So you won?" Dienox scratched his head. "But Oot . . ." Dienox reached for his axe, the chipped crystal returning to his hand as he unleashed a sigh of obvious disgust. He peered down at the fourteen statues there.

"Sometimes losing is winning," Minapsis answered.

Torgrimm joined her and they kissed.

Awfully affectionate all of a sudden.

"It is indeed." Sedvinia rose and curtsied, forcing Kilke to avert his eyes to avoid gagging at the nauseating politeness of it all. Skulking back to his corner, the god of secrets and shadow cupped his hands together, peering with his leftmost eye into the ball of darkness he'd created. Things went well in the world as far as he could see.

His warlord would soon imbibe the third and last type of blood for the ritual and be transformed, just as Kilke's severed head had promised. The winged boy, the crystal twist, Caius, progressed nicely, well on his way to being prepared for the next game. Rin'Saen Gorge would fall to the Zaur, as would Albren Pass. The sweltering lake of magma that would no doubt soon pool in the midst of The Parliament of Ages, though a defeat, would also provide the potential for a foothold in the forest. He was impressed by the warsuits and their stratagems, but . . .

Warsuits!

"Where did they go?" Kilke demanded as he spun back to face the room. "Torgrimm and my sister! Where?"

"To bed one another," Dienox sulked. "Repeatedly, I have no doubt. They act like rutting newlyweds."

"Of course, they do," Kilke answered. *And I think I might know why.* "What have you been doing, Harvester? Or are you the Harvester at all anymore?" he whispered into his cupped hands. "It is a secret," he told the borrowed shadow within. "His location. Find him for me. If Torgrimm lives and Kholster's statue stands at Oot next to it, find me Kholster."

CHAPTER 64
SOUGHT

A patch of sentient shadow the size of a small mouse slid liquidly across the Eldren Plains. It left the White Road near Porthost and streaked north across *Jun'ghri'kul*, "the Broken Table." Pockmarked and dotted with buttes and mesas, the landscape still bore the marks of geomantic assault against the Aern. Large expanses of ground had been melted into glass, and, in places, shards of the cracked glass jutted up like massive daggers.

Fort Sunder stood at the rough center of *Jun'ghri'kul*, equidistant between Porthost and Stone Watch, a dark and imposing wedge that almost looked as if a tremendous block of onyx had fallen from the stars impacting the middle of the slowly eroding caprock of the mesa upon which it stood.

A small village huddled along the base of the mesa itself, but the living shadow ignored it, slipping past the settlement without slowing, darting amongst the Eldrennai of Bark's Bend as they went about their day. It did slow momentarily when it reached the bridge which served as the main crossing over the cool, deep waters of the Shard River. An Eldrennai male threw a bolt of light into the shadows beneath the bridge then gestured for his son to do the same. Once it was certain that the two were simply practicing, not seeking it, the shadow crossed the white, seamless bridge unnoticed.

It was not long before the shadow found itself in the yawning shade cast by Fort Sunder, sliding beneath its massive triangular gate and moving across the refurbished fortress. Bone-steel had been used to enforce the walls and replace most of the old iron work, rendering it a castle of Aernese bones. Newly woven banners announcing the power and presence of the mighty Aern army hung in reforged banner stands. To the shadow, the once-abandoned fortress appeared ready for war.

Kilke's shadow emissary slithered through the seam between two bone-steel doors and down a long, brightly lit hallway where light glowed regularly from sconces, once magic, now replaced within Dwarven lanterns. It sought the armor of Torgrimm and sensed the artifact's presence deep within Fort Sunder. Passing an inactive Port Gate, the shadow skittered to a halt. The shadow was not alone.

Where the Life Forge once stood, the bone-steel statue of an Aern clad in the very armor the shadow had been sent to find stood at a new bone-steel forge. Tentative, the shadow crept closer. The figure was an Aernese male, worked in metal, clad in Torgrimm's warsuit, its arms resting in front of its body, gripping a bone warpick so that the haft of the weapon lay flush against the statue's thighs, perpendicular to its spine.

Where the light caught the eyes of the statue, it was reflected and amplified by the strange black crystal, shot through with shades of green and amber, which formed them.

"Do you think I do not see you?" the statue asked. As they moved, the lips of the statue became flesh and the crystal eyes softened, the scleras flowing black, the amber pupils tinged with jade. Statue no longer, the Aern turned, the air about him crackling with power and distorting the edges of his form. "Do you think I do not know who seeks me?"

Sharply tipped gauntlets seized the shadow between thumb and forefinger, lifting it up to eye level. "You move between the realms of the gods and mortals, because Kilke gave you life and sent you to seek me. There is an old Aernese rhyme that he would do well to remember:

The Harvester knows when he is sought
The Harvester knows when life is bought.
He feels the call of every soul
Whether aged man or morning foal

The Harvester knows when warriors clash
The Harvester knows when weapons slash.
When battles fought are lost or won
When heroes die with quests undone

He comes for them with tender care
As farmer to field in harvest fair
In bliss, in terror, or forlorn
Like sheep of wool, their souls are shorn

The Harvester feels when it is time
The Harvester reads the final rhyme
He knows the text of every soul
Each love, each loss, each labored goal

He takes them to their final rest
As once he placed them in the nest
At birth, he doth deliver, then
At death, he takes them home again.

*

The shadow-thing quivered with fear, eliciting a sigh from Kholster. Kholster closed his eyes. Such deceptively simple words: "Because I need your help . . ."

The instant Torgrimm had spoken them to him, Kholster had known that he would agree to help the god, no matter what he asked. Kholster recalled the second time he'd met the deity . . .

An Aern had lain dying on the battlefield, the first Aern to die, and Kholster had seen Torgrimm walking toward him across the blood-soaked plain littered with Zaur. The battle had been over for days, yet the Aernese army had remained in place, because of Irka.

Irka, after whom Kholster had named his Freeborn son, had been Ninety-Second of One Hundred. He had never been comfortable with the fighting. He had fought because he was Oathbound and because he was Aern, but when he lay dead, his body turned to iron and was broken and not re-forming, not even slowly. After several days he had even begun to rust.

In those days, Torgrimm had worn a rich blue cloak and dressed like a human nobleman, a sword belted to his waist. A vague point had begun to show at the tips of his ears, and his canines had been only slightly sharpened. He had walked across the field to Kholster and been instantly recognized. Kholster remembered snarling at the god and knowing, yet still not believing, why the Harvester had come.

"He is dead, General," Torgrimm had said tenderly.

"Aern do not die!" Kholster had shouted. "We are warriors eternal. Not even death can stop us! I will take his bones back to the Life Forge." Kholster began to gather Irka's iron into a pile as he spoke, leaning over it protectively. "Maybe he just needs help re-forming. I will work him back together. If I cannot do it then I will beseech Uled . . ."

"You could," the god had agreed. "I would allow it. But he is tired. You know that he has never been happy with this." The god gestured to the battlefield where the gnawed-upon bones of the Zaur lay scattered, blood still mingling with the dew. Kholster had ignored him, busying himself with Irka's remains.

"His children," Torgrimm had continued, "are like the rest of you, but an unintended gentleness was worked into Irka." Torgrimm had stepped closer to Kholster, kneeling next to him. "If you command it, I am certain that he would return. He would do anything for you. You are his general."

Kholster paused with Irka's rusted iron hand held gently in his as he considered it. "What will happen to him?" he asked finally. "Will he be required to go to an afterlife like the one of which the Eldrennai speak . . . with white towers and endless singing of praises to the gods?"

"I'm not certain." Torgrimm stood, wiping a thin layer of rust from the knees of his breeches. "You see, his soul was not made by the Artificer's will. He, like you, is entirely of the mortal realm. I could allow it. Is that what you think the Aern who have perished would want?"

"What do you mean?" Kholster had asked, dropping the hand and standing to face the god. "He is the only dead Aern. He will be the only dead Aern."

"I do not believe that will be so, General. Time can make even the strongest soul wish for release."

"You are the god of death and birth."

"I am."

Kholster, less than a century old at that point, his name not yet a verb or a rank, had stared blankly at the Harvester, eyes searching him for falsehood. Finding none, he had allowed himself to continue. "What does Irka want?"

"He wants to help you, all of you, wants to be with you, but he is so tired . . ."

"Fine," Kholster snapped. "Then add him back to us somehow. No Aern would want white towers anyway. No Aern would want to spend day after day singing songs to frivolous deities in idiotic robes any more than we enjoy bowing and scraping before the masters we already serve."

Torgrimm had seemed surprised, pulling his robe self-consciously close. "Add him back to you?"

"His soul, his essence," Kholster had continued slowly and then with more confidence as the idea took shape in his thoughts. "Divide it between us so that when one Aern dies, all Aern are strengthened. In death, we will empower our brothers. In this way, those who choose death can do so with honor, knowing that their knowledge will not be lost, that they do not abandon us, and yet their suffering will still be at an end. Can that be done?"

"I believe it can. You are all linked as it is, by the Life Forge upon which you were made. . . . This does mean that some of you may die without wanting to, those whose bodies are too far gone to recover. Your bodies will no longer turn to metal, will no longer repair themselves if you die within my reach. They will remain flesh. The bones will still be metal, but the flesh will rot . . ."

"Fine," Kholster had said brusquely with a wave of one gauntleted hand. "Do it. We are not afraid of death, merely unprepared for it."

"Irka has one request, General."

"What?"

"He asks that if ever there comes a time when Aern can be free not to fight . . . then he asks that you name a son after him. If you look into the metal of an unawakened Freeborn son and feel it is right, name him Irka."

"That will never happen," Kholster had said, laughing, "but if it does then I promise I will grant his request."

In the present, Kholster laughed again, echolessly within the empty forge chamber. He examined the quivering shadow and drew out the spark of life that dwelled within it as he pondered his third meeting with Torgrimm, when he'd gone into the water, burning.

"Did you kill it?" asked a ghostly figure, stepping free of a wall.

"Yes, Marcus."

The ghost of Marcus Conwrath eyed a space near the forge expectantly. With a gesture, Kholster summoned a perfect replica of Conwrath's grandmother's table and chairs.

"They don't make chairs like this in paradise." Conwrath settled into his favorite seat and sighed contently. "Too perfect. I don't think Minapsis has the understanding of mortals her husband does."

"A body could get lost in this place, Hundert," said another familiar ghost as he climbed out of the forge itself, "not to mention a soul."

"I trust you to find your way, Japesh." Kholster smiled as Japesh settled into an empty chair across from Conwrath.

"Did I hear you say you killed that little shade?"

"Yes, I did, Japesh."

"I thought t'other one said he weren't after slaying and such?"

"Quite clearly," Kholster said softly, summoning food he felt the two ghosts might crave, watching it appear on the table between them, "I'm not him."

Master? a voice, cold, calm, and mercenary whispered in his mind, banishing the smile from Kholster's lips. It had been Torgrimm's armor, but it was truly his now that Kholster had reforged it. He had given it the only name that seemed appropriate: Harvester.

Not master, Kholster corrected. **My name is Kholster. We work as one, not as owner and slave.**

Yes, Harvester replied. **Yes, I comprehend that, but it is not as I expected.**

Few things ever are, Kholster replied. He held out his warpick, and once again he felt the presence of the other gods. He wondered if they knew that he could do so, wondered if they realized that even they were subject to his grim harvest. He knew them with a thought. So far, only four of the gods he had pondered were exempt from his fury. Yhask, the god of the air, and Queelay, the goddess of water, rarely assumed their human aspects except when communicating to the other gods. They had rarely participated in the games the gods played with mortal souls. Jun, the great builder, had once played but had long since seen the folly of the games, actively protesting each new game . . . and of course, Kholster could find no fault with Torgrimm.

Which left the others vulnerable. Chiefmost of the offenders in Kholster's mind were Kilke, Shidarva, Dienox, and Aldo. Each one bore watching. If he relaxed and let his mind unfocus, he could sense every soul in the entire living world. He knew where they were, or, if he focused on them, could see what they were doing.

He did so, waiting for a sign of interference and concentrating his detection on the living beings with whom he felt the gods might interact. Dienox, he expected, would be first to commit an offense. One by one, Kholster would wait for them to step across the line, and he would teach them a lesson. If the lessons did not take, if they refused to relearn and to resume their proper roles, then one by one, Kholster would reap them.

"Could be war, you know?" the shade of Marcus Conwrath whispered. "Lots of killing in a war."

"Yep. Could be war." Japesh took a bite of his food, a comforting concoction of fruit, sugar, and day-old biscuits he called "slump."

Kholster smiled, refreshing the tray of food on the table with a sizzling steak and skillet potatoes for Conwrath, more slump for Japesh, and a dark draught of beer for both of them.

"What war may I, who reap the gods, not wage and win?"

ACKNOWLEDGMENTS

Thanks to my wife, Janet, for putting up with the worlds in my head and the way they overflow into discussions that she might prefer remain grounded in reality. Absent her feedback and that of our close friends Mary Ann, Karen, Dan, Rob, and Rich, I might yet be lost in a quagmire of edits.

As always, I owe a huge debt of gratitude to my Mom and Dad . . . without them there would be no me. Special thanks are due to Gail Z. Martin, author of many excellent epic fantasy novels, for looking at an early draft and asking the simple question it took me hundreds of pages to answer: "Why doesn't Kholster simply break his oath?" Thanks also to my editor and friend, Lou Anders, for agreeing the world should get a chance to read this book; you should read his, too.

ABOUT THE AUTHOR

J. F. Lewis is the author of The Grudgebearer Trilogy and The Void City series. Jeremy is an internationally published author and thinks it's pretty cool that his books have been translated into other languages. He doesn't eat people, but some of his characters do. After dark, he can usually be found typing into the wee hours of the morning while his wife, sons, and dog sleep soundly.

Track him down at www.authoratlarge.com.

Photo by Janet Lewis